THE COLOUR OF RUBIES

The Colour of Rubies

A Sebastian Foxley Medieval Mystery
Book 10

M
MadeGlobal Publishing

For more information on
MadeGlobal Publishing, visit our
website
www.madeglobal.com

For my History Group who have remained loyal via Zoom throughout two years of Covid 19 lockdowns and continue to be an inspiration to me.

Toni.

Why not visit
Sebastian Foxley's web page
to discover more about his
life and times?
www.SebastianFoxley.com

Prologue

The Palace of Westminster

BY LISTENING at doors, lurking in dark corners and hiding behind faded tapestries, the espier had learned much to his master's advantage. He was now alone in the clerks' dormitory, foregoing a decent dinner to compose the letter. His hands were cramped with cold, no fire being lit in the hearth until the day's work was done. He kept stirring the ink to prevent it freezing. In the guise of a complaint about the English weather and the foolishness of the people with whom he had to live and work, whilst longing to see home, the intelligencer encoded his secret information for his master, Ludovico Sforza, Regent of Milan.

It was complicated to explain. Not that the use of Italian was a problem, being his native tongue, nor even the use of a cypher. The difficulty was the convoluted politics of kings, princes and dukes – how to explain the situation. Milan had had its eye on the Principality of Piedmont for years, lying as it did in a strategic position between France and the Italian City State. But Louis of France had similar intentions for Piedmont. The King of France was ever a thorn in Milan's side, thwarting any possibility of expansion.

But now King Edward had in mind a plan that would play well into Milan's aspirations – not that the stupid, bellicose English monarch would realise it. The espier had overheard a Privy Council meeting yesterday and learned this juicy morsel of intelligence. In his message, he revealed that King Edward was grown tired of his troublesome neighbour, the King of Scots, and since the treaty signed with them at York ten years before had now expired, he was determined to make war upon Scotland during this coming summer of 1480. By the terms of some Old Alliance, such action would require Louis of France to aid his Scots allies, distracting his attention to the northern end of his kingdom, far away from Piedmont. The espier did not dare to presume to tell his master that this would be the perfect opportunity to march the Milanese forces into Piedmont. Still, Ludovico Sforza was an intelligent man: he would understand.

Having made a fair copy of his draft, the intelligencer signed it: *per mano dello Scudiero del Rubino*; 'by the hand of the Esquire of the Ruby', folded and sealed it. He would now deliver it to the courier in Lombard Street, in the City of London. As for the original draft copy, he tossed the paper into the hearth as kindling for the fire when it was lit later.

The servant came to prepare the clerks' dormitory for the evening. His first task was to get the fire going, to warm the large chamber. But what was this? It looked to be a letter lying in the hearth. One of the clerks had been careless indeed. The servant could not read, so the words meant naught to him but he was a conscientious soul. He would give it to the chief clerk, whom he knew by sight. That should solve the problem. He would know what to do with the letter.

Chapter 1

Friday, the twenty-seventh day of January in the Year of Our Lord 1480

Westminster

WHAT A BLOODY MISERABLE way to celebrate his nine-and-twentieth birthday.

He should never have come to work as a royal clerk. Secretary Oliver, who now ruled his days, was an utter bastard, sitting there, snug, amid cushions with the chamber's solitary brazier warming his feet whilst his eight clerks shivered at their desks before him.

The pen wavered unsteadily in Jude Foxley's chilled fingers. Pellets of snow beat against the glazed window such that candles were needed to work by even at mid-morn. Jude was unsure whether the ink was drying or freezing on the page as he wrote. It was hours since he last felt his toes, the cold leeching into his shoes from the bare flagstones of the King's Scriptorium.

Jude cursed Oliver and thought longingly of the Foxley workshop in Paternoster Row, back in London, where his brother Seb would also be cosy beside a glowing brazier, sipping mulled ale when he liked, taking time to leave his desk, stretch his back and walk about to thaw his feet. He should never have left.

He reached for a fresh sheet of parchment – the eighth or tenth, was it? He'd lost count of how many summonses to

Parliament he had copied out, leaving a blank space for the name of the lord to whom each would be sent. Couldn't King Edward simply send out heralds to announce it? Damn it all. He'd never had such a tedious task. His mind was as numb with boredom as his fingers with cold, aye, and his arse with perching on this misshapen wooden stool with the split seat that pinched his buttocks. The draught blowing in the door gnawed at his ankles like a starveling rat every time it opened. That was the penalty he paid for being the newcomer to the scriptorium: the worst stool by the door. Mind, to sit by the window with icy airs rolling down the wall from the glass panes above wasn't much of an improvement, though there was more light to see what you were doing. Flickering candlelight glimmered off the wet – or frozen – ink of his last few words.

At the desk beside him, Piers Creed's teeth were chattering loud enough to be annoying. But then everything about Piers was irritating. Worse was his constant foul farting. God knew what he ate to cause such noisome stinks that so frequently disturbed his fellow clerks. The ominous purring rumble of another assault on the senses had Jude covering his nose with his sleeve in good time.

'For Christ's sake, can't you cease that?' Jude muttered from behind his sleeve which proved inadequate. 'Stop eating bloody horse-beans or whatever...'

'Silence!' Secretary Oliver bellowed from his exalted cushioned chair at the far end of the scriptorium. 'I've warned you before, Foxley. You speak again and your pay will be reduced by two pence since this is your second offence. Now get on with your work.'

Piers Creed is the bloody offence, Jude thought, stabbing his pen into the inkwell over hard and ruining the nib. But he knew better than to answer back to Oliver, the pompous bastard who served as the king's French and Italian secretary. In truth, there wasn't much work for this particular royal office through the winter months, when ships weren't voyaging to foreign lands to collect or deliver correspondence. Hence, their current employment in helping out the clerks of the Lord Chancellor's Office who were supposed to write out the numerous summonses to attend Parliament before Easter.

Jude's much-exaggerated knowledge of Italian tongues had gained him this position – with his brother's aid – and now he wished most heartily that he hadn't bothered to lie about his skills. Still, the clerkship earned him coin in his purse. Besides, a month since, King Edward had celebrated Christmas in fine style, including everyone who worked at Westminster Palace in the feasting and entertainment. Jude had appreciated that, as did his young bride, Chesca – Francesca-Antonia Baldesi. She had made quite an impression at court, wearing her one remaining Venetian gown of silk and bits of finery, making quite a show. Men had been so envious of him with her on his arm, dancing with him, laughing at his wit. He grinned at the memory, reshaping his quill with his penknife. But Christmas seemed long ago now as he sat, freezing his bollocks off, scribbling endlessly even as the ink turned to ice in the well.

Christ be thanked for the mercy of the bell, calling them to dinner in the Great Hall.

'Coming, Piers?' Jude asked, setting down his pen and pushing back his stool which grated on the flagstones fit to set teeth on edge. Despite his vile personal problem, Creed was the closest thing to a friend Jude had made among the clerks since coming to Westminster.

'I've nigh finished this summons. I'll join you shortly. Save me a place at the board.' Creed went on scribbling without looking up.

Jude shrugged, gazing down on his industrious companion. The fellow's lank hair was sparse, his nose bulbous and his build so skinny he made Jude's lean-limbed brother Seb seem plump in comparison. In truth, Creed's only asset was that he made a splendid foil for Jude: a fine figure, broad of shoulder, taller than most, good-looking with a full head of fair hair.

At least, that was how Jude saw himself, refusing to acknowledge that incipient and unwelcome roll of flesh that began to do daily battle with his belt buckle or, of late, the receding hairline Chesca took malicious delight in pointing out. ''Tis but a high forehead,' he'd told her, 'The sign of a large brain and great intelligence.' The young hussy had laughed, devil take her, and earned a slap for her mischief.

Mistress Baxter's Lodging House, Thieving Lane, Westminster

Chilled and miserable, Jude trudged home in the dark through the deepening snow. But a surprise awaited when he returned to the upper chamber where he and Chesca dwelt at present, unable to afford anything better. He came bearing a cold supper of white bread and cheese, napkin-wrapped, filched at dinner. Living on a pittance, most of his fellow clerks did likewise, those who did not live at court. The unwed clerks had bed and board within the ramshackle parts of the palace but wives weren't allowed. Thus, Jude lodged in this single chamber with barely space to spread his arms and a roof too low for him to stand to his full height of just six feet. Mind, at this rate, what with being bent over his desk all day at Secretary Oliver's behest and stooping here at Mistress Baxter's place, he'd be a bloody crouchback before he was five-and-thirty – not that he intended his life to go on in this dismal way for that long. He had plans.

Jude gawped at the sight that greeted him at the head of the rickety stair: Chesca decked in all her finery, her hair loose, gleaming, black as midnight, being the least of it. A good fire burned in the hearth, the room had been swept and the draping cobwebs removed. A table-board he'd never seen before was spread with a pristine cloth and all manner of food set out in pewter dishes: a whole salmon, jellies, cheeses and sweetmeats. And wine!

'Sweet Christ alive, Chesca. What have you bloody done?' Jude waved his arms to encompass the chamber. Even the bed was neatly made.

'Are you pleased, Jood? This for your birthday. I pouring wine for you... good wine, no dog's pees now.' She served him the red wine in a chased silver cup fit for royalty. God alone knew how she'd come by such luxuries. It was a fine Gascon wine, as had been served at King Edward's Twelfth Night feast.

Jude sipped it cautiously, wondering how much each swallow cost him. Money he didn't possess.

'Everything looks... so clean. Did you do it yourself?'

'You no spoiling it.' Chesca pouted like the child she was at just sixteen summers of age.

'You didn't, did you?'

'Servants clean. Baldesis no clean.'

'You're not a Baldesi now; you're a Foxley. We can't afford bloody servants... nor all this food and drink.'

'Your brother having servant; why no us?'

'You mean, Nessie? That foolish chit costs him more to feed than she does in labour. She doesn't count and answer my damn question, woman.'

'Mistress Basster. I paying her to making clean.'

'Mistress Baxter? You paid our bloody landlady to do the work? How much did that cost?'

'Leettle, leettle money, I swearing. Pleease now we eating good food.'

'Did you steal it or borrow the money?'

'An' I no meaning Nessie. Rosa – she serving or no?' Chesca changed the subject.

'Rose? She's a special case.'

Chesca cut flakes of salmon with her knife and arranged them on a piece of fresh white bread.

'I knowing. Nessie telling me how you an' Rosa were marrying an' you never coming to the church. Why you no coming to her? She fine woman.'

''Tis none of your bloody business! Besides, you should be grateful I never wed her, else I couldn't have saved you from that filthy old lecher your family wanted you to marry.'

Chesca sat in his lap and fed him the fine fish.

'You liking?' She raised her eyebrows in question, wriggled provocatively and began to unlace the doublet he wore beneath his clerk's gown. 'You liking other things more?'

'We're bloody eating, Chesca. I'm tired...'

'Never too tired. Eating later... after.'

'Don't take my clothes off, you little harlot. It's still chilly in here.'

'Warming in bed, Jood. Come now, husband.'

Thoroughly satisfied regarding all bodily requirements, Jude lay awake in bed, thinking – a bad habit of his brother's but, for the most part, one he rarely bothered to indulge. He reached out for his wine cup upon the floor, careful not to knock it over. Such good wine; how in Christ's name had Chesca paid for it? The possibilities stewed in his head, all of them bad. Had she taken up thievery? It seemed unlikely, seeing how much food and drink had appeared, as if by magick. Stealing on that scale could not have gone unnoticed. Maybe she'd run up a great account and he would suffer such a shock when the reckoning arrived with demand for immediate payment. God knows where the coin would come from in order to settle it.

But it was a third possibility that wormed its way insidiously into his head, like a small but venomous serpent: that somebody else had paid for everything. And why would that be? No one did favours out of kindness these days; they expected the favour returned – in full. He had nothing to give... but Chesca. What had the hussy done? Or rather *who* had she done? That little minnekin! If she'd lain in another man's bed, he'd kill the bastard, whoever he was.

Of a sudden, he was convinced he had struck upon the truth and the rich food – paid for by some snot-nosed knave – roiled in his belly until he felt quite sick. He looked at his wife curled close beside him: young, beautiful, aye, and desirable, devil take her. In the fading firelight, she looked so innocent, sleeping like a well-fed kitten. No wonder the adulterous bitch hadn't answered his questions, avoiding the issue. Well, she'd bloody regret it; that was certain, but he couldn't be bothered now. He turned his back on her and spent much of the long night plotting his revenge on the shit-monger scawager who'd cuckolded him, whoever it was. The worse the punishment he could devise for the pillaging prick the better.

Saturday, the twenty-eighth day of January

Beyond the frosted horn-paned window, as best he could make out, Jude saw a world shrouded white. Damn the snow. Damn the cold. His breath fogged the air even indoors. Last eve's welcoming blaze was now grey ash in the hearth with not a splinter of wood to revive it to life. His anger had likewise cooled overnight but he knew it wouldn't take much to rekindle it. One word amiss from Chesca and he'd skin her like a bloody cat so it was as well then that she slept on, huddled in the warm bed – no early riser she in any case, but 'neath the blankets was the best place to stay on such a day. He'd wring the truth out of her later.

Jude donned his clerk's gown over almost every item of clothing he possessed: three shirts; doublet; jerkin; two pairs of hose and breeches. He could hardly move in so many clothes, and pulling on his boots proved a struggle. The debris of his birthday feast still littered the cloth. There was no point in wasting good food, whoever had paid for it. Jude cut a fat wedge of cheese which he put in his scrip for later, along with a handful of marchpane-stuffed figs. He piled flakes of salmon on a slice of white loaf and folded it to eat on his walk to work. It wasn't a mannerly way to break his fast but he didn't care. He swung his cloak around his shoulders and pulled his coif and plain clerk's cap as low over his ears as possible, cursed at finding his cheap gloves were splitting. Thank God it was Saturday, a half-day only of scribbling and shivering in that devil-damned place with Piers Creed farting and stinking beside him. It was no life for a red-blooded Englishman and definitely not for Jude Foxley.

Hard pellets of snow gusted in his face, stinging like icy sand. It was difficult to tell if this was fresh snow falling from the dour, leaden clouds, or simply blowing off the roofs. Underfoot was treacherous ice, hid by a soft layer of innocent-looking virgin white. He and others forced, complaining, from their firesides, slipped and slithered, ungainly. As Jude turned off King Street and entered Westminster Palace's outer courtyard through Great Gate, a fellow in front of him lost his footing and collided with a baker's lad carrying a tray of still-warm bread, fresh from the ovens. Small loaves scattered in the snow but not for long. Folk swooped upon the scene of the mishap like scavenging kites and the bread disappeared, four *pains de main* finding their way into Jude's scrip to join the cheese and sweetmeats. Waste not; want not, as the old saying goes.

He trudged on towards the Exchequer Offices and the scriptorium adjoining the Great Hall. At the threshold of Secretary Oliver's cold little kingdom, he knocked the snow off his boots, shook it out of his cap, removed his useless gloves to chafe his numb fingers into life and prepared to work. The door whined like a lost soul – as it always did – when he pushed it open on its time-worn iron hinges.

As ever, first to arrive and last to leave, the industrious Creed was already at his desk, aye, and had begun his daily production of farts, to judge by the stink.

'Don't you have anything better to bloody do, Piers?' Jude greeted him.

'I'm not an idle layabout like the rest of you. Besides, since Secretary Oliver entrusted me as key-holder, I have to be first here and leave last.'

'You have that wrong: he only gave you the key because you're so bloody eager to start work every morn. You give the rest of us a bad name, you foolish bugger. Here, have a sweetmeat.' Jude put a stuffed fig on Piers desk.

'What's this for? You want me to copy out your quota of summonses?'

'You suspicious old curmudgeon. 'Twas my birthday yesterday and a few morsels were left after.'

'Secretary Oliver'll be in a rage if he finds out we're eating at our desks, getting crumbs and grease marks on the parchment.'

'I won't tell him, if you don't.'

'Oh, I don't know, Jude.'

'Well, damn it then, I'll bloody have it.' Jude took back the sweetmeat and ate it in two bites. 'Dilemma solved! Now, what's the old goat got for us this morn, eh?' he spoke through a mouthful of fruit and marchpane, wiping sticky fingers on his gown. 'More bloody summonses, no doubt.' He rubbed his hands together vigorously to warm them, so he could hold a pen and sat on the stool with the split seat that pinched his arse, if he didn't take care.

'Aye. He left us instructions to do another thirty: fifteen each.'

'What? Us alone? What are the other buggers doing, then?' Creed shrugged.

'Something just as boring, I suppose, when they get here. They'll be blaming the snow for their tardiness. They always do. Snow makes a fine excuse for being late to work.'

'Even those who live here? I had to walk from Thieving Lane.'

'That's not so far.'

'Farther than you had to come from your bloody dormitory above stairs. Oh, shit. My damned ink's frozen solid.' Jude threw down his pen in disgust. 'Well, I can't work 'til that thaws out.' He took the inkpot and set it beside the solitary brazier the clerks were permitted in their icy den. He stood close as he dared to the glimmer of warmth bestowed by the feeble glow of charcoal without scorching his threadbare gown. It had been his predecessor's cast-off and, therefore, was too short to keep his knees warm when he sat to write – yet another reason for complaint about his current employment.

'While you're waiting for your ink, last night, after you'd gone, Chief Clerk Sowbury put a sheaf of papers on the shelf up there.' Creed nodded towards an untidy-looking pile of mismatched sheets in danger of sliding to the floor. 'He said we're to sort them out, see what's relevant and send them to the appropriate offices.'

Jude took the papers to his desk and began to straighten dog-ears and smooth out creases. Some were torn.

'Reckon this could all go for bloody fire-lighting.' He leafed through them, muttering under his breath: 'Laundry list... order for parchment... memo to self: "don't forget M's birthday"... another laundry list... an anonymous tailor's demand for payment... Whose stuff is this? Each one in a different hand...'

'Don't ask me. Mayhap, some servant was finally setting about cleaning behind a coffer. Could be years old, some of it.' Creed fidgeted and let out a long rumbling fart.

'Can't you go outside to do that, you disgusting wretch? I have to breathe in your bloody stink.'

'It's a penance we both have to bear.' Creed sighed and repeated the offence for good measure before dipping his pen to complete the document he was writing.

Jude made no answer, frowning over a paper. Smoothing out the wrinkles where it had been screwed up, he followed a line of wording with his finger, puzzling to make sense of it. It seemed to be in some Italian form but not of Venice, which he would recognise for certain, nor of Florence, with which he had some acquaintance. The hand was tiny, cramped and execrable with many crossings-out and insertion marks, dots and under-scoring.

'Something of interest?' Creed asked, finishing another summons and reaching for a fresh parchment to commence with 'Right Trusty and Well-Beloved, We Greet You Well...' – the customary royal greeting.

'Doubt it. Someone's first draft for a letter home, by the look of it. Just rubbish.' Despite his words, Jude set the paper aside for perusal later, if he could be bothered. If it contained a bit of juicy court gossip, it might be worth the trouble to interpret. A few extra coin for 'information' could always be of use to a poor clerk with a spendthrift wife.

Their fellow scribes arrived in twos and threes, all blaming the weather for their late arrival, as Creed had predicted, moaning about the pitiful brazier that did naught to warm them. They, too, found their inkwells frozen – another reason to delay working, so they trooped off in search of mulled ale whilst the ink thawed, the door screeching closed behind them.

'Hal, Lawrence, bring some drink for us!' Creed called out with little hope that they would, he and Jude being the lowest of the low in the clerks' unspoken hierarchy.

Unsurprisingly, the clerks returned without any ale for Jude or Creed.

'What have you two been doing?' Hal Sowbury, the chief clerk, demanded. He was heavyset but of short stature, dark-browed. Jude hadn't liked him on sight, the pompous, puffed-up toad. In Jude's opinion, Chief Groveller and Arse-Licker Extraordinary were better titles for him. And he possessed a nasty temper.

'More summonses. What else?' Creed told him.

'Foxley. What of you, you lazy cur? I don't see any summonses on your desk.' Sowbury leaned back in Secretary Oliver's vacant chair, arms folded, making the most of their master's absence to sit close to the brazier.

'My ink was frozen as yours. Meantime, I've been going through a pile of waste papers from somewhere or other. You said to make certain there's naught important among them before putting it all on the fire. Wouldn't do to accidentally burn your love letters, Hal, from your latest mistress, would it now?'

'Shut your mouth, Foxley.' Sowbury leapt towards him, fist raised.

Jude stood up, straightening to full height. Up on his toes, he added an extra couple of inches, towering over the angry clerk.

'Touch me, Sowbury, and you'll bloody regret it,' he said, sounding utterly calm and composed. No note of ire in his voice.

'I'm your superior!'

'I don't care if you're Pope Sixtus himself,' Jude continued in the same easy tone. 'No man lays a finger on me.'

Sowbury thought better of it and backed down but his scowl promised retribution to follow.

'You'll be the one in trouble when I inform Secretary Oliver of your behaviour.'

'*My* behaviour? You're the one threatening to strike me, you ridiculous little prick.'

Sowbury had been goaded beyond bearing and went so far as to climb upon Jude's desk to get at him. His eyes blazed and his penknife was in his hand.

Jude stepped back, avoiding a clumsy thrust, laughing.

'Get off my desk before you fall and hurt yourself. We don't want blood splashing the parchment, do we? That would upset Secretary Oliver, wouldn't it? God knows, he might even chastise us, then we'd all be in tears.'

'Stop it, Jude, don't mock him,' Creed said softly. 'You're making matters worse with every word. You don't want him for an enemy. He's a sly one.'

The situation was ended by the entrance of Secretary Oliver himself, fur-swathed and red-nosed, sniffing. He croaked a greeting of sorts – or it might have been a reprimand, it was hard to tell – and slumped in his comfortable chair. Lord of all he surveyed here in the clerks' office, if he was afflicted by an excess of rheumy phlegm and a chill, then everyone else should be made to suffer the same. Leastwise, that seemed to be his purpose as he sneezed and coughed and spat his contagion right freely upon all.

Jude now had reason to be glad of his draughty place, farthest from the brazier, well away from Oliver. The fellow looked pitiful and, for once, uninterested in what his underlings were doing, whether working or wasting time. Creed, of course, was writing out yet more summonses. Such diligence should be commended, though it rarely was. More likely, poor Creed was derided by his fellows and given far more than his fair share of work.

'Take a breath, Piers,' Jude whispered, nudging him. 'They'll only give you more work to do, if you finish those damned summonses. Look around: Sowbury and the rest are doing nothing at all, fiddling with their cod-pieces, picking their noses, scratching their arses. We're the only ones working.'

'I'd rather be doing something to pass the time 'til dinner.'

'Here, take a look at this.' Jude handed Creed the creased paper that caught his attention earlier. 'What do you make of it, eh? Interesting?'

'Not much, in truth,' Creed admitted after a deal of squinting and thumb-chewing. 'Italian tongues aren't my strong point. What do you think it says?'

'I best not tell you too much. 'Tis a love letter to King Edward's latest mistress. We don't want that to become common knowledge, do we now? The king might throw us in the Tower of London and feed the key – or us – to the bloody lions in the Menagerie.' Despite his words of doom, Jude was laughing, watching Creed's horror-stricken face. 'I'm jesting, Piers. Don't take everything so damned seriously. Of course it's not a bloody letter from the king. Why would it be when the king doesn't know any Italian? If he did, he wouldn't need me and I wouldn't be freezing my bollocks off in the pest hole. See sense, you daft fool.'

'What does the letter say?'

Jude shrugged.

'Ah, now, 'tis a difficult hand to make out, is it not? I'll take it home; work on it there. I can't concentrate here, what with you farting and him sneezing all the time.' Jude cocked his chin at Secretary Oliver, who appeared to have nodded off.

''Tis most conscientious of you, to work at home when you'll not be paid for it.' Creed sounded surprised – as well he might – if not impressed.

'That's me, Piers: a most hard-working fellow indeed,' Jude said as he surreptitiously folded the letter out of sight, beneath his desk and slipped it into the sleeve of his gown. In truth, he had no idea what it said; his Italian was not that good. But to keep up the pretence of fluency, he had his secret assistant: Chesca.

Chapter 2

Saturday afternoon

SEB FOXLEY had struggled through the snow, from Paternoster Row in London, out by Ludgate, across the half-frozen River Fleet and along the Strand. He paused to catch his breath by Charing Cross, the first King Edward's great memorial to his much-loved queen. It was a long walk on so bitter a day. Seb turned southward onto King Street, finally reaching his destination of Mistress Baxter's lodging house in Thieving Lane. The snow underfoot had been by turns packed hard into ice, grubby and slushy or, in less frequented parts, soft and pristine as swans' down. Whatever the case, for Seb anything but a firm footing made his journey hazardous, his hip aching and not to be relied upon. Thus, he had resorted to using a staff, as of old, before his injury had been improved by a miracle, as he reckoned it, some time since. After all his efforts, he prayed that his brother would be at home.

He knocked at the door, bleached of all colour by years of weathering, and waited. His dog, a great lolloping black and white creature, was busy sniffing at all the new scents Westminster had to offer, pushing his nose into a heap of discoloured snow.

'Leave be, Gawain. Who can say what horrors you may find hid there. Leave be, I tell you.'

The door was opened by a plump matron of middling years.

'Oh, Master Foxley, fancy you coming all this way in

17

such weather.'

'God give you good day, Mistress Baxter.' Seb lowered his hood, removed his cap and began kicking the snow from his boots. 'Yesterday was the anniversary of my brother's birth. I have brought a gift. I hope he may be here?'

'Aye, the idle lummox is upstairs, having traipsed lumps of snow all through my house. Mistress Foxley's there too. I must say, they had quite the celebration last eve.'

Seb was yet unused to anyone but his late, beloved Emily being spoken of as 'Mistress Foxley'. Her death in childbed at Easter last was a hurt from which he had still to recover. Chesca seemed to him too young to bear the gravity of the title.

Saturday, being a half-day for most traders, craftsmen and labourers, was the time for visiting. Seb made his careful way up the stair to Jude's room at the top of the old house, Gawain threatening to trip him as he hastened past on four paws. Draughts emanated from every window, doorway and crevice in the walls. Seb noticed a dust-laden cobweb lifting in the draughts. It felt hardly any warmer within than without and he shivered inside his new winter cloak, despite its generous lining of rabbit fur.

'Jude... 'tis me, Seb.' He tapped upon the door. It was wrenched open with difficulty.

'Bloody door sticks,' Jude complained, shoving it closed again with his shoulder. 'What have you come for? You shouldn't be out in this, what with the streets so treacherous. You'll break your damned foolish neck for sure. You haven't got me to hold you upright these days.'

'Mistress... Chesca,' Seb said, making his courtesy to his sister by marriage. 'I managed well enough with my staff, Jude. I be all of a piece, as you see. I had to bring your gift. It was intended for yesterday but...'

'Seb!' the young lass cried, rushing to embrace him and kiss him heartily upon both cheeks. 'It being good to see you. And Gawain, *il mio cane preferito*.' She hugged the dog who licked her chin.

'It could've bloody waited, whatever it is.' Jude muttered. 'You want wine? There's a drop left from last night. Pour it for him, Chesca.' The lass was feeding Gawain with titbits strewn upon the board. 'Come on, leave that damned dog alone and play the goodwife, can't you, you little minnekin.' Jude slapped her backside, laughing.

Seb looked away. Such actions might be allowed privily or in low-life taverns and bawdy houses but he did not want to see such behaviour.

'What have you brought me, then?' Jude continued. 'And take your cloak off, if you're staying, little brother.'

Seb obeyed, despite being reluctant. The fire was pitiful and gave out so little warmth that their speech formed mist clouds as they spoke. He sat down on the edge of the rumpled bed, there being too few stools. Still eyeing the remaining sweetmeats, the dog stood by the board, looking hopeful. Chesca fed him another stuffed date that was rather squashed.

Jude took Seb's cloak, admiring it, stroking the fur.

'New, is it? Fine wool... decent bit o' fur. Expensive, no doubt.'

'Mayhap. Rose, Adam, Mercy and Ralf all contributed to buy it for me upon my birth anniversary afore Christmas. They complained that my old cloak had suffered overmuch misuse and was hardly fit to wear to church any longer. 'Tis quite the bold hue though... too bold, as I first thought. What say you, Jude?'

'Aye. Crimson's not your colour; far too grand for you. You'll be acting the prosperous bloody merchant before long, wearing such a thing.'

'Well, I thinking it handsome, Seb,' Chesca said, giving him a cup with a skim of wine in the bottom. 'Taking no notice of Jood. He being dull sort. You wanting sweetmeats? We having some still. Gawain is liking them.'

'My thanks, Chesca.' Seb accepted a dried apricock before delving into his scrip. He fetched out a cloth-wrapped bundle and gave it to Jude.

Jude opened it, eager as a child.

'Gloves! Thank Christ for that. How did you know I was in need?'

'You complained sufficiently of your old pair. Rose not only advised my choosing of the leather but sewed them so finely, as you would expect of the best glover in London. And see there? She embroidered the letters 'JF' upon them so none of your fellow clerks may filch them.'

Jude examined the perfectly matched silken initials on the cuffs, ran his fingertips across the supple kid-skin.

'Rose made these? Why would she? She hates me, surely? Probably left a needle in the leather to have her little revenge on me.'

'You think she would do so mean a thing? Rose has forgiven you long since for abandoning her at the church door. She has me now.'

'A miserable bloody exchange though: you for me.' Jude pulled on the gloves. 'Mm. A reasonable fit, I grant.' He flexed his fingers. 'Not sure I like grey. No doubt but you chose the colour.'

'I did. A practical hue, I thought; not likely to show every mark and speck of dirt. I be sorry if you disapprove.'

'They'll serve me well enough, I suppose,' Jude said, reluctant to give praise even when due. He went to the shelf where his old holey gloves lay. He threw them at Seb. 'There. You can give those to some deserving beggar on your way home.'

''Tis a kindly act, Jude. I be grateful. But pray tell me of your work for Secretary Oliver: does the Italian tongue come any easier to you than it did afore?'

'Jood finding it easy when I doing it for him.'

'Be quiet, Chesca. I bloody warned you...'

'He being your brother, he no telling anybody.'

'Walls have ears in this place; I told you that.'

Chesca looked startled.

'Ears? How they having ears? England strange place if...'

"'Tis an English expression, Chesca,' Seb said, smiling at her confusion. 'Jude be saying "you can never know who maybe listening". Whether at the door, the window or concealed within the shadows.'

'Westminster's a bloody nest of eavesdroppers and I don't mean only in the palace. I don't trust that Mistress Baxter an inch. She's the worst of gossips and has ears like a bloody hare. If she hears what you say of an evening, Chesca, the whole of Westminster will know of it by morn. So you keep quiet, if you know what's good for you – for us. You understand?'

'*Si*. I understanding, Jood. I no speaking to any walls or hares in Westminster.'

'Christ give me bloody strength,' Jude said under his breath, gazing up at the roof beams. 'What am I to do with the silly bitch?'

'Why you calling me bad name, you *grasso sciocco*!' Chesca cried, stamping her foot. '*Tu non sai nulla.*'

'What did you say? What did you call me, you little hussy? How dare you spout your filthy alien nonsense at me.'

'I calling you a fat fool not knowing a thing. How else will you be learning my tongue if I not teaching it to you, eh, husband?'

'Seems to me,' Seb said, laughing, 'Chesca's English be better than your Italian. Mayhap, she should serve as the king's clerk in your stead.'

'Don't you take her part, you wretch. Bloody woman, I've had enough of her,' Jude said. 'Tell you what, little brother, what say you we go into the palace. I'll show you that stained glass in St Stephen's Chapel that I told you of. I know the colours will dazzle you.'

'*Si*, Jood. I coming also. I want seeing glass with Seb.'

'Not you. You caused enough bloody trouble at the Twelfth Night feast.' Jude handed Seb that fine new cloak, feeling envious of such luxury.

'You not fairly!' Chesca flung her arms in the air. '*Ti odio!*'

'Surely Chesca may join us?' Seb said. 'She must find this solitary chamber tiresome and lonely.'

'Too bad; she's not coming. That's my final word on the matter.' Jude pulled on his gloves, admiring Rose's embroidery. 'Besides, she hasn't got any boots to wear in this bloody snow. She'll ruin her shoes and I can't afford new ones. Come, brother, let's go before the snow comes down again.'

'*Maledite voi uomini!*' Chesca shouted after them as Jude slammed the door.

He didn't want to know what she had called him this time.

'*Ti odio,* Jood Fossley. I hating you so.' She beat on the door with her fists as tears ran down her plump cheeks. They had grown pale of late. '*Vi odio inglesi... Odio l'Inghilterra!*' she sobbed. The warmth, the sunshine, the family and friends she had in Venice all seemed so far away now. No wonder she hated cold, lonely, miserable England.

Jude led the way along Thieving Lane, looking back frequently to assure himself Seb was keeping up and not tripping over the dog that kept so close at his knee. Having his little brother fall into the grey slush would be too much like old times – not to mention the ruination of that enviable hooded cloak. Seb was a fool to have worn it on such a day but, doubtless, he felt the cold – as he always did – and had need of its fine thick wool and coney fur lining.

'Come on!' Jude urged, 'Else it'll be dark and you won't see the stained glass at its best.'

Seb didn't make answer, being concerned to negotiate a particularly miry patch on the corner of King Street.

Jude went back, offering his brother a sturdy arm to assist. Seb accepted it with a sigh.

'Apologies,' he said. 'My hip has been no bother 'til the weather turned so chill and damp. All summer, it was right well...'

'Fortunately for you, little brother, servants are paid to remove the snow from the palace courtyards and strew ashes underfoot, so you'll do well enough once we're through the gate.'

The Great Gate was impressive, its ancient stone ivy-clad, its turrets snow-capped and the Royal Standard flapping above in the fitful flurries of icy flakes. The guards in their bright liveries stamped their boots and blew on their hands, puffing out white clouds with every breath. Keeping watch in January was a duty none enjoyed. They recognised Jude and waved him through, ignoring Seb as a person of little consequence, unlikely to endanger King Edward in any way.

The Inner Gate into Green Yard was far less imposing but the solitary guard there demanded to know their business. Mayhap, he was in need of some activity or company to pass the time.

'Who goes there?' he demanded, barring the way with his halberd.

'Walter, you bloody nincompoop, it's me,' Jude said. 'You know me better than your own father – if you ever knew him at all.'

'Bloody Foxley,' the guard growled. 'What brings you back on a Saturday afternoon? And who's this?' He nodded at Seb.

'My brother. He's a scribe like me and we've got work to do for Secretary Oliver – not that it's any business of yours.'

'Mind your mouth, Foxley. I can throw you in the lock-up anytime I like and you'll freeze to death in there afore you can say your Paternoster. And why's your brother here? He ain't a king's clerk and if he's half the bloody trouble you are, he's not welcome.'

'He has permission; a written warrant.' Jude took a paper from his purse and offered it to the guard, fully aware that Walter was illiterate as a blind sheep. 'You want to read it?'

The guard shook his head.

'Just keep out of my sight, the pair of you. Any trouble and you'll have my halberd shoved up your arse with a ribbon on it.'

Jude was sniggering as he led Seb to the side door.

'You upset him. Why did you taunt him so, not to mention the lies you told?' Seb asked, knocking a dark mess of slush and ashes off his boots against the stone step.

Jude didn't bother, treading mucky footsteps along the passage within.

'Forwhy Walter's an ignorant pig. He knows I have the measure of him, the damned jackanapes, and lying is just the Westminster way – nobody tells the truth here. Besides, this clerkship job would be unutterably tedious if I didn't have folk like him and Piers Creed to make mock of. Did I tell you about Creed the Farter?'

'Aye, you did, more than once.'

'This here is Secretary Oliver's joyous house of entertainment,' Jude announced, stopping at a closed door. 'Scene of my life-wasting scribbling and associated tortures. Coldest place on earth, if I know anything, where we sit and feel our bollocks shrivel and fall off, if we're not careful. You want to see inside, if it's not locked? Creed is probably still working like an idiot.'

Jude tried the door, lifted the latch. It squealed open and, sure enough, there was Piers Creed, as Jude had half expected, bent over his desk, pen in hand. Despite the noise, the clerk didn't look up.

'Jesu's sake, Piers, you farting, foolish fucker, can't you think of anything better to do on our free afternoon? Go play bloody snowballs or something. Hey! Don't ignore me. How can you sleep in here? It's too damned cold.' Jude kicked the clerk's stool to rouse him from his nap.

But Piers did not waken. He slid across his desk and toppled off the stool, the pen yet held fast in his fingers.

'Wake up, you idiot.' Jude grabbed his fellow before he should fall to the floor and hurt himself. He shook him but it did no good.

Seb lowered himself to the flagstones with care. He removed his gloves and touched the clerk's cheek.

'His skin be icy.'

'So would any man's be in this place. See? The brazier isn't alight. Come on, Piers, rouse yourself, you idle...'

'Shouting at him will have no effect, I fear.' Seb put his fingers to the pulse point under the angle of the jaw. ''Tis a sorrowful thing, Jude, but your friend be dead. We must fetch a priest to him, straightway.'

'What? Dead? Can't be. Don't prattle such nonsense. He was well enough before dinner.' Jude bent closer. 'You're certain of it?'

'Aye. There be no doubt.'

'Hell's name, Seb, you think he's perished of the bloody cold? It'll serve that bastard Oliver right to lose a clerk. He shouldn't be so bloody mean with charcoal for the brazier.'

'I have no doubt of his death, Jude, but as to the cold being his killer...' Seb pushed himself upright, using the desk as an aid. 'Look at this chamber.' He gestured to the other desks, the shelves and the coffers. 'Do you usually work amid such disarray?'

Jude hadn't noticed until then the chaos of papers flung about, coffers gaping and overturned. He appeared shocked, running his fingers through his hair.

'Oliver'll have bloody apoplexy when he sees this. And he'll vent his spleen on us. Christ, what a mess, Seb.' He began to pick up papers and sheets of parchment.

'Best leave them,' Seb said, touching his brother's shoulder. 'The coroner should observe all as it lies. Just fetch a priest to see to this unfortunate soul.'

Jude dropped the sheaf of Creed's neatly written summonses back on the floor.

'Aye. There'll be someone in St Stephen's Chapel. Wait here.'

Seb had no intention of leaving. Once Jude had gone off upon his errand, he went on his knees again to examine the clerk's body more closely. There was naught to see; no blood on the clothing, no marks of strangulation at the throat. Mind, it would not have been so quiet a death if there were. Mayhap, he had died of cold or some natural cause but it seemed too great a coincidence that someone had then turned all the paperwork on its head. Unless Creed himself had suffered some fit of frenzy, ransacking the scriptorium, then sat down, took up his pen and calmly died. How likely was that? Nay. Someone had been searching for something.

Seb elbowed Gawain aside and turned the body onto its front.

'Keep back, lad. Do not put your nose where 'tis not required.' Seb parted the sparse hair, feeling for any injury to the head. His fingers explored the scalp and the hairline behind the ears and along the back of the neck. There was naught untoward. No bruising; no swelling. Either none had occurred or death came so swiftly, there was not time enough for such signs of violence to develop. But then, an inch or two lower down the neck, he found what he was looking for.

Before Jude's return, Seb had laid the clerk's body straight and seemly and closed those clouded eyes. He and the dog kept watch by the door.

The priest attended to the corpse, giving unction and doing all he could to aid the departing soul. Others gathered, summoned like carrion crows by the scent of death: gawpers and idlers all, whether kitchen scullions or velvet-coated courtiers. Folk were all the same, whatever their breeding.

As first-finders, Seb and Jude were required to wait for the coroner to arrive and ask his questions. Still, at least it wouldn't be London's Coroner Fyssher, that inefficient, unfeeling rogue who, in the past, had been the Foxley brothers' occasional employer. Westminster would have its own official and, whatever his nature, he could be no worse than Fyssher.

'What did you find?' Jude asked as they shivered in the passageway outside the scriptorium to allow the priest to minister to the dead, undisturbed. 'I know you couldn't resist the temptation to look whilst I was gone.'

Seb huddled deeper into his cloak, avoiding the press of the ever-growing crowd in the narrow way. His hip ached and he used his staff to fend off an over-eager servitor craning his neck to see, fearful of being jostled off balance. At least Gawain, lying close, was keeping the draughts from his feet.

'You know me too well, Jude,' Seb whispered. 'Aye, I admit I did look closely, as you surmise. As a result, I can tell you that the victim knew his killer and trusted him utterly. He was taken quite unawares.'

'Killed, you say? How? I saw no blood, no injury.'

'But it was there, even so, 'neath his hair, where none would look.'

'Except you.'

Seb shrugged.

'As you say: except me. I found a small puncture wound at the back of the neck, betwixt the vertebrae. Just a speck or two of dried blood marked the place; the cause of instant death inflicted as the scribe was writing, bending forward over his work, most like. He would have had no time for a last prayer nor even for one final thought, poor soul.'

Saturday eve

Seb had the opportunity to see the stained glass in St Stephen's Chapel but it didn't come with the leisure to study it in detail; neither was there daylight sufficient to appreciate its jewel-like colours.

The king had reluctantly given permission for the inquest to be held in the chapel nave. The torches had been lit and set in sconces; candles illuminated the steps of the chancel where a chair had been placed beneath the arch of the Rood Screen for the coroner.

Coroner Sir Thomas Burns was a man of middling years

with a beaming, cherubic face – anyone less like the dour Fyssher was hard to imagine. Yet such a merry countenance seemed much at odds with his solemn office, dealing with unexpected or inexplicable deaths. A jury of Piers Creed's fellows of like social standing had been summoned in haste. The fourteen men chosen to serve included two palace cooks, three valets, a stable groom, four servitors, two wardrobe attendants and three clerks from the King's Scriptorium.

'That's Hal Sowbury, the chief clerk, the bane of our lives and his miserable toady, Lawrence Duffield.' Jude spoke low at his brother's ear, pointing out the clerks, distinguished by their dusty black gowns and ink-stained fingers. 'I wouldn't trust either of those buggers any more than I would a bunch of starving curs to guard a haunch of beef.'

'And the third clerk? Is he one from your office also?' Seb asked, indicating a skinny fellow standing behind Sowbury and Duffield, seemingly hoping to fade into the mural painting on the nave wall beyond.

'Aye. That's Andre le Clerc – most aptly named. Supposedly, his father's French, so that's how he got the bloody job. Bit of a mouse though; not a sociable fellow, worse even than poor old Piers, God rest him.' Jude crossed himself, as did Seb.

Secretary Oliver, impressively rotund, had given his testimony as Piers Creed's employer. It amounted to naught, made betwixt coughs and sneezes. Oliver claimed he knew nothing of the circumstances as to why one of his clerks had been working when the office should be closed. He was unacquainted with any of Creed's family or friends, if indeed he had any of either. No, he had not been informed that the clerk in question was unwell in any way likely to cause his sudden demise. In truth, according to Oliver, this was just typical of his pestilent clerks, ever determined to put him to the worst inconvenience they might devise. Dropping dead in the scriptorium was simply another way of wasting his precious time. And now he would be put to the trouble of finding a replacement.

'A sympathetic man, is he not, your master?' Seb whispered to Jude behind his hand.

'He's a bloody tyrant; make no mistake, little brother.'

A surgeon, Master Curran, was then summoned to take his oath, state his qualifications and guild membership before giving his learned opinion upon the cause of death. It involved a deal of convoluted speech, Latin medical terms and astrological conundrums but, so he said, Creed had died of heart failure… or cold… or some aberration of the brain. Finally, after a lengthy testimony, the surgeon's conclusions were summed up in three words: *mortem naturae debitum:* death by natural causes.

'He be mistaken,' Seb said. 'Creed was murdered.'

'You're certain of that? You can't be mistaken?'

Before Seb could reply, Jude, as a first-finder, was called to take his oath and answer Coroner Burns's questions. Stating his name, age, current place of residence and profession was straightforward; explaining why he was in the scriptorium on a Saturday, after it had closed for the half-day, was less easily done.

'My brother asked me to show him where I worked, so I did. He wanted to see inside the king's palace. He's just bloody nosy like that.'

I might have known it would be my doing, Seb thought.

'So I brought him, never expecting the scriptorium would be unlocked,' Jude continued. 'But, since it was, we looked in. My brother's also a scribe and was eager to see my desk and situation – having a professional interest, somewhat. We saw Creed sitting at his desk, as if he was working. I couldn't believe it – it was too bloody cold in there without the brazier burning and the ink would've frozen again since this morning.'

'Why would he be there, working alone on a Saturday afternoon? Do you know?'

'Creed held the key to the scriptorium so he could go there any time and he loved the damned work. The fool seemed to enjoy writing endless writs, warrants, summonses and the like. God alone knows why; the rest of us don't.' A murmur rippled around the assembly at Jude's comment, though whether it betokened agreement – from the clerks, perhaps – or disapproval from those in authority was hard to determine.

'The deceased was sitting at his desk, working, you say?' Burns asked, raising a quizzical eyebrow.

'He was still holding his pen but looked as if he'd dozed off. He didn't answer when I spoke to him. I tried to wake him but he fell off the stool.'

'And you believe he was already dead, not simply senseless?'

'My brother said it was the case. He knows of such matters better than most.'

'How so? Did you not tell this inquest your brother was a scribe, like you?'

'Aye but he's oft assisted both City Bailiff Turner and Coroner Fyssher back in London, solving a number of perplexing murder cases.' Jude turned his head slightly, caught Seb's eye and grinned.

Seb sighed and rolled his eyes. Why did Jude have to reveal that? Was he determined as ever to make Seb's life more difficult than need be? Such a statement would surely mire them more deeply in this unsavoury matter.

'At what hour did you discover the deceased?' the coroner asked Jude.

Jude shrugged.

'Well, it wasn't yet dark. My brother wanted to see the stained glass here, in the chapel. You can only see it at its best in daylight, so... I don't think we'd heard the bell chime for Nones in the Abbey over yonder. I suppose it must have been sometime before three o' the clock.'

'And when had you last seen the deceased alive?'

'He was fit and well enough when we were summoned to dinner. The rest of us went to the Great Hall; I was bloody starving, I can tell you.' A muffled tittering ensued amongst those gathered. Such levity was unseemly, in Seb's opinion.

Coroner Burns seemed to concur and frowned at Jude. He

had no interest in the state of the witness's belly.

'What of the deceased? Did he accompany you and your fellows to the hall?'

'Nay, I think not. Creed was often late to dinner, lingering over his bloody work. I usually keep – or kept – his place at the board, save some pottage and bread for him, though it's mostly cold by the time he arrives.'

'How long after did he arrive in the hall this morn?'

'Well, now I think on it, I'm not sure he did come, not before I left to hasten home, leastwise.'

'Was that a common occurrence?'

'Don't know really, regarding Saturdays. Most other days, he would turn up eventually, just in time to have to bolt down a cold dinner. Why don't you ask the other clerks? Most of them live here in the palace, as Creed does – did. I bide elsewhere; I'm not Creed's bloody nursemaid to know his every move.'

'So death could have occurred anytime betwixt the hours of eleven and three o' the clock?'

'I wasn't here all that while. How should I bloody know when he shuffled off? Ask the others. They could have gone back to the scriptorium any time. Not that they would.'

'Why do you say that, Master Foxley?'

'Because no man in his right mind goes to that damned icy box unless he's forced to – except Creed, of course. But then he's a bloody idiot – or was.'

Chapter 3

Saturday eve
St Stephen's Chapel nave

S EB REMOVED his cap, pledged his oath with his right
hand upon the Gospels and stood before the jury to answer
the coroner's questions and give his testimony. He most heartily
wished he'd remained at home this day and not ventured out
in such vile weather, only to stumble across a dead body and
all that its discovery entailed for a first-finder. He could have
been at his cosy fireside with Rose and the little ones, having
enjoyed a goodly supper. Rose would be worrying about him
by this time, fearing he had come to grief on a patch of ice and
suffered some hurt.

Having recited his particulars, as required, including his
recent elevation as an Assistant to the Warden-Master of the
Stationers' Guild, Seb met the coroner's eyes directly. He was
a most honest citizen with naught to hide and would have Sir
Thomas Burns realise that.

'Master Foxley, you say you manage your own business as a
stationer in Paternoster Row in the City of London and I see you
require a staff to aid your walking. So tell the court what caused
you to risk coming all the way to Westminster in the snow?'

''Twas the anniversary of my brother's birth yesterday. I
brought him a gift, sir. Besides, the staff be but a precautionary
measure. I make use of it but rarely.'

'How did giving your brother a gift – I recall that he said

he dwells in Thieving Lane – necessitate a visit to Westminster Palace? I would know your explanation.'

'Sir, my brother offered to show me the stained glass in the chapel here. I heard tell it be of the finest workmanship. My own craft involves illuminating manuscripts and observing the use of colours and pigments used elsewhere, in other arts, assists me to improve my skills.'

'Then why were you in the scriptorium?'

'We passed the door upon our way from the courtyard. Jude – my brother – told me it was his place of work. He lifted the latch and, finding it was unlocked, he pushed the door open. We went within forwhy, when Jude spoke to the unfortunate Master Creed, he failed to reply or even look up. The door creaked loudly: anyone who was not stone deaf must have heard it but the clerk did not move. His behaviour – or rather the lack thereof – made us think something was amiss with him. As turned out to be the case.'

'What do you know of the deceased?'

'Naught at all, sir, I never saw him afore this day. We have never been introduced.'

'But you know who he was?'

'I have heard my brother mention his name in conversation but that be all. We were not acquainted. I did not know him by sight either but Jude called out to him from the doorway.'

'What did your brother say?'

'He, er, said "Piers, why be you working still?" Or something like.' Seb felt his cheeks redden. These were not Jude's words but he couldn't repeat what his brother had truly said, not here, in God's house, before witnesses. Yet to tell a lie under oath was a sin.

'We would know the exact nature of what was said,' Burns insisted, his pleasant features taking on a solemn cast.

Seb squirmed, shuffling his feet, staring at the floor tiles.

'I called out to him "Piers, you farting foolish fucker, can't you think of anything better to do?" Jude shouted out. Laughter ensued among those gathered. 'Just spare my brother's blushes, can't you?'

Burns rapped his knuckles on the lectern to restore order.

'Were those the precise words used?' he asked.

'I believe they were, sir,' Seb answered, still knotting his fingers and feeling hot 'neath his fine cloak.

'Tell us what you saw when you entered the scriptorium – in your own words.'

'Thank you, sir. I noticed that Master Creed did not turn towards us but I had greater interest in seeing how the King's Scriptorium be organised. I felt shocked to see the place in so great a condition of disarray. Confusion was all, regarding the papers: parchment strewn about, coffers open, their contents flung aside. Since it appeared unlikely to my mind that anyone might work efficiently amid such chaos, I could but conclude that the place had been searched in considerable haste and carelessly.'

'Searched?'

'It seemed most likely to me but then I have never set eyes upon the scriptorium until now. I cannot think that the king's clerks be so unruly and untidy in their work.'

'Indeed. The possibilities will be looked into. For the present, tell us what you did next.'

'It was then that my brother called my attention to Master Creed who was now slumped upon the floor beside his desk. Jude attempted to wake him but could not. I saw that Master Creed's eyes were open but their sight veiled. I feared we were too late to aid him. I felt beneath his ear, here...' Seb demonstrated. 'I found no beating of his pulse. I then suggested to Jude that he fetch a priest, since he knows the ways about the palace as I do not. After he was gone, I put my ear to Master Creed's chest to make certain his heart had stopped. I could find no sign of life. I turned him upon his front, the better to examine him...'

'Why would you do that? 'Tis a surgeon's business to examine the body, not yours.'

'Forgive me, sir. I fear 'tis somewhat of a custom of mine. As my brother mentioned afore, I have assisted both Coroner Fyssher and City Bailiff Turner in London with similar occurrences in the past, in the event of no surgeon being available – to wit: I have dealt with dead bodies and looked into the possible causes of their demise.'

Burns cleared his throat.

'We'll pass over the appropriateness or otherwise of your unsolicited actions for now. In the meantime, describe what you did.'

'I half-expected to find some evidence of a blow to the head but there was none, so next I...'

'Why would you – or anyone – expect to find such a sign of violence?' the coroner interrupted.

'Er, well, in my experience, limited though it be, a death from natural causes rarely comes to pass upon an instant. A few moments of pain would ensue and, likely register upon the features as shock or agony, yet Master Creed seemed to have departed so peacefully.'

'Wherefore, again, I ask why you thought to see any sign of violence?'

'A blow to the head may stun a man utterly, whether it kills him immediately or if some further means of extinguishing life be applied after. I thought that could account for him dying unaware that his end drew nigh. At which moment, the bladder and bowels usually evacuate in the final struggle to survive, to take one more breath.'

'And had they? And did you find a head wound? Indeed, we know you did not for the surgeon has already testified that no injury was found of any kind.'

'Nay, sir, on both counts. But the surgeon be mistaken. There was an injury – small but proving mortal upon the instant. Master Creed was murdered, sir.'

The assembly in St Stephen's Chapel rose in a clamour. Murdered? In the king's Palace of Westminster? Outrageous!

The surgeon shouted out, quite truthfully, that this upstart had no medical training and no right to question his findings as the expert in such matters. This Foxley fellow was but a charlatan and a fool and should be fined for his presumption. Others agreed, in particular the clerks on the jury, fearing things might become awkward for them in the scriptorium, if one of their number was suspected of having died by murderous means and intent.

'You've set the fox among the chickens now, little brother,' Jude called out. 'Should have kept your mouth shut.'

'Silence! Silence!' thundered Coroner Burns, grabbing the nearest thing to hand – the Gospel book – and thudding it against the solid oak of the lectern. Order returned slowly. 'This inquest will adjourn until Monday morn at nine o' the clock. Tempers will be cooled by then but all witnesses must attend on pain of contempt. Dismiss.'

Darkness had long since fallen but the paleness of snow seemed to light the streets and overlay them in an eerie quietude. Seb and Jude could see their way well enough, back to Jude's lodgings in Thieving Lane. Seb felt torn betwixt hastening home to reassure Rose he had come to no harm and the need to draw a few calming breaths over a cup of ale with Jude. Thinking another half hour would make little difference to Rose's anxiety, whereas a measure of ale would fortify him for the long, cold walk back to Paternoster Row, he elected to do the latter.

'I had to speak out. Justice demands it,' Seb was saying as they clomped up the stairs to the cramped lodgings, Gawain following behind. 'Your fellow clerk deserves his due under the law; I care not what some slip-shod surgeon says. He be gravely mistaken, calling it death by natural causes when it be naught of the kind. Besides, 'twas you who set matters in train, telling the inquest of my work with Fyssher and Thaddeus Turner.'

'Keep your bloody voice down,' Jude told him. 'We have

neighbours who'll hear every word and I don't want them knowing all our damned business.' He pushed open the door at the top of the stair. 'Chesca! Pour us some ale, for pity's sake.'

'There is no ale. You telling me not to go out, so how I getting any ale?' Chesca, swathed in a tattered blanket, was seated at the board, looking at papers, scribbling with a frayed pen and half-frozen ink as best she could. She waved the pen at them without taking her eyes from the page before her. 'There is little wine but pour it yourself. I being busy.'

'How dare you speak to me so, you little bitch. Don't answer me back or I'll...' Jude raised his hand to strike her but, seeing the expression on Seb's face, he changed his mind, knowing his brother had such strong opinions concerning corporal punishment. They had enough to deal with as it was without causing a fraternal argument now. He could deal with Chesca later when Seb was gone home.

'There!' Chesca declared, throwing down the pen. 'I having done the letter in English for you. It not important. Just about weather and courtly fashion and other things but it looking oddly.'

'A letter from home, Chesca?' Seb asked, taking an interest in anything requiring pen and ink.

'No!' Jude snatched the pages from Chesca before Seb could see them.

'Jood bringing it from work. He not knowing what it means. I doing it in English for him, he thinking it might be important but it not.'

'How many times do I have to bloody tell you, Chesca? You mustn't tell anyone.'

'Seb your brother. He no telling.'

'You say it looks odd? Why is that?' Seb asked. 'May I look at it?'

Jude sighed impatiently and thrust the paper at him.

'Look, if you must, though it has naught to do with you.'

Seb took the English translation and studied it with creased brows. He kept glancing at the Italian original lying on the board, sticky with marchpane from the sweetmeats Chesca had finished off. It meant no more to him than a letter in the strange writings of Araby.

'These marks betwixt certain words...' He pointed a few of them out. 'Have you copied them faithfully from the original letter?'

'I know how to do good copying. My mother teaching me to write out copies of my father's *effetti di vendita* – how you saying... bills of sale. Those marks being anywhere. They making no sense.'

Seb compared the two. Both were dotted with symbols, each like a small figure seven. Sometimes a similar mark – the Tironian nota – was used by scribes as an abbreviation for 'and' or 'et' in Latin but, in this case, as Chesca said, it was used here and there throughout the letter, without meaning and quite at random.

Chesca's translation told of the recent English bad weather and the author's dislike of the cold and damp. It mentioned the style at court for men's doublets with heavily padded shoulders – no doubt just to keep the wearer from freezing to death – and the out-moded shoes with long points that were still worn in this backwater that was England, unlike the square toes of fashionable Milano. It described the Christmas entertainments of a month ago at Westminster and other innocuous subject matter. And the whole was spattered with that little symbol.

'There would seem to be naught of any consequence there,' Seb concluded, returning the translation. He picked up his gloves off the table. 'I should bid you both good eve. Rose will be concerned for me and my walk home will not be swift on such a night. God keep you, Jude; Chesca.' Since there was no ale to be had to give him strength, nor a decent fire to thaw his benumbed feet, thoughts of Paternoster Row tugged at him, invitingly. 'Would you both come dine with us on the morrow?' he asked as he made for the door. The thought of Jude and

Chesca shivering over their meagre fire, eating the last crumbs of Friday's supper dismayed him.

Out in Thieving Lane, Seb found one of a group of lads waiting around with torches to light travellers on their way home for a penny. On such a bitter night, it was a wonder there were any torch-boys out on the streets at all. He chose the smallest, skinniest lad, thinking a tall, well-built fellow would attempt to make him hasten more than was wise in these icy conditions. He could keep pace safely with a little lad. Pulling on his gloves, Seb realised he had also picked up the original Italian letter with them, stuck to the leather with a morsel of marchpane. No matter, he could return it later. Jude would not have need of it until Monday, if at all, after the inquest was concluded.

Sunday, the twenty-ninth day of January
The Foxley House in Paternoster Row, London

Before the household attended mass at St Michael le Querne's Church, Seb had rummaged through the clothes coffer in his bedchamber. Coming in to make his bed, Rose found him upon his knees amongst piles of his late wife's clothing.

'I suppose 'tis time I ought to do something of use with these items,' he said out loud. 'Em's been gone a while now – God assoil her soul. But I do not have the heart.' He held a gown of sapphire blue wool, put it to his nose and breathed deep. Emily's Sunday best, it smelled of lavender but, so he fancied, there was yet a hint of her scent lingering in the cloth. How could he give it away when it bore the last trace of his beloved? Then there was the fine gown of rose-coloured silk velvet that he had purchased at such cost so long ago for Em. She had worn it but a handful of times, fearing being fined for breaking the sumptuary laws. He had quite forgotten it, smoothing the soft knap under his fingers, recalling how he had chosen it with love, knowing the colour would have so suited Em's complexion. He wondered if Rose might have a use for it but dare not enquire for fear it might seem to be a gift given with certain 'expectations' on his part. He set the folded gown aside with its sorrowful memories.

'Are you looking for anything in particular?' Rose asked, plumping pillows with enthusiasm.

'Em's boots. I would send them to Westminster for Chesca. She has only shoes unsuited to the snow. She may as well have Em's, rather than leaving them lying here, unworn. Ah! I have found them. I shall pay a messenger to take them afore church. You recall that I invited them to dine with us? She may wear them for the walk here, if I send them straightway. Jude be reluctant to permit her to go out in the snow for fear of spoiling her shoes. He says he has no money to buy another pair.'

'Are they truly so badly off? I thought Jude's clerkship paid well.' Rose tucked in the last corner of the sheepskin coverlet and brushed off a few stray bits of fleece. 'Were you warm enough last night?' she asked. 'There are spare blankets from Adam's bed, if you have need.'

'Do you and Kate not require another blanket in this bitter cold?'

'Nay. We keep each other warm in our bed and often share it with little Dickon and Julia too. We have such a cosy nest but I worry for you in your lonely bed.'

'I do well enough. The cloak you gave me makes a fine extra coverlet, if I should have need. Come, we must hasten, else we shall be late for mass and I must find a lad to take these boots to Westminster aforehand.'

Sunday dinner at Paternoster Row was quite a gathering, as usual. Rose was ever delighted to feed a crowd and these days, what with the workshop's increasingly lucrative commissions from certain lords, Richard, Duke of Gloucester, and King Edward himself, no less, they could afford it. Not only was it a charitable act, it also gave Seb and Rose a deal of pleasure to feed family and friends on the Lord's Day, whenever possible.

Besides Seb, Rose, Kate, the talented apprentice, Nessie and Ralf, the live-in journeyman, little Dickon and the babe, Julia, Adam Armitage – Seb's relation and fellow stationer – came with his new wife, Mercy Hutchinson, as was, and her three lads. Stephen Appleyard, lately Seb's father-by-marriage, and Jack, his assistant of sorts, for no one ever quite knew what Jack Tabor was, were at the board, along with Old Symkyn, the beggar who held a special place in Seb's affections.

Only Dame Ellen had refused the invitation to dine, sending word that she was too old to risk the walk from her house in Cheapside in such bad weather, what with the snow still treacherous upon the ground. Rose had since dispatched a covered platter of the finest morsels to the old silkwoman, sending young Kate. Nessie would do naught but moan and bewail her ill-treatment, if Rose sent her on so cold an errand, despite her being the serving wench who should do as she was instructed.

Jude and Chesca arrived in haste, breathless from running. Chesca, an ebony-haired beauty who seldomly observed the English custom of a married woman concealing her tresses, glowed with cold upon her flawless cheeks. She was laughing.

Seb supposed the young lass was delighted to have escaped her icy imprisonment in Mistress Baxter's lodging-house, now that she had a decent pair of boots to wear. He checked at the snow-damp hem of her gown but she saw him and lifted her skirts.

'*Si,* Seb, I wearing the boots you sent. *Grazie.*' She kissed him heartily, cold lips against both his cheeks. 'You liking?' she asked the company. Everyone agreed that the boots looked well, if somewhat familiar of old.

'Do they fit you?' Seb asked. He had wondered whether Emily's feet were larger than Chesca's, though wearing a second pair of hose would solve that difficulty, but if they were smaller, he feared that could be a problem.

'They fitting good and warming.'

Dinner was a fine meal of roasted pig with sage and apples, pigeons with dried apricocks in a coffin, buttered turnips with grated ginger – to warm the belly – red cabbage with caraway and anise and an almond cream tart with dried plums. Rose had excelled with her culinary delights once more. She was making quite a name for herself as a cook of some renown.

When the meal was done and the womenfolk had cleared the board and scoured the pots and dishes, everyone but Julia, who was too young, went out into the garden plot where much of the snow lay pristine. But for Nessie's footprints, down to the henhouse and back, to feed the chickens, it lay soft and sparkling in the weak winter sun beneath a colourless sky. A snowball tournament ensued. Jack, Kate, Chesca and Adam – old enough to know better – were flinging snowballs at each other. Simon, Mercy's eldest, joined in, as did her young scamp, Nicholas. Their shouts and shrieks of merriment brought out the neighbours, Jonathan and Mary Caldicott, who began throwing snowballs over the fence.

Jude shoved a handful of snow down Chesca's neck, making her squeal with shock. What names she called him were best not translated into English, but she took it in good part. Rose and Mercy showed the youngest, Edmund and little Dickon, how to heap up the snow to build a mountain. Stephen, Ralf and Old Symkyn were exchanging tales of their youth when, no doubt, the snow had lain deeper and for far longer, giving rise to great adventures for them but dire consequences for others.

Seb had thrown a few snowballs, not wishing to spoil the fun, but the cold was gnawing at his hip. Thus, he welcomed Jude's suggestion that they return within doors.

'I would speak with you, little brother, away from the others.'

Seb nodded. He expected to hear another plea for coin. However much Jude was supposed to be earning at the King's Scriptorium, somehow his purse was ever empty, or so it seemed. Therefore, he was surprised when no such request was forthcoming. They sat either side of the cheerful blaze in the parlour. Seb added another log to the fire and held out his hands to the warmth.

'How much do you need?' he asked while Jude poured him a cup of spiced ale from the jug Rose had left to warm on the hearthstone. Everyone would be in want later, after playing in the snow.

'Need?' Jude echoed. 'Aye, well, a couple of marks always comes in useful if you're offering, but that's not what I have to talk about. This morn, I was summoned before church to attend upon Coroner Burns and that bastard Oliver in the scriptorium. On a bloody Sunday too! They have no right...'

'It must have been important...'

'To them; not to me. But then, of all people, Lord Hastings turns up. The lord bloody chamberlain, in person, so I knew it meant we were in trouble.'

'Do you mean you and your fellow scribes?' Seb took a sip of his mulled ale.

'No. I mean us; me and you. Or, rather, *you*.'

'Me? How can I be in trouble with the lord chamberlain? Has he decided I overcharged him for that Book of Hours he commissioned? I most assuredly did not.'

'It has naught to do with that.'

'Thank Jesu for His mercy. It was an honest piece of work...'

'Stop your prattling and listen to what I have to say. Oliver needs a clerk to replace Piers Creed, preferably someone who doesn't bloody fart all the time.'

'You need to enquire of Richard Collop, then. He will suggest a suitable fellow from the guild.'

'Don't interrupt. I knew you'd say that. The fact is that "The Powers-That-Be" – or at least the coroner and Lord Hastings – already have somebody in mind.'

'Who? Anyone we know? I wish them the best of it.'

'They want you, little brother.'

'What? But that be absurd. I have a workshop to run. And why would they want me? I be no common copy clerk.'

'Well, thank you for the insult – calling us "common copy clerks". You think you're so bloody high and mighty...'

'I meant no such insult, Jude. Besides, you are no common clerk since you know Italian. But you have not answered my question: why me?'

'Because, little brother, you are known in high places. They've heard of you. You made that copy of Vegetius' *De Re Militari* for the king last twelvemonth and Lord Hastings' Book of Hours and stuff for Duke Richard of Gloucester. It all adds up and gets your name known.'

'But they do not want an illuminator. Tell me truly, Jude. Why me?'

'You told them at the inquest about how you've solved crimes here in London.'

'I had no choice, did I? You had said as much afore I was called to make my oath.'

'It seems that the coroner had the surgeon take a second look at the corpse last eve and they now agree with you that Piers Creed was murdered. With the king's sanction, they want you to work in the scriptorium alongside the rest of us clerks and sniff out the villain... all very mantle-and-sword, if you ask me.'

'I cannot afford to abandon the workshop here. I have a livelihood to earn.'

'It will pay well...' Jude took out a purse and threw it at Seb's feet. It landed with a weighty thud. 'That's come straight from the royal coffers which just goes to show how bloody desperate they are. They want you to start work in the morn, directly after you've finished giving your testimony to the inquest. No one will discuss it; you'll just come to the scriptorium and take Piers Creed's place. Or rather, you'll be sitting on my arse-biting stool and I shall move up a desk, away from the draughty door, seeing you'll now be the poor bloody newcomer. Hard luck, little brother.'

'I have not agreed to do it, as yet,' Seb said, looking at the purse upon the floor. He did not pick it up but let it lie. 'And, mayhap, I shall not.'

'You would refuse the king's chamberlain? He's the one organising this. The king doesn't want a bloody killer running loose in the palace. For Christ's sake, take the damned money afore the others come back in.'

'I have no need of it.' Seb drank his ale.

'Don't be so bloody stubborn. If you don't need the coin, the king needs you to solve this crime. How can I tell him you've refused? His wrath will come down on me. You have to do it, Seb; for my sake if not the king's.'

'I cannot go to and fro twice a day from London to Westminster and back.' Seb stumbled upon an excuse. 'And there be not room enough for me to bide at your place.'

''Tis taken care of. You'll have Piers's bed in the clerks' dormitory. 'Tis all arranged. I warn you though, don't bring anything you value forwhy the clerks' are light-fingered as any cut-purse ever was but wear as many shirts as you can. Those clerical gowns are hardly worth the wearing; they're of such poor thin stuff and well-worn by those who went before.'

'I have not agreed...' Seb repeated.

'But you will. We both know that. You never could resist poking your nose into someone else's puzzle. Am I right?'

Chapter 4

Monday, the thirtieth day of January

SEB WAS YET in two minds about Lord Hastings' proposal that he should be employed in the King's Scriptorium, working for Secretary Oliver in order to discover Piers Creed's killer. Even so, he had no choice about braving the hazards of the long walk to Westminster because he must complete his testimony to the inquest at nine o' the clock. It meant an earlier rising than usual to see the workshop settled for the next few days. He hoped this business would take no longer than that.

Adam and Ralf were capable and reliable. They could deal with most of the orders in hand and run the shop. But a recent commission required Seb's artistic talents: the new lord mayor, Bartholomew James, a wealthy draper, wanted his portrait painted in his mayoral robes and chain of office. A sitting had been arranged at Guildhall for this afternoon and Seb had had to send a message, cancelling it – something he was ever reluctant to do.

Then young Kate, the apprentice, had to have some task set to occupy her for a while. He had given her a copy of Geoffrey Chaucer's *A Prayer to Our Lady*. It was an acrostic poem with each verse commencing with the letters of the alphabet in order, from 'Almighty and all merciable Queen' as the opening line of the first verse, to 'Zachary you calleth the open well' beginning the final verse. The language was somewhat old fashioned these days but Seb would have Kate invent individual illuminated capitals for the entire alphabet. Such an exercise would give her good practice and take days to complete. It was also a task of the kind Kate enjoyed.

Seb had made sure of a good breakfast before leaving home and was wearing three shirts under his jerkin – as Jude had suggested. Without consciously deciding, it seemed he was likely destined for that cold scriptorium. Huddled in his crimson cloak with the fur-lined hood about his ears, he took a few minutes to seek out the beggar, Old Symkyn, back at his previous post by the northern entrance into St Paul's Cathedral precinct, nigh opposite the Foxley House in Paternoster Row. Despite the cold, the elderly man was there upon his stool with the begging bowl at his feet.

'God aid you this day, my friend,' Seb greeted him.

'And you also, Master Seb. That was a fine dinner we had yesterday. Your Rose is an accomplished cook. A chill day we have ahead of us but a thaw tomorrow, I reckon.'

'Then I shall expect it. You be rarely mistaken concerning the weather. In the meantime, I know you may make good use of these.' Seb gave Symkyn Jude's old gloves. 'They were my brother's and much worn, but Rose has made neat repairs that they may serve a while yet.'

'Your Rose is a treasure indeed, young master. Thank her right heartily for me. When are you going to make an honest woman of her? I think it's time you did before some other less deserving fellow sweeps her up.'

Seb felt his cheeks redden, and the cold east wind was not the cause.

'I must be upon my way, Symkyn... business at Westminster. I dare not be late.'

'Farewell! God keep you, young master.'

Seb hurried across the cathedral's precinct and left the city by Ludgate, using his staff to steady himself on yesterday's snow which had frozen hard overnight. He had left the faithful Gawain at home and felt but half-clad without his companion but the King's Scriptorium was no place for a dog. He sighed, realising his decision was made: he would do as Lord Hastings required.

Westminster

Seb arrived in St Stephen's Chapel at the appointed hour for the inquest without getting completely lost in the rabbit warren that was Westminster Palace, an unintended detour by way of a linen and napery storeroom notwithstanding. It was hardly any warmer in the chapel than outside, so Seb kept his cloak on, despite the vivid red colour being at odds with the gravity of the occasion. It was too bad: he refused to stand shivering before the court; some might interpret that as fear and conclude he had something to hide.

Coroner Sir Thomas Burns was there at the lectern, ready to resume his interrogation of Seb as one of the first-finders. Jude was absent, having completed his testimony on Saturday eve but three of his fellow clerks were there as jurors, as before. Sowbury, Duffield and le Clerc, if Seb recalled their names correctly. He would need to learn more of his new colleagues in the scriptorium. Jude particularly disliked Hal Sowbury, the chief clerk, and Seb wondered why. But then his brother ne'er had a liking for his superiors in any situation.

'Master Sebastian Foxley,' the coroner began, 'Remember you are still under oath to speak the truth before this court. Are you prepared to continue giving your testimony under that condition?'

'Aye, sir. I shall do my best.'

'Would you refresh the jury's memory concerning your discovery of Piers Creed's body in the king's scriptorium upon Saturday last? I believe that may be helpful.'

Seb recounted all that he had said upon Saturday eve about

how he had examined Piers Creed's body.

'I concluded he had been murdered forwhy there was a small wound upon the back of his neck, 'neath his long hair: an incision which, nevertheless, went deep, betwixt the bones of the spine. Likely, a long thin blade was used. I believe 'tis called a *stiletto* in the Italian tongue. I read once in a surgical text that a penetrating incision in just such a place may cause death upon an instant. I believe that was the case here.'

'Do you make a habit of reading surgical texts?' Burns asked, more out of curiosity than in search of information.

'Nay, sir, I was copying out the text for a commission but the passage caught my attention and I remembered it. Seeing the wound upon Piers Creed's neck brought it to mind once more. That was all.'

'So, Master Foxley, in your expert opinion...' Burns paused to allow a titter of ironic laughter in the court to subside. 'How long had the deceased been dead when you and your brother discovered the body?'

''Tis difficult to determine, sir. The body was cold to the touch but there was no sign of *rigor mortis* – that is the stiffening of a corpse after death...' Seb explained.

'I'm the coroner,' Burns said loudly. 'I am aware what *rigor mortis* means.'

'Of course you do, sir, but I would explain for the benefit of the jurors.'

'Very well,' Burns said with a sigh. 'Continue.'

'In normal circumstances, the onset of *rigor mortis* commences in the extremities within an hour or so of death, so it could be assumed that Piers Creed had been dead for an hour perhaps. However, the process is slowed by the cold, so he could have been dead for somewhat longer when we found him shortly afore three o' the clock. Yet I think not. I believe he was killed not long afore our finding.'

'Why do you say that?'

'The scriptorium was become icy since the brazier was alight no longer. The body would have cooled swiftly but I be certain, when I turned it, taking hold under the arms, there was yet some vestige of warmth remaining. By my reckoning, Piers Creed had likely been dead for less than one hour but for more than half an hour; closer to the latter.'

'That is most helpful to this court,' Burns said, though his tone lacked sincerity. "Tis a wonder that you did not see the perpetrator leaving the scene.'

'You speak truly, sir, for the searching of the papers would have taken some time, I think. It seems most probable that we did not miss the murderer by many minutes.'

Seb had given his testimony and was dismissed from the inquest. He felt quite wearied by the ordeal. Coroner Burns might have the face of a cherub but he possessed a core of stone. Seb had been discomfited, unsure whether the coroner was mocking him or if the man had believed any word that he said. No matter. That part was done with now and he made his way to the scriptorium to begin the next: the pretence of working for Secretary Oliver.

Jude awaited him in the passage outside the creaky door.

'You're late,' Jude said by way of greeting. 'Oliver is spitting venom at your tardiness even before you bloody start.'

'I was at the inquest,' Seb said.

'Aye, and Oliver bloody knows it but he has to treat you as a miserable menial, like the rest of us, so prepare yourself for a tirade. Here, take off your cloak and put this on.' Jude held out a clerk's black gown, faded and fraying. 'Did you wear extra shirts, as I told you?'

'I did.' Seb removed his bright cloak and put on the gown. He sniffed it and felt the thinness of the cheap woollen cloth, rubbing it between his ink-stained fingers. 'Is this Piers Creed's?'

'Nay, fear not,' Jude lied, knowing how sensitive was his brother about such things. It was fortunate the murdered man hadn't bled, else the lie would be found out by Seb's observant eye. 'They all stink the same. I'll take your cloak home with me later. It'll not be safe in the clerk's dormitory. As I told you, the clerks are all bloody thieves.'

'Suppose I have need of it?'

'We'll keep it safe for you. Don't worry, I won't let Chesca sell it to a fripperer. Besides, I get my month's pay tomorrow, so we'll have money enough for another few weeks. You must come to supper; we'll have a decent meal. Otherwise, you'll have to put up with the victuals they serve here in hall.'

'Be the food so bad?'

'We get a generous helping at dinner and it usually tastes well enough but supper – so I've heard tell – is always a gamble, depends whether anything decent was left from dinner or not. Unless the king is presiding, in which case it'll be lavish fare and mind your manners.'

'I always do.'

'But the others don't. Like scavenging curs, the entire pack of them, I bloody warn you. Snatch what you can or you'll go hungry to bed. Ready?'

Seb nodded, readjusting his gown in seemly wise.

With Seb's cloak under his arm, Jude pushed the scriptorium door open. It squealed in protest.

They stood before the secretary's lectern.

'Where have you been, Foxley? Work began an hour since. I'm docking your pay accordingly,' Secretary Oliver snarled.

'I was waiting for my brother. We were attending Coroner Burns's inquest, as you know full well.' Jude's tone was not going to earn him any favour with the secretary, neither was his mutinous, scowling expression. 'This is my brother, Sebastian, come to take Creed's place, as arranged.'

'Another damned Foxley to plague us, eh?' Oliver said, addressing Seb and looking him up and down with narrowed eyes. 'I know not why Lord Hastings thinks you'll be an asset to this scriptorium, if you're half as idle as your sibling...' Oliver shrugged and didn't trouble to complete the sentence. He wiped his nose on his sleeve. 'Sowbury!'

'Sowbury is serving on the coroner's jury, sir,' a fellow with a red beard spoke up. 'Along with Duffield and le Clerc.'

Looking around, Seb saw only three clerks, apart from Jude and himself, and several vacant desks.

'Waste of time,' Oliver muttered. 'Very well, Newson, you'll have to show him what's required. I have business elsewhere.' With that, Oliver stalked out, the door protesting behind him.

Seb was told to sit at the desk closest to the door, as Jude had warned, so he checked the stool seat. Sure enough, the wood was split across and likely to pinch the sitter, so Seb settled himself hesitantly but without hurt.

'Copy this letter out four times in a good secretary hand,' Barnabas Newson instructed, putting a paper before him. Seb saw it had been written in haste with numerous deletions and insertions but was legible – just. 'Ink is in that bottle by the brazier; pens in the box on the shelf over there. Mark one copy for the muniment room, one for the Signet Office, one for the Exchequer Office and the best copy goes to Lord Hastings for King Edward's signature. Understand?'

'Aye,' Seb nodded. He had barely set his mind to what was required when the door squealed open and the remaining clerks entered, having finished their jury service.

'What was the verdict?' Newson asked them.

'Unlawful killing.' The speaker was a swarthy fellow with bushy brows – Hal Sowbury, the chief clerk, Seb recalled. 'What else would it be? Took us all of a minute to reach it.'

'This is the new clerk,' Newson nodded towards Seb. 'Another damned Foxley, worst luck for us.'

'I know. He's just given his testimony at the inquest.' Sowbury regarded the newcomer, glaring at him for so long Seb felt his palms growing sweaty. 'You know what's required?' Sowbury demanded.

Seb swallowed.

'Aye,' he managed to say.

'Aye, MASTER SOWBURY, you oaf. I'm the chief clerk here and you'd better remember it. And the letters must be accurate and neat. Got that? Else I'll make you do them all again.'

'Aye, Master Sowbury. I understand.'

'Then get on with it. All four copies must be made before dinner and, if they're not finished, you'll stay at your desk until they are, even if you miss dinner in the hall.'

Seb didn't answer. He took his inkwell to the bottle by the brazier and filled it, collected half a dozen pens from the box and resumed his seat. He trimmed and shaped all the pens with his penknife, smoothed out the first of the blank parchment sheets provided and began writing. The scribbled letter consisted of about thirty lines of cramped script. Seb gauged the required line spacing with a practised eye in order to make it fit the page, copying swiftly in a fine, even, secretary hand. No mistakes; no ink splotches. It was no more than he would expect in his own workshop. In a little over half an hour, he had completed the four copies required. Sowbury had said to choose the neatest to go for the king's signature but, since all were identically perfect, Seb decided the chief clerk could select which it should be.

Seb left his desk and presented the parchment sheets to Sowbury who now occupied the comfortable chair at the lectern in the secretary's absence.

'Finished already?' the chief clerk sneered. 'How many errors will I find in such hasty workmanship?'

'Not one,' Seb said, confidently, knowing he spoke the truth. He was capable of copying entire manuscripts faultlessly. A short letter hardly made use of his talents, even if it required the deciphering of a poorly written document. He'd read worse.

Sowbury perused the sheets, taking his time.

Seb wondered if the clerk was going to find faults, if only for the sake of putting the newcomer in his rightful place. But he didn't.

'Not bad,' he conceded at last. 'Now file them: that pile goes to the muniment room, that for the Signet Office, that for the Exchequer Office and one to await King Edward's signature. Then take the next letter from that central pile. They're all to be dealt with in the like manner. Don't touch the right-hand pile: those are warrants. The central pile is correspondence and the left-hand pile is for accountings. And the papers in that box,' he said, waving at a wooden tray on the shelf beside the pens, 'Are miscellaneous, so leave them be unless instructed.'

Seb obeyed, taking the next piece of correspondence to his desk but he eyed the tray of 'miscellaneous' stuff. If the chance offered, it might be worth looking through as part of his covert investigation. After all, that was the true purpose of his working here: to discover a killer. Besides, copying letters for hour after hour was mind-numbing, as Seb had soon realised. There was no camaraderie here as there was in most workshops. Scribing in silence was no way to build friendship with your fellows. Worse yet, it was unlikely to reveal any clues towards unmasking a murderer. Dinnertime would likely present a better opportunity to get to know his new colleagues.

Later, as Seb followed the other clerks towards the Great Hall for the communal dinner, Jude pulled him aside in the passageway.

'For Christ's sake, Seb, you'll get the rest of us a bad name.'

'How so? What be your meaning?' Seb asked, frowning in puzzlement.

'All those bloody letters you've copied out in one morn. And I saw even that bugger, Sowbury, couldn't find fault with your efforts. Don't work so bloody hard and eagerly, else we'll all be expected to do the same.'

'I thought that was the purpose of a clerk in the king's employ. What would you have me do? Twiddle my thumbs, pick my nose and stare at the roof beams, as the rest of you do half the time. I should rather work and have the hours pass more quickly.'

'You're worse than bloody Creed, being so damned keen. Remember, we get paid the same, whether we do two letters or a score. Don't you see? If we get all the paperwork done today, then they'll not need us on the morrow and we lose a day's pay. See sense, little brother.'

'Oh. I had not thought so far.'

'Forwhy you're a bloody idiot, Seb.'

'I shall work less diligently this afternoon but I cannot be idle, you know that.'

'Aye. But work slowly. There's no hurry. None of it is that important.'

On their way to the Great Hall, Seb was appalled to see one of the clerks step into an alcove, open his gown and unlace his breeches.

'Are there no latrines here?' he asked Jude. 'I have a need.'

'Do as everyone else does. You saw Beckton...'

'I shall not! I have more respect for the king's palace. 'Tis disgusting. Even wild beasts do not befoul their own den. I pray you, tell me where I may find the house of easement.'

''Tis quite a walk – which is why no one else takes the time and trouble – and you'll be missing dinner. Besides, the conduit that flushes everything away is frozen. Trust me: you don't want to use that stinking cess-pit.'

'Just tell me where...'

'Oh, very well, if you must. Return to the Inner Gate, where we came in, and watch out for that miserable bastard, Walter. Turn to your right-hand, towards the river. On the far side of Outer Courtyard you'll see the Great Clock Tower and beyond that, closest to the river, you'll find the jakes. Don't break your damned-fool neck slipping on the ice and don't freeze your bollocks off. Have a care, you mad idiot. I'll save you some dinner.'

Seb followed the directions, stepping carefully. Things were thawing, as Old Symkyn had predicted. Water drip-

drip-dripped from the eaves and the snow was turning to slush underfoot; in its own way, no less treacherous than afore. In the winter-bare branches of a quickthorn bush beside the entrance to the house of easement, a flock of sparrows huddled, damp feathers fluffed, sulking like disgruntled scholars. Seb could sympathise. An icy trickle found a way down his neck, making him shiver. And Jude was correct about the stink. Seb could not hold his breath long enough, so he wasted not a moment. Jude was also right about nobody else using the place. He was alone in the foul-smelling gloom.

Seb returned to the Great Hall. The clamour of voices, the clatter of knives and spoons were over-loud after the silence of the scriptorium. The hall was chill even with so many persons present, the tapestries wafting in the draught as the servitors went to and fro, removing empty dishes and bringing new ones piled high with food.

Seb washed his hands in the laver bowl provided before squeezing onto a bench betwixt Lawrence Duffield and Robin Beckton, making his apologies. The pair obliged by shuffling apart to make room for him. Jude gave him a disapproving glare from across the board but pushed a pewter platter towards him. There was white bread, slices of capon in some kind of sauce – with ginger, Seb decided – and a curd tart with lemon, no matter that they were seated at a lower table where less exalted dishes were provided. As Jude had said, the victuals served at dinner were good indeed, despite King Edward's absence from the dais. Chamberlain Lord Hastings presided instead, sitting to one side, avoiding the carven chair 'neath the canopy of estate: the king's place.

'How come you're too high and mighty to sit with me now?' Jude asked when the meal was done and they made their way back to the scriptorium at a leisurely pace. No one hastened to work at Westminster, Seb was coming to realise. It was a wonder that England was governed at all.

'You think I was avoiding you? I was not.' He brushed a few pastry crumbs from his sombre robe. 'But how shall my investigation proceed unless I win the trust of my fellows? I cannot interrogate them openly, can I? They would probably tell me to mind my business and let them alone. My hope be to have them talking freely in my presence, mayhap, to guide the conversation somewhat towards a productive destination. I must become better acquainted with the others and I shall not achieve that if I do but keep company with you. I apologise if I offend you but I do so with purpose and reason.'

'Mm, I suppose that makes sense of a sort. So, did you learn anything useful?'

'Within so short a space? Hardly. But did you know Lawrence Duffield is planning to depart his clerkship here? That will leave the scriptorium short-handed again, seeing my position be but a temporary one until we find out the felon.'

'Duffield's such a lazy dog, we'll not miss him,' Jude said, shrugging.

'Truly? It seemed to me this morn he was more conscientious than some. He put a fair number of letters to be filed. Who does that task? The filing, I mean.'

'Andre le Clerc is responsible for all the filing. He likes the job, probably because it gets him out of the scriptorium. He seems to spend hours in the muniment room and taking copies to the appropriate offices. It's just an excuse to put down his bloody pen, of course.'

As the clerks reached the scriptorium door, Seb recalled something he had meant to say to Jude.

'By the by, upon Saturday eve, at your place, that Italian letter that you had been translating...' Seb hoped the falsehood did not cause his face to flush. 'The one telling of the English weather, if you remember?'

'What of it? I haven't seen it since.'

'Nay, for it became adhered to my gloves with marchpane

but I have it safe. Remind me to return it to you.'

'Don't bother. It wasn't of any interest anyway. No tasty morsels of gossip. Forget it, little brother.'

During the short afternoon, afore darkness fell so early, Seb made four copies each of three further letters. He could have done more but heeded Jude's warning. One concerned an application for a licence to crenellate a lord's new manor house at some place Seb had not heard of – Oswestry, wherever that was. The king was refusing to grant permission without stating any reason. But that was the king's prerogative.

Another was a letter of thanks for the New Year's gift of an enamelled silver cup from the Mayor of Exeter to the king. From the tone, Seb thought the king had not appreciated the gift over much. Mayhap, it was of poor quality and craftsmanship, or else his grace had expected a more significant item and was disappointed.

However, the third letter requiring to be copied quite shocked Seb. In his opinion, a matter of so confidential a nature should have been kept more privily, not laid open to the gaze of curious clerks. Yet there it was: King Edward's grovelling apology to his lady-mother, Cecily, Dowager Duchess of York.

As he read and copied, Seb learned that mother and son had argued during Christmastide and, so it seemed, the king was in the wrong. Or, at least, he had lost the argument, though the subject of the dispute was not mentioned. Seb flushed hotly as he wrote, wishing this once that he was one of those scribes who reproduced a text without ever consciously registering the meaning of the words. The king sounded like an errant schoolboy caught out in some mischief or other, pleading, making excuses, denying and laying blame elsewhere by turns. It did not sound as a royal missive ought but showed the king in a poor light, as all too human, fallible. It made uncomfortable reading for Seb. He felt tempted to conceal the additional copies away from other eyes and not file them, a source of malicious gossip if ever there was. But then such decisions were not his to make. He filed them as required, shaking his head at the folly of his betters.

'I saw you looking puzzled over that last letter,' Jude said as they left the scriptorium when their labours were ended. He had Seb's crimson cloak around his broad shoulders, taking it home for safe-keeping, as he insisted was necessary. 'Was it anything interesting? I could do with some amusement after the bloody tedious day I've suffered.'

Seb winced, scuffed his boots on the flagstones, aware that the king's letter to his mother was exactly the kind of amusement his brother had in mind.

'Nay. Naught but an accounting I found difficult to transcribe.'

'You're lying. Your cheeks have flushed red as this cloak.' Jude stroked the good quality wool. 'Come, little brother, you know you're the world's worst at lying. Besides, I put my copies of a letter to Richard, Duke of Gloucester, atop yours. I'll tell you what the king wrote to your precious patron, if you tell me what he said to the duchess. Aye, I saw that much, the addressee, at least. Come now, you know I can keep a bloody secret well enough.'

In truth, Seb knew no such thing. Jude could gossip like a fishwife, if the mood were upon him, especially after a few ales.

'It was just thanking the duchess for her New Year's gift. Naught of importance.'

'What was the gift?'

'A-an enamelled cup.'

The way Jude looked at him, Seb knew his brother did not believe the lie.

'You can tell me the truth later,' Jude said. 'Meanwhile, I have a wife to go home to. Oh, and fear not, I'll take good care of your cloak.' He grinned, knowing Seb was loath to part with it, desiring its warmth. But it was too fine a garment to leave unguarded in the communal dormitory where Seb would be spending the night – or so Jude told him, repeatedly.

'That's your bed there,' Hal Sowbury directed Seb. Predictably, it was the one closest to the door and most distant from the consolation of the hearth where a goodly fire blazed. But the situation was not so bad. Supper had consisted of bread, cold capon left from dinner and a thick pottage well flavoured with onions and leeks.

'May I put my belongings in this coffer?' A small chest stood beside each bed with a tallow candle in a wooden sconce set upon it.

Sowbury shrugged.

'It's yours, if you want to risk it. I wouldn't leave anything valuable. Some in here are not to be trusted. There's a piss-pot in the corner – handy for you but we all make use of it. The servant hasn't brought our night livery yet but there'll be bread and ale left on that sideboard. We help ourselves but there's never enough ale to last, so take your share quickly, that's my advice. Make yourself at home.'

'My thanks, Master Sowbury. You be kind indeed.'

'Away from the scriptorium, you may call me Hal.'

'And they call me Seb.'

'Good. Two Foxleys is too confusing. One's one too many with that scoundrel of a brother of yours. Sebastian is a bit of a mouthful, so you'll be plain old Seb from now on for all purposes.'

Seb smiled and Hal did likewise. Jude was mistaken concerning the chief clerk, Seb decided. Sowbury was not a bad sort at all. He was also pleased to have made a little progress in getting to know his fellows.

What pleased him less was the bed. When he sat upon it, he

could feel the mattress was thin as paper. The sheets were clean – a blessing – but well worn and the solitary blanket was moth-eaten and of little substance. Again, he resented Jude having taken his cloak. He could have used it as a warm coverlet. It was going to be a chill night as the fire burned low. As it was, his feet were cold within his boots, despite his wearing two pairs of hose.

Seb counted three-and-twenty beds in the long, narrow dormitory, lined up against the walls: a dozen on his side of the chamber and eleven on the opposite side with a gap in the midst for the fireplace and chimney – a coveted position, no doubt. He noted that Hal was seated on the bed closest to the hearth. By now, he knew the names of his fellows in Secretary Oliver's office but others also wore clerks' gowns, though not all. He wondered what their duties might be but then recognised a servitor from dinner earlier. A mixed bag of sleepers shared the dormitory.

Recalling his payment in advance from Lord Hastings and, therefore, his purpose here, Seb would join his colleagues on the benches around the hearth, enjoying the warmth whilst it lasted. Hal and Lawrence Duffield were playing draughts on a make-shift board drawn on a stool-seat. Robin Beckton – he who had used the alcove as a jakes, to Seb's disgust – was dicing with a group Seb did not know. Andre le Clerc, the gaunt, skinny fellow said to have French blood in his veins, was reading from a tiny volume, holding it awkwardly towards the firelight to better make out the text. Barnabas Newson, the red-bearded clerk who had first instructed Seb, was stretched out upon his bed, eyes closed, maybe dozing, maybe not. The only other scribe from the scriptorium was Eustace Dane, an elderly fellow, bald 'neath his greasy coif. He was curled in his bed, the blanket drawn up to his double chin, snoring already.

Seb approached Andre to enquire about the book he was reading.

'I enjoy reading greatly,' Seb said. 'What be the subject of your book, if I may ask?'

'The text is French. You will not comprehend it.' Andre closed the book and set it aside.

'I be familiar with the French tongue, written as well as spoken. Not fluent, I grant, but I do well enough.'

Andre wasn't to be persuaded. He left his seat by the fire and moved away, taking his book with him. Seb grabbed the chance of a good place by the hearth but it seemed the French clerk was less inclined to friendliness than the others.

Chapter 5

Tuesday, the thirty-first day of January
Westminster

JUDE GREETED his brother with a cheerful grin and a
hearty slap on the back forwhy it was plain that Seb was
miserable this morn.

'How did you enjoy sleeping with your fellows, eh?'

'My bed was cold and hard as a tombstone with but a rag
of a blanket for warmth. I could not sleep for shivering. The
others snored, coughed, talked, farted and used the piss-pot
beside my bed so many times it was overflowing by morn. I
must inform them they be requiring a larger receptacle for so
many men. How might I sleep amid so much noise, suffering
such discomfort that my bones ache from cold and weariness?'

'You'll get bloody used to it.' Jude was never one to feel
much sympathy but the dark shadows below his brother's eyes
were too obvious to ignore. 'No doubt but breaking your fast
improved matters.'

'Last eve's pottage served cold did little to improve my lot,
though the bread was fresh and yet warm from the oven – the
only warmth I have felt this morn. I had to break the ice in
the ewer to wash. No one else took the trouble. Little wonder,
I suppose.'

'Poor old Seb. But at least the brazier will be alight in the
scriptorium. Come on. There'll be time to thaw your hands
before it, as well as the bloody ink. Did you uncover any clues

to the murderer you're supposed to be searching out?'

'Ssh. Do not speak so loudly of it.'

The door gave its usual squeal of protest as they entered. Barnabas Newson was within, looking peeved, having been chosen as the key-holder in Piers Creed's place. The task required him to unlock the scriptorium right early, kindle the brazier and set the inkwells and bottle to thaw – a duty the red-beard did not relish.

'God give you good day, Barnabas,' Seb greeted him. 'I did not see you at breakfast, so I have brought you some bread. 'Twas new baked and warm earlier but has cooled by now.' He held out a folded napkin.

'Why?' Barnabas asked, giving Seb a wary glance.

'I thought you might be hungry.'

'That's not what I mean. Why would you do me any favour? What do you want in return?' The clerk had not accepted Seb's offering.

'Naught at all. 'Tis a gesture of friendship, if you will? I expect naught from you.' Seb put the bread on Barnabas' desk and went to warm his hands at the brazier. He wondered why the fellow was so suspicious of accepting a heel of bread. Glancing over, though, Seb saw Barnabas eating the new bread, eager as a half-starved street urchin.

When Secretary Oliver arrived to take his chair beside the brazier, those not already at work – namely Jude, Barnabas and Robin – scurried to their desks and took up their pens. The clerks stood, scraping stool-legs on flagstones, bowing their heads to acknowledge the master's arrival.

'Worse than bloody school used to be,' Jude muttered.

'What was that you said, Foxley?' Oliver demanded.

'Nothing, sir. Clearing my throat was all,' Jude said. 'Bastard,' he added in an undertone.

Seb promptly completed four copies of a long letter to the Lord Mayor of York regarding unlawful fish traps in the River Ouse. It was mentioned in the missive that the Duke of

Gloucester had brought the problem to the king's notice. Seb smiled to himself, thinking how like Lord Richard it was to have remembered and taken the trouble over an issue that was of importance to none but humble folk.

Engrossed in his work, Seb forgot his brother's warning not to be so diligent. He transcribed the copies required of eight different documents before dinner, a pause to fetch more ink and flex stiffening fingers, notwithstanding. Otherwise, the only distraction had occurred when Secretary Oliver roused himself to come and stand at Seb's shoulder, overseeing his work for what seemed an hour but was probably far less. It made him nervous, fearful of making an error or knocking the inkwell. He breathed more easily when Oliver left him alone. He hoped the man was satisfied with his efforts. At least, he made no complaint.

'Come sit with us.' Sowbury beckoned to Seb when he entered the Great Hall for dinner after a chill expedition to the distant house of easement across the Outer Court. Fortunately, most of the snow and slush had melted away, making things easier for Seb's occasional less certain step. It made for a safer and more rapid journey.

Jude was already piling his platter high with mutton in gravy with parsnips and he ignored Seb when he seated himself betwixt the chief clerk and Lawrence. Seb silently congratulated himself on his progress in befriending his colleagues, though it was a melancholy thought that his true purpose in doing so had naught to do with friendship. He had ever to keep in mind that he was here to find out a cold-blooded killer. Even so, he could not set aside the likelihood that all but one of the clerks was innocent of that foul crime and any companionable action on their part might well be genuine, whilst his was but pretence.

Seb had an abhorrence of such deceit, yet here he was, playing a false part like a mountebank. It did not sit well with him; no wonder he had not slept last night. Noisy bedfellows and a thin mattress were not the only causes. A troublesome conscience ne'er aided blissful slumber. And Seb had an unforeseen difficulty: he was beginning to like most of his fellow clerks. Barnabas was a wary soul, Andre seemed cold and Eustace he had yet to speak with but the others were pleasant enough, if he made some little effort to get to know them.

'How are you liking the work here?' Sowbury asked, spooning gravy over his meat before scooping a generous portion into his mouth.

'Well enough,' Seb answered cautiously. It would sound unconvincing to be overly keen. Neither did he want to offend his fellows. 'I quite enjoy transcribing. 'Tis somewhat of a challenge, I find.'

Sowbury laughed, spraying gravy.

'Reading those dolts' unintelligible scribbles, you mean. They ought to teach the damned secretaries to write properly. Oliver's hand isn't so bad but some of them… A fellow named Crabtree – crabbed hand, more like – if he takes the king's dictation, there's no making head nor tail of it. Fortunately for us, he slipped on the ice last week and broke his wrist, so no pen-wielding for him for a while. Mind you, when he returns, his scrawl will likely be worse than ever. Creed is – was – the only one who could be bothered to labour over Crabtree's notes. We'll be relying upon you, Seb, to do that in his stead, if you can?'

Seb did not tell them that his clerkship was but a temporary position. None knew that but Lord Hastings, Secretary Oliver and Jude, of course.

'What of Piers Creed: what manner of man was he? Was he easy to work with?' Seb asked, looking at his platter, not at his colleagues. He took up a gobbet of mutton on his knife, popped it in his mouth and chewed. It would not do for them to realise the importance of his innocent-sounding enquiries.

'Hard to say. We never really came to know him, did we, Lawrie?' Sowbury picked at a piece of meat caught betwixt his teeth.

'No, despite us being clerks together for... how long? Five years for me. Longer for you, eh, Hal?' Lawrence added. 'He never joined us in any pastime. His scribing seemed to be his only interest. Not like the rest of us. Barnabas has his wenches – outside the palace only. Eustace goes to his daughter when he's not working or sleeping. Robin has his gambling cronies. Andre reads books. Your brother has that luscious young wife of his, the lucky rogue. Me and Hal... we like games and musick and... other things.' The pair exchanged knowing grins. 'What's your pastime, Seb?'

'I draw and sing... a little,' Seb said, wiping the platter clean with the last of his bread. 'So Creed was a solitary fellow. He must have worked diligently to fill his lonely hours.'

'Aye, he did. Evenings, Saturday afternoons and occasional Sundays. A good thing, too, since it meant the paperwork didn't pile so high as it might. I've noticed the difference this week. Without Creed's efforts, the work to be done outweighs that accomplished and matters can but get worse. I don't suppose you feel so inclined, Seb...' Sowbury asked, raising his bushy brows in hopeful expectation.

'Not I. I have my own family in the city. I shall spend Saturday afternoon and Sunday with them.'

'I suppose you've got a merry goodwife like your brother?' Lawrence asked, his ale cup halfway to his lips.

'I be a widower... for a twelvemonth, come Eastertide.' Seb could not disguise the sorrow in his voice.

'Oh, our condolences for your loss. But you say you still have family.'

'Aye, two small children, Dickon and Julia. My cousin, Adam, my colleague, and his wife and her youngsters... I see them daily. Kate, my apprentice, and Ralf, my journeyman, bide with us also along with Nessie, our serving wench. And Rose...'

'Rose? Is she your sister or another cousin?' Sowbury chuckled and nudged Lawrence with his elbow. 'Nay, Seb, I see by your eye she's more than that to you. Your mistress, more like.'

'Indeed, 'tis not the case!'

'But you wish it was.' The pair was now laughing heartily, rocking the bench, and others at the board were joining in the merriment, even if they knew not the cause of such mirth.

Jude alone, seated opposite was frowning. It angered him whenever his brother was mocked. It had been so since their days of childhood. He would ever defend Seb against the taunts and jests of others, even those well-meant and all the while poking fun himself. But, being brothers, that was different.

'I keep a decent house and Rose be my...' Seb's words trailed off. In truth, he never knew how to speak of Rose nor to describe how greatly she mattered to him. And now his colleagues had found him out, on that score, at least.

'Have you heard?' Barnabas was saying, speaking with his mouth full, dribbling meat juices into his beard. 'The little Prince of Wales is coming here from Ludlow to spend Easter.'

'So what?' Robin asked. 'What's that to us?'

'You know the king will be in a fine mood for celebration with his lad joining him. Easter will be a great feast for us all.'

'But we've got forty days of Lenten misery before that,' Robin moaned.

'Well then, that'll make Easter even better, won't it?' Barnabas was not to be dismayed.

Upon the clerks' return from dinner, Barnabas unlocked the scriptorium door. Everyone went to their desk but Seb. He wanted to speak to Secretary Oliver and begged leave to conduct the conversation privily in the passageway.

'What do you want, Foxley? This isn't the way we work here. You don't tell me you want a private word. I'm your superior.' Oliver stood with his arms folded, glaring at his lowliest clerk.

'Forgive me, sir, but you know full well my employment here be for another purpose than clerkship. I have a question regarding the filing of documents.'

'Then ask one of your fellows.' Oliver made to go back inside the scriptorium but Seb put a detaining hand upon the secretary's arm. Oliver's eyes blazed and he pulled away. 'How dare you.'

'I apologise to you but I cannot ask the others for fear of raising their suspicions. You must understand that, sir. After all, 'tis possibly the case that one of them be the killer.' Seb kept his voice to a whisper.

'And I don't know why that should be,' Oliver shouted. 'Why are my clerks suspected so, there being no evidence whatsoever?'

'I admit, 'tis no more than logic that makes one of them the most likely perpetrator. But I need to know...'

'Then explain this damnable logic to me, for I see it not.' Oliver gave a violent sneeze and dabbed his nose with the hem of his fur-lined gown.

Seb put his hands inside his sleeves. The passage was icy and this conversation was becoming longer than expected. He shivered and did his best not to sound exasperated as he began his explanation. Oliver's impatient foot-tapping did not help.

'Creed's killer came here upon Saturday last, after dinner. He knew Creed was likely to be working, even beyond the official hours but that was his only course of action. Elsewise, if Creed were not working, the door would be locked. The guilty one knew that, so must be aware Creed was a key-holder.'

'Others could know that much and be aware of Creed's love of his work,' Oliver said.

'True. But then there was Creed's reaction to the newcomer.'

'Maybe he was so engrossed, he neither saw nor heard... was quite unaware.'

'Sir, we all know well the screeching of that door each time it opens. A man must be deaf not to hear it and none have mentioned that Creed was thus afflicted. And even if he was, I now work at Creed's desk and can testify to the vicious cold draught that bites at my legs upon every occasion of that door opening. Believe me, sir, Creed knew someone had entered the scriptorium yet thought little of it. Thus, I think it can be assumed that whoever came in was not out of place here.'

'How can you say what Creed thought? He might have been instantly in terror, fearing for his life.'

Seb sighed, wondering at Oliver's lack of insight.

'Creed was not in fear. The newcomer concerned him not in the least. This we know forwhy Creed sat at his desk and resumed his writing. The killer has to be one of the clerks. Anyone else and Creed would have asked questions, raised the alarum or, at the very least, put aside the confidential documents upon which he was working. Yet he was slain as he sat, his back turned, pen in hand. Only after he had dispatched Creed could the felon begin searching the paperwork – the very purpose of his coming. Which brings me to my query...'

'Why did he kill Creed? If the fellow was a clerk, he could have leafed through the documents, making some excuse – it was mislaid in the wrong pile, a likely error in transcription recalled. Creed would have assisted the search. Or why not come when the scriptorium was empty?'

'Because Creed had the key for the door; else it would take an axe to get it open. As for Creed assisting in the search, I suspect that was the last thing the killer wanted. Whatever he was looking for, it was of a confidential nature and not meant to be here at all. So, to my question, sir... I noted upon Saturday last that there were certain neat piles of papers, untouched during the desperate search. I now know them to be the documents for filing as warrants, correspondence and accountings. 'Twas the stuff in the 'miscellaneous' box that lay flung about in disorder, along with the contents of the coffers. So, I ask you, sir, what manner of papers was in that box on Saturday?'

'You expect me to remember? I have not the least knowledge. Now, be done with your foolishness, Foxley, and get back to work, or your pay will be docked considerably this eve.'

Seb recalled, it being the last day of January, the clerks would receive their salaries when work was ended. And I would remind you, he thought to say to Secretary Oliver, that you are not the man paying me. But he bit his tongue on the words. He was in Lord Hastings' employ, for better or worse. And at present, it was most definitely for the worse, his enquiries proving fruitless. Two days' labour in the scriptorium had garnered him not a solitary morsel of useful information.

That eve, despite everyone's purse chinking with coin, few of Seb's fellows in the dormitory had elected to spend time and money in the local taverns, as was their habit on payday. Instead, one or two had ventured out into the steadily falling sleet – likely, it would turn to snow, if it continued in the night – and brought back wine, cider and pies from various establishments along King Street. The mood was merrier and musical instruments were retrieved by those with talents for such things.

Seb was enjoying the musick, humming along to a ballad concerning a country lad's search for a sweetheart. Some of the words were too bawdy for his liking but there was no denying a tuneful melody.

'Hey, Seb!' Hal Sowbury called to him. 'Come join us. You said that you sing. Give us song, then. I can play most anything on this.' He patted his lute – a thing of beauty. 'What shall it be?'

Seb thought for a moment, going over to the benches set around the hearth.

'What of *Green Grow the Rushes-o*? Everyone knows that and may join in.'

For a while, Seb entertained his fellows and a lively time was had but the songs they suggested were less and less of a kind he wished to lend his voice to. He pleaded a dry throat and fetched some ale, allowing one of the servitors to take his place and closing his ears to the roistering songs which followed.

He sat upon the edge of his bed, huddling in the thin cloth

of his clerk's gown, which did little to warm him at this distance from the fire. Lawrence came to join him.

'You don't like their grubby little lays, do you? Neither do I. My dear mother would have apoplexy, if she knew I listened to such words, so it makes me feel guilty to do so. How about we play Nine-Men's-Morris?'

Seb nodded.

'I fear I be unpractised at such games but I shall do my best, if you will remind me of the rules of play.'

Needless to say, Seb lost three games in quick succession, having to pay his debt of sixpence to Lawrence. Unlike the other clerk's, Seb's purse wasn't full. He had left most of Lord Hastings' payment at home, both for safety's sake and to supplement the housekeeping money for Rose to care for the family.

'No more, Lawrie... I can afford to lose no more coin,' he protested with a laugh.

'Pity. I was about to suggest we play draughts.' Lawrence was grinning. 'But if your purse can't withstand it... and the bawdy songs are done with now. Come back to the fire. You told us you draw: what is it that you draw?'

'People, animals, buildings... what you will,' Seb said. 'I could draw your likeness, if you wish, Lawrie?'

'You think I'm a fitting subject, then? Handsome? Elegant? Of noble mien?' Lawrence raised his chin, assuming a pose in profile.

'I shall do what I may with the material provided, my friend,' Seb said, chuckling. 'As you say, we should return to the fire; the light there will better serve my purpose.'

Seb fetched his scrip from the coffer beside his bed and went to sit with his fellows as before. Hal, Barnabas, Andre and Robin watched as he took out his drawing board, his chalks – both red and white – and charcoal, each kept separate in a special wooden box with its sliding lid, to avoid exchange of colour. Searching in his scrip for a suitable sheet of paper, he found a pot of salve

Rose had given him some while before, when he had cut his thumb, but frowned over a folded piece of paper he couldn't call to mind. Pulling it out and unfolding it, he remembered:

'Ah, *mea culpa,* I had forgotten the Italian letter that my brother was translating. I must return it to him, that he may file it correctly.' Seb returned the letter to his scrip, making a note to himself to put it in his purse, to return it to Jude. 'Now, Lawrie, sit comfortably that you may remain still for a few minutes.' Seb found some other paper and pinned it to the board. He then observed his sitter for fully five minutes before making a single mark with the red chalk.

'Have you begun?' Lawrie asked.

'Aye. Afore long you shall have your portrait.' Seb drew unerringly with the red chalk, creating a perfect likeness as his hand moved swiftly over the paper. With the basic sketch done, he used white chalk to highlight and charcoal to create shadow, rounding out the under-drawing to a lifelike image. 'There. I have completed it.' Seb unpinned the paper, shook off the chalk and charcoal dust and passed it to Lawrence for inspection.

Lawrence's eyes were round with wonder.

'How did you do this?' he asked.

'You watched me. 'Tis no mystery. I make marks upon the paper according to what I have observed. There be no cunning magick to it.'

'Well, I certainly couldn't do it. What say you, Hal? Robin?' Lawrence showed the others the drawing. Of a sudden, it seemed as though everyone wanted their portrait drawn, crowding around, leaning close, to see the next likeness appear. Seb was kept busy for the remainder of the evening until he had no more paper.

'We'll get you some paper for the morrow,' Hal insisted. 'You haven't drawn Eustace and Andre yet. They'll want their portraits done, too.' Eustace was sleeping soundly in his bed long since and Andre was no longer in the dormitory. Hal took his portrait and pinned it to the wall above his bed. Man and image stared boldly at each other, both smiling with a prideful air. The chief clerk was well pleased with his portrait.

Wednesday, the first day of February

Seb had slept better last night and was determined that the first day of the new month would find him in a more confident mood. Having broken his fast with his fellows in the Great Hall, they awaited Barnabas Newson's juggling with the key to the scriptorium.

Jude arrived somewhat tardily and a blind man could have seen he was in as ill-humour as a bear with toothache.

'God give you good day, brother,' Seb greeted him in the passageway forwhy Barnabas was still wrestling with the lock and key.

A snarl was his only response but, as Jude turned towards him, Seb saw his brother's face.

'In sweet heaven's name, what came to pass?' Seb asked, reaching out towards his brother's cheek.

Jude batted his hand away.

'Nothing. A bloody bastard door ...'

Seb shook his head but said naught. A door ne'er made three parallel gouges like that; but fingernails might well have.

'Hey, Foxley,' Barnabas said, catching sight of Jude's injury as they crowded into the scriptorium. 'I hope the bitch was worth it. Or did that feisty little piece of yours catch you at it, eh?'

'Shut your trap!' Jude leapt over a desk to get at the key holder, fist drawn back in readiness to land a blow. Seb grabbed his arm.

'Jude! Brother. Be calm, I say. Barnabas meant no harm. 'Tis but a few words spoken in jest.'

'We'll see how he jests when I shove his bloody teeth down his throat. I'll have my revenge on you, Newson. Just you wait, you shit-hole rat.'

'No more of this, Jude,' Seb said, speaking softly, still gripping his arm. 'Sit down at your desk, for I hear Oliver's voice in the passage.'

'Get off me, Seb. Let me go, you stupid little fool.' Despite his verbal protest, Jude had the good sense to take his place at his desk, just as Secretary Oliver arrived, fat and breathless, to fall into his chair with a groan of relief. He, too, looked to be out of sorts this morn.

'Get on with your work,' Oliver yelled when he'd caught his breath enough to assert himself as a master should and survey his underlings. 'Where's le Clerc, that damned imbecile? He's late.' As he spoke, Andre le Clerc pushed the door open with a squeal. 'Where have you been? That's a penny docked for you already on the first of the month. Now, get to work.'

'Forgive me, sir. I was, er, detained,' le Clerc said, hastening to his place. The scowl upon his features announced another for whom the day had not begun well.

Back at his workshop in Paternoster Row, Seb knew there were many projects requiring his attention, every one of them of greater interest than mindlessly copying out someone else's deplorable scribblings. But it couldn't be helped. Lord Hastings had paid him, in advance, to discover a murderer and there was no other way to achieve that end, insofar as Seb could see, than sitting here, in an icy draught, acting the part of a clerk. So he resumed the act, transcribing documents, as required, becoming engrossed in the work, as was ever his way.

'Cease that damned singing,' Oliver roared. Everyone looked up from their silent penmanship. 'You; Foxley. Stop your noise. Christmas was over weeks ago.'

Seb was slow to realise he was the culprit. Singing whilst he worked was so natural an occurrence to him, he did not register that he was giving voice to some melody or other out loud.

'Forgive me, sir, but I often sing as I write. I ne'er realised I was doing so. What was I singing? I apologise if it disturbed anyone.'

'Some damned Christmas tune. Now keep quiet and get on

with your work. You're as big a bloody nuisance as your brother.'

Seb heard Jude muttering threateningly as he sat at the next desk. There came a hint, too, of muffled laughter from some other quarter. Seb bowed his head and continued copying, wondering how he might ensure he did not commence singing again when it was an unconscious habit, of which he was hardly aware. At home, no one would have mentioned it, or, mayhap, they might have joined in.

'Hey, Seb,' Lawrence Duffield called out as they made their way to the Great Hall for dinner. 'That was a merry air you were singing earlier. I approved it. The scriptorium is worse than a charnel house; it needs something to liven it up. How does the song go? *Gaudete, Gaudete, Christus est natus...*' Lawrence sang in a reasonably tuneful voice, deeper than his normal speech would suggest.

'Was that the song I sang? I was quite unaware,' Seb admitted. 'We choristers did sing it in St Paul's upon Christmas Eve and the melody has remained in my head since then. Now and then, it bursts forth without my knowing, however untimely or out of season.'

'You're a Paul's chorister? Then you must sing it properly for us this eve, in the dormitory. That should wake you up, eh, Eustace?' Lawrence said, prodding the elderly clerk who made some mumbled reply. Seb had yet to have a conversation with the old fellow who seemed to sleep more than he worked. It was of concern to Seb, though, that his colleagues were coming to know more about him than he was learning of them. That was not the way it was intended to come to pass.

At the board, Seb sat with Jude as they dined. The coney stew with dumplings was hot and filling, just what was needed. But Jude was in need of something else also.

'Your cheek looks to be somewhat inflamed,' Seb said. 'Did you bathe it with wine and put honey on those gashes?'

'Don't bloody nag me. You're worse than an old woman,' Jude said betwixt mouthfuls, reaching across to spoon another herb dumpling onto his platter before someone else took it. 'Where would I come by honey?'

'You need some salve upon it, at least. I have some in my scrip, upstairs in the dormitory. Come. Cease stuffing your face with food and I shall tend to it for you. If we be fortunate, there may yet be a little wine remaining from last eve to wash those cuts.'

'Wine? Wine's for drinking, not for wasting on a little nick.'

'You did not bathe it at all, did you? What if it should fester?'

'I told you not to nag me but let's go to the dorm now. I'll have that wine – to drink, not to wash with.'

Chapter 6

Wednesday afternoon

SEB AND JUDE climbed the stair to the dormitory but their hopes of a little wine left from last night to cleanse Jude's cheek were dashed.

'I fear the servants have cleared all away,' Seb said when they saw the sideboard was bare of any remnants of yesterday's payday feast.

'Drunk it, more like,' Jude said. 'No matter. It doesn't need bathing. Where's that salve you said you have?'

'In my scrip. I put it in the coffer by my bed.' Seb lifted the coffer lid and stared, dismayed, at what lay within. 'Oh, Jude. Look. My belongings ... See what has come to pass.'

'I warned you not to leave anything of worth in this bloody place. Why did you bring your damned scrip? You should've left it at home, as I told you, but do you ever listen to me?'

Seb knelt to take his things from the coffer. His scrip was there but emptied of all its contents. His box of chalks and charcoal had been opened, the lid thrown aside and the contents tipped out, colours mingling. Charcoal dust and crumbs besmirched everything. His one clean shirt and nether clouts were filthy with black dust and smears of red chalk.

'What has been stolen?' Jude asked, sitting on the bed, feeling the wooden frame through the thin mattress and covers.

'Naught at all,' Seb answered, frowning. 'My decent gloves be here; my shirt, grubby now, but undamaged otherwise; my drawing stuff, though the charcoal be but useless bits … and the pot of salve we require. Naught has been taken. I do not understand.'

'Well, last eve, we were all paid, weren't we – except you,' Jude said. 'No doubt, the bloody thief didn't know that and hoped you'd put your money in the coffer. Probably, every other coffer has been ransacked as well.' Without a by-your-leave, Jude opened the coffer beside the bed opposite. 'They didn't bother with this one; it seems undisturbed.' He did the same with the next coffer. 'This one could've been looted.'

Seb joined him, peering into a mare's nest of clothing and odd items of gaming paraphernalia.

'Nay. 'Tis Robin's coffer. He being so untidy, it always looks thus. But see here.' Seb found a purse, weighty with coin. 'Robin's winnings at dice last eve be safe and untouched.'

Jude went to the next coffer beside Lawrence Duffield's bed.

'Shit! Damn it,' Jude cursed, sucking his finger. 'Why does any man need so many bloody pins?' He slammed the lid down.

Hal Sowbury's coffer was undisturbed; his precious lute lay atop his neatly-folded spare garments. As they examined the other bedside chests, it became apparent that Seb's was the only coffer to have been raked over.

'Mayhap, some bugger wants to make sure you know your place as the newcomer,' Jude suggested, sitting on his brother's bed whilst Seb smeared salve on the gouges on his cheek as gently as possible.

'That may be so,' Seb said. 'These scratches look sore. How did you come by them?'

'Ow! Have a care, damn it.' Jude shoved Seb aside. 'How do you think?'

'Men be inclined to use their fists in a fight. Therefore, I would suppose they were made by a woman's hand, using her fingernails.'

'Bloody Chesca. She's due a sound beating when I get home.'

'Chesca did this to you?'

'Who bloody else would it be? That little bitch …'

'Were you arguing? It must have been a matter of considerable concern.'

'Keep your bloody long nose out of my business,' Jude said, jumping to his feet and elbowing past Seb.

'Keep the salve,' Seb said, closing the lid on the little pot. 'You may need it, if the inflammation is no better.'

Jude snatched the pot, shoving it into his purse without a word of thanks.

'We must hasten,' Seb went on. 'Secretary Oliver will chastise us, if we be late returning.'

'That man's a shit-house arse-wipe. I don't bloody care what he does.'

'You'll care if he docks your pay; you know you will.'

'Bastard. He's worse than a bloody galley-master, bellowing at us to pull harder on the oars, standing over us with a bloody whip. The fat, buggering bastard. One of these days, he'll drive me too far and I'll …'

'You'll do naught, if you have but a moment of sensible thought. How else will you earn a living, Jude?'

'Anything's better than this. I have ideas in mind.'

'You do? Then pray tell me. I have little liking for my pretending to be a clerk whilst espying for Lord Hastings. If you have some better way of uncovering a murderer …'

'No, I didn't mean that,' Jude said as they went down the stairs from the dormitory. 'I have other ideas about a means of earning my living. But you won't approve and neither will your precious bloody guild.'

'Sweet Jesu, Jude, 'tis not something illegal you have in mind, is it? I could not condone anything of a criminal nature.' Seb's face was such an image of horror, Jude laughed.

'Nothing illegal, I swear, but you'll most likely consider it criminal and certainly won't condone it. Now shut your clacking. Don't say a word.'

Seb fell silent as they went into the scriptorium but he greatly feared what his brother's next money-making scheme might be. His expectation was that it would not be entirely honest and Jude would fall into yet another cauldron of trouble. All afternoon, he worried at it like a tongue at a loosened tooth, so distracted that he made two errors in copying a single document. Fortunately, he corrected them before anyone saw but was concerned that he could have made more mistakes and not noticed them. Oh, well, it was too bad, if he had. He doubted the other clerks ne'er made errors.

That eve, having been invited to sup with Jude and Chesca in Thieving Lane, Seb did his utmost to make his spare shirt look respectable, trying to brush off the charcoal dust and smears of chalk. In truth, it would not show so much 'neath his doublet, jerkin and clerk's gown. He straightened his belt and glanced at the purse he wore there. Thieving Lane? Supposing it proved true to its name? He unstrapped the purse, wondering if it would be any safer here, in the dormitory. He recalled that Robin's gambling money had not been troubled, even though someone had rummaged through his own coffer.

Having made certain none were looking in his direction, Seb flattened his purse as much as possible and slipped it betwixt the thin mattress of his bed and the supporting ropes. Did it make a noticeable lump or was that naught but his imagination? It would have to serve.

Washing the worst of the day's ink-stains from his fingers, Seb set out from Westminster Palace and went through the Great Gate into King Street. A cruel easterly wind blew off the river, snatching at the thin cloth of his gown. But at least he wore his good gloves. He regretted not having his crimson cloak to wear over all on a night so bitter; yesterday's thaw being short-lived. He had brought his staff for safety's sake, in case the way proved icy.

At Mistress Brewster's lodging house, Seb was hoping for a

warm fire and a good meal now that Jude had been paid but he found no welcome at his brother's place. Instead, Chesca was in tears beside a cold hearth. Her gown was besmirched with mud. Even her hair hung in wet, muddy clumps. And there was no sign of any supper either.

'Whatever befell here?' Seb asked, going to Chesca's side. 'Be you harmed, lass?' Seb feared that Jude might have carried out his threat and administered a beating but that would not explain the mud.

'No. No harming done,' Chesca said, pushing her hair back into some semblance of order. 'Excepting your fine cloak, Seb. I so sorry I wearing it when he pushing me. Now it being all mud-covered and ruined.'

'Who pushed you?'

'Some bastard who's going to bloody regret it,' Jude answered for her. 'Grabbed her and pushed her over in the filth. Look at the state of her! And the foolish bitch dropped the basket with our supper in it. She's more bloody worried about your damned cloak than whether there's kindling for the fire and food upon the board. Bloody useless wife she is.'

'Oh, come now, Jude. Cease your complaining. Chesca has been much affrighted.' Seb found a cloth and there was water in a pot beside the hearth that was not yet gone quite cold. He dipped the cloth and wiped the mud from Chesca's face.

She managed a wan smile and took the cloth to make a more thorough job of cleaning up. Jude stalked up and down, fuming in a temper but doing naught of any use.

'Why do you not go out and buy us all some supper, somewhere?' Seb suggested. 'And some wood for the fire will not go amiss.'

'Who do you think you are, bloody ordering me around in my own house?' Jude growled.

'Well, you seem to be at a loss what else to do,' Seb said, bending to assist Chesca to remove her wet boots. 'At least you might find us something from a pie-shop or an inn. I be certain we are all hungry.'

Jude cursed but put on his cloak and went out, slamming the door loud enough that the royal court could have heard it across the way. It shook dust from the roof beams and a shower of soot in the hearth.

'Your beautiful cloak, Seb,' Chesca said, tears welling up anew. 'I so sorry. I wearing it because it warmer than mine and it looking so fine ...' Her voice trailed away. 'I so sorry,' she repeated.

''Tis but a garment. I be certain the mud will brush off when dry. Did the rascal rob you? Or harm you in any way? We should report the incident to the watch.'

'I not hurting. He grabbing me by the shoulders, turning me around. I dropping my basket of foods and drinks all in the mud. He looking at my face and cursing then throwing me down so I falling in the mud with the bread and rabbit-pie. He taking nothing but running away.'

'Did anyone else see what came to pass?'

'*Si*. The street being busy. It so oddly yet ... I thinking he cursing in my tongue. Then I coming home. A man and woman helping me.'

'Do you mean that the rascal spoke in Italian?'

'It sounding so but maybe I mistaking it. He saying *cazzo*! And calling me *puttana*!'

''Tis quite a coincidence, if he did.'

'Coindisense? What is that?'

'A coincidence means two unlikely circumstances occurring together – you being attacked by an Italian when there be so few of your kind in Westminster.'

'I could be not hearing him correctly.'

'What do you think he said? What do those words mean in English?'

'If I hearing rightly, he saying 'shit' and calling me 'bitch'. Just as Jood doing but in Italian.'

'And he did not attempt to rob you or molest you elsewise?'

Chesca shook her head.

'No. He just throwing me aside like useless thing and spoiling your fine cloak.'

Jude returned, feet pounding on the stairs then shoving the door open as far as the hinges allowed, so it banged back, knocking a lump of plaster from the wall. He flung a few items on the board before removing his cloak, shaking snow off it and dropping it in a wet heap on the floor.

'No bloody kindling to be had; no sodding ale and no decent fucking food. Pie-shop's closed and that bastard innkeeper didn't want to serve a non-bloody-resident, so there's stale bread and hard cheese. Barely enough for two of us. And if you're thirsty, you'll have to drink water like a fucking French peasant. No bloody ale! This is all your fault, Chesca, damn your eyes, you stupid wench.' He raised his hand to her.

'Jude! Enough! It was not Chesca's fault that she was attacked. Let her be, you inconsiderate wretch. Have pity on the lass, for Jesu's sake.'

Jude turned away, grabbed a hunk of bread and cut off a wedge of dry-looking cheese. He didn't offer anything to his goodwife or brother but lay on the bed to eat it, propped against the pillow. Since the room was chill, he pulled the blankets over him without bothering to remove his filthy boots.

Seb tucked his once-handsome, now-soiled cloak around Chesca's shoulders as she sat by the dead embers.

'God keep you this night, Chesca,' he said as he made to leave. 'You also, brother.'

'Don't forget your staff,' Jude said through a mouthful of bread. 'It's bloody snowing a blizzard out there now.'

The snow came in gusts as the wind blew, stinging his eyes and numbing his nose and cheeks. It was not a lengthy walk in any other weather but long enough that Seb felt frozen to the core by the time he entered the dormitory. As for his hands and feet, he had no feeling in them at all, despite wearing good gloves and boots.

Hal Sowbury took pity on him and gave up his stool beside the fire.

'I trust the good supper with your brother was worth the effort?' he said. 'You look blue with cold, my friend.'

'There was no supper,' Seb mumbled through benumbed lips, removing his gloves and holding his hands out to the warmth of dancing flames.

Hal took Seb's wet gown and spread it on a bench to dry. The rest of his attire was damp also, especially across the shoulders.

'You'd best get undressed and wrap yourself in a blanket before you take a chill,' Hal advised.

Lawrence Duffield chuckled.

'The weather wasn't so bad when I was out there, earlier. Stop fussing like a mother hen, Hal. He's a man grown; not a babe-in-arms.'

'He's a decent scribe and we're short of clerks as it is,' Hal protested. 'We don't need another falling sick. Get off your idle arse, Lawrie, and fetch him some ale and meat, if you pigs have left anything of our night livery.'

Under the chief clerk's watchful eye, Seb ate a far better supper than Jude and Chesca had and, once his fingers and toes had ceased stinging and tingling as feeling returned, he sat by the fire and thought through the eve's events.

Poor Chesca. Her experience must have been frightening indeed: flung to the ground by some cut-purse or vagabond. It seemed strange that the rascal had then run off, taking neither money nor the strewn victuals for his trouble. What was it Chesca had said? "He looked at my face, cursed, then threw me down." It was as if her attacker had expected her to be someone else. Mayhap, robbery had not been his intent. Why did he accost her in the first place? What did he see that attracted his notice? Not the basket of provisions, otherwise he would have taken it. Chesca was wearing his crimson cloak but, if the fellow had a fancy for its value and warmth, why did he run off without it? The crimson cloak: the thought lodged in Seb's mind and would not depart.

Later, Seb awoke, shivering in his cold bed under a thin blanket. But it was not the chill that roused him. His crimson cloak! That had attracted the assailant's notice but it was not a young lass he expected to be wearing it. The scoundrel had thought it would be him. Everyone who had attended the inquest had seen him wearing his bright cloak. The wretch had not been after Chesca but thought to attack Seb Foxley. The more he considered the possibility, the more probable it became. But why? What did he possess that someone else wanted so badly as to make an attack when the streets were busy? Also, since the rascal had realised his mistake in assaulting Chesca, was there a likelihood he would try again and, this time, make certain of his target? It was a worrying thought.

No wonder Seb got little sleep for the remainder of the night.

Thursday, the Feast of Candlemas, the second day of February Westminster

As if to welcome this day of the Virgin Mary's purification six weeks after she gave birth to the Christ Child, the morning was bright with sunshine and the snow was gone from all but the most shadowed corners. Light danced on meltwater dripping from the eaves, droplets hanging like pearls, momentarily, before falling into the puddles below.

Seb should have felt heartened by this gladsome change in the weather. Instead, it added to his concerns. He had decided to exaggerate his need of the staff when walking in the snow and keep it by his side. If an assailant moved against him, the staff would serve as a means of defending himself. But, with the snow no longer lying, gone was his reason for carrying the stout support. Seb was no brawler. His balance was too uncertain to kick an opponent. His hands were shaped for wielding pen and brush, not landing blows. Neither had he bodyweight upon his side, if matched against any but some starveling child. He was no coward but violence was ne'er his way. So far as he could see, the only solution would be to remain with a group of his fellows and thus deny any foe the opportunity to attack him whilst alone.

Seb stood with his fellow clerks in the Chapel of St Stephen for the Candlemas Day office of celebration, welcoming the Virgin Mary back into society after her time of confinement. The sun streamed through the great east window and, for the first time, Seb saw the wondrous colours of the stained glass in their full glory. Patches of ruby, sapphire, emerald and gold were strewn across the floor like discarded jewels. Jude was right: the glass was well worth seeing.

But the company of clerks huddled together like hoody-crows in their sombre black. Seb's gown was yet damp from last eve's snowfall and, though the sun was bright, it gave little warmth. They stood, shivering, 'neath a breath-fog of their own making. Jude was not among them, Seb noted without surprise. Of late, his brother was not one of the Church's most ardent supporters, attending only as often as required to avoid paying a fine. Little wonder he had failed to make the effort to rise early when the working day was to begin a half-hour later than usual, to allow everyone to celebrate the special High Mass. Jude would regard spending more time in a warm bed as a bonus. Seb chided himself for assuming the worst of his brother. Mayhap, Jude was attending mass in St Margaret's, the parish church across the way. But then another array of bejewelled wonder diverted his attention.

King Edward himself processed up the aisle, Queen Elizabeth at his side and a gaggle of befeathered, beribboned courtiers trailed behind the royal couple.

Seb craned his neck to get a better view. He had never been this close to the king before. Edward, though, was hard to miss, tall as Zeus and broader than a warhorse. He wore a glittering diadem about his brow – as if he needed it to mark him out a king – and a wide grin that verged upon outright laughter. Someone must have told him a fine jest. Quite the opposite, when Seb caught a glimpse of the queen, was her expression akin to that of someone who had a mouth full of lemons or had swallowed vinegar. This was his first-ever look at Elizabeth Woodville. She was a rare beauty in her youth, so it was said, but he thought she was become a gaunt, sour matron and could see little to attract any man now. Her pale hair, alabaster skin and robes of cloth-of-silver, trimmed with white fox, made her seem a creature carved from ice and did but add to the chill of the chapel.

Edward wore an ermine-lined gown of purple velvet over a doublet of green cloth-of-gold. The bejewelled belt at his waist would encircle Seb three times with length to spare. Behind the king, Seb caught sight of Lord Hastings's hat over the heads of the congregation. It was of pearl-studded black velvet adorned with a golden ostrich plume. Once the royal couple were seated, the plume was easily visible, bobbing each time Hastings moved in his position, standing by the king's chair.

Then the High Mass began with the lighting of a thousand candles or it seemed at least that many to Seb. But their light was of little significance compared to the sun streaming through the stained glass, turning the chapel into a living illuminated miniature of the most marvellous colours. How joyously it lifted Seb's spirit!

But later, after so bright an interlude, the scriptorium was as dour as ever. Its windows faced north and were of plain glass. No hint of colour cheered this place and Seb's joy abated all too swiftly. Secretary Oliver was disgruntled and caustic as usual as his clerks settled at their desks. Fortunately, Barnabas had done his duty before mass, kindling the brazier and setting the ink to thaw so work could commence without delay.

Jude arrived in the nick of time to avoid a reprimand and took his place next to Seb.

'God give you good day, brother,' Seb whispered. 'I needs must speak with you later concerning the attack upon Chesca. I trust she has suffered no after-effects?'

'She's well. Better than she deserves, being so bloody careless. She'd spent fourteen pence of my hard-earned money – a damned fortune – on wine and food and then leaves it lying in the bloody gutter. Stupid mare. I told her ...'

'Silence, Foxley!' Oliver bellowed, rapping his knuckles on the arm of his cushioned chair. 'Get on with your work or I'll dock you sixpence.'

'How much! You can't do that. Nobody gets stopped a full day's pay just for speaking a few bloody words.' Jude came to his feet, blustering and outraged, overturning his stool with a crash.

'I'll stop you a whole shilling for insolence, if you don't get on with it.'

'You wouldn't dare.'

'Jude,' Seb said, righting the stool and pulling his brother back down onto it. 'Have a care. Say naught more, I beg of you.'

Jude tugged his gown from Seb's grasp.

'Keep out of this, you. You started it by talking to me.'

'I gave you good day ...'

'I should've bloody ignored you,' Jude shouted.

'Silence!' Oliver roared, leaving his chair. 'Outside, both of you. Now!' He waved his staff of office in threatening wise. 'I'll not have my scriptorium turned into a bear-pit nor my clerks yelling at each other like drunken fishwives.'

They followed the secretary out into the passageway. Seb left the door ajar. The excited babble of the other clerks could be heard at their departure like schoolboys eagerly anticipating their fellows' punishment at the hands of the master. But Oliver went back and closed the door. There would be no eavesdropping by the others – and no witnesses to whatever was said or befell.

Jude stood tall, defiant as ever. His eyes were dark with the fires of rage. He had the advantage of being half a head above the secretary. Seb less so, but even he could look Oliver in the eye, if he dared. However, the king's secretary had the advantage of royal authority, making it less than a fair match.

'You!' Oliver poked Seb in the chest with a fat finger. 'I'll be speaking with Lord Hastings about you. I will have you removed from this office. You're a disruptive influence. All ran smoothly until you came.' He turned his attention to Jude. 'As for you, you tardy, idle, good-for-nothing trouble-maker …' He stabbed at Jude with his finger.

Jude grabbed the man's finger, twisted it and bent it backwards. The audible snap of bone was sickening.

Oliver went white as bleached parchment. It was a long moment before he was able to cry out. Then he crumpled in a swoon, falling on the cold flagstones.

'God have mercy, Jude. What have you done?' Seb knelt beside the secretary's limp form.

'A broken finger never killed anybody. He bloody got what he deserved, treating me like a bloody menial, the bastard.'

'But he's a scribe, like us, and you've broken his right forefinger. How will he hold a pen now?'

'I don't bloody care. He can stick the pen up his fat arse. I'm leaving and I'm not coming back. I've had enough of this bloody place.' Jude made for the door out into Green Yard.

'Wait, Jude.' Seb hastened after. 'We can't leave him lying there in this cold …'

'I can. You do what you want with the devil. Set fire to him. That'll warm up the bugger.' With which parting suggestion, Jude strode from Westminster Palace, discarding his clerk's gown on the way, dropping it in the mud.

Seb stared after his brother; his dismay hung heavy upon his shoulders. What to do? He knew that, for the present, Jude's anger had taken him beyond reasoning. There was no point in attempting to call him back. Secretary Oliver was unlikely to allow his return in any case after what he had done. Jude would be fortunate to avoid a charge of assault. Seb knelt on the cold flagstones beside the slumped form of the secretary.

'Secretary Oliver? Come, rouse yourself,' Seb encouraged. To no avail. He returned to the scriptorium, pushing open the squealing door. 'Master Sowbury. Everyone,' Seb called out. 'The secretary be in need of aid. Help me. I fear he requires a surgeon.'

In moments, the scriptorium arose in uproar. Sowbury and Beckton managed to lift the secretary's bulk with difficulty and lugged him back to his chair by the brazier. Beckton began chafing the man's hands in an effort to revive him from his swoon.

'Not his right hand,' Seb said. 'I fear he has broken bones there.'

'Blood of Christ! What did you do to him?'

'He made the error of poking at my brother with his finger. Jude grabbed it. I fear he knows not his own strength. Then Secretary Oliver fell into a swoon.'

Sowbury came and leaned over to peer at their master.

'How's he faring, Robin?' the chief clerk asked. Beckton shook his head and held out Oliver's damaged hand for inspection. The index finger was swollen and misaligned in quite the wrong direction; red and black bruises were already visible.

'Not good. Has anyone gone to fetch the surgeon?'

'I sent Lawrie. And Barnabas has gone to the buttery for wine. He'll need it when he wakens.'

'I need it now,' Beckton said. 'I hope Barney brings enough for us all.'

Sowbury turned to Seb.

'And where's that wretched brother of yours? You say he did this?'

'He left. I know not where he may be. He was more angry than I have seen in many years but Oliver provoked him. I misdoubt that Jude intended …'

'But the deed stands, nonetheless. Your brother is in serious trouble now.'

Seb nodded. Jude and trouble were ever close companions. His brother was a fool, too readily governed by his temper. Seb wondered how acts of violence against superior officers were dealt with in the king's own palace. Not leniently, he feared. At the very least, Jude would likely be barred from Westminster. But what of his physical punishment? Seb dared not think on it.

That eve, Seb had no interest in attempting to glean information from his fellow clerks regarding a murder. Nor did he care for warming himself by the hearth in the dormitory. Instead, he hastened out into the chill blackness beyond the Great Gate, making for Mistress Baxter's lodging house.

Thieving Lane looked to be living up to its reputation for dark deeds. Not a light showed anywhere among the hovels and leaning tenement houses. Seb realised he had been wise to leave his purse behind as last time, 'neath the mattress. Only on the corner with King Street was there any sign of life where an ale-house door stood ajar, allowing the escape of light and the sounds of drinking and carousing to drift out into the night. The street stretched away before Seb into the tunnel of night. Somewhere, a dog howled like a mourner and a babe wailed close at hand. Seb shivered, pulling his clerk's gown around him. If he did but know it, he was nigh invisible to human eyes.

He jumped at a sudden sound. But it was just a door slamming shut farther up the lane. A night owl swooped low, setting his heart a-flutter. It flew off like a ghost, disappearing over the huddle of rooftops into the water meadows beyond. Seb almost broke into a run in his haste to reach safety and such was never his way.

Breathless and with his heart thudding, he hammered on Mistress Baxter's door.

'Whatever's amiss?' Mistress Baxter greeted him. 'You trying to break down my door?'

'Good e-eve, mistress,' Seb stuttered, recalling courtesy even so. 'I must speak with my brother, if you please.'

'Then you've come to the wrong place. He's not here.'

'Oh, then I needs must speak with Chesca – Mistress Foxley.'

'She's not here either.'

'Do you know where they be?'

The woman shrugged.

'I've not seen him since he went out this morn – and tardily, I might add. Though I heard them for certain an hour or two later, so he must have returned whilst I was at market. They had the most almighty row: hollering and cursing. Things got thrown about, I can tell you. Then he thundered down my stairs fit to rock the house and slammed this door so the ground shook. Mistress Foxley left after the dinner hour, all primped and tricked out in her best, so she was, and wearing that fine new red cloak of hers. Don't know where she was going but it isn't the first time she's done that. Neither of them has come back. You could try the Fighting Cock on the corner, or the Garter Inn off King Street or ...' Mistress Baxter lowered her voice to a whisper and mouthed 'Or the Maiden's Head on up the lane but I wouldn't go there alone, master. You know not what mischief brews there.'

'My thanks, mistress. I bid you good night.' Seb turned away as the door closed. With drooping shoulders, he returned the way he had come. What should he do now? If Jude was not returned home, where could he be? Paternoster Row? That was a possibility. Or he could be drowning his sorrows in some ale-house or other.

A cat shot out of an alleyway, startling Seb from his thoughts and almost oversetting him as it dashed betwixt his legs. He had hardly steadied himself against the nearest wall when another sudden movement caught his eye, a darker shade of night in the satanic shadows. He turned to see but the blow came out of the blackness. Stars burst across his sight and Seb went down, sprawled in the mud. He felt himself roughly handled; his body searched, yet could make naught but the most feeble of protests. Then it ended and he was left lying in the lane, knowing no more.

Chapter 7

Friday, the third day of February
Mistress Baxter's Lodging House

LAST EVE, Jude had drunk a bellyful of ale, visiting every tavern and ale-house in Westminster, by his reckoning. He knew he shouldn't waste his coin on drink. A jobless scrivener must be frugal but what was a man to do? Bloody Oliver had driven him to this – devil take the bastard – and breaking his finger had been well deserved but didn't placate Jude's temper by much. So he'd gone out, looking to get drunk and spoiling for a fight. He'd succeeded on both accounts and was now paying the price with a heavy head, a roiling belly and bruises aplenty. He couldn't recall where or how he had come by them and didn't much care.

'Chesca! Will you shut your bloody noise,' he complained from the bed, pulling the pillow over his ears.

'I putting your breakfast out, Jood. I getting bread and eggs for you.' Chesca was bright as sunshine this morn, rattling platters and singing some Venice song or other. Whatever she lacked in melody, she made up the deficit with volume.

'For sweet Christ's sake, be quiet. And I don't want bloody breakfast.'

'You be feeling better if you eating something. Having the eggs before they cooling, Jood.'

Jude groaned and turned over in bed, burying his head under the blankets. The smell of eggs was nauseating.

'And I having good tidings for you, husband. A messenger coming to speak with you when you not being here.' Chesca plumped down on the bed beside him. The unexpected movement of the frame and mattress was the final assault. He leaned over the side of the bed, grabbed the piss-pot and threw up in it.

'Go away. Leave me be.'

'It being all your own fault, Jood Fossley. Now get up, eat and I telling you the tidings.'

'I don't want to bloody hear them. I don't care.' Even so, he eased himself more upright against the bolster. 'A messenger, you say? Where's the letter, then?'

'There being no letter. He just telling me.' A long pause followed. Chesca sat, chewing her nether lip and winding her fingers through her raven tresses.

'Well? Who sent him – this messenger? Who was he?'

'How I knowing? I not knowing everybody in Wessminter.'

'For Christ's sake tell me, you foolish woman. What did he say?'

Chesca pouted and turned away from the bed but he grabbed her arm.

'Tell me, you little bitch, or must I knock the bloody words out of you?'

'You hurting me! Italian man not treating ladies like this. The sons learning to respect and adore their *madri*. They loving their mothers so well and being good to women.' She pulled free and went to stand by the door – a way to escape, if needed.

'Well, I never had a mother and never felt the lack.'

'That why you being the *animali*, Jood Fossley.'

Jude swore a long string of oaths and flung back the blankets, headache and bellyache forgotten. Naked as God made him, he could still be intimidating. He strode towards her.

'You started this, you bitch. You said a message came for me. Now tell me or I'll make you regret it.'

Chesca put on her most haughty Venetian expression.

'I telling when I want.'

Jude's hand moved quicker than a serpent. He slapped her hard across the shoulder.

'I bloody warned you,' he growled.

She was sobbing, hugging her hurts.

'*Ti odio, mostro!*'

'Don't use your barbarian tongue on me. What did the messenger say?'

'He saying... saying you go back to scriptorium on Monday.'

'You're lying. They'll not want me there, not now, not ever.'

'No, no, it true... I swearing. They needing you.'

'I don't believe you. Who sent this messenger? Not bloody Oliver, that's for certain.'

Chesca pulled her dignity about her like a tattered cloak.

'He saying the lord chamberlain sent him. Lord Haysling.'

'Hastings? Why should he involve himself in my affairs?'

Chesca shrugged.

'How you think I knowing this? I only telling what the messenger saying.'

'They want me back in Oliver's bloody icy pest-hole. Why would that be? What is it that you're not bloody telling me?'

'Naught, I swearing.'

Jude didn't believe her, not for one moment.

Westminster

Seb was lying upon his hard bed in the clerks' dormitory. Like his brother across the way, he had a pounding headache for company.

'Not so clever now, are you?' said the surgeon as he finished binding the linen strips in place over the stitched wound. It was Master Curran, the same surgeon with whom Seb had disagreed at the inquest concerning the cause of Piers Creed's death.

Pointing out another man's failings in his craft when it was not your own was no way to gain a friend, as Seb discovered. The surgeon had been less than gentle with his needle. 'Got what you deserved, no doubt, you young upstart.' The surgeon's glee was obvious in his grin. Sympathy was not part of the treatment.

'Thank you, Master Curran, I believe that will suffice,' Seb muttered. 'I shall manage well enough now – unless you have some remedy for an aching head?'

The surgeon put a small, black vial on the coffer beside the bed.

'Two drops in a cup of ale. No more than that. And tell Secretary Oliver I'll be adding it to his reckoning, along with the charges for treating his broken hand and your stitchery and bindings.'

'But I thought the king paid you a retainer to treat all his staff.'

'There you go again: poking your nose into other folks' business where it don't belong. I wonder that it ain't been the death of you long since. Rest! Plenty of rest is what you need now.'

When Master Curran had departed, Seb was alone in the dormitory. The others were all at their work, leaving him to lie against the pillow and consider his situation. Head wounds being notorious for the amount of gore they produced, his clothes were blood-soaked and whosoever had attacked him had nigh torn them from his back. Filthy mud and horse dung caked everything. Ripped and stained, he had no garments sufficiently clean, undamaged and respectable to wear. The clerk's gown was a heap of evil-smelling rags kicked under his bed.

He had not the least idea how he had made the journey from Thieving Lane to the dormitory, whether he managed it by himself or by the aid of another. He seemed to have been the victim of a vicious robbery and yet he still had his boots and gloves – both worth stealing. Was it not fortunate his purse was left here? No thief could have resisted that.

With utmost care, Seb eased off the bed. The walls spun somewhat but settled. He removed the vial from the coffer top and crouched to open the lid. The few items of clothing within should all have gone for laundering but at least they were of a piece. He pulled on nether-clouts and a pair of hose, a grubby shirt, ink-splotched at the sleeve-ends, but it would have to serve. He had brought but one doublet from home and was wearing it last eve. Now all the eyelets were torn through and it could be laced no longer, in addition to bloodstains, dried black as ink, marring its once-woad-blue wool. The worst damage had befallen his thick woollen and leather jerkin, cut through with a blade, by the look of it, and gore-drenched. How easily that blade might have gone deeper and sliced flesh – his flesh. It did not bear thinking upon. But what to do? He possessed but one jerkin and it was the warmest thing he had to wear. Now it looked to be beyond repair.

Seb fished the clerk's gown from under the bed. It had ever been a sorry piece, its thin cloth faded and the seams failing. He shook it out and held it up, wrinkling his nose at the stink. He must have lain in a pile of dung. Now stained and rent, the gown was hardly fit to wipe the floor, never mind wear. His hands came away bloodied where it had not yet dried completely.

Looking over at the serving table, hoping there was a little ale left from last eve to slake his thirst and to take the remedy for his headache, the board was bare – not so much as a crumb remained to break his fast. Not that he had any desire for food, feeling somewhat queasy, but he was thirsty indeed. He wondered at the hour. There was no sign of the sun beyond the dirty window, the sky grey and featureless as a blank page of poor-quality paper. Disconsolate, he returned to his bed and wrapped the meagre blanket around himself. Without clothing, he could not go to the scriptorium to work nor to the hall for dinner. What was expected of him?

Seb's query was answered when one of the servitors who slept in the bed in the farthest corner by the window came in bearing a tray and some clothing draped over his arm. James Penny by name, if he recalled aright.

'Hal Sowbury bade me look in on you, if I had the chance,' James said, setting the tray on the end of the bed. 'And he said to find you something to wear. No idea if these'll fit but they're better than naught. And you can borrow his spare gown to go down to dinner, if you're able? It's in his coffer.'

'I be grateful indeed to both you and Master Sowbury for taking the trouble.'

James laughed.

''Tis no act of charity. The scriptorium is short of two clerks now. He wants you back at your desk before the paperwork buries them all.'

'I shall do so as soon as I be decent,' Seb said. 'What be the hour?'

'The bell for Terce rang in the abbey just a while since. Dinner isn't for nigh on two hours. If I were you, I'd make the most of this unexpected leisure. Enjoy your breakfast.'

When James Penny left, closing the door, Seb straightway reached for the cup of ale on the tray. He unstoppered the vial and added just two drops of the remedy into it and stirred it with his finger. It did not taste too bad but gave the ale a bitter edge. He would rather have taken the meadowsweet cure Rose made at home to treat pains of all sorts, especially headaches, but this would have to do. Hopefully, by dinnertime, the throbbing would have eased enough for his thoughts to be better ordered. At present, thinking was a difficult process, he discovered.

He was unsure about eating the fresh bread and cheese James had brought but a few tentative bites settled his queasiness and he ate most of the food before turning his attention to the items of clothing. A clean shirt – a mercy for sure. A pair of brown hose, darned and repaired but, likewise, clean though they might be too wide for him. No matter. A brown doublet of well-worn wool, darned and not of recent fashion, being unpadded at the shoulders and untailored at the waist. Not that Seb cared for courtly fashion anyway. It must once have been a splendid garment for the braiding was of silver thread, now tarnished black. At least the cloth was yet thick enough to give some warmth. But there was no jerkin nor any additional layers. Seb decided to keep his own dirty shirt on and put the clean one atop it. As he feared, the hose hung in wrinkles at thigh and knee but were of a good length for him, otherwise. The doublet also had room to spare but, mayhap, the styles had been looser in the past. Pulling on his own boots – still muddied and, he suspected, bloodied – he felt warm at last.

The only problem now was headwear. The clerks were expected to wear a coif 'neath the hood of their gown. Seb's coif had been lost last eve and even had it been found, it was probably bloodstained like everything else. Anyhow, a coif was never going to fit over his bandages. He touched his hair with tentative fingers. It was stiff and set hard on the left side, below the bindings. Should he attempt to comb it? Finding his comb in the bottom of the coffer, he made an effort to tease out his hair, to no avail. Wetting the comb in the laver bowl produced some results but the water was quickly turned to rust-colour by a mix of old blood and mud. He did his best but had no mirror to assess whether there was any noticeable improvement. His hair still felt stiff and spiky as a faggot of kindling and his efforts made him wince as the stitches pulled. He conceded defeat, fearing to tear the wound open. However dishevelled his appearance, his fellow clerks would not care, so long as he could hold a pen.

Wearing Hal Sowbury's third-best gown – though patched, it was of far better quality than the one he had been wearing – Seb went down the stair when the bell rang to announce dinner in the Great Hall. He trod carefully, keeping one hand against the wall forwhy he felt a little light-headed and feared falling. Mayhap, he was not so well recovered as he thought. Mayhap, it was the surgeon's potion. No doubt but some hot food would help.

'You look as though you should have stayed abed.' Lawrence Duffield's greeting was less than heartening.

'Are you well enough to be in hall, Seb?' Hal Sowbury asked, passing the ale jug.

Seb tried to pour some into his cup but his hand shook, spilling it.

'Here, let me do that.' Barnabas, sitting opposite, obliged him. They were all giving him wary glances.

'I be grateful for the use of your gown, Hal. Mine be beyond redemption, I fear. But how did I get back here last eve?' Seb asked his fellows. The mystery had been plaguing him since the question first occurred to him.

'You were fortunate indeed,' Lawrence told him. 'The guards upon the Great Gate found you when they opened up this morn. Nigh frozen to death in a heap you were. Any longer spent lying there and all you'd be needing is a winding sheet. The impertinent rogue must have attacked you right outside the palace.'

'It's a wonder the guards didn't hear anything. Drunk most likely.' Barnabas munched on a mouthful of herring and spat out a bone.

'I do not believe I was assaulted there but in Thieving Lane.'

'Well, I'm sure you never walked from there to the gateway, not in your wretched condition.' Hal added his opinion. 'Either you dragged yourself, which I doubt, or someone else did. Then they left you to perish of cold. Why would anyone do that? Bring you halfway then leave you to freeze: it makes no sense. They could've roused the guard. I reckon you've misremembered where you were when you were attacked. They took your purse; no doubt you know that much.'

'Nay, Hal. I did not have my purse with me. I was not robbed.'

'Oh. That's another stroke of good fortune for you, then.'

Seb sipped his ale gratefully but the scent of fish stew was turning his stomach. He should not have come.

'Barnabas, if you would lend me the key, I shall await you in the scriptorium. 'Tis quieter there.' Seb left the bench but had to steady himself, leaning on Hal's shoulder.

'Head still aches, then?' Hal enquired.

'Somewhat. I shall do well enough, seated at my desk,' Seb assured the chief clerk.

The colder air outside the hall – unperfumed by fish – improved Seb's case. Even so, his way to the scriptorium was a wandering one as he meandered like a Saturday-night drunkard along the passageway. He was relieved to reach the door of the scriptorium without falling or staggering into anything. Having struggled to fit the key in the lock and flinched as the door squealed open, he stumbled over the threshold. Sagging onto his stool, unmindful of the split seat, he folded his arms upon the desk to pillow his head and swiftly fell asleep as the effects of the surgeon's potion overwhelmed him.

A sudden bolt of pain brought him stark awake. All was dark, yet he was certain his eyes were open. Had he gone blind? He put his hands to his face; discovered that the bindings had slipped down, covering them.

'Leave that,' a muffled voice instructed behind him, 'Unless you want this in your belly?'

Seb felt cold steel against his neck and took his hands away from the bandages.

'W-what…' His voice sounded weak as water. His mind could form no coherent thought.

'Where is the letter?'

'Let… what letter?' His head was pulled back by his hair and he gasped, feeling the stitches in his scalp split asunder. Hot blood dribbled down his temple until it soaked into the bindings but Seb was more afeared of the blade pressing against his throat.

'The Italian letter, you imbecile.'

'I-I kn-now not. In t-truth… I know not.'

'You had it. You told your brother so.'

'I cannot think…'

The sound of feet upon the flagstones and raised voices beyond the door saved Seb. The blade was gone and his head was shoved hard against the desk as the door screeched upon its hinges. The clerks crowded in. They would apprehend his assailant. Seb eased his bandages back into place, expecting an outcry when his attacker was taken. But naught happened. Was the devil invisible? Or escaped through the high window?

'Oh, Seb. Look at you,' Hal Sowbury said, putting his hand on Seb's arm. Seb pulled away in alarm. 'Steady, my friend. You're bleeding afresh. Did you knock your head? You must have fallen against your desk. See the blood here? God be thanked Secretary Oliver isn't here to see it too. He'd be suffering apoplexy, fearing bloodstains on the parchment.'

'There was someone here...' Seb began to explain. 'He pulled the bindings over my eyes. I could not see. He held a knife to my neck...'

'You're confused and no wonder, Seb. There's no one here but you and us. You must be recalling last night. Now you've reopened the gash, we'll have to summon the surgeon to stitch it again.'

'I know there was somebody... he demanded a letter but...'

'Hush now. We'll take you back to your bed. You can't work today, not in this sorry wise.'

Had he dreamt this second assault? Imagined it? Was he so confused as that?

Saturday, the fourth day of February
Mistress Baxter's Lodging House

Jude was perfectly sober this morn but his temper had not improved over much with the passage of another day. He was in two minds concerning the supposed message from Lord Hastings. It did not ring true. If he returned to work on Monday morn and the message proved to be a ruse just to taunt him, how humiliating that would be, to be flung out of Westminster. It would be insupportable. Last time, it was his choice to leave. On the other hand, last month's pay was already considerably depleted, spent mostly on ale. He would soon need the money.

Chesca was quiet indeed. She had hardly said a word to him since yesterday but glared whenever their eyes met.

Jude determined to go out. He would go to Paternoster Row and talk things through with Seb. Anything to get away from *her*. He couldn't bear to look at her with her martyr's face on, accusing him with every glance. It was like torture.

And where was his other bloody boot? He didn't need this aggravation. He went on his knees, groping under the bed. No boot. But what was this? He brought out a small silk-wrapped bundle. The contents were oddly shaped and jangled. He let the cloth fall open. Bright objects clattered to the floor.

'Nooo!' Chesca screamed and flung herself down to cover the objects, trying to gather them to her. But Jude put his foot on something bright and picked it up. A heavy brooch, gold, by the look and weight of it, set with an emerald that gleamed like a malevolent green eye, surrounded by pearls.

'What devil's work is this?' Jude roared. 'You've been bloody thieving, you stupid bitch. Get up. Let me see what else you've stolen.'

'No thieving, I swear on my life, Jood. I stealing no things, ever.'

'Don't lie to me. How else do you come by these… these trinkets?' Jude turned an amethyst ring on the palm of his hand. It was exquisitely worked. A pendant formed of golden wire scrolls was set with sapphires. These things would cost five years' wages – each.

'They being gifts to me.'

'Who in hell's name do we bloody know who can afford such "gifts", eh? You're a lying bitch, Chesca, and a damned thief.'

'I no lying… nor thieving. *He* gave them to me.'

'He!' Jude shrieked, grabbing his wife by the shoulders and shaking her so hard. 'Who is this *he?*'

'I cannot say. Oh, pleeease, Jood. How you thinking I buy your birthday supper... and wine?'

'You unfaithful, adulterous little slut!' He struck her across the mouth, splitting her lip.

'No marking my face. He liking me beautiful. If I looking ugly...' Tears fell like rain. Only Chesca could still look enticing even as she wept.

Jude hit her again.

'See how he likes you now. Tell me his fucking name. I'll have his bollocks off with a blunt knife and stuff 'em down his throat an' choke him. Cuckolding me... I'll gut him like a codfish, the bastard. Who is he? I have the bloody right to know. You didn't get jewels like this for some hasty, drink-sodden fumble at the back of the ale-house. You're a whore, Francesca, a fucking whore, you ungrateful bitch.' He threw her down and kicked her. 'I should kill you for this.'

'It not being my fault. I having no choice.'

'You could say no, for God's sake, you filthy slut.'

'No, I not refusing Edoardo. How can I be saying no to him?'

'Another buggering, shit-hole Italian then. I should've left you in Venice to marry that pox-ridden old man your father promised you to. And what have I got for my pains, eh? A wife who cuckolds me with the first Venetian she sees.'

'He *Inglese* as you. He the king! How I telling him "no!"?'

Jude staggered back and slumped on the bed. He felt as though some accursed leech had drained every last drop of blood from his veins.

'What did you say? King Edward? The king is your lover? You lying bitch. Tell me the truth.'

'I telling you true. The king wanting me. I swearing it true.'

'Since when did the King of England take a fancy to a jade like you?'

'He seeing me at the Twelve Night feast. He liking me. Next

day, a messenger coming from Lord Haysling, asking me to go to Wessminter. And Eduardo waiting there for me. He kind and give me gifts. How you think I getting your job back for you?'

'And what am I supposed to feel? Honoured and grateful that the king chooses to fuck my wife?'

'We could be selling the jewels and buying a fine house,' Chesca suggested. 'We could be having servants and fine wine...'

'And that would make me a kept man!'

Westminster

Seb had slept for most of Friday afternoon and eve and through the night hours also. He awoke upon Saturday morn feeling greatly improved. The re-stitched gash was yet sore but the accompanying headache was but a dull reminder of yesterday's throbbing. And he was hungry.

He hastened down the stair to the Great Hall with his fellows, pleased to realise the light-headed dizziness was no more and eager as any man to break his fast. He helped himself from the communal platter of cheese and cold ham, took a cup of ale and a heel of fresh-baked bread and joined Hal, Lawrence and the others at the board. Hal grinned at him, watching him eating with enthusiasm.

'You're a fairer sight this morn. Up to wielding a pen, I trust?'

'Aye, I be much improved. I shall work the harder to make good what I failed to do yesterday.'

'Just do what you can, Seb. We don't want you exhausting yourself and having to take to your bed again. Besides, 'tis but a half day. Will you be going home after dinner to see your beloved Rose?'

Seb flushed hotly as he always did at mention of her name. The other clerks did not forget to say it at every opportunity to tease him. It was well-meant but embarrassed him all the same.

'I shall be glad indeed to see my little ones. I have ne'er passed a whole se'ennight without them.'

"Tis but five days since you came here,' Hal corrected.

'Aye but it seems a deal longer. I miss them. And I would find my brother.'

Hal merely grunted, having no interest in the whereabouts of Jude Foxley. In his opinion, the scriptorium was better off without that idle troublemaker. He ne'er did any work when he was there, anyway.

Chapter 8

Saturday afternoon
From Westminster to the Foxley House

IN THE SCRIPTORIUM, Seb had worked diligently throughout the morning, oblivious to noise, cold or draughts from the door, so determined was he to make amends for Friday's lost hours of labour. But when the bell rang out, summoning everyone to dinner in the Great Hall, Seb was first to wipe his pen, put his documents into the correct piles and leave. The half-written letter upon his desk would needs await the arrival of Monday's hours of work.

Seb did not accompany his fellow clerks to dinner. Instead, he hastened from Westminster Palace to undertake the lengthy walk back to Paternoster Row in the city, eager to see Rose and the children. He would forego dinner in the hall to see them the sooner. Besides, Rose's cooking was more to his taste and she would have set a portion aside for him, anticipating his return as keenly as he did. At least, he hoped that was the case. Dearest Rose – how he had missed her. He set off, still clad in Hal Sowbury's old gown, a borrowed coif, having cast aside the bindings for his injury, and the brown wool doublet. He had naught else to wear.

It was fortunate that the snow was gone. Seb did not want anything to slow his walk to London. Even so, by Charing Cross, when he saw a woman with a tray, selling marchpane sweetmeats, he stopped to buy some for the little ones. Then he espied a pedlar, hawking ribbons, braid, blue papers of pins and other haberdashery wares. The jewel-like hues of one particular braid caught his eye, as bright colours ever did. He stopped and asked the pedlar to show it to him.

'Aye, master, this is the best quality stuff.' The pedlar gave a gap-toothed grin. 'Kings and queens've bought my wares before now. I'm on my way to Westminster and I'm expecting to sell this to them fine court ladies.'

'If they permit you beyond the Great Gate,' Seb said.

The pedlar chuckled throatily, coughed and spat.

'They always does. They knows me well. Jake Parslow's the name, master. Royalty buys my ribbons and this braid...' The fellow turned a length this way and that, so it caught the sunlight. 'Woven with gold threads, see? They'll want this fer sure... unless you're buying it before I get there.'

The braid sparkled. Strands of blue, red and green, vivid as stained glass, were interlaced with the gold.

'What be the cost?' Seb asked, wondering how much was required to go around the hem of a woman's gown.

'Threepence per clothyard, depending...'

'Depending upon what?'

'When did you last buy braid, eh? Never, I reckon. Depending how much you buy, o' course. More you buy; cheaper it is, see?'

'I should hope so. Threepence be an extortionate price. How much per clothyard, if I purchase a half dozen yards?'

'You want so much? That's all my stock of it.'

'Well, how much does it take to trim the hem of a woman's gown?'

The pedlar shrugged and squinted, gauging his reply.

'A gown with a train... who knows?'

'No train. She be a fine woman but not a duchess. 'Tis for a straight, plain gown.

'Plain? And you would use this braid upon it? Fie, master, what a waste that will be.'

'Do you wish my custom or no?' Seb was exasperated,

wondering how the simple act of buying a length of braid had become a battle of wits. 'How much for five yards?'

'One shilling and three pence.'

'But that's no reduction at all.'

'Well now, if you was buying them six yards, like you said...'

'I'll take all you have for one shilling.'

'No, I can't do that. I would make not a farthing's-worth of profit. This braid comes all the way from Araby.'

'From Flanders more like. Thirteen pence for the entire bundle.'

'Fifteen.'

'Fourteen for it and a paper of pins. Take it or leave it.'

'Done!'

Seb was surprised when applause commenced behind him. A crowd of goodwives had gathered to watch the bargaining.

'Reckon you made a good purchase there, master,' a middle-aged matron told him.

'I hope so, mistress. I truly hope so.' Seb unlatched his purse, now back upon his belt, to sort out the coin: three groats and two pennies. It was a deal of money to spend on so frivolous an item. He tipped the coins into the pedlar's eager hand. Upon fishing deep in his purse, he had seen the crumpled page of Jude's Italian letter, quite forgotten. Still, with his brother no longer working in the scriptorium, what did it matter now? And Jude had said it was of no consequence.

'Is she worth it, though?' another goodwife asked.

'Most assuredly.' Seb smiled as he put the bundle of braid in his scrip atop his soiled clothing and fastened the buckle on his purse. 'There be no better woman living on God's good earth.' And, he realised, he meant what he said.

A casual passer-by might have thought he must have been gone for years, sailing the Seven Seas or traipsing the Silk Road through faraway lands, to judge from Seb's greeting at the door of his home.

Rose embraced and kissed him heartily upon both cheeks. The little ones clamoured at his feet for attention, Dickon grabbing at his clerk's gown, shouting 'Papa, Papa', and little Julia pulling herself upright by clinging to his ill-fitting borrowed hose. He kissed them all, then swept Julia up in one arm. Then the faithful Gawain nosed through the press of folk to give his master's hand a thorough licking, tail wagging so hard his entire furry body swayed from side to side.

'What are you wearing? Where's your cloak?' Rose asked as she led him through to the kitchen as if a week's absence could have caused him to forget the way. 'Come, you must be hungry after your long walk. I saved the best meats for you. What is it like, working in the King's Scriptorium? Do they treat you well? Is your bed warm enough?'

Seb laughed and kissed her again.

'All in good time, my dear one. 'Tis a long story. Have the children behaved in seemly wise, this week past?'

'Aye, they're a credit to their Papa... for the most part, like other children.'

'Then shall they have a sweetmeat each.' He searched out the marchpane delicacies and two small hands took them eagerly. Dickon ate his straightway. Julia thought to wear hers in her mousy curls before taking a bite. That just one sweet could make such a sticky mess was another source of work for Rose's cleaning skills.

Seb put Hal Sowbury's gown to one side, removed his borrowed coif and washed his face and hands in the laver bowl. In the warmth of the kitchen, he did not need to wear them. Of course, it was too much to hope that Rose wouldn't notice his gore-stiffened hair and the stitches in his scalp.

'Merciful Jesu save us! What have they done to you, Seb?' Rose put down the ladle and left the stewpot to rush to examine his injuries. 'When did this happen? How? Who did it?'

'I was assaulted last Thursday eve in Thieving Lane but a

surgeon has tended the wound, as you see. I be none the worse for it now and 'tis healing well, so they tell me. Does it look so bad then?'

Rose fingered his head, frowning.

'I suppose the surgeon has done a passable job though he has used the cheapest horse-hair and his stitches wouldn't meet with a decent glover's approval but, as for your hair! Did they not think to clean it just a little? It's stuck together in clumps and in need of a thorough wash but I suppose that must wait until the gash has healed. Does it pain you?'

'Nay.' Seb's reply was too swift.

'I'll fetch you some meadowsweet remedy. 'Tis but two days since and no wonder if you are bruised and in discomfort.'

'And I did not have my sweet Rose to tend me.' He smiled and put his arm around her waist.

'Come, sit, eat your dinner before it goes cold. I'll put Julia in her cradle for a nap. Dickon shall play on the floor and you can tell me everything.'

Seb tucked into the choicest mutton pie he had ever eaten, served with parsnips and sippets in a creamy mustard sauce. There was but the slightest hint of pepper. Not like the dishes served in the Great Hall, as he explained to Rose, which were so laden with garlic and ginger and coloured with sanders or turnsole that you could not tell whether it be capon or coney, pork or partridge. Rose put the royal cooks to shame, so he told her, as he set to on a second helping.

''Tis over quiet here. Where be the others?' he asked, leaning back with a sigh of pleasure and pushing his empty platter aside.

'Kate and Nessie are visiting Dame Ellen. She's frailer by the day, Seb. You should visit her, too; pay your respects while you may. Ralf is resting abed. He has a nasty cold and feels right sorry for himself, his humours in quite a distemper. I've given him a posset and horehound syrup for his chest. He'll mend in a day or so. Adam went home to Distaff Lane after closing the shop and eating three helpings of my pie. He'll get fat that one, for I think Mercy likely cooks him a dinner, too. Now. I will hear what has come to pass at Westminster. Everything.'

Rose brought two cups of ale and sat at the board, facing Seb. He realised there would be no escape until he had told her all she wanted to know. How different she was to Emily who would have shown little if any interest in what had befallen him.

And so he related his tale, making light of the worst moments: Jude's departure for one and the attacks on Chesca and himself, though he did explain that he had left his cloak at their lodgings for safe-keeping and said naught of its spoiling. He omitted to mention that his coffer had been rootled through and his horrid imaginings of yesterday in the scriptorium. He was yet uncertain whether he had been assaulted for a second time or dreamt it, so he did not tell of it. He described his fellow clerks, his bed and every meal in detail, as Rose demanded.

'I fear that I have brought you a deal of muddied and bloodied garments in need of laundering and repair and my jerkin be beyond saving. 'Tis a poor gift for you upon my home-coming but...' Seb reached for his scrip beneath the board. He sorted through its contents, took out the filthy clothes and dropped them in a heap. Rose stooped to pick them up. 'Leave those for the present, lass. I have something better here for you: a worthy gift.' With a broad smile, he gave her the bundle of braid.

'For me?' Her eyes went wide with wonderment.

'I purchased the sweetmeats for the children. Did you think I would not bring a token of some sort for the dearest woman in England? I trust you like it. I believe a new gown may be in order for you to make best use of the trimming. And I even thought to purchase pins to pin it in place.' He tossed the blue paper with the pins in it on the board.

'Oh, Seb!' Rose flung her arms about him. 'You're the dearest, kindest, most generous man... I don't deserve such a fine gift. Though I have pins aplenty already, a woman can never have too many and these are of good quality.' She straightened a length of the braid along the table, smoothing it with her hand. Then she gathered it up and took it to the back door where the light of a fading February afternoon showed off the colours to better advantage. 'It's so beautiful. I know not what to say...'

Seb laughed.

'You seem to find words enough and you deserve every inch of it.'

'Thank you, Seb. I never thought the day would come when I, poor Rose Glover, possessed such...'

Her gratitude was cut short by the back gate slamming and a shout:

'Where the bloody hell are you, Seb? Are you here?'

Seb went to the kitchen door.

'Jude, whatever be amiss, brother?'

'Every bloody thing's amiss. I've been trying to find you.'

'Come, sit down by the fire. Have some ale. Tell me what troubles you.' Seb led Jude within and pulled a bench close to the fire. Rose poured him ale. 'You came without a cloak in this chill?'

'Never mind the damned cloak. I've never been so bloody humiliated. I'll never hold my head high again.' Jude sat running his fingers through his pale hair, turning it into a thicket.

Seb, standing beside him, was surprised to see how much grey intertwined the fair these days.

'How could the bitch do this to me?'

'Chesca? What has the lass done now?'

'She's no lass. She's a slut, a whore, a harlot... another man's fuck.'

Seb took a step back.

'Chesca?'

'Aye, bloody Chesca, God rot her, the filthy bitch. And I don't know what to do.'

'Oh, Jude. I be so sorry.'

'What are you bloody sorry for? You didn't fuck her as well, did you?'

'Nay. Merciful Christ. What manner of man do you take me

for? I be your brother.' Seb sat upon a stool, too shocked to trust his legs to hold him up. He had never seen Jude so distraught and angry. 'We must be calm and rational… think what be for the best.'

'The best would be if I killed the bastard, sliced off his pox-riddled prick and fed him his own bollocks. But I can't.'

'Of course you cannot. Your anger be justified but it would still be murder.' Seb was relieved that Jude's wrath had not robbed him of all reason. 'You must speak with this rapscallion. Tell him you will drag him to the Court of Arches for trial by the Church. I shall help you afford a lawyer, if needed. The devil must pay for cuckolding and dishonouring you. A sizeable amount of compensation be due at the very least.'

'Ha! If only that were possible.' Jude put his head in his hands. 'A rapscallion, you say? If you did but know…' Then he began to laugh but there was no mirth in it. He continued to make a sound so dreadful as a moonstruck Bedlamite.

Seb and Rose exchanged anxious glances as Jude seemed upon the verge of madness.

'Jude. Brother. Stop this.' Seb gripped his shoulders and shook him. 'Jude! Cease your noise. Now, I say!' He gripped harder, digging his fingers into flesh and shook him again. 'Stop it!' he shouted to no avail whatever.

Rose pushed Seb aside, a jug of cold water in hand and threw it in Jude's face. It worked far better than words.

Jude leapt to his feet, trying to wrench the jug from Rose, calling her every wicked name he could find upon his tongue. She shoved him back on the bench.

'Sit down and hold your peace, Jude Foxley, and stop behaving like a spoilt brat lost his toy. You're not the first man in London to be cuckolded and you won't be the last. When I think how many unfaithful husbands there are – and I met a good many when I was forced to earn my bread at the Pewter Pot – I wonder that men dare make such a fuss when a woman contrives to do the same. Don't tell me you haven't gone astray since you wed Chesca because I know otherwise: at the Cardinal's Hat and the Sun in Splendour to name but two. We women talk, you know. You men have no secrets from us.'

Jude sat with his jaw dropped. Rose – the woman he once thought to marry – had never spoken so before.

Seb was taken aback and could find not a word to say. Instead, he poured more ale, blinking at this revelation of womankind.

'There's something you don't bloody know, you stupid witch.' Jude found his voice. 'She isn't fucking some neighbour nor merchant nor even the bloody Lord Mayor of London. The whoreson bastard who's fucking my wife is the King of England! There. What do you say to that, eh? That's silenced you, you yowling alley-cat.'

Seb spilt the ale and didn't notice.

'T-the king? Edward?'

'Well, it ain't bloody Herod. She calls him Edoardo, if you please. Stupid bitch. Now do you see why I can't kill the bastard? Any other man and I'd have him gutted and spitted and roasting over a bloody fire. But the king? What am I to do?' Jude was frantic again, a wild look in his eye, tearing at his hair. 'For Christ's bloody sake, tell me what to do, Seb.'

After a long silence, Seb asked:

'What of Chesca?'

'What of the little slut?'

'What does she say of this? Did she have a choice in the matter?'

'How do I bloody know? I don't care what she says. I can't bear to look at the bitch. I don't want to talk to her – ever – and I'm not about to ask her bloody opinion, am I?'

'How did you discover what was happening?'

'I found all the bloody geegaws and expensive trinkets he's been giving her.'

'You did her no harm, did you, Jude? When you found out.' Seb felt fearful of a sudden for Chesca's safety. 'Where be

Chesca now?'

'With him, most likely, drinking fine wine and fucking on silken sheets.'

'She was not hurt by you?'

Jude scowled.

'A scratch or two. She deserves far worse and I'd be within my rights.'

'Aye. I suppose you would at that. But she be little more than a child.'

'She's woman enough to suit him.'

'Do you think she, at so tender an age, would be able to say him nay? Would you have courage sufficient to refuse a king?'

'I'm not a woman.'

'Do not be perverse. You understand my meaning. Could any young lass gainsay such a man to his face? Have a little sympathy for her plight, Jude.'

'She's not in need of your misplaced sympathy; I am. She bloody enjoys the jewels and gifts. Being a king's mistress pleases her too bloody well.'

'Does it? Be you certain of that?'

'A rich and powerful man's pet? What woman wouldn't want that, given the chance? Of course she's bloody delighted.'

Seb was uncertain of the wisdom of his proposal but what else could he do? He offered Jude bed and board for the night. His brother could make use of the chamber that had been his exclusively, the one at the head of the outside stair. More recently, Adam had slept there, sharing with old Ralf Reepham. Now Adam bided with his wife Mercy in Distaff Lane, Ralf was become the sole occupant – and just as well forwhy Ralf snored like a bear at the best of times. At present, with his cold rheum at its worst, the elderly scribe's snores, according to Rose, could be heard above St Martin's loudest bell. Was it fair to have Jude, in so angry a humour, share a room with Ralf? Ralf might not live to see another dawn, if he did.

'You may share my bed,' Seb suggested, half hoping his brother would refuse.

Jude glowered in ominous wise and said neither aye nor nay, so the matter of his lodging for the night went undetermined. But, when supper was done – a sombre and nigh-silent occasion at which no one dared speak to Jude nor hardly to each other for fear of setting the betrayed husband off on another rant – the cause of such disquiet departed of his own accord. As the kitchen door slammed to, followed by the back gate crashing shut, the household breathed easy once more.

'I'm glad that devil's gone,' Nessie declared, clattering dishes in the washtub. 'I couldn't stand him much longer. I hope he don't come back.' Although everyone else was too courteous to say as much, it was obvious they too agreed.

Seb was in need of some pleasant distraction to settle his jangling humours and his workshop seemed a goodly place.

'Come, Kate, show me your work on Master Chaucer's poem, the *Prayer to Our Lady*? How far have you progressed through the alphabet of the acrostic?'

Kate, eager to please as ever, laughed and skipped along the passage to the workshop, her untameable dark curls bouncing. What a balm was she for a disquieted soul, Seb thought.

'I've almost finished the illuminated initial for 'Redress me, Mother...'

'The letter 'R' already? The remainder of the letters will not keep you occupied for another week. I shall have to find you some other task since I must return to Westminster upon Monday morn, regrettably.'

'See here, Master Seb,' Kate sorted through her beautifully written pages, each commencing with a large, colourful initial. 'I like 'M' the best. I thought monkeys – for the letter 'M' – should climb about the letter. Do you like the one wearing the little hat? I was right pleased with him.' Kate's delightful little creatures seemed somewhat at odds with the subject matter of the patriarch Moses and the Burning Bush but there was no denying their appeal. 'And I did popinjays for 'P'. What do you think, master? Pretty, are they not?'

Seb had to laugh. Within the verse, reference was made to the Archangel Gabriel and Kate had him flying with the popinjays, his wings as colourful as the birds'.

'I ne'er could have imagined an angel thus, Kate. What wonders you have contrived. 'Tis fine craftsmanship indeed. As a reward, when you be done with the acrostic, what would you like to do next? You may choose your task.'

Kate pulled a wry face.

'Well, master, in truth, I'd like to make a copy of *Reynard the Fox* with many miniatures, like the book of fables you made for the Duke of Gloucester that while since but...'

'But?'

'Master Adam says it's time I learned other skills so that I can be more useful in the workshop. He says he will teach me how to collate, block, stitch and bind the pages of this poem together. I should like to see it put into a proper book but Master Adam says only if you approve of it and give me permission to learn from him.'

'Of course you may, lass. You could have no finer teacher than Adam and, if you complete the remaining pages to the same fine standard as those you have finished already, I think they will make a most worthy book.' Seb leafed back through the loose sheets, smiling at the horse with its head stuck betwixt the uprights of the letter 'H', over the cross stroke, as if looking out of a stable half-door. Kate had painted the letter itself as though made of timbers. 'F' was decorated with – unsurprisingly perhaps – a family of foxes. He laughed at the dog, tongue lolling – obviously Gawain – leaping through the letter 'D' and their cat, Grayling, entwined around the letter 'C' in its endeavours to catch a tiny mouse perched upon the serif at the letter's head. It was all right cleverly done, he thought, demonstrating both talent and imagination.

Elsewhere in the workshop, a neat pile of cheap primers sat, finished and ready for sale, upon the collating table. Adam's desk had a sheaf of pages ruled for yet another of the kind. These little booklets were ever in demand for young scholars but dull indeed to make with no call for the least imagination. It was tedious work for a man of Adam's abilities.

Upon Ralf's desk were the most recent pages for a little psalter on parchment, no larger than a man's hand. It was after the style of the tiny French *Books of Psalms*, currently so fashionable. This one had been commissioned by a wealthy grocer for his new wife – as much to impress his fellow guildsmen, Seb suspected, as to please the bride. It was to have gilded initials to each psalm and gilding applied to the page edges when it was bound. Ralf had made good progress and Psalm 132, beginning *Ecce quam bonum,* was well in hand. Seb nodded approval.

He checked the storeroom and found it well stocked, although Adam had written a note that more chalk pounce would soon be needed for whitening parchment. It seemed all was well in his beloved workshop in his absence. In a way, it was almost a disappointment to realise that work progressed quite satisfactorily without his presence.

When he found his thoughts wandering back to Jude's predicament, Seb required some other subject to distract him else he would get no sleep that night. Thus, he lit another tallow candle and sat at his empty desk. His stool was much more comfortable compared to the one in the scriptorium, and there were fewer draughts. But how to occupy his mind? He fetched pen, ink and paper and doodled a few scrolls, ornamenting them with acanthus leaves. Then he sketched Gawain, lying by the door. Yet naught was sufficient to prevent his thinking of Jude and Chesca, aye, and the king. What a coil was that!

Then Seb recalled the Italian letter folded up in his purse and what he thought his imagined assailant in the scriptorium had said: 'Where's the Italian letter?' Seb had believed from the beginning that there was more to the letter than Chesca's translation implied. So much innocuous stuff concerning the weather and English fashions in dress might hide something more significant. He took out the crumpled paper and smoothed it on his desk, staring at the words in a foreign tongue. He noted the haphazard use of the little symbol that oftentimes indicated the word 'and' but, in this case, was strewn all about. In Master Chaucer's *Prayer to Our Lady*, something akin to this Tironian nota was employed to fill space at the end of the shorter lines. Suppose in the letter it likewise marked the end of a line?

Taking great care to copy the unfamiliar words correctly, Seb rewrote the letter in the form of a poem, taking the first word after each symbol as beginning a new line with a capital letter. It took time, what with so many deletions and insertions to take account of, and the tallow candle was reduced to a guttering stub by the time Seb had completed it. He swiftly saw that he could have spared himself much labour. The whole need not have been copied out but only those first letters after the symbol. It was obvious now that the capital letters formed an acrostic. Seb could not read Italian but it took little wit to recognise EDOARDO – the king's name. SCOZIA. Might that be the Italian word for Scotland? Seb wondered. And FRANCIA was likely to be France. The word ALLEANZA was repeated. Did it mean alliance, mayhap? In which case, this was no innocent letter home.

Chapter 9

Sunday, the fifth day of February
The Foxley House

SEB AWOKE in his warm bed after a surprisingly good
night of rest. Jude hadn't disturbed him, if he had returned
at all. Seb suspected that his brother might have sought solace
in some obliging woman's bed, if only to have his petty revenge
upon Chesca.

Unlike Jude, he was not convinced that the young lass went
willingly to the king. He might well be rich and powerful, but
he also had the appearance of a good many more years than
his true age of less than two score and was grown mightily fat.
There seemed little about King Edward to attract one so young,
except for the obvious: that he wore a crown.

Seb's mind had also come to a firm conclusion during
the night, concerning that other matter as to whether he had
imagined the attack upon him in the scriptorium on Friday
afternoon. He was now sure it had come to pass in fact.
Moreover, in some ways, it was like unto the murderous attack
upon Piers Creed – without the fatal outcome, fortunately
for him. But, just as then, the assailant had disappeared into
nothingness, or else he simply merged into the group of clerks.
Seb was now certain, beyond reasonable doubt, that the killer
for whom he searched was, indeed, one of the clerks. But which?

Hal Sowbury seemed a reasonable, friendly fellow, though
Jude disliked him and the feeling was mutual. But then Jude

always resented anyone who ordered him about and offended them at every opportunity. Lawrence Duffield was pleasant and good-natured. These two did not appear to be the murderous sort. Neither did Barnabas Newson for all his rough ways. Of the others, Seb realised he yet knew little of them. Robin Beckton was a gambler and preferred to spend his leisure hours playing dice with his like-minded friends but possessing one vice of which Seb did not approve hardly made him guilty of a serious crime. As for Eustace Dane and Andre le Clerc, Seb knew only that the elderly scribe slept a great deal and Andre was a solitary man who preferred reading books to idle conversation. Seb could not blame him for that: others had accused him of the same in the past.

At St Michael le Querne Church later that morn, Seb did his utmost to concentrate upon the office of High Mass. Old Father Thomas's sonorous voice was all too readily drowned out by the chattering of the congregation and noises from the street outside. Then Julia set up such a din of wailing. Rose said the little lass had a new tooth coming through and the infant's one burning cheek made it most likely true, so Rose took her outside to calm her. Yet Seb smiled – problems there ever were but it was good to be with his family and household. He did not relish the thought of returning to Westminster tomorrow.

When mass was ended, he lit a candle for Jude and Chesca, beseeching Our Lady's aid in putting to rights the conflict betwixt them. Hopefully, the king's wandering eye would alight on some other fair lady soon enough and Chesca could be reconciled with her goodman – if Jude was amenable. But his brother was not much the forgiving sort. Seb wondered if either of them would come to dinner this day, as was their custom upon a Sunday. If both came, then sparks would likely fly.

But Seb need not have worried. Chesca arrived in time to share their Lord's Day meal but of Jude there was no sign. The lass looked wary as she stood at the kitchen door, hesitant upon the step.

'Chesca!' Rose was first to greet her with a smile. 'Welcome. Let me take your cloak and set it to dry. Such a day of drizzle is soaking everything.'

'I be right glad you came, sister,' Seb said, giving her the kiss of greeting.

Chesca sighed and returned their smiles, much relieved that she hadn't been turned away, as she feared might happen. Then another thought occurred: mayhap Jude had not been here and they did not know.

'Have some mulled wine,' Rose said, guessing at Chesca's thoughts and offering her a steaming, spicy cup. 'And worry not. *He* isn't here but he told us his side of the story. None of us blames you, however it has come to pass. Now drink up.'

Chesca laughed.

'I not knowing what you would think of me. What Jood must be telling you... And, Seb, I thinking you must take your brother's part.'

'Chesca, dear lass, I know Jude too well to believe every word he tells me. Ever the master of elaboration, his tales be rarely the whole truth and naught else. An exaggeration here, an embellishment there. He was ne'er a man to permit truth to restrain a more exciting version of a story; *his* version. And every story has two sides. We would hear yours afore we pass comment. But after we have dined.' Seb took her hand and gave it a reassuring pat, then wondered if he had just touched flesh where the king had done likewise.

Adam Armitage and Mercy arrived with the Hutchinson youngsters in tow. Nicholas – Mercy's second son of three – was ever a trial and grizzling as the family came into the kitchen, wiping his snotty nose on his sleeve.

'Stop your racket, Nick. You know Uncle Seb hates such noise. If you hadn't been misbehaving, you wouldn't have hurt yourself.' The child's stepfather of six months was already short on sympathy and patience with the little lad.

'And stop wiping snot on your Sunday best sleeves, child,' his mother put in, slapping his hand and sighing with exasperation.

There was now quite a cluster of little ones getting in the way in the kitchen whilst Rose, Kate and Nessie, now with Mercy's assistance, were attempting to prepare the meal. It was so wet outside there was no possibility of their playing in the yard or the garden plot without becoming begrimed with mud. The workshop was no place for children, so it either had to be the shop itself or the parlour with its few but most precious furnishings. The parlour it must be. Seb could not afford for the books to be pulled off the shelf in the shop and mishandled, making them no longer fit for sale.

Chesca sat on the cushioned settle with little Julia on her knee and Grayling the cat beside her. Both babe and cat were attempting to catch a scrap of rag which Chesca bounced upon a string. All three seemed to be enjoying the game and Seb was pleased to see his sister-by-marriage could put aside her difficulties so readily.

Simon, Mercy's eldest of twelve summers in age, asked if he might look at the book Seb had left lying on a stool. Seb, ever eager to permit youngsters to learn, agreed. Simon was a scholar at Paul's School and well able to read. That left Seb and Adam to amuse the smaller lads, Nicholas, Dickon and Mundy. Most of the time, Dickon and Mundy were biddable enough and cheerful little souls. Nicholas was quite different.

'I want to play with the sand-tray,' Nicholas whined. The wooden tray of fine sand was kept in the workshop. With the sand wetted, it was used to teach new apprentices the correct forms of letters, drawing with a finger, instead of wasting ink and paper on their earliest attempts. In the past, Seb had discovered by this means that Nicholas had quite a talent for a four-year-old in drawing pleasing shapes in the sand and spending much time doing so without becoming tired of it. He often set the tray out in the yard where spillages mattered not. Dickon enjoyed the sand also.

'No,' Adam said. 'The parlour is no place for sand, you'll get it everywhere. Uncle Seb has better things to do than watch you making a mess.'

Nicholas's face puckered; his small fists clenched, ready for another outburst of tantrum.

Seb's only recourse in such a situation was to sing. His beautiful voice soon worked its usual magick, calming the unruly and cheering the downhearted. By the time he had sung through all seventeen verses of *Froggie went a-Wooing*, accompanied by much thigh-slapping and 'a-ha-ing', others had arrived to dine. Stephen Appleyard – Seb's father-by-marriage when Emily was alive – and Jack Tabor – currently Stephen's apprentice to the craft of carpentry – were made welcome and Rose was summoning them to the kitchen to dinner.

Seb was half-expecting Jude to burst into the kitchen, as he had the previous afternoon but, God be praised, there came no thumping of boots on the cobbles of the yard. So Seb said a grace in Latin and everyone picked up their knives and spoons, prepared to do justice to Rose's undoubted culinary skills. Hare in a quince sauce was served with a hearty bacon pudding to chase away the February chills. Buttered turnips and beets came with a crumb topping and crisp onion fritters. The meats and a sweet egg tart flavoured with rose water, even the butter on the worts had to be appreciated to the utmost, for the forty-days fasting of Lententide would begin in just over a week's time.

With dinner done and the dishes soaking in the washtub, Rose and Mercy settled the little ones for a nap, although Nicholas protested until the last, when sleep claimed him. Now the menfolk and Chesca sat over their cups in the parlour whilst the other women set the kitchen to rights. Chesca had been raised in Venice as a fine lady and, although she was come down in the world, household chores were not for her.

'So, Chesca,' Adam began, stretching his long legs towards the fire and moving the cat aside with his foot. 'How is it you come alone this day? I trust that husband of yours hasn't got himself into trouble again?' Adam had little liking for Jude, his kinsman, whom he regarded as idle, feckless and a millstone around Seb's neck. On the other hand, Seb was his greatly esteemed and beloved relative.

Chesca shook her head but made no answer.

'Jack, we be in need of more wood for the fire, if you would oblige us and fetch it from the yard, please?' Seb said. 'Simon, why do you not go into the shop and choose something for yourself to read? Do not spoil the pages though, as it must remain fit for sale.'

Jack slouched off, grumbling. Simon raced from the parlour, delighted with his quest.

'Now, lass, why do you not tell us your side of the story? Adam and Stephen can be trusted not to spread a word of it abroad,' Seb assured her.

'Story?' Adam's interest was engaged. 'What have I missed?

'I doubting that matters now. Jood will be telling everybody what he thinking of me. My name will be dragging in the filth.' Chesca sighed and sipped her wine. 'It beginning on Twelve Night when Jood taking me to the celebrations in the palace. I dressing in my best gown and looking fine. There was food and drinking; musick and dancing. When Jood dancing with me, everybody looking. The king looking too. The king coming to me to dance the next measure. Jood angry but what I doing? I cannot tell the king to be off. I dancing with Edoardo two times. He liking me. Next day, I getting message telling me to come to the Great Gate tomorrow when the Clock Tower bell ringing for noon. I doing as he says. How can I not? Lord Haysling meeting me there. Now I going to the palace two or three times in a week. Edoardo liking me very much. He calling me his lively mistress. When Jood finding out, when he seeing the jewels Edoardo give to me... he going like madman. I not knowing what to do.'

Adam blew out a long breath. Stephen's jaw hung slack. For some moments, no one spoke. Words seemed inadequate.

'Mistress to the king himself? Well, whatever's going to come of that?' Stephen spoke at last.

'Jude will likely do something rash,' was Adam's comment. 'Something we'll all have cause to regret. You know how reckless he is, the great fool.'

'I ain't reckless,' Jack said, returning with a huge armful of firewood and spilling it by the hearth with a clatter, startling Gawain from his slumbers by the fire and sending Graying bolting for the door with a yowl of feline protest.

'Nobody's talking about you – this once,' Adam said, refilling cups from the ale jug.

'And 'tis naught for you to go yammering about in every tavern and ale-house across London, young Jack,' Stephen told his erstwhile apprentice. 'I know you're one for gossiping at the least excuse. Now restack that wood in orderly wise.'

''Ow can I bloody gossip when I don't know wot yer talking about?' Surprisingly, Jack obeyed his master without argument, bending to arrange the kindling into a pile, if haphazardly. Neatness was never Jack's way. If he laced his jerkin straight in the morn, it was a matter worthy of note.

'And mind your language on the Lord's Day!' Adam warned in an undertone, scowling at the youngster.

Jack might lack years but he lacked little in height and strength, as Adam knew to his cost.

Everyone heard the back door slam and voices in the kitchen.

'Oh, Jude! 'Tis you.' Rose's voice was audible in the parlour – clearly a warning but unnecessary. All had guessed who caused the racket.

'Is the bitch here?' Jude shouted, his footsteps thudding along the passage. 'Come here, you bloody harlot! I know you're hiding behind my brother's back. Well, he won't bloody save you this time.' Jude burst into the parlour like a horde of Vikings on the rampage. 'Where is she?'

Adam and Jack blocked his path. Seb and Stephen stood either side of Chesca who was pale and trembling.

'Out!' Adam roared. 'You're not welcome here if you intend

trouble. There are four of us against you…'

Jude did not waste words. With the strength of overwhelming rage, he grabbed both Adam and Jack by the hair and slammed their heads together with such a buffet the pair staggered off balance. Adam groped for the door jamb to support him. Jack fell to the floor, groaning and clutching his head.

This was Seb's house. He had to do something but he was a man of words, not action, and his brother was of no mind to give heed to reason. Seb braced himself and stepped forth, his face not much more than a hand's span from Jude's furious countenance. Seb could smell the drink on his breath.

'Out of my way, you!' Jude roared, his hands gripping Seb by the shoulders, the fingers digging deep as he tried to drag him aside to get at Chesca who was sobbing in Stephen's protective embrace. The carpenter was brawny enough but, like Seb, he was a peaceable man, disinclined to violence.

Seb stood firm, trying hard not to wince in his brother's fearsome grasp.

'Jude. Harken to me. Chesca be a guest in my house. You will desist from this madness. Do not harm her – nor anyone else. Do you hear me?'

For answer, Jude swatted Seb aside like an irritating fly, shoving him back onto the settle and seizing hold of Chesca. He did not expect the heavy pewter wine jug, still half full, with which Stephen clouted him across the nose. Chesca was released and fled the parlour to the safety of the kitchen and the other womenfolk as wine sloshed among the scented rushes on the floor.

'You bastard, Appleyard. You'll bloody regret that.' Jude spoke through his hands as he nursed his nose. Blood seeped betwixt his fingers as he slumped on the settle beside Seb who hastily removed himself.

No apology was forthcoming from the carpenter who turned to Seb.

'We thank you for your hospitality, Master Seb, and a fine

dinner as always but I think it best that Jack and I go home now.'
He then whispered so only Seb could hear: 'Shall I send the lad
to fetch Bailiff Turner? A night in the lock-up might quiet him.'
Stephen nodded towards Jude who was now dripping gore on
the embroidered cushions Emily had once stitched with pride.

Seb shook his head.

'I think not, Stephen, but thank you for the thought.
Rather...' Seb lowered his voice. 'I would ask you and Jack to
escort Chesca to Dame Ellen's house... until Jude calms and
be in his good senses once more. Enough hurt has been done
already.' He went to Jude, to assist him. 'Come. Let me see
your injury.'

'Get away from me,' Jude snarled. 'I'm your damned brother
yet you take that bitch's side against me.'

'Chesca be but a child – '

'She's my bloody wife! Supposedly.'

Seb heard Stephen, Jack and Chesca departing by
the back way.

'Let us go to the kitchen and tend your nose; cleanse your
face. Rose has violet oil for bruises and knit-bone salve, if your
nose be broken...'

'Just pour me wine...'

'I believe you have had an excess as it is.'

'Just give me a drink, you sanctimonious little prick... to
wash away the taste of blood in my mouth. Wait 'til I get my
hands on Appleyard. I'll wring his neck like a bloody chicken.'

'You will not. Now sit quietly and hold your tongue
whilst Rose tends you.' Seb guided Jude onto a bench at the
kitchen board.

Rose brought cloths and icy water.

'You're such a fool, Jude,' she said, wringing out a wet cloth
and folding it to make a pad to staunch the bleeding.

'Don't you start bloody scolding me. You're not my wife,
thank God. Ouch! You ham-fisted drab. Have a little pity,
can't you?'

'Keep still.'

'It's broken, I know.'

'Nay. Bruised but not broken. You're fortunate and deserve worse. Stephen should have struck you harder. Now hold this as a cold compress on the bridge of your nose.'

'I knew not to expect sympathy from you, you heartless cow. Leave me be.'

'As you please. Tend your own hurts. The violet oil is here, if you want it, and don't go dripping more blood on my fresh-scrubbed board, either.'

'I apologise for all this, Rose,' Seb said, watching as his brother slopped gore-tinted water everywhere. 'And there be bloodstains upon the cushions and wine spilt in the parlour. Such a sorry mess.'

'I'll see to it, directly.' Rose hastened to inspect the chaos in the parlour.

'She be the finest of women,' Seb said to no one in particular when she was gone.

'She's an overbearing bloody cow, like every woman you've ever taken a fancy to,' Jude attempted to remove the greased stopper from the violet oil whilst keeping his head well back. 'Don't stand there watching; bloody help me with this, you damned fool.'

Seb obliged.

'Do not speak ill of Rose or I shall strike you myself and add to your pain.' He smeared the pleasant-smelling oil around Jude's swelling nose and between his eyes which were blackening with bruises already.

'You wouldn't dare.'

'Do not try me further, Jude. I grow tired of your actions and grave discourtesies this day. There. 'Tis the best I may do but your battle scars will look quite the fearful sight upon the morrow.'

'Then we'll make a fine bloody pair in the scriptorium in the morning. You look like a beaten bloody egg from your mishap with some bugger's cudgel the other night.'

'I be aware of that and have made use of this oil myself.'

'Hasn't done you much good then.'

'I know the bruises look bad but they do not hurt as they might. But you mentioned the scriptorium? I thought you had walked out after...'

'Well, I walked back in again, didn't I? Or will do.'

'How did that come to pass? Master Oliver's broken hand is yet...'

'Words have been spoken from on high. I still have a place, whether bloody Oliver likes it or not.'

'Chesca persuaded the...'

'Shut up! Don't say her name in my hearing... or you-know-whose, the bloody lecherous prick.'

Mercy and Kate came down the stairs bringing the little ones hardly awake from their naps. Mercy glanced at Jude and the gory cloths.

'Where's that goodman of mine, then?' she asked, setting her youngest, Mundy, down on the flagstones.

'Nursing an aching head in the parlour, I fear,' Seb said.

'Adam's ever too eager for a brawl,' she said with an exasperated sigh.

''Tis not as you think, Mercy.'

'Him and Jude? You may as well tie a cat and a dog by their tails. It'll end in a fight, no matter what.'

'Mind what you say, mistress,' Jude put in. 'I'm in no mood to suffer more insults from anyone.'

'Adam was protecting Chesca. We all were,' Seb explained, speaking quietly.

'From him? That one will cause trouble wherever she goes. You mark my words,' Mercy said.

'You may well be correct,' Seb said, sounding weary, lifting little Dickon into his arms. 'Come, little man. Let us go greet the hens in their run, shall we? I believe the rain has ceased and the fresh air will be welcome indeed.'

Later, Jude had calmed down. His nose ached and throbbed but bled no more. Under Seb's sufferance, he was permitted to stay to supper.

Adam and Mercy had taken their family home to Distaff Lane, so it was much like old times: Seb, Jude, Rose, Kate and Nessie, supping at the board. Ralf returned, belatedly, from spending the day with Joanie Alder, his love of many years' standing, but he did not linger, except to bid everyone good night, before retiring to the room above the outside stairs that had once been Jude's.

When the women, too, were gone to their beds, Seb and Jude sat over their ale as the kitchen hearth gave out the last of its heat. Few words had been exchanged betwixt the brothers throughout the evening. Neither knew what to say. Seb feared rousing Jude's wrath again with an incautious word spoken out of place. Jude had a headache the size of St Paul's and preferred silence. In truth, he had much to dwell upon – mostly dark thoughts and a mountain of regret.

Seb, as ever, hated to sit idle and fetched his scrip from the workshop. Searching through its contents, among the fresh paper and other drawing stuff to replace what had been damaged the previous week by some rogue rummaging through his possessions, Seb was reminded of the mysterious letter in his purse. He had the leisure now to think upon the acrostic in Italian and attempt to understand it. What a pity Chesca was not here to unravel the words for him.

He smoothed it out on the board and moved the solitary candle to better illuminate his writing of an unfamiliar tongue. As he had seen yestereve, a few words were clear enough, names of people – EDOARDO, for one – and places, maybe. FRANCIA was likely France. But what the words betwixt them meant, to make sense of it all, he knew not.

'What are you frowning over, little brother?' Jude asked. 'Last week's accounting all gone astray has it? Are you as deep in bloody debt as the rest of us?'

'Nay. 'Tis a puzzle but half solved. If only I knew more of this tongue.'

'Give it here. Let me see.' Jude took the paper and Seb waited, expecting a shout of anger at the least sight of something written in Italian. It did not happen.

'Who wrote this?'

'I did.'

'But you don't know any Italian.'

'And therein lies my difficulty. Are you able to read any of it?'

'Why would I want to?'

'You will recall the page of correspondence you found in the miscellaneous documents pile? I kept it. See here.' Seb handed Jude the much-creased letter. 'And Chesca translated it, saying it was but harmless comments about the weather and fashion but pointed out those symbols, somewhat like figure sevens, dotted throughout the text in a seemingly random manner? They made a nonsense of it but I rewrote the text, commencing a new line after every symbol.'

'Why did you bother?'

'Forwhy, in truth, I was attacked not once but twice; the first upon Thursday eve, when I was battered and my attire ripped and despoiled. The second occasion was after dinner, Friday, in the scriptorium, a blade held against my neck. At first, I believed I had dreamt it, the result of the surgeon's potion. In my befuddled state, I thought that I heard my assailant demanding that I give him the Italian letter. But now I know I was not mistaken. I have deciphered the letter and discovered it to be an acrostic.'

'A what?'

'Like Master Chaucer's ABC Prayer. The first letters of every line spell out quite a different message from the letter which contained them. This be that new message. I can make out a few words, enough to suggest its importance, else why would it be encoded in a cypher? I must know what it means afore I act upon it.'

'Act upon it?'

'Aye. Suppose 'tis information concerning... I know not what. King Edward's plans to go on Crusade against the Turks... Who can say?'

'Why would I give a damn about what that bastard plans? He can rot in hell's pit for all I care.'

'But it may contain information that England's enemies ought not to know.'

'You really think that could be the case?'

Seb shrugged.

'We cannot be certain unless we learn what it says.'

'It could earn us a goodly reward, if we save England from a costly war.' The possibility of additional money in his purse ever enlivened Jude. 'Bring another candle that we can see it better. My knowledge of Italian isn't so lacking I can't make out a few sentences. It's a pity you wrote it in such a scrawl.'

'I have yet to make a fair copy.'

'So some other bugger knows of this? Are you certain this is what they demanded of you? Who knows you have the letter?'

'It was no secret. We spoke about it, did we not?'

'Then we'd better hurry and work this out before he does. That is, if he knows any Italian.'

Seb did not say what he believed: that the man who demanded the letter was the same who had written it in the first place; that he would fear his secret message was known to others. Seb's life could be at hazard over this and Jude's too. He was also convinced now that the man was one of the clerks in the scriptorium. How else could he have 'disappeared' on Friday except by mingling with his fellow scribes?

The brothers sat, heads together – the dark and the fair – frowning and pummelling their brains. St Martin's bell had chimed for Matins before they achieved the best they might, dragging forth the meaning from a mass of unfamiliar words.

'I'll have to ask audience with Lord Hastings first thing in the morn. We cannot keep silent upon this matter,' Seb said, reading through his final fair copy, translated to the best of their combined abilities. If they had it correctly, it was disquieting indeed.

'I'll come with you,' Jude said, pushing back his stool and draining the dregs in his ale cup. 'If there's a reward to be had out of this, I want my share.'

Chapter 10

Monday, the sixth day of February
Westminster

JUDE HAD STAYED the night at Paternoster Row, sharing Seb's comfortable bed though, as he complained, a woman would have made a more satisfactory bed mate.

At first light, the brothers hastened to Westminster, walking quickly through the cold drizzle. Seb missed his good crimson cloak more than ever as the rain soaked into his thin clerk's gown despite his wearing his old faded mantle and a hood. He did not wish to stand in Lord Hastings' presence looking like a half-drowned dog.

'You have the translation?' Jude asked for the third time since they had left the warmth of the kitchen.

'In my purse, as I told you afore.'

'You think Hastings will see us?'

'I be in his pay, searching out the murderer of Piers Creed. He will suppose I have urgent tidings on that score and likely grant us an audience.' Seb side-stepped a particularly noisome-looking puddle and Jude caught his arm to steady him. It was like times past.

'Suppose he doesn't?'

'Then I shall have to put our findings in writing to his lordship, I suppose.'

'Best not. We know not who we can trust, what with a killer on the loose and a bloody espier?'

'We shall have to trust Secretary Oliver since 'tis through him that my request must be sent to Hastings.'

'I would rather go into the Great Hall and find him at breakfast; tell him straight, there and then. None of this time-wasting, courtly etiquette, mantle-and-sword nonsense. This is important, Seb.'

'You think I do not know as well as you? I be following my instructions: to inform Secretary Oliver and he will arrange matters with Lord Hastings. What concerns me is that Oliver might expect to simply pass on a message, rather than allow me – us – a meeting with the king's chamberlain in person.'

'We daren't risk involving a third party, especially not that conniving bastard Oliver. He'll want a fat share of our reward. Besides, I don't trust the bugger. For all we know, he could be the culprit in all this. I've always said his eyes are those of a criminal sort. Don't you agree?'

'He seems a reasonable man. I know you dislike him…'

'I hate the whole scabby bunch of them in the scriptorium. There's little to choose between them. Sowbury and Duffield think they're God's gift; Beckton's a cheat, robbing me at dice; Newson's a dolt; Dane's an idle bugger and le Clerc's the most miserable sod since Job first started complaining.'

'Job did not complain…'

'Oh, shut up, Master Know-it-all. You understand my meaning, so don't contradict me. And high-and-mighty Oliver is the most obnoxious of all. I did so enjoy breaking his damned finger, as he well deserved for poking me like a pudding to see if I was done. Bastard.'

'Shall I await you here?' Seb asked as they came to the Great Gate of Westminster Palace.'

'Why? I'm coming with you.'

'But Jude, if we stand before Lord Hastings… well, you have worn that same attire since Friday and it stinks of the numerous taverns you have frequented. Do you not wish to go to your lodgings and change your shirt, at least?'

'Bugger Hastings. If he can't suffer the smell of an honest man's toil, then that's too bad. I'm not bothering for the likes of some jumped-up baron.'

'But what of the rest of us working beside you in the scriptorium? Do we not deserve a little consideration?' Seb wrinkled his nose and sniffed. His brother used to be so concerned for both his appearance and cleanliness. Seb wondered how Jude had changed since his travels in strange lands.

'You're a worse nag than any wife. You realise that? Well, I'm not going to trouble with my clothes just to please you, either. Come on. Let's go find that bastard Oliver and get this done.' With that, Jude dragged Seb into Westminster's Outer Courtyard, towards the Inner Gate.'

'Tardy again, Foxley, you idle devil?' Walter, the guard on the gate, acknowledged Jude, coughing and spitting a gobbet of green phlegm as a question mark to his observation.

Jude ignored him and made for the entrance to the Exchequer and other offices, Seb hastening to keep up. In truth, they were early, as intended, and found the scriptorium yet locked. Neither was there any sign of Secretary Oliver. Since he always arrived last, after the clerks, that was to be expected.

'Great Hall. They'll all be feeding their bellies still,' Jude said, continuing his rapid strides along the passageway towards the hall, grinning to himself when they passed the very spot where he had snapped the secretary's finger the previous week.

The first meal of the day was never an organised affair. Those of rank usually broke their fast in their chambers, either finishing whatever remained of their generous night livery allowance, or sending their servants to fetch fresh food and drink from the kitchens and buttery. It was the lesser mortals who gleaned from the offerings laid out in the Great Hall, a proper meal at such an hour being reckoned necessary only to those who laboured, if they could afford it. Even so, the king being a man who required a full belly at any time of day, the food available at dawn for the royal court was plenteous and of a goodly standard. Thus, breakfast was becoming more important these days, even among the noble early-risers.

William, Lord Hastings was a keen trencherman himself, evidenced by the paunch which grew more generous by the week, though he was but a novice in gluttony compared to his king. Therefore, it came as no surprise to see the chamberlain upon the dais, helping himself to morsels from a platter of cold meats as he spoke with two men of about his age, the one grizzled and greying – Lord Howard – the other bald as a hardboiled egg.

Seb knew John, Lord Howard, for whom he had completed certain commissions, including a fine coat-of-arms, but did not recognise the bald man who must be a person of note, judging by his fine attire. Seb was shocked when Jude pulled him straight towards the dais and he tried to hang back. This was not how courteous folk approached their betters, without an introduction or a by-your-leave.

'Nay, Jude…' he hissed, attempting to prise his sleeve from his brother's grip, but it was too late.

'My Lord Hastings,' Jude said, sketching a hasty bow that was little more than a bob, although he did have grace enough to remove his hood, leaving his clerk's coif in place. 'My brother, Sebastian Foxley – who is known to you – requires speech with you, urgently… and privily, sir.' Jude shoved Seb forward before retreating in haste to a board where ale jugs and cups stood ready.

Seb went on one knee, baring his head, awaiting a response – if there was to be one, other than his instant removal by his lordship's servants or the guards summoned to cart him off to some filthy dungeon in the bowels of the palace. He imagined the worst but Lord Hastings only snorted his disapproval.

'Well, at least you have better manners than the oaf who accompanied you. Get up, Foxley, and tell me what can possibly be so urgent that you require an audience without the proper procedure and civilities.'

Seb stood, realising everyone in the Great Hall was observing the spectacle of a scruffy clerk demanding an audience with the lord chamberlain.

'F-forgive me, my lord. I apologise for this ill-mannered intrusion but 'tis a matter of some import... regarding certain... m-matters of, er, consequence.' Seb bit his lip. He was sounding like a lack-wit.

Lord Howard grinned at him, came down the steps from the dais and clapped him hard on the shoulder.

'Never expected to see an honest citizen such as my favourite artist in this den of iniquity. How do you fare, Foxley?' The grey-haired lord leaned close. 'Watch yourself, Seb,' he said under his breath. 'Come away, Thomas,' he waved to the bald man. 'Let's leave Will to his privy business. I'll show you that fine new gelding of mine; put him through his paces. What say you?' With that, Lord Howard and his companion departed.

Arms folded across his belly, Hastings looked at Seb and sighed, as though such lowly persons were a constant irritant and vexation, like gnats on a summer's eve, spoiling an otherwise pleasant day.

'Follow me,' he said after a lengthy silence during which Seb grew hotter and increasingly anxious. The chamberlain came down the steps and led the way to a door set off to one side of the dais, concealed behind a fine tapestry, pausing to let a servant lift it away so they could pass through, unimpeded. The chamber beyond gave the air of magnificence but Seb had no chance to admire the sumptuous luxuries. His eyes did not stray from Hastings' velvet- and fur-clad back.

Hastings' flung himself into a cushioned chair – almost grand enough for a throne – signed to a waiting servant to bring him wine and then sent the fellow away, telling him to stand beyond the door and admit none but the king himself.

Seb swallowed in panic. The king? Edward... in person! But the king did not come, to Seb's immense relief. Hastings crossed his legs, displaying silken hose of thrush-egg blue, and sipped his wine, keeping Seb on tenterhooks, waiting and fretting as the minutes stretched out.

'So... who murdered that clerk? Thank God it has taken but a week to find him out. Name the rascal and I'll see him hanged before sunset.' Hastings set down his wine cup and picked at a hang-nail. 'Well? I don't have all day to wait upon your answer. Tell me.'

'I f-fear, my lord, I cannot name the miscreant but –'

'Then don't waste my time. Get out!'

'But I have this, my lord.' Seb held out the crumpled page of the Italian letter, his acrostic version and his neatly written message, translated from the Italian as best he and Jude could achieve.

'What are these? Pleas for more money? I paid you at the beginning sufficient for two months' work, at least.'

''The first is a letter my brother discovered, left by accident among papers in the scriptorium. 'Tis encoded in a cypher, my lord, in the Italian tongue. I solved the code and we – my brother and I – have made it out into English and think you may have concerns regarding it.'

Hastings snatched the papers and squinted at them. His eyes were, mayhap, not so good for reading small writing any longer.

'You invented this.' He shook the paper bearing Seb's version of the code in English:

Alliance with Scotland ended. Edward to invade. France alliance with Scotland.

'Nay. As I shall attempt to explain, I worked it out. The original letter, as you see, is in the form of an acrostic and we...'

'A what?'

'A word puzzle, my lord. The first letters of each line spell out words anew. But they are in Italian, of course. We have translated them.'

Hastings was only interested in the English, not knowing other tongues save French and some little Latin.

'How could you know of these matters? The king and his

closest advisors have discussed them in council only. How did you learn of these intentions? You have been listening at doors. Are you an espier? An intelligencer?'

'Nay, I did but unravel the meaning of the cypher. If there be any truth in what I have written there, it has been uncovered by a very real espier, not by me.'

'This is not the letter itself then? Bring that to me.'

'I believe that to be but a first draft, to enable the message to be encoded. It has numerous deletions and insertions but neither signature nor seal. I know not the whereabouts of the completed letter. Mayhap, it has been dispatched to...'

'You make this business murkier and more foul by the moment. Why should I believe there ever was such a letter? You could have made this up as a malicious prank to set the Privy Council by the ears.'

'Why would I do such a thing, my lord? How could I or anyone profit from such mischief?'

'I dare say there are ways. Sell this to England's enemies for a goodly price...'

'But I brought it to you.'

'And who's to know if this is the only copy and you haven't sold the same to the Scotch, the French, the Spaniards and whoever else might benefit from this knowledge?'

'Have me swear upon God's sacred Word... a pile of Bibles, Gospels, Psalters and Books of Hours and I will so swear, to the peril of my soul, that all I have told you be the truth. I know not how else to prove my honesty, my lord.'

'Oh, cease your prating, Foxley. His Grace of Gloucester and Lord Howard vouched for your honesty before I employed you. The king himself has put his trust in you. Now go to and find the murderer and then you have an espier to track down also. Well? Don't stand there like a graven image. Go and do what I've paid you to do.'

'Aye, my lord.' Seb sketched a bow and withdrew in haste. It was all he could do to restrain himself from bolting like a startled hare. A last glance back as he went through the door, back into the Great Hall, showed Lord Hastings frowning at the papers once again.

'What happened in there?' Jude was waiting in the hall. 'Is Hastings going to do anything about the message we worked out? Tell me, damn you.'

'I know not.' Seb paused to catch his breath like one who had run a league or more. 'I know not whether he will do anything. He went so far as to suggest we invented it but I hope I convinced him otherwise. We can do no more. 'Tis up to him and the king now... except that...'

'Except what?'

'He has charged me with uncovering the espier as well as Creed's killer. As if I have not more to do than the hours, days and weeks allow.'

Work had long since commenced in the scriptorium. Master Oliver was seated by the brazier, his injured hand supported in a blue silken sling. When they entered, Seb expected an outburst of anger from the secretary but, surprisingly, naught of the kind came to pass, although the scowl Oliver cast at Jude could have turned best butter rancid. Had the man been forewarned of their late arrival or was he now wary of Jude's temper? It seemed odd indeed that not a word was said concerning Jude's appalling past behaviour nor were his apparent resignation last Thursday and absence upon Friday and Saturday mentioned. Seb wondered why but dared not enquire.

The brothers took their places and began the endless task of neatly copying out ill-scrawled missives as clear and elegant letters from the king. Seb had hardly settled on his cracked stool and was puzzling over a name half obliterated by an unfortunate inkblot the size of his thumbnail when someone knocked upon the door.

'Come!' Oliver bellowed. Since, inexplicably by the king's

own command, he could not vent his spleen upon the Foxleys, another would have to suffer the consequences. Why the king should have the least interest in this pair of misbegotten knaves was beyond the secretary's comprehension but it was not his place to question a royal order.

The man who entered was well known about Westminster as a groom of the king's chamber, so Oliver curbed his ire and rethought the words on the tip of his tongue. It did not do to shout at the king's personal servants. The man approached the secretary and whispered his message. Oliver's sigh of exasperation was audible.

'Foxley!'

Both Seb and Jude looked up.

'Not you.' He sneered at Jude. 'Sebastian. King Edward has summoned you. Go with Sir Nicholas FitzAlan. Now.'

Seb dropped his pen and sent his stool toppling and crashing in his haste to rise. The king! What had he done amiss that he should be summoned? His knees felt like unravelling string and he doubted they would support him long enough to stand afore Edward himself. 'Sweet Jesu and St Mary aid me,' he prayed silently as he scurried along, attempting to keep up with Sir Nicholas's long strides.

They returned to the chamber where Seb had spoken to Lord Hastings earlier. Sir Nicholas FitzAlan did not pause but continued on, through a further door, into another splendid chamber even more grand than the one before, draped with velvet of deepest blue, fringed with gold tassels. A canopy of estate overhung a gilded throne with cushions of the same velvet - the Presence Chamber. A congregation of finely-clad courtiers milled around, speaking in undertones. At first, they ignored Seb like a man invisible. Not one deigned to openly acknowledge so humble a subject, clad in a faded, threadbare gown like a moulting sparrow amongst peacocks in their pride. Seb's unease increased. A few sideways glances fell upon him, hastily turning away as though drabness might be a contagion.

'Wait here,' Sir Nicholas instructed before advancing upon a third doorway, guarded by two stout fellows in full royal livery. Despite the law which stated none should bear naked blades within a mile of the king's person, both wore swords at their side and Seb did not doubt they had permission to unsheathe them, if necessary. His wait, 'neath the covert scrutiny of so many hostile eyes, seemed long indeed and the discomfiture weighed heavily. If only he could sit afore his trembling knees gave way but the chamber was bare of any chair, bench or stool except for the throne itself. None sat in the presence of the monarch.

Sir Nicholas returned.

'Come. The King's Grace will speak with you in the privy chamber.'

Seb gulped. The king was going to speak with him! He had spoken with the king's brother, Richard, Duke of Gloucester, more than once in the past, having painted his likeness, carried out other commissions for him and once presented the gift of a book to his lordship. The duke had ever put him at his ease. But the King of England was another matter entirely. His bodily person alone was more than intimidating at a distance. The fact that he was Almighty God's Anointed One made it worse yet.

As Sir Nicholas led the way into the privy chamber, Seb was relieved to see that King Edward reclined in idle wise upon a day bed, lessening his towering presence. Seb bent the knee and pulled off his clerk's coif, feeling the criticising eyes upon him of those select few gathered around. It was as well that he could not know how, having removed his coif, his dark hair now stood up in tufts, all unruly, else it would have further added to his embarrassment and nervous humour. Seb was not a vain man but to look so unkempt in the presence of his king was a discourtesy indeed. But either Edward did not notice or paid it no mind.

'Stand, Master Foxley. Let me see the face of my brother's favoured artist. I have heard much of you... some of it not so uncomplimentary.' The king laughed heartily at his little jest and everyone else present pretended laughter also.

Seb thought it wise to smile too. Taking offence was not permitted. From the corner of his eye, he saw Lord Hastings, the bald-headed lord whose name he did not know and one he remembered all too well and prayed the remembrance was not mutual: Anthony Woodville, Lord Scales, the queen's brother. There had been occurrences in the past concerning that man, which Seb did not want to suffer again.

The king bestirred himself and sat up on the damask-cushioned bed. Even seated, he was looking at Seb straightly, eye to eye. Edward's eyes were keen and clear, blue as lapis lazuli. They would see all and miss naught, Seb was sure.

'Ah! Not so much the little mouse, eh? Sebastian Foxley has courage enough to look at his king. An artist's prerogative, no doubt.' Edward chuckled, his humour genuine as Seb hastily lowered his gaze to the king's black-and-silver piked shoes of finest Cordovan leather. He had not meant to stare.

'I-I intended no offence, Your Grace, and beg pardon most contritely.'

'Don't play the courtier with me. They all pretend that I don't shit, fart and fornicate like other men but you know better, I suspect.' Edward waved an encompassing hand at the handful of men in this inner sanctum. 'My brother Dickon says you're too honest to be a flatterer; that you see men for what they are underneath the baubles and finery, the insincere courtesies and counterfeit smiles.' The king did not seem to care if the others in the chamber heard his opinion of them. Mayhap, it was no secret. Neither did he appear the least concerned as he continued to speak openly:

'My court is a pit of vipers. Did you know that, Master Foxley? Everyone out to poison the prospects of his rivals. They all love their king whilst he pleases them but one move amiss and they'll fling him to the serpents. I know that from experience. Few are the men I can rely upon in adversity. My brother Dickon is one; Hastings another and Lord Scales would hope to account himself along with them, as would Lord Stanley, I have no doubt.' The king directed a half-smile at the bald-headed man who looked away. 'Are you one of those few, Master Foxley; a fellow in whom his king can trust, whatever befalls?'

'I will serve you in all honesty, Highness, to my utmost ability.'

'Well said. I like not empty words. We will talk privily, you and me.' Edward stood to his full height and raised his voice. 'Out! Leave us... all of you, save Lord Hastings.'

Seb was glad to see Anthony Woodville was leaving.

The king waved him to a stool and once more reclined upon the day bed. Hastings also sat on a comfortable chair.

'Now,' Edward began. 'This is a fine coil, is it not? So tell me, Foxley, what you know of this Italian quagmire. What has your brother said of the affair?'

Seb looked both shocked and bewildered, as well he might. To which 'affair' did the king refer? To the espier or to Chesca as his new mistress? How was he supposed to answer?'

'M-my brother, Jude, was most helpful in translating the deciphered message from the Italian, my lord.'

'I don't doubt it but his wife's knowledge of the tongue is far superior, for obvious reasons. We have suspected there to be an Italian intelligencer at court for some time, calling himself the Esquire of the Ruby. Two letters, thus signed, were intercepted last leaf-fall; there may well have been others that succeeded in escaping my agents – who knows. But if the epistles were innocuous as Secretary Oliver, with his moderate knowledge of Italian, believed them to be, why were they not signed with a proper name? Esquire of the Ruby indeed! Thus, we suspected a code, a cypher of some kind, but could not unravel it. In truth, we have reason to believe there is – as I said – a vipers' nest of enemies within these very walls.

'Your sister-by-marriage, whilst in guise as my mistress, has been translating these letters with her greater knowledge of the tongue and agreed for the most part with Secretary Oliver's conclusions regarding their innocent subject matter. She, too, has tried to find some other meaning therein, in order to assist us in uncovering her countrymen who wish evil upon us. But now it seems you, Master Foxley, have met with success where others failed. What more natural than a brother and sister to talk together? Therefore, you and Francesca shall work in concert to find out our ill-wishers and reveal what it was they would tell our enemies.'

'W-what of my brother? Does he know of this a-arrangement?' Seb asked, all uncertain, hardly able to force the question from his lips.

'Your brother assumes that I cuckold him and so let him believe what he will. He has no further part in this, except as the wronged husband, and thus it must remain. His hot temperament and loose tongue are not to be trusted with this knowledge and you will not speak of it with him. Not one word. Do you understand?'

Seb nodded, swallowing down his fear at the look in the king's eyes. Edward might act the mild monarch but there was Plantagenet fire at his core. The king continued in a more amiable tone:

'However, your brother shall be compensated most generously for my 'use' of his pretty wife. Money appeals to him, so I'm told. Or property, if he prefers. In the meantime, Master Foxley, you and Francesca, when she arrives at midday, shall have the use of Lord Hastings' chamber. None will disturb you there. Food, drink and writing stuff will be provided. You work your magick and decipher the code in these letters we have already. Francesca can then translate your findings into English. Can you accomplish this by suppertime?'

'I believe so, my lord, if the letters be not over long.'

The king clicked his fingers as a man might call his hound to heel. Lord Hastings fetched a small coffer, inlaid and enamelled, and set it before Edward. The king drew forth a small gold key upon a chain around his neck, hid 'neath his attire, opened the box and lifted out a tray of such jewels as Seb had never imagined could exist – rings, brooches, pendants and necklaces. He set the tray aside and took some folded papers from the bottom. These he handed to Seb.

'Have a care with those,' he said. 'Is the remainder of the day sufficient for your work?'

Seb leafed through the pages of small, close written script – nine in all. The writing was clear and unhampered by corrections and deletions, as had been the case with the draft copy he had struggled to make sense of previously.

'Aye, my lord; more than enough.'

'Good. I shall expect the results before I sup. Let us hope your revelations do not put me off my meal.' Edward laughed as he lifted the jewel tray to replace it in the ornate coffer, noting Seb's wide-eyed wonderment. 'I hear of your delight in colour, Master Foxley, as proven by the illuminated copy of Vegetius' *De Re Militari* you made for me last summer. A worthy and most pleasing book indeed. Mayhap, you deserve some little reward for your efforts this day?' The king poked about among the priceless objects upon the tray and selected a ring. Too small for Edward's large hands but suitable for an artist's slender fingers. 'Here, take this trinket for your trouble as a sign of my favour. Appropriate, is it not? A fine ruby for one about to uncover the secrets of this damnable Esquire of the Ruby.'

Seb accepted the ring, barely able to find words to express his gratitude as he slipped it on the little finger of his left hand. The king waved aside his stuttered and inadequate thanks.

'Sir Nicholas FitzAlan will take you to Lord Hastings' chamber and see you settled with all requirements. The door will be guarded to ensure your privacy and Francesca will join you later to complete the task. Do you have any questions? No. Then go to and solve these riddles for us.'

Chapter 11

Monday afternoon
Westminster

LORD HASTINGS' chamber was fine indeed, as was to be expected of the king's chamberlain's abode. Hangings of figured damask around the great bed were threaded through with gold that glimmered opulently in the pale light from the glass windows. Seb looked out upon the privy gardens to the wall and the River Thames beyond, all shrouded in murky, February drizzle. Even so, there was ample daylight by which to work – better than the taper-lit gloom of the scriptorium. The flames of a goodly fire burned in the hearth, warming the chamber, with more logs of scented applewood stacked beside to replenish them.

Two servants came, lugging a heavy writing desk. Another followed with a cushioned stool – the epitome of luxury for a humble clerk. Mind, Seb thought, how many humble clerks wore a ruby upon their finger? He held his hand to the window, twisting it this way and that, to better admire the play of light upon the beauty of the blood-red stone.

At his instruction, the desk was set by the window and the stool placed just so, before a third fellow arrived with enough scrivener's paraphernalia to satisfy a workshop for a fortnight, including the finest beeswax candles, in case Seb should require them. Finally, a pair of servitors came bearing platters of cold meats, cheeses, fruit, the whitest, wheaten pain de main bread and a flagon of wine with matching cups. To Seb's eye, it looked sufficient to feed his family, friends and every neighbour in Paternoster Row for a feast day. Did the king really believe so much sustenance was needed to last one man until suppertime? Oh, aye, and one lass, when Chesca should arrive. If this was accounted a mere clerk's dinner, how much would serve for a monarch's meal? Little wonder Edward was grown so large.

Once alone, Seb poured himself a generous measure of wine. He was not one to partake of wine, unless upon a day of celebration, but there was no ale and he felt sore in need of a reviving drink after an audience with the King of England in person. What a morn it had been! One to tax the courage and sinews of any man. Cup in hand, he sat on the stool and relished the comfort of its padded seat. The scriptorium would be a place of torture after this.

Having enjoyed the wine and soaking up the pleasant heat of the fire, Seb set out pens, ink and paper, feeling only the slightest twinge of guilt, thinking of his fellows under the eye of Secretary Oliver, all of them dry of throat and shivering. He reminded himself of the unwelcome likelihood that he would be suffering alongside them once more upon the morrow, unless some miracle came to pass and he uncovered the murderer this day. But that was not going to happen whilst he sat at ease in Lord Hastings' chamber. Best get these letters deciphered.

Seb sat, head down, concentrating his efforts on the first letter written by the Esquire of the Ruby, intercepted by the king's agents the previous October, a four-page epistle. It was addressed to *Il Leone d'Oro*, whoever that might be. Seb thought it meant 'The Golden Lion', if the comparison to Latin was not misleading – a man of importance, no doubt, to bear so noble a by-name.

As with the draft letter, the Tironian nota symbols, like little figure sevens, were scattered throughout the text. Knowing now how the cypher worked, Seb simply wrote down the first letter of the next word that followed the symbol. The result was a lengthy line of letters without any indication of where gaps betwixt the words should be. No doubt but Chesca would unravel that mystery soon enough.

As though she had heard his thoughts, the chamber door opened to admit his sister-by-marriage. Chesca wore her raven locks loose as usual in her own fashion, ignoring English tradition and propriety. What looked to be a new gown of amethyst satin showed off the perfection of her olive-tinted complexion. Seeing her beauty, Seb misdoubted that the king's dalliance with her was entirely fictitious; that there was truth enough in the story besides her use as a translator.

'God give you good day, Chesca,' Seb greeted her afore forcing his eyes back to the papers upon the desk. 'I have nigh completed the decipherment of this first letter. You can begin translating the message shortly.'

'Scribbling, scribbling, scribbling... is that all you doing all your life, Seb?' Chesca helped herself to wine and sat by the fire.

''Tis how I earn my living, lass. Shirking ne'er earned a bent penny.'

'You could be a troubadour, singing in palaces, living in chambers like this every day.' Chesca began wandering about, examining the bed-hangings, fingering the carpet draped upon the board, admiring the silver candlesticks.

'I doubt the troubadours get such fine lodgings. Having sung for their supper, they probably have to share a straw pallet in the stables.' Seb continued writing, completing the decoding. 'Here. The first message be done. You may have it now.' But Chesca ignored the proffered page.

'We having damask hangings like these at home... just as fine but blue.' She sounded wistful indeed. 'My *Mamma* loving blue, the colouring of the gown of *Santa Maria*. And *Papa* making certain we having good wine like this every day.'

'You miss your home in Venice, do you not?'

'*Si*. I missing it very much, Seb. It being lonely here in London and so cold. I wanting to go home.'

Seb was shocked when Chesca flung herself at him, sobbing, nigh upsetting the inkwell which he managed to save, by God's grace, from spilling its contents over the fine desk, the letters and all else.

'There now, lass. Calm yourself,' he consoled, leading her away from his desk to sit upon the bed. He fetched more wine for them both then sat beside her, his hand upon hers in comforting wise. But still she sobbed and Seb ne'er knew how best to aid a weeping woman.

'Jood no loving me anymore... I all alone now.'

'But you have us, Chesca. We will not cast you aside; you know that. We be your sure and certain friends.'

'*Si.* I knowing you love me, Seb. You being kind man. Better than Jood. You never hurting me like him.' Chesca clung to him like one drowning to a floating spar. He stroked her dark hair, feeling it soft against his fingers, letting the silken strands run through them, as he used to do with his beloved Emily. Memories stirred and he held Chesca close against him, hushing her.

The warmth of the fire, fine wine and a comfortable bed... When Chesca turned her tear-streaked face to his and their lips were so close he felt her breath upon his mouth, the kiss was inevitable. Just a gesture of comfort; no more than that. Yet now she was entwined in his embrace, whispering '*mio caro cuore*', pulling him back upon the bed. Her lips were hot upon his skin, her hands seeking out...

For a few wild heartbeats, he responded in kind, relishing the closeness, the heat, the taste of a woman. Lust burned in his soul and set his desires ablaze.

'Nay!' He broke away from her, breathing hard. 'Nay, Chesca. This cannot be. I – we cannot betray Jude. He suffers enough, thinking of you and the king. He be my brother...'

'But I loving you, Seb. Not Jood. Not Edoardo. You!' She seized his arm and he was hard put to loosen his fingers.

'Nay, lass, you do but deceive yourself. 'Tis not love but

loneliness. You need companions of your own age. Kate be a more fitting confidante for you.'

Chesca tried to drag him back to the bed.

'Pleeease, Seb, I needing you to love me, now. I wanting you...'

'Nay! And let there be an end of it. No more, I say. We have gone too far as it is. Now compose yourself. We have the king's work to complete afore suppertime.' He resumed his seat at the desk, making an effort to steady his uneven breath and calm the thudding beat of his heart.

'You not fair. You treating me bad as Jood doing.' Chesca's tears flowed free once more but Seb ignored them.

What was far more difficult to ignore once it was aroused from its twelve-month and more of slumbering was his longing for a woman and – worse yet – his guilt at what had so nearly come to pass. He wiped the beaded sweat of passion from his brow and took up his pen, yet the Italian words of the second letter danced afore his eyes, defeating his efforts to concentrate upon them. Five pages of script – the longer of the two letters – and the day wore on.

Seb debated the wisdom of consuming yet more wine but refilled his cup all the same. He put another log upon the fire and returned to the desk by the window. Never once looking at Chesca, now lying, sulking, on Lord Hastings' splendid bed, he stared out at the privy garden, deserted upon so miserable an afternoon.

But no – not deserted after all. A black-gowned clerk was attempting to shelter from the drizzle 'neath the bare branches of a tree. His hood was pulled close about his face, so Seb could not see who it was. Then a second figure came to join the clerk, striding across the wet turf. Despite the heavy cloak and hood worn by the newcomer, Seb recognised Sir Nicholas FitzAlan, a groom of the king's chamber, by the length of his steps. As he watched, Sir Nicholas appeared to be explaining something and the clerk became agitated, gesturing with his arms. At one point, both men looked up at the window, as though they knew he was observing them. Had it not been for the rain upon the glass panes distorting their features, Seb might have been able to recognise his colleague from the scriptorium but a blurred, pale disc of a face was all he could discern within the shadow of the wet hood.

What possible business could cause a humble clerk to meet with a groom of the king's chamber? And why did they look towards Hastings' chamber? Of a sudden, Seb felt an uncomfortable pricking sensation betwixt his shoulder blades and liked not the direction in which his thoughts were inclined. Below, the two men went their separate ways as the dreary daylight faded into premature dusk.

Seb left the window and returned to his task of deciphering the second letter. He gave his entire mind to the work, realising the hours were passing in haste.

'I finished the first letter a while since,' he told Chesca, pushing the paper towards the edge of his desk. 'You may translate that whilst I complete the second. Take what paper and pens you require but we must share the inkwell.' Seb continued writing.

Chesca made no move to leave the bed and did not respond.

Seb finished puzzling out the second letter, wiped his pen and tidied the pages, refolding the original letters and setting them aside.

'Chesca. We must translate these messages, now that I have deciphered them. Come, else the supper bell will be rung afore we finish. The king...'

'I not caring anymore.' Chesca sat up, pouting and flouncing her satin skirts. 'I not helping you now.'

Seb felt irritation stir, gnawing at him. She was playing a foolish, childish game.

'The king has given us the responsibility of performing this task which may concern the safety of the whole realm. 'Tis our duty.'

'*Your* duty; not mine. Why I caring about *your* king or this

Inghilterra? I hating you and your brother and your country and your king. I hating it all!'

'Chesca, lass, please. I cannot translate these as you can. I be too ignorant of your tongue to make sense of them. Please, I beg your aid.'

'Now you wanting me; I saying no! How you liking that, huh? *Cosa orribile!*'

Seb was at a loss what to do.

'You like jewels, do you not, Chesca? See here. You may have my fine ruby ring, if you translate…' He removed the king's gift from his hand, sorrowful at having to part with it for such a cause. He had taken a liking to wearing it, feeling its weight and the warmth of gold upon his finger.

'I got many rings. Edoardo giving me rings. I not wanting yours.'

''Tis a beautiful gemstone in an exquisite setting,' he said, hoping to tempt her.

'I saying no!' Chesca shouted, jumping from the bed and hastening to the door. When she lifted the latch, it would not open, so she hammered upon the oak with both fists. 'Let me out of here,' she screeched. 'I no prisoner. Let me out, *voi bastardi!*'

The door was opened from the outside. Seb caught a glimpse of a man-at-arms in royal livery but Chesca was gone, fleeing the chamber.

'Chesca! Do not go, I pray you,' he called out.

The man-at-arms winked and gave him a conspiratorial grin.

'You lucky knave! What did you do to her?'

'I did naught.' Seb slammed the door in the fellow's face. His burning cheeks were caused by anger, he told himself. It was no lie: he had done naught amiss. Well, little enough. Adultery, bigamy, immorality: these were grave sins – true – but it had been a case of wrongful thoughts, rather than deeds, had it not? He had resisted temptation; refused to succumb to the Devil's wiles. He should be proud of that. But he was not.

He had betrayed Jude, his own flesh and blood. Guilt was an ugly burden.

Alone now, he knew not what to do. Could the situation deteriorate any further? He prayed it did not.

So far as he could see, there was no other solution but to attempt the translations himself. To have his brother here would be an asset now... if he could e'er look him in the eye again? At least Jude knew a little Italian. Seb had acquired a few words from their previous efforts together and from Chesca's occasional reversions to her mother tongue but not sufficient for these messages. Knowing how to say 'my favoured dog' in Italian was of no assistance whatever. He was already aware that in some instances Latin was helpful but, equally, at other times, it proved a false friend. His misunderstandings could have fearful consequences for England if his translations were at fault. He hardly dared think upon King Edward's anger if he made mistakes that might not be uncovered until it was too late.

Seb looked longingly at the wine jug but decided against drinking any more. A clear head was required for this work and his thoughts were in disarray as it was. Befuddlement would not serve. As it was, a headache gnawed like a rat behind his eyes. Too much wine? Or the delayed effects of last week's injuries returned to plague him?

The summons came. Seb followed Sir Nicholas out of Lord Hastings' well-appointed chamber, clutching the original Italian letters in one hand and his acrostic codes in the other. Tucked within the sleeve of his gown, out of sight, were his neatly written English translations of the two acrostics. Just because they looked well did not mean the translations were correct but he had done his best. Mind, he suspected that his best, in this case, was not particularly good and likely to be replete with inaccuracies. God help England if his arrows fell too wide of the true mark and he was about to warn King Edward of things that were not intended whilst failing to tell correctly of a plot that was being hatched. And God help Seb Foxley. Men had been executed for less.

Once again, Seb stood before King Edward. If anything, this second audience was yet more frightening than the first but the king seemed in fair humour, drinking wine and nibbling sweetmeats as he lounged upon the day bed. Hastings was present, as was Anthony Woodville, unfortunately, along with the bald man. Lord Stanley, was it? And Lord Howard.

'Well, Foxley, have you deciphered those rascally Italian epistles?' the king asked, inspecting the marchpane delicacy he held betwixt his fingers before popping it in his mouth.

'I have, Your Grace.'

Edward chewed and swallowed then sipped his wine.

'And young Francesca has translated them for us out of her barbarian tongue?'

'I fear not, my lord. Francesca became, er, indisposed.' Seb faltered upon the lie, crumpling the papers in his grasp in agitation, but what else could he say? 'I have made what I might of the acrostics without her aid.'

Hastings held out his hand for the letters afore Seb ruined them beyond reading, smoothing the creases before offering them to the king. Edward waved them away.

'Then tell us what they say. We have wasted time enough upon this business.' The king spoke through a mouthful of sweetmeat.

'Indeed, my lord. The first message reads, in as far as I may make out, *Io consiglio rapire il Galles.*'

'And what in the name of Our Lady does that mean?'

'I know that *consilium* means 'advice' in Latin and *rapire* means to plunder or seize. So since Italian must surely be the daughter of Latin, I believe it says 'I advise the plundering of France' – Gaul being the way the Romans referred to France.'

'At least that's of no consequence for us,' the king said, sighing with relief. 'And the other?'

''Tis more cryptic, my lord. It says *Prima di Pasqua. Confermare* which I think means 'Before Eastertide. Confirm'. But I cannot tell to what it refers that must be done before Easter. I apologise, my lord.'

'No matter. Whatever it is, it doesn't seem to involve us. Although why an Italian in England should be writing of such matters, who can say? In any case, if these people intend to invade France before Easter, they'll have to hasten to it. Lent begins next week.' He laughed loudly. 'If you wish to organise an efficient campaign against your enemies, ask an Englishman to do it for you. These foreign fellows are always at a loss how to wage war effectively, leaving things too late, as ever.'

'Indeed, my lord,' Seb agreed without the false enthusiasm being shown by Hastings, Anthony Woodville and the other courtiers standing around. Why did he have the feeling he had missed something important? If only Chesca could confirm his translations.

'Go to your supper, Master Foxley. You have done well. Find out these Italian correspondents for us, oh, and the murderer, of course, and your work here will be ended.'

And the end could not come soon enough for Seb.

That evening, in the dormitory, Seb was in need of some distraction. Lawrence came and sat beside him upon Seb's bed, curious as to what Seb had been doing all day, Seb shook his head.

'I would rather forget it,' he said.

'But rumour says you had an audience with the king and spent hours in Lord Hastings' chamber. What were you doing?' Lawrence glanced at the beautiful ruby ring on Seb's finger. 'Robbing the royal treasury, by the look of it.'

Seb removed the jewel in haste and put it in his purse – something he should have done hours before.

''Tis a gift,' was all he could think to say.

'Quite a token for writing out the royal laundry list. Ah, I have it: the king required you to compose his love letters for him.' Lawrence laughed and slapped Seb on the back. 'No wonder it's all so secretive and he rewarded you well.'

Eager to escape his inquisitor, Seb was relieved when Hal called him over to the fire. The chief clerk was tuning his lute.

'Come, Seb, give us a song: something lively would suit. Bring us some ale from the night livery first. That new fellow, Jackson, is far too meagre with our rations. James Penny always found us a few additional morsels.' Hal sat ready, his lute resting on his thigh and tuned as required. He strummed a melodious chord. 'Well? What shall it be?'

'I know not.' Seb shrugged. He was not of a humour for singing this eve and would change the subject somewhat. 'But what of James? He be our servitor by rights, is he not?'

'We haven't seen him since Saturday eve. Mayhap, he has been given duties elsewhere. Lawrie reckons he must have offended someone important and been banished to scouring kitchen pots or mucking out the stables.'

'Would you not have been informed?' Seb glanced at the neatly made bed in the far corner, not slept in since Saturday last.

'Why would anyone tell us? Jackson serves in James's place, making our beds, emptying the piss-pot and bringing our livery, and that's all we are supposed to care about. Nobody thinks we should care about the lad himself, that having a bed in our dormitory has made him a friend of ours.'

'Does Jackson not know his whereabouts?'

'I asked him on Sunday eve when first he came in James's stead. He said he didn't know. Not sure I believe him. Servants know far more than anyone else about what comes to pass in this place. I'm just relieved he isn't sleeping here. The fellow reeks of wet dog and garlic. Now, Seb. What of that song?'

'I be not of a humour to sing, Hal, if you will forgive me,' Seb confessed honestly. He reached out and ran a finger along the edge of Hal's lute. 'Your lute be of most beauteous craftsmanship. Who made it?'

'Some Genoese fellow, I believe. My father is a merchant out of Hampton on the south coast. We were wealthy – once. My father had two ships trading with the Levant, importing silks and spices. But, in a single fearful year, one ship was taken by Barbary pirates off the north coast of Africa and the other foundered, sunk in a storm off the Isles of Scilly. Both crews and cargoes were lost and my father's business ruined. You see now why I'm a simple scrivener?

'But my lute is the one reminder of more prosperous times. In those days, my father paid tutors to school me and my lessons included musick, of course, since I was the son of a wealthy gentleman. He hired a Genoese to teach me how to play the lute. When we fell on hard times, all our trappings of prosperity were sold off but I begged to be allowed to keep this one thing and my father did not insist upon its sale. He told me, if I kept it, I must use it to cheer the family through those desperate months... years, in truth, before the situation improved somewhat. But it will never be as it once was.

'So come, Seb, before I become maudlin. I pray you sing one hearty song for us to gladden a gloomy evening.'

But Seb was more interested in Hal's lute. The wood felt silken, glossy as satin. He admired the intricate carving in the centre, its rose-window type tracery.

'Do you play?' Hal asked.

'Nay.' Seb shook his head. 'I have ne'er learnt any instrument. My brother plays the pipe but our father always said my voice was instrument enough. Besides, we could not have afforded anything so fine as this. But I have oftentimes thought upon learning to play and make musick other than by singing for fear that one day my voice might fail me.'

'I could teach you,' Hal offered. 'Come sit by me and I'll show you how to hold it to the best advantage and for ease of playing.'

Seb moved to sit on the bench with Hal and the chief clerk

settled the bowl of the lute upon Seb's right thigh.

'Comfortable?'

'Aye, but so many strings...'

Hal laughed.

'There are lutes with far more courses than this. Here we have but four courses – these pairs of strings – and the single string at the bottom, called the chanterelle. Now take the neck in your left hand to support it and rest your right hand, so your fingers are parallel to the courses. That's the way... and keep your little finger ever against the wood of the instrument.'

Seb was surprised how natural it felt to hold the lute but all those strings were a daunting prospect indeed.

'To pluck a string – and it's not so much like plucking a chicken but more like brushing its feathers with a delicate touch – brush down with your thumb and then up with your fore-finger. Softly does it.'

Seb did as Hal instructed. The first note he made sounded harsh.

'Light of touch, Seb, as I told you. There... that sounds better, does it not? Keep your fingers along the line of the courses. Do not move your hand so much; you aren't shaking the moths out of a blanket. Aye, much better.'

Slowly, slowly, Seb coaxed the basic notes out of the instrument, watching every time to see his fingers were correctly positioned.

'Why so many strings, Hal?' he asked.

'Think of each course as a separate voice, like those in St Paul's choir. In polyphony, you sing one part and the choristers sing other parts in harmony but not necessarily the same tune. Likely, you know that better than I do. Just think of it as a choir singing but the player is a lone performer yet makes so many sounds at once.'

''Tis a marvellous thing that one man can be a choir but...'

'This is your first lesson. It takes a deal of practice but you will come to find your fingers know what to do without your looking to see. When first you were taught penmanship, you had to learn how to hold the quill and every letter stroke required thought but now you do it without thinking. The lute is the same. You'll get the way of it. Your next lesson will be concerning how to tune it. With your ear for musick, that should be easy for you and then I'll show you what the left hand does. In the meantime, borrow the lute to practise when you have time but, I pray you, take care with it.'

''Tis most kindly of you, Hal. I have enjoyed my lesson.'

Aye, a lesson concerning musick making had been the perfect distraction for Seb, or so he assumed until he awoke in the night with certain most disturbing thoughts.

So Hal's family had connections with Italy. Hal had had an Italian tutor. Supposing Hal... Seb did not want him to be the espier and definitely not a murderer. He found Hal friendly and likeable. Could he be so mistaken in feeling the chief clerk to be a trustworthy fellow? In truth, he did not want any of his colleagues to be guilty of such dreadful crimes but there was little room for doubt that one of them was the evil-doer – he had argued the logic of that assumption himself with Secretary Oliver. Was he wrong?

And what of the incident he had observed in the privy garden that afternoon? The clerk involved – if that had not been a disguise – behaved in so furtive a manner, awaiting the coming of Sir Nicholas. Of course, those in the secretary's office were not the only clerks at court; lawyers, too, dressed in similar garments. What did that meeting have to do with the espier, if anything? Mayhap, it was not a meeting planned at all but rather that Sir Nicholas saw someone in the privy garden who had no right to be there and berated them for the intrusion. Aye, that could well have been the case, unless Sir Nicholas was also involved in the espying. If only Seb had been able to hear the subject matter of that acrimonious exchange.

Seb hoped it was not Hal whom he had seen. He did not think it was, Hal being broader set and not so tall, yet it was difficult to be certain of the fellow's stature when looking down upon him and he hunched in the drizzle. Most disturbing had been the way both men had glanced up at the window where he stood. Did they see Seb and know he watched them? No, no, for certain the rain would have obscured their view. At least, he prayed that was so. Could he convince himself?

Chapter 12

Tuesday, the seventh day of February
Westminster

NEXT MORN, with the sun making a valiant effort to disperse yesterday's louring clouds, Seb shrugged off his fears of last night like a worn-out cloak and put a smile upon his face. Of course Hal was not the espier. The meeting in the privy garden was of no significance at all – just Sir Nicholas sending some fellow upon his way who had taken a wrongful turn in the coney warren that was the Palace of Westminster. Seb had become lost himself more than once since coming to work here.

Having broken his fast in the hall with his colleagues, he made for the house of easement across the Outer Court, as usual. His visits were always as brief as possible for the stink was no better, even with the conduit now free of ice. Still, he refused to disrespect the royal abode as others did, relieving themselves in any convenient corner or alcove. Did those guilty parties behave in like manner in their own homes? If they did, he would not care to visit them in their filthy dwellings.

His return across the courtyard removed all unsavoury thoughts for the birds in the trees and bushes of Green Yard were carolling right joyously and Seb paused to harken to their anthems. A speckled thrush repeated his couplets of song; the wren rolled his rrrs in the midst of each chorus and a redbreast gave voice to his sweetest melody. A heavenly choir indeed and Seb was content to listen.

'Hey! Are you going to work with us this morning or stand there like a moonstruck noddlehead, getting in everyone's way?' Lawrence Duffield appeared at Seb's shoulder and nudged him towards the doorway to the offices in the Exchequer building.

'Oh, I beg pardon. I was listening to the birdsong.' Seb stepped aside to let Lawrence pass within.

'Wasting time more like.' Well, here was one who took no pleasure in the sunshine and musick of spring. What was amiss with Lawrence? He was not cross-grained by nature most mornings.

Seb noticed that Lawrence carried a few green ribbons and a square of beeswax of the kind tailors used to draw their threads through to keep them from tangling. Mayhap a pedlar had come by. Indeed, Lawrence also had a blue paper of pins. It must be that same pedlar from whom Seb had purchased the braid for Rose by Charing Cross. What was the fellow's name? He said he often came to Westminster. Seb could not recall the name, if it had e'er been mentioned. He wondered for whom Lawrence had brought the ribbons.

Within the secretary's office, confusion reigned when Seb entered. Barnabas was cursing and flailing his arms like a windmill.

'Be gone, accursed bird!' he shouted, flapping his hands in the direction of a panicked ball of feathers. 'Away with you, I say.'

Andre le Clerc and Eustace Dane joined in, attempting to harass the little creature into flying out of the door. But it flew in the wrong direction, collided with the window and fell, stunned, behind a coffer.

'I have it trapped,' Andre said. 'I'll kill the wretched thing.'

'Nay! Do not,' Seb cried, elbowing Andre aside. 'What harm has it done you? What offence has it committed that you would destroy it? 'Tis one of God's own creatures as well as you and me. I shall give it its freedom.' Seb reached behind the coffer and lifted out the bird, cradling it in his cupped hands. It appeared to be recovering its senses. ''Tis as well you did not kill it for 'tis a redbreast.'

Eustace crossed himself, knowing he had narrowly escaped bringing ill-fortune down upon his head.

'Why do you foolish English so revere those birds? They're as good in a pie as any other kind.'

'Do you not know how the redbreast came by its crimson feathers?' Seb asked Andre who had posed the question. ''Tis said that when our Lord Jesu Christ was dying upon the cross at Calvary, a bird came and sang sweetly to Him to calm His spirits. The bird perched so close to the Lord that a barb from the Crown of Thorns pierced the white feathers of its breast so that they became stained with blood. Almighty God was so pleased with the courage and kindliness of the little bird, He determined that all its descendants should bear the redbreast forever. Since they be so blessed by God, who would dare destroy such a one?'

'You English believe such nonsense?' Andre scoffed.

'And who's to say it's not true?' Eustace put in.

Seeing the bird was now fluttering against his fingers, Seb left the scriptorium and retraced his steps down the passageway and back out into Green Yard. There, he opened his hands and released the redbreast which flew to the nearest bare tree, seeming none the worse for its ordeal.

'Sing, little one. Sing for joy.'

'Sing for joy? Not bloody likely when I've got to spend the day in Oliver's icy pest-hole, working my fingers to the bone.' Jude had arrived, tardy as usual.

'God give you good day, brother,' Seb said.

'Where's that miserable arse-wipe Oliver? Is he here yet?'

'Nay, so you may escape a reprimand.' Together, Seb and Jude took their places at their desks, Seb taking care when sitting upon his split seat.

Since Secretary Oliver was not present, Hal, as chief clerk, gave out the day's tasks.

'There are a few extra summonses to attend Parliament to

add to the list, so Barnabas and Eustace can do those, then that's the last of them, God be praised. There are no French papers for you, Andre, so you and Seb can furrow your brows over these documents from the Welsh Marches – some dispute betwixt Chepstow Castle and a neighbouring priory, by the look of it, with a few Welsh phrases for you to puzzle out. Lawrence, Jude and Robin, there are letters to be copied – naught complicated. At least the ink isn't frozen this morning so, to work, everyone.'

'And what are you bloody doing, Sowbury? Putting your feet up, as usual, while the rest of us work, no doubt, you idle bloody dog.' Jude could never hide his great dislike of Hal. The feeling was mutual.

'Keep your mouth shut, Foxley, else it'll be the worse for you. And we all know about what your buxom little wife gets up to whilst you're here, scribbling.'

The speed with which Jude left his desk to smite the chief clerk was remarkable but Hal was quicker, putting out his foot to trip his opponent, sending Jude sprawling.

Seb aided Jude to his feet. Fortunately, Secretary Oliver arrived before any harm was done, though Jude was seething, white-lipped with anger – that was obvious.

Seb was not sorry to exchange places with Eustace, enabling him and Andre le Clerc to peruse the Welsh documents together, warning the elderly clerk to beware the stool when he sat at Seb's desk.

'Le Gallois... the language makes no sense to me,' said le Clerc under his breath. 'I hope there is little of that barbarian tongue in these documents.'

'I know naught of Welsh either,' Seb admitted. 'Why does Hal think we be the best suited of the clerks to work on these?'

'We have more patience than the others? I know no other reason, unless to taunt us with our ignorance.'

'Hal would not stoop to so petty a spite. Does anyone else here know Welsh?'

'Robin comes from Shrewsbury way. He would likely know

more of the Pays de Galles than we do but he is not of a humour to puzzle his head over difficult words.'

The morning's labours had hardly begun when a messenger arrived bringing a sealed letter. Expecting to be the recipient, Secretary Oliver took delivery of it only to see it wasn't addressed to him but to 'Master Sebastian Foxley of Paternoster Row, London'. It was no common occurrence for a mere clerk to receive a letter and although the secretary passed it to Seb, he forbade him wasting valuable time on a personal matter and refused to permit him to read it until the dinner hour.

Having noted that the letter bore the fox-head seal, Seb knew it must be from Adam and was consumed with anxiety as to the contents, wondering how he might give his full attention to the work demanded of him.

Fortunately, the Welsh documents that he and Andre le Clerc had to transcribe, as things turned out, were not so difficult as they had first feared. The unpronounceable Welsh words seemed to be place names for the most part and it was not their task to explain the geography of Wales, though whosoever's task it was, Seb did not envy them.

The pair – or rather Seb – was writing out the last sentence in a clear hand when they were summoned to dine in the Great Hall. Glad to stretch his legs and straighten his back, Seb thought a short walk around Green Yard would refresh both body and mind. And he had Adam's letter to read but, now that he was allowed to do so, he felt reluctant, fearing it must bear ill-tidings. As he broke the fox-head seal and began to read, Jude leaned over his shoulder, trying to make out the words.

'So who's dead? Someone must be. I can't think what else could be so urgent that it can't bloody wait 'til you see Adam on Saturday.'

'None has died, Christ Jesu be thanked.' Seb continued to read, his face showing first surprise and then concern. 'If only this wretched business here could be done with. I be sorely needed in the workshop.'

'What's Adam done? Bloody made a mess of things, no doubt.' Jude's dislike of his kinsman was evident.

'Nay, not in the least. In my absence yesterday, no less than three offers of commissions have been made, all requiring my skills. Adam would know whether to accept or refuse them and, if he accepts one or all, what date he may give the customers as a likely time for completion. In other words, how much longer am I to be here at Westminster, scribbling the weeks away to so little effect?'

'Commissions mean money, little brother. Tell him to accept them all and worry about the time needed later. That's my advice.'

'Aye, and you would pay no heed to an irate customer when you fail him? I cannot risk our reputation so.'

'What are the commissions and who's offering them?' Jude was still trying to read the letter.

'St Mary-le-Bow Church wants a large illuminated version of the Gospels for reading aloud to the congregation…'

'In Latin? They won't understand a bloody word. What else?'

'Bennett Hepton wants a little Book of Hours for Peronelle… you recall they were wed last year? It seems Peronelle be with child but feels afeared for the outcome. 'Tis unsurprising, I suppose. Peronelle spent much time at my Emily's bedside when things went so t-tragically a-awry a twelve-month since. Little wonder at her apprehension. Bennett hopes the book will give her comfort and courage.'

'Well done, Bennett! Didn't know the bloody fishmonger had it in him, the skinny wretch. Still, I suppose you managed it – twice! What a shock to mankind that was. What's the third job?'

'Another portrait. I be set already upon an image of Lord Mayor Bartholomew James which I have had to delay, despite his first payment having been advanced at New Year last.'

'And which other conceited devil wants to preserve his likeness to plague posterity now?'

'Hush, Jude. Do not say such things 'Tis Robert Stillington, the Bishop of Bath and Wells, no less. He who was the King's Chancellor a few years since.'

'Well, only you can do the portraits, Seb. You'll have to let somebody else do the book illumination.'

'Nay, I wish to do the book for Peronelle. She was a good friend to Em, so it will be a personal matter. I would make certain of that. A gift for her deserves the best.'

'Then the others must do the Gospels.'

'But 'tis God's Word and must be of the highest standard.'

'God's bloody bones, Seb, you can't do everything. You'll have to learn to trust the others. Or take on more journeymen.'

'Aye, you be correct, Jude, but...'

'But you're bloody perfect and no one else can match you. You're as conceited as the damned bishop.'

'Nay. I be far from perfect, I know, and more accomplished hands to work on the commissions would be a great asset. My difficulties lie in the size of the workshop. You know that four desks and the collating table fill the place. It has ever been that way since we were journeymen to Matthew Bowen, you and I, working alongside Kit Philpot, may God rest both their souls. Another desk or two and we would be tripping o'er each other, jostling elbows, knocking inkwells and spilling precious pigment. All would be chaos and the work suffer as a result.'

'You could shift the collating table upstairs into my old chamber. Only old what's-his-name sleeps there now, doesn't he?'

'Ralf. His name be Ralf.'

'Aye, well, there'd be space enough for him and the table upstairs and you could put an extra desk in the workshop downstairs. So get yourself a decent new journeyman.'

'You?'

'Not bloody likely. I told you before, I have plans and they don't include doing your bidding forever, little brother. Nor am I going to continue working in this pest-hole for bloody Oliver for much longer. Besides, what use would I be to you? I'm a scribe – and a bloody good one – but I leave the drawing and prettifying of pictures to you.'

'But you were reinstated by the guild…'

'So I was but I haven't paid my quarterly dues for December and don't intend to. Sod the guild. I don't want to have to abide by their stupid regulations, not with what I have planned.'

'What do you have planned, Jude?'

'Mind your own bloody business. Come. I want my dinner.'

'I shall join you shortly.'

Jude shrugged and made haste to the Great Hall, aware that the tastiest morsels would be gone if he arrived too tardily. Those greedy buggers wouldn't think to save a platter for him, though they might do so for Seb, he being well-liked by his fellows. God alone knew why that should be.

Seb stood in Green Yard. The kitchens across the way were busy, industrious as a bee skep, but sufficiently distant that the clanging of pots and pans and the shouts of the cooks would not disturb him. Seb required peace to think. Something that Andre had said earlier had raised an alarum somewhere in the back of his mind but he could not quite bring it to the fore. Mayhap, a little quiet contemplation would retrieve the errant thought.

Seb's sharp eye had spotted a few specks of azure strewn around the foot of an elder bush. Speedwell flowers, even so early in the year, had survived the snow in the shelter of the bare branches. These tiny, unexpected heralds of spring deserved a closer look. Seb picked a sprig of blue blossoms and noted the perfection of colour and form. Mayhap, he would draw them later. He watched sparrows in the bushes, unruly as young scholars in Paul's Song School, chattering and chirruping. He cleared his mind, gazing up at the sky but, whatever he did, the lost thought was not to be recovered – gone as surely as mist on the Thames in the warmth of a summer morning.

Eventually, he followed Jude to the hall. No point in going hungry. The remainder of the day passed uneventfully in the scriptorium. Seb worked unstintingly, as he ever did, earning frequent scowls from Jude for his excess of diligence. No matter. He could not sit idle. But, ever in the dim recesses at the back of his mind lurked that wayward thought. It was like an itch he could not scratch, a splinter too small to get a hold of and remove but an annoyance all the same.

In the dormitory that eve, Hal was proving to be a fair teacher with infinite patience. And he required every grain of it, Seb knew as he made so many errors with his fingering on the lute. An hour and more was spent with Seb attempting to make his left hand do one thing and his right hand another. Brushing the strings with his right hand was not a difficulty and he was learning the correct positions for the fingers of his left hand upon the frets, changing the note of each course. But performing the two actions together at one time was proving an elusive skill indeed. He was unable to watch both hands and the result was a fearful cacophony of mistakes. Even so, Seb and Hal would have persevered longer, if their fellows had not complained.

'Cease strangling that damned cat, you two,' Barnabas cried, rolling the dice Robin handed him. 'Give us some peace, can't you? There! See what you've caused me to throw: a bloody three and a deuce. What use is that? And your devilish racket is shredding my nerves.' Everyone else agreed, except Eustace, who was sleeping soundly already. The fellow must surely be stone deaf.

'You're a useless teacher, Hal, if that's the best you can do with your lute,' Robin muttered, gathering up his winnings. 'Use it for firewood is my advice; let us get some sleep.'

Seb apologised to all, well aware that his dismal efforts had more to do with his lack of attention than to any failing of Hal's. He was surprised when Hal came and sat beside him upon his bed and brought the lute.

'You can practise the fingering, Seb, silently. As you become used to the feel of the positioning, you won't need to look at what your fingers do.' Hal put the lute in Seb's hands. 'Just don't pluck the strings.' Hal picked up the drawing board Seb had left on the coffer. 'Flowers? I thought you did portraits.'

'I draw whatever catches my eye,' Seb said, attempting to finger an 'A' chord correctly without looking. When he checked, he was an entire fret amiss. Hopeless. 'I found those speedwell blossoms out in Green Yard – a welcome harbinger of spring.' He showed Hal the now-wilting sprig. 'The flowers fade all too swiftly but a drawing will live on after, a constant reminder of their ephemeral beauty, if so desired.'

Hal nodded.

'How did you and Andre fare, working together?

'We finished the transcription well enough. The Welsh words were place names, so did not need translating into English.'

'That wasn't quite what I meant,' said Hal, adjusting Seb's left hand on the neck of the lute and straightening his forefinger. 'There. Try again. Close your eyes so you can't cheat and finger the 'D' chord without looking. Aye. Much better. You'll soon have the way of it. Keep practising.

'What I meant was: how do you feel about working with Andre? He's a strange bird, that one. Says so little. Ne'er holds a conversation with anyone. The others do not like working closely with him. I wondered if you felt the same.'

'So our efforts with the Chepstow documents were by way of a test for me?'

'Not so much of a test, Seb. I've been wondering all along, since poor Piers was slain, if his killer was one of us. I find Andre the most secretive and difficult to know beyond his skin-deep appearance. I wondered what you think of him.'

'Beyond the superficial, I know less of him than you do, Hal. He was determined that I should not draw his portrait, unlike the rest of you, but some folk have a superstition about any re-creating of their image, believing the making of a man be God's prerogative alone. Mayhap, Andre believes that also. But he proved easy to work alongside. He has a good eye for the tiniest details of nigh-illegible handwriting. He made this morn's task easier than it might have been.'

Hal sighed and moved as close to Seb as possible, adjusting his pupil's fingering once again.

'Then I'll ask you plainly,' he whispered. 'Do you think Andre could be the killer?'

Seb made no reply straightway, not wanting to admit that his thoughts had travelled in a similar direction. Lacking any evidence whatsoever, it was wrong to lay blame upon a man simply because he preferred to keep his own company, reading rather than sharing in any communal activity. That was no crime. After all, by inclination, Seb was as guilty of that as anyone. Only the need to know his colleagues more nearly, as Lord Hastings required, forced Seb to be convivial beyond his usual disposition. He found that hard but such activities as singing, drawing and now learning to play the lute assisted in this unaccustomed necessity of being companionable to men he little knew.

'You're new to the scriptorium and a fresh eye may see more,' Hal was saying.

'I cannot venture an opinion, Hal, not on so short an acquaintance. I should not presume so far without just cause.' Seb knew his answer was an excuse. Hal was unaware of Seb's true purpose in working with the clerks: his appointment by the lord chamberlain to uncover, firstly, a murderer and now, secondly, an espier. Therefore, it was most discomforting to have Hal asking him so pertinent a question – almost as though he guessed Seb was not just an innocent scribe employed to fill Piers Creed's empty desk.

'Think on it, Seb. I want your opinion. I dare not ask the others, not knowing who to trust... apart from Lawrie, of course. I've known him long enough.'

'And what does Lawrence think?'

'He agrees with me. But you have doubts? So you must think the killer could be another of us. Who?'

'As I said: I cannot venture an opinion concerning Andre, Lawrie, you or anyone else. 'Tis not my place to hazard a guess.' Seb stared down at his hand resting on the lute strings. The lie had brought a flush to his face; he could feel his cheeks burn. He prayed that Hal had not noticed. When he felt the heat fade, he looked up and returned the instrument to its owner. 'I be right grateful for the lesson, Hal, but I believe our companions' ears should suffer no further assault this eve. On the morrow, maybe?'

'Aye. But you'll consider my question.'

Seb nodded. Consider it? Certainly. Make his reasoning known? How could he when he was yet stumbling in the dark? There was not so much as the dot above an 'i' in evidence against anyone.

Seb came awake in an instant and sat stark upright in his bed. The dormitory was shrouded in darkness; silence ruled. What had snatched Seb from his slumbers? Ah. That errant thought that Andre conjured earlier had been there, balanced upon the threshold betwixt sleeping and waking. Now it was gone, elusive as a dream. Despondent at the loss, Seb turned on his side, pulled the thin blanket up to his ears, hoping to return to sleep and, mayhap, cleave hold of that thought once again. But sleep would not come.

What first seemed like silence in the dormitory was not the case. Sleepers coughed and mumbled. Someone – probably Eustace – snored and snorted fit to disturb the saints in heaven afore falling quiet. A bed frame creaked. Soft footsteps padded on the boards. Seb awaited the inevitable sound of someone making use of the piss-pot by his bed but nobody did. Instead, a cold draught blew for a moment and the door latch clicked back in its hasp. Somebody had gone out of the dormitory at dead of night. If that was not a suspicious act, what else could it be?

Seb left his bed, shrouding himself in his clerk's black gown and slipping on his shoes before following the night-wanderer through the door. He closed it as quietly as he could behind him, thanking Dame Fortune for well-greased hinges. The figure was halfway down the stair, lit by infrequent cressets burning in the sconces. Like Seb, he wore a dark gown but had pulled up his hood. He appeared jerky in his movements as his shadow leapt along the wall, jumping from one source of light to the next. Seb crept after, placing his feet with care to the sides of the stair treads to avoid a loose board revealing his pursuit but if his quarry should look back, there was no hiding from him. Seb began to regret this foolhardy, nocturnal venture.

The figure did not look back. At the stair foot, he turned to the right along the passageway as though making for the Great Hall.

Seb hastened his descent but, upon reaching the passage, he saw no sign of anyone to right or left. Then, towards the hall, the flames of one of the cressets danced wildly. Seb moved upon tip-toe. Opposite the cresset – now steadied – was a door he had failed to notice previously, despite the clerks walking this way for every meal. Perhaps it was not so surprising; Westminster Palace was replete with nooks and crannies, alcoves and corridors to nowhere. The building had stood for centuries with every king rebuilding, adding to and modifying the structure. Folk did not call it a 'coney warren' without reason.

Seb opened the door, noting its hinges, too, were recently greased. Within, all was black as any tomb but he could make out a faint, flickering light ahead as his eyes adjusted. He moved forward and stumbled, stifling a yelp. There were steps here. He prayed the man ahead of him had not heard his muffled cry. Five steps, then the floor ahead was flat but the light was no more than a distant glimmer. Seb had lost time, having to feel his way with such care. Then the darkness was absolute. Blind, Seb stopped. There must be a turn in the passage or another door. He continued, hands outstretched, but progress was even slower than before. His hands hit solid stone and he reached out to either hand, hoping for a way forward.

To the left, the wall continued until he reached a corner where it turned back the way he had come. Proceeding to the right, the same thing happened. A dead end. But it could not be. The man he was following had not walked through solid walls. There must be a doorway or passage off somewhere. Seb felt a gap in the stone, then rough planking 'neath his fingertips. Groping around, he found a wooden latch, lifted it and pushed. The door creaked open, not so well-greased as those he encountered previously.

He was outside. A fitful half-moon came and went behind gusting clouds, illuminating weeds and brambles in this forgotten corner of the palace. Later in the year, this spot would likely be overgrown entirely. Seb smelled something rotten: a dead creature trapped here, mayhap, unable to find a means of escape forwhy the moonlight revealed walls bounding this place on all sides. The hairs upon his neck prickled. He shivered. There was no sign of the man he had followed nor any torchlight. A mystery indeed.

And then two pairs of strong hands grabbed him from behind and some kind of cloth bag was pulled over his head.

'You damned fool. Why did you follow me?' a voice snarled in his ear, muffled by layers of foul cloth.

'Use the stiletto and be done with him. We're wasting time,' a second voice insisted.

'I did not bring it. I wasn't expecting any unwanted eavesdroppers to attend our meeting.'

Chapter 13

Wednesday, the eighth day of February
Westminster

SEB COULD hardly draw breath. His mouth and nose were tight covered, his eyes bound. He attempted to move. Something sharp jabbed him in the back. A knife? He lay still.

When he tried to move a second time, he realised his wrists were tied behind him, as were his ankles, but his fingers found thorns and prickles beneath him. There was no knife.

The night airs were bitter cold and he realised he now wore only his nether clouts. His gown was gone. His teeth would have chattered had his face not been smothered in some vile-smelling cloth. He would likely die if he did not get back within doors. Writhing and shuffling as best he might, he managed to sit and move upon his backside until he reached a wall. If he could find the door...

What good would that do? He could not open it, nor walk, nor shout out for aid. First, he must somehow break free of his bonds and the effort required would warm him. If only he might cut the bindings around his wrists. He now regretted that it had not been a knife pricking him earlier. Might the bramble thorns tear him free? Nay. More like they would tear the flesh from his hands.

Was such a contortion possible? He had watched acrobats do such things at St Bartholomew's fair. There was but one way to find out. Seb tried to sit on his tied hands, thinking to pass his backside through the loop of his arms and bring his hands to the front. A youngster could do it, no doubt. But he was grown stiff with cold and was far less supple. How long had he lain here? He must have swooned at some point forwhy he could not recall being tied up.

He lowered his shoulders as far as he might and succeeded in getting his hands 'neath his backside – but only just. He paused to rest, panting inside the foul cloth that swathed his face. The cloth was becoming wet with moisture from his breath and sweat, making it increasingly difficult to draw air into his lungs, stifling him. Be calm, he told himself. Be calm. He prayed silently to Almighty God, Our Lady and his own St Sebastian for aid.

He tried again, wriggling backwards through his arms but too many of Rose's fine cooked dinners meant his backside was too broad to fit through so small a gap. Thinking of Rose... and Dickon and little Julia... he could not leave his children orphaned. Having lost their mother, they must not lose their father also. He had to get free.

Twisting until his ribs would go no further, he tried one buttock at a time. His shoulders, elbows and wrists burned in agony. Inch by tormented inch, choking on the pain, he moved his hands forward. At last, slick with blood where the bonds had stripped his skin, his hands were in his lap and he tore off the cloth that bound his head. It looked to be his gown, ripped into lengths. Exhausted, he breathed in great gulps of air, panting, only to heave upon the renewed stench of death. He had forgotten that.

It took a while to recover afore further effort was required to untie his ankles. He discovered they, too, had been bound with lengths torn from his clerk's gown. Looking upward, the square of sky showed faintly with the coming light of dawn. Stark against it, like the stumps of black and broken teeth, were the remains of roof beams jutting from the walls. This place had once been a chamber, a storeroom or some such, but now the roof was fallen in. A pile of rotted timber and twisted lead lay in the corner as proof; a few remnants of crumbling plaster yet adhered to the more sheltered parts of the walls. Perhaps it had once been a grand chamber but Nature ruled here now, strewing the floor with nettles and brambles, draping the walls with ivy and studding the timbers with moss and fungi.

Now he was able to see, Seb realised the knots at his ankles had been done in haste and not so securely as they might have been. He sat and picked at them for what felt like hours, although the sky overhead told otherwise. It just seemed to take so long with aching fingers and hands still bound and bloody. He kept losing hold. And then one knot came undone and he was able to free his left foot. He left the black cloth dangling from his right ankle and stood to stretch and straighten his body, groaning as his spine clicked and his shoulder joints eased back into their accustomed positions. He would hurt for a month.

In the meanwhile, concentrating so hard on the knots, he had nigh forgotten the stink. It was not hard to find the cause. He had known of it since removing the cloth from his eyes. In the strengthening light, a form lay unmoving amidst the tangle of last year's weeds. Splashes of bright colour showed the royal arms upon it. Had it been summer, flies would have buzzed and swarmed. Seb had little doubt of the unfortunate soul's identity; the servitor's tabard suggested a name but he would make certain, if recognition were possible.

James Penny stared up, eyeless, at a sky he would not see. Seb swallowed down tears and whispered a prayer for the departed soul. There was no great wound apparent, apart from those inflicted by the unkindness of crows, but Seb held his breath and turned the body of young James face down. As he expected, there was just light enough to make out the small incision at the back of the lad's neck – in likeness of the wound inflicted on Piers Creed. The poor lad had not deserved so pitiful an end, dying in this forsaken place. The perpetrator would pay for this. Or rather: *they* would pay forwhy Seb now knew there were two men involved at the least and one most definitely slept in the dormitory.

Determined upon avenging James's death, Seb squared his aching shoulders and tried the doorway that returned within. Suppose it was barred or locked? It was neither. Still trailing the length of cloth from one ankle, he made his way back. Daylight revealed high window slits along the passage he had taken in the stygian darkness last night, giving just sufficient illumination to see his way clearly. Carven stone figures alternated with the window embrasures. Worn with age and unrecognisable, their paint flaking, they told that this must once have been a grand entranceway to a chapel or royal chamber.

Seb reached the five stone steps on which he had stumbled last time and then the door to freedom. But this one was locked or barred on the other side. Whatever the case, he could not open it. He pounded the wood with his fists and shouted. If the hour was close to the time when the palace denizens broke their fast – as he thought it was – the passage beyond would be busy with comings and goings. Someone must hear him.

Someone did.

Seb nigh tumbled through the doorway in his desperate haste, into the arms of a man he recognised as a clerk of the Exchequer who slept in the same dormitory and played dice with Robin. This was Seb's saviour who had unlatched the door. The man set him upon his feet and regarded him with raised eyebrows

'So the secretary's clerks don't bother with dressing of a morn these days,' he jested but then saw the blood on Seb's hands and changed his tone to one of concern. 'Hal Sowbury!' he called out. 'One of yours in trouble here.'

Hal, Lawrie and the other clerks were coming along the passage from the hall, ready to begin the day's duties. They all came running. Seb felt weary beyond belief but was alert of a sudden. Every one of his fellow scribes was there and one of them had left him to die. 'Why did you follow me?' he had said. But whose voice had spoken those words? Seb's ears had been muffled and his mind in a turmoil of shock and fear at the time. He was unable to recall the sound of that dreadful voice precisely, yet he must do so. It was a matter of life and death – most likely his own.

'I know what became of James Penny,' he told Hal. 'Through that door.' Seb pointed and Hal saw the damage to his hands, raw and bloodied. 'He be much in need of a priest.'

'Is he alive?' Hal asked, taking his dinner knife from his belt and sawing through the remnants of cloth to unloose Seb's wrists.

Seb shook his head, relieved to be free but dismayed at the mangling of his hands.

'In which case,' the chief clerk continued, 'We'll tend to you first. Barnabas: go open the scriptorium as usual. Robin, Eustace and Andre: go to your desks. You'll have to explain the situation to Secretary Oliver. Lawrie: find a priest for James Penny. Where is the lad, Seb?'

'Go through that door from whence I came and follow the passage. The way cannot be missed in daylight. The lad lies beyond a second door, outside. I think 'twas once a chamber but now stands open to the sky. James was slain in like manner to Piers Creed. His killer be the same man, I fear. But there were two of them last eve and they left me to die.'

'Left you to die? Merciful God. Who would do that to you? And why murder a humble servitor? What harm has either of you ever done? Come, Seb. We needs must get you cleansed and clad and your hands tended.'

Hal guided Seb towards the stairs to the dormitory.

'I have not the time for this,' Seb objected. 'I must speak with Lord Hastings without delay.'

'In your nether clouts? I think not.'

In truth, Seb had forgotten his state of undress as Hal gave him his own gown to conceal it. How many gowns had he ruined since coming to Westminster? The one that was rent to truss him up like a Christmas goose had been Hal's second-best, he remembered – or was it his third?.

An hour later, Seb was waiting to speak with the lord chamberlain, wearing doublet and hose but without a clerk's gown.

Jude had come racing to the dormitory as soon as he learned of his brother's nocturnal misadventures, abandoning any pretence of working in the scriptorium. It was a valid excuse, not that Jude cared whether it was or not.

Seb was right glad to have Jude with him. Hal acted with naught but care and concern but Seb dared trust none of his colleagues now. Alone in the dormitory with Hal washing and binding his wrists with soft linen, Seb had been rigid with apprehension until Jude came.

'I be that glad of your company,' he told Jude as they made their way across the Great Hall to the curtained door beside the dais. They knocked and awaited a response.

'Changed your tune now, then? Usually, you can't bloody wait to throw me aside.'

'That be untrue. 'Tis not that way in the least. But now, I confess to being truly afeared. I dare not sleep in the dormitory again else I shall be slain in my bed.'

'They wouldn't dare.'

'Oh, I think they might. Likely, James Penny was snatched from his bed upon Saturday night last, yet Hal swears none were awakened by any commotion. Could a score of men honestly sleep through the sounds of abduction?'

'Mayhap, he wasn't abducted, as you put it, but enticed away. Maybe the bastard asked the lad for aid, as it were. "I'm feeling poorly. Fetch me some wine – and don't wake the others." James would've crept out, much as you did, straight into the waiting clutches of the bastard's partner in crime. You said there were two of them.'

'Aye, Jude. That sounds most plausible. You could well be correct. Even so, I should rather pass the night on the floor of your lodgings than sleep here again.'

'You're welcome. Chesca stays away these days. Sleeping in that cuckolding devil's bed, no doubt, the little bitch. Still… I won't be living in that rat hole for much longer, nor working here. Matters are moving on apace, little brother.'

'Oh? Pray, tell…'

The door opened at last and Sir Nicholas FitzAlan stood before them. His eyes went wide with shock when he saw them.

'Y-you have no appointment. L-Lord Hastings is unavailable. You have no warrant. Be gone.'

'This is our warrant.' Jude bunched a formidable fist, scarred by legion tavern brawls. 'Tell Hastings this is a matter of life and death or you'll be swallowing your own damn teeth… sir,' Jude added, his tone dripping contempt.

'This is an act of intimidation,' Sir Nicholas said, attempting to resume his customary haughty manner.

'The man isn't quite as stupid as he looks, Seb. We must give him credit for that. Now, tell Hastings, you incompetent whelp, or we'll enter, uninvited, and tell him ourselves.'

Sir Nicholas retreated, nose held high, pushing the door to.

'He was right shocked to see me, Jude,' Seb murmured, frowning in thought.

'Well, we didn't plan this audience beforehand.'

'Nay. Not that. 'Twas as though he ne'er thought to see me again. I wonder if…'

The groom of the chamber returned, smiling in triumph.

'The lord chamberlain is not here. He cannot see you.' He flicked an invisible dust mote from his silken sleeve.

'You're a bloody liar.' Jude shoved Sir Nicholas to one side and barged past him. 'Come, Seb. We just made our appointment.'

'I'll summon the guard,' the groom protested unconvincingly.

'Do as you will,' Jude said without looking back. 'It'll be the worse for you. Make haste, little brother.'

Seb obeyed but he did look back over his shoulder at Sir Nicholas and saw a scowl of menace crease the courtier's handsome features. He also observed a series of snagged threads in the man's hose of the kind a cat's claws might make. Or last year's brambles, could it be? He hoped most fervently the man would not come with them and hear what he had to tell Lord Hastings. But that was too much to hope for. Sir Nicholas was just one pace behind them when Jude knocked and entered the chamberlain's room.

Lord Hastings glanced up at Seb and Jude.

'How come it now takes two clerks to collect a handful of papers? The draft copies of the arrest warrants for those Northumberland malefactors are over there.' The chamberlain nodded towards a side table with a small pile of documents.

'My Lord Hastings,' Seb began, bowing low, 'Those are not the purpose of our visit. I beg pardon for this intrusion but I may have information concerning a malefactor far closer to home, in this very palace.'

Hastings set aside his wine cup.

'May have? Not certain, then. I require facts, not maybes and suppositions, Foxley.'

'Forgive me. I did not speak plain. Last night, another attempt was made upon my life and I discovered that a servitor from our dormitory, not seen since Saturday morn last, has been murdered. And I be able to confirm that one of the perpetrators also shares the dormitory.'

'One of?'

'Aye, my lord, for I was assaulted and left to die by two men.'

'Dear God save us. What is going on here? This is the king's residence, yet it's becoming a den of criminals: traitors, espiers and murderers. Who attacked you, Foxley? Incompetents, obviously, since they failed to kill you. Unless that was not their intent? Perhaps they meant only to warn you. Either way, name the devils and they shall be apprehended immediately.'

'I fear that I cannot. Their faces were hid from view and

then my eyes were covered but they did intend my death for certain. They bound me and left me exposed to the cold of night. They had also slain poor James Penny, a servitor, whose body I found in that same place. He had been murdered in the same manner as Piers Creed, the clerk killed in the scriptorium a while since. A thin-bladed knife was used, inserted betwixt the neck bones. I suppose I was fortunate in that the same was not done to me. I succeeded in escaping my bonds and raising the alarum. My wrists bear the marks.' Seb held out his bandaged hands. The linen had slipped somewhat and ugly red weals and flayed skin showed.

'If you saw them not, how do you know they were of your dormitory?'

'Forwhy I followed one man, swathed in a clerk's gown with the hood up, when he crept out in stealthy wise. As for the other... I only know that two pairs of hands grabbed me and they spoke. However, by that time, my head was smothered by my gown, so I ne'er saw the second man, nor could I put a name to either voice. I apologise for this failing...'

'As indeed you should,' Hastings growled. 'I paid you a substantial fee, in advance, to find out Creed's murderer and you're no closer to doing so than on the first day. And now we have two killings and an espier to deal with as well.' Hastings left his chair, adjusting his jewelled belt over his belly, and went to the board where wine and sweetmeats were set out. He helped himself to a handful of sugared almonds.

Seb caught sight of Sir Nicholas gloating over this scene of his humiliation. No doubt the rascal was delighted.

'My lord, I-I will endeavour to find out these miscreants,' Seb stuttered, 'As soon as may be but...'

'There are no "buts", Foxley. You'll do so before Lent begins next week or repay me every penny. And if you've spent a solitary coin of it already, you can pass all of Ash Wednesday sitting in the stocks as punishment. You hear me?'

'I hear you, my lord.'

Sir Nicholas was laughing, quietly but maliciously, as he ushered them out of Hastings' chamber.

'You'll fail. You know that don't you?' he sneered.

'I'm going to rip off his balls and stuff them in his mouth,' Jude said as they were crossing the hall.

'Forget him, brother. I – we have more important matters to concern us. If I could but think who were my assailants last eve.'

'Did you break your fast this morning? Watching that bloated lord scoffing nuts has set my belly rumbling.'

'Well, nay. There was not the opportunity, being nigh naked and my hands bleeding.

'Then no wonder you can't think. No man can think properly on an empty belly. Hey, you!' Jude beckoned to a servant, jug in hand, making his way through the hall. 'If that's ale, we'll have it here.'

'This is ale for the Exchequer clerks.'

'But we're in Lord Hastings' employ upon the king's business. We take precedence, my good man, so fetch us cups and some bread and cheese. And make haste, else I shall inform the lord chamberlain of your slovenliness in performing your duties and your tardiness in complying with the orders of your superiors.'

Seb shook his head. Jude knew how to play a part but this was going too far.

'You want food and drink, don't you?' Jude asked, seeing Seb's dubious expression.

'Aye, but...'

'As Hasting said just now: there are no "buts". We'll cudgel your lapsed memory as we eat. Something will come to you; then we'll know who are the guilty bastards.'

They sat at a board already set up for dinner at the lower end of the hall. Seb drank the ale, realising how parched he was. Jude broke the bread in half and sliced the cheese into wedges.

'Now, little brother, let's think logically. You say you followed the devil from the dormitory last night. He wore a clerk's gown and we've already determined it had to be someone from the scriptorium who killed Creed and attacked you on Friday last. Presumably, it was the same man who roughed you up and left you to your fate. So tell me what you saw of him last night.'

'He wore his hood up. I could not see his face.'

'But you saw his shape. Was he tall, short, fat, thin? Think, Seb. You can't afford to return Hastings' money after all this.'

'I was above him upon the stair, looking down.' Seb chewed a piece of bread, considering what he had observed. ''Twas difficult to tell his height then but, when he grabbed me, I sensed...'

'What?'

'That he was somewhat taller than me but not by much... not so tall as you. And lean of frame but not thin, I would think.'

'Good.' Jude took a hefty swallow of ale before setting down his cup. 'So, it can't be that skinny little prick Robin Beckton.' Jude counted off on his fingers. 'It's a pity but I suppose that excludes that pompous sod Sowbury as well. I was so hoping he's the murderer. I'd like to see him swinging from the gibbet.'

'I be right glad to remove Hal from the list,' Seb said. 'I like him well and he be instructing me how to play the lute.'

'He's teaching you the lute?' Jude sounded incredulous. 'Is that what you're bloody doing every eve in that dormitory? No wonder you haven't solved these damnable crimes. What a bloody waste of time but, of course, any lute-player couldn't possibly be a killer.'

'Do not take that tone, brother. I saw it as a means to better know my fellows. Besides, Hal says I be an apt pupil.'

Jude laughed out loud in mockery.

'Sweet Jesu and Mary save us but you're a gullible idiot, Seb. More likely he was trying to look innocent and it seems he succeeded. Sowbury stays on the list.'

'Forwhy you dislike him and no better reason. You be mistaken, Jude: Hal is no killer, I be certain.'

'No matter. To continue: you couldn't have been following old Eustace Dane. He's fat and wouldn't have the strength to overcome even you.' Jude ticked off another finger. 'What about Barnabas Newson? He's tall, though I wouldn't call him lean.'

'Nay, not Barnabas. The wretch was nigh silent-footed. Barnabas clumps around like a clod-hopping ploughman. It could not be him.'

'So... who remains?' Jude scratched his chin, considering. 'Lawrence bloody-thinks-he's-God-Almighty Duffield. As Sowbury's crony, I'd be content to see him as our killer. The pair of them could swing together on the gallows-tree. Or Andre le Clerc. It could well be him: a bloody foreigner. He's the most likely espier for the same reason. Tall and quite lean. What say you, Seb? Is le Clerc the killer?'

'I have no evidence against him, although Hal, too, has his suspicions regarding Andre since he wants so little to do with the rest of us,' Seb acknowledged. 'I cannot accuse a man forwhy he be tall, lean, of a solitary disposition and only of English birth upon his mother's side.'

'If that's even true. So we have Duffield, le Clerc and Sowbury...'

'Not Hal. He be too short of stature.'

'But he could be the second man, the one who was already below, waiting last night.'

'I think not. I sensed the pair to be much of a height...'

'And he's casting doubt upon le Clerc to distract you from accounting himself. Anyhow, Seb, it seems to me you're living too bloody dangerously of late. Three times you could have met your end this week past. Have you made your will, little brother? As your next of kin, I don't want it falling to me to have to sort out your bloody affairs, if the buggers succeed in killing you?'

Seb looked shocked, unsure whether Jude was jesting or not. The matter of a will had ne'er occurred to him.

'And you know your beloved Rose will get nothing unless you sort out that situation,' Jude went on. Clearly, he was not jesting.

'What is it you say? "Sort out that situation?" What do you mean?'

'You know full bloody well what I mean.' Jude drank the last of the ale in his cup and brushed crumbs from the board with a sweep of his hand. He stood, pushing back his stool with a squeal of wood on stone. 'Marry her, Seb, and make haste about it whilst you can. London custom will care for her as your widow but not as your bloody maid-of-all-work.'

'My widow! But...'

'No "buts", as Hastings said already.'

'But he also said, rightly, that Lent commences upon Wednesday next. There be no time to arrange a marriage afore the forbidden period.'

'How long does it take a man to make a vow and a woman to respond in kind before they go to bed and fuck to make it a binding union?'

'Rose deserves better than that. A proper ceremony, a nuptial feast, a celebration with family and friends, as Adam and Mercy had last leaf-fall. I could not force her into marriage like a Saturday eve drunkard and his wench of choice. 'Tis hardly decent nor respectable.'

'Yet it's all that's necessary. Think on it, little brother, the way your life is at hazard now, waiting until Lent ends in forty days could be too late for you... and Rose. That way, she'll be your next of kin and you can appoint her as your executrix; save me the trouble of dealing with the mess you leave behind.'

'I have not so much as asked her whether she wishes to be my wife or no.'

'Oh, no more excuses! Just do it, Seb. Rose'll say 'aye'; you know she will. Come. Let's go to my lodgings.'

'What of our work in the scriptorium? Master Oliver will be expecting...'

'What of it? You can't work with those hands like that. You're wincing each time you lift your cup. How will you hold a pen?'

'I shall manage well enough.'

'No, you won't. I'm taking you to my lodgings. I yet have that salve you gave me. I think you need it now. We can be back here in time for dinner, if we hasten. Come, Seb. Do as I bloody tell you this once.'

'Aye, but in truth, I should return to Paternoster Row, to answer Adam's queries concerning those new commissions. I had forgotten his urgent letter of yesterday until now.'

'And whilst you're there, you can ask Rose the great question as she tends your hands with proper care. I'll tell bloody Oliver your hands are too swollen to work. I reckon that's the truth, this once.' Jude took Seb's right hand and inspected the bindings which had slipped once more, revealing puffy red flesh and oozing lacerations. He tutted and pulled a face. 'True enough, little brother,' he muttered, releasing hold. 'Get them tended before they turn morbid.'

Chapter 14

Wednesday afternoon
The Foxley house

THE BROTHERS had not gone to Jude's lodgings in Thieving Lane but parted company by the door of the nearest tavern in King Street. Jude promised to return to the palace in time for dinner and pass on Seb's apologies to Master Oliver. Seb had doubts upon the matter but Jude was correct: he could not wield a pen as yet and must have his injuries attended to by one skilled in such arts.

He hastened past Charing Cross and along the Strand, eager to be home but half fearful. What would Rose say? Not about his hands, although she would likely have words concerning them. He turned towards Ludgate, crossing the bridge over the Fleet. What would she answer when he proposed marriage and one without due ceremony at that? Was he ready to take a new wife? Em's year-mind day was not yet come. He made his way through St Paul's precinct. Was it too soon? He acknowledged Old Symkyn, sitting with his begging bowl by the north gate. Would Rose refuse to be rushed into a union all unplanned? He tossed a coin into the old man's bowl – a farthing or a noble: he did not notice. Did she wish to marry him at all?

Plagued by so many questions and doubts, Seb found himself upon his own threshold before having an answer to a single one.

'Seb! God be thanked. We're running about like piglets gone amok in the workshop. Hardly time to draw breath.' Such

195

was Adam's greeting as Seb entered the shop. 'All those new commissions I wrote to you concerning... you did get my letter?'

'Indeed I did, cousin.' Seb held up his hands to still Adam's interrogation. But then Adam saw the bandages.

'What have you done now? Can you still work, Seb? We need you here... How did that happen?'

'I shall do well enough upon the morrow, God willing, but my work be not yet completed at Westminster. I must return in the morn. But where be Rose?'

'In the kitchen most like...'

'No, I am here. I heard your voice, dearest Seb.' Rose was drying her hands upon her apron as she came into the shop. Once dry, she put her hands on his shoulders and drew him close, kissing him on either cheek. 'I miss you when you're away.'

'And I you, dearest Rose.'

'Your hands! Oh, my poor dear Seb. Let me fetch...'

'Later. Firstly, I would speak privily. Is anyone else in the kitchen at present?'

'Nessie is peeling carrots.'

'Send her upon some errand.'

'But we need naught from the market and she just returned from taking bread and meats to Dame Ellen. The old woman is most unwell, Seb. You should visit her...'

'Never mind Dame Ellen. Please, Rose, we must speak alone.'

Rose frowned. This was unlike Seb.

In the kitchen, she bade Nessie fetch some extra leeks from Cheapside whilst Gawain greeted his master with tail-wagging enthusiasm and little Dickon hugged his parent's knees with sticky fingers.

'But we've got plenty o' leeks,' the plump wench objected, as she ever did.

'Do as Rose instructs you, Nessie,' Seb ordered.

'She ain't my mistress.'

'Get you gone!' he told her.

As Nessie grabbed her cloak from the hook, demanded

money for the leeks and departed the kitchen, scowling, Seb turned to Rose.

'We may be about to change that,' he said softly.

'Change what?'

'The fact that you are not the mistress of this house.' Seb went down on one knee and took Rose's hands in his, bloodied bindings notwithstanding. He looked up at her, grey eyes meeting hazel-green. 'Rose Glover... my dearest Rose, would you consider doing me the greatest of honours by consenting to become my wife?'

'Seb? I... this comes as a shock to me. I never thought...' Rose blushed. 'Oh, I...'

'Does it truly shock you so, sweetheart? Do you not know how much and for how long I have loved you and dared not admit the truth, even to myself? Oh, Rose... wrong as it was, I loved you since first I saw you in that dreadful tavern.'

'Did you, Seb?' Rose was close to tears but uncertain of the cause. 'What of Emily?'

'I adored her, aye, and believed she loved me in return. But hers was an infatuation, I now realise, a brief passion, not a lasting love. My love for her was blighted when she turned from me. I tried to keep it burning but she threw water on any fire of love I held in my heart for her 'til the embers went cold. But my love for you, Rose, has increased, growing slowly but strongly, inexorable as the passing seasons. I know that now.

'Rose, will you marry me? Will you overlook my failings and shortcomings? Will you consent to being mistress of my house and mother to my children? As God be my witness, I, Sebastian Foxley, vow to love you, Rose Glover, and be faithful unto you, to share all that I have, heart and soul, hearth and home, with you, to honour and cherish you until death.'

There. It was done; the vow made. Seb was surprised at his own rash act. He had intended to make as much of a marriage as possible in the few days remaining before Lent began. But, mayhap, it was as well to have said the words ere his courage failed him.

'What say you, Rose?' he asked, shy of a sudden and fearful of refusal.

Rose knelt before him upon the cold flagstones of the kitchen floor, little Dickon and Gawain the dog serving as witnesses.

'As God be my witness, I, Rose Glover, vow to love you, Sebastian Foxley, and to be ever faithful and obedient unto you as my lawful wedded husband, to share all that I have, heart and soul, with you, to honour and cherish you to my life's end and, thus, I plight my troth.' Hands still clasped, they sealed their vows with a kiss. Seb fumbled in his purse and found the ring given him lately by the king. The ruby gleamed, warm and red as fire.

'Then I pray you wear this token of our love.' He placed the ring upon her finger. It fitted as well as it ever could, as though always intended for Rose.

A hearty round of cheers and applause caused the couple to draw apart and get up off their knees.

'Praise be unto God, Seb, I never thought you'd get around to it.' Adam stood in the doorway to the passage, grinning like a gargoyle.

Ralf, Kate, customers and neighbours stood behind Adam.

'This calls for celebration,' someone shouted.

'Not until I have tended to my husband's hands.' Rose stressed the words 'my husband', delighted by the sound of them. 'My husband,' she repeated softly in Seb's ear.

'That be musick to me, indeed, *wife*,' he said, kissing her cheek, his face an image of rapture. He had done right by Rose and rejoiced in their new status. 'Mistress Rose Foxley: my dearest goodwife,' he cried aloud. 'Let all London know of it... all England! The whole world! Tell them Seb Foxley be the happiest of men.'

As Rose bathed and soothed his hands with salve, Seb kept on smiling, despite the hurt.

'We may have a proper ceremony, with a priest and all, in

St Paul's, after Easter,' he told her. 'You shall have a new gown and everyone we know shall be invited.'

'Seb, there is no need. I have you; I have this ring. We are wed. What more is necessary?'

'I want everyone to know.'

Joyful tidings travelled fast as fire through the streets – a marriage, no matter whose, was an occasion, or an excuse, to make merry. Food and drink appeared as though conjured by alchemy, as did revellers by the dozen. The house was soon crowded and the celebrations spilt out into Paternoster Row. Seb and Rose were loved and respected and well-wishers arrived in haste.

Rose, embarrassed to be seen in her work-a-day gown on her wedding day, patched and neatly darned though it was, retired to her chamber – the one she had shared with Kate for so long – to put on her Sunday best. Kate and Mercy came to her and presented an ivy coronet for her hair, woven about with ribbons of rainbow hues. It should have been a flower garland but winter had not yet released its hold and blossoms were not to be found.

'Take off your cap,' Mercy said. 'You're yet a virgin bride. Comb out your hair, just this once.'

'But I am no virgin, Mercy, you know that,' Rose whispered. 'My life before I came to live here was...'

'No matter,' Mercy insisted, 'For these few hours upon her marriage day, every woman can be accounted a virgin. Come, loose your hair and put on this ivy garland.' They aided Rose in dressing her hair. The transformation was wondrous. With her hair now a cascade of ripe-wheaten curls few even knew existed beneath her cap and veil, she appeared to have shed a decade of years – a young lass once more. Her hazel-green eyes sparkled and her soft lips curved in a perfect smile.

'Master Seb will love you even more now,' Kate said. 'And shall I have our bed to myself this night?'

'You surely shall,' Mercy answered for Rose who was blushing like her flowery namesake, 'And for every night to come. Are you ready to face the world, Mistress Foxley?'

Rose's cheeks were now aflame. Mistress Foxley! Mistress Rose Foxley. How well that sounded. As she descended the stairs to the kitchen, she felt like the Queen of England. Her crown might have been of pearls and rubies from far off Araby or Cathay, rather than ivy from the garden plot and a few pedlar's ribbons.

Seb's desire that everyone should know of his union with Rose seemed likely to be achieved before morn. His one regret was that Jude, instigator of this momentous event in the Foxley family, was still at Westminster and knew naught of it. Thus, Seb sent a messenger to seek out his brother. As for Jude's wife, Chesca, likely biding in the chamber of the king, if not some other lord's, there was little possibility of informing her. Neighbours, Seb's fellow guildsmen, the precentor and choristers from St Paul's were sharing cups and platters with his relatives or even casual passers-by. Old Symkyn sat at his usual place, not begging but beaming and drinking fine wine from a cracked wooden cup.

As Rose came along the passage from the kitchen to stand beside Seb at their front door all heads turned. A gasp gave way to hearty cheers. Seb had heard of unexpected visions taking folks' breath away but ne'er had he experienced it himself – until now. He knew Rose to be a handsome woman: tall and slender and fine of feature but the bride beside him now outshone Helen of Troy, Aphrodite and all the other beauties of classical myth and legend.

'Close your mouth, Seb,' Adam told him, nudging his kinsman. 'You're gaping. You'll be drooling next. She's lovely, is she not? I never realised and it seems you didn't either. You're a lucky dog, cousin.'

Upon the instant, every man was pushing forward, eager for the customary kiss from the bride. The queue was long indeed, elbowing and shoving in good-natured eagerness to claim the prize. Rose survived the ordeal in good heart, although Seb feared for her being bruised 'neath the press of menfolk.

Not long after the working day ended and darkness had fallen, Jude arrived, accompanied – to Seb's great surprise – by some of their colleagues in the scriptorium: Hal, Lawrence, Barnabas and Robin.

'Eustace sends his apologies,' Hal explained, 'But has given money for a jug of good ale. Andre sends naught.' Hal pulled a face. As Seb had learned, the chief clerk disliked the Frenchman. 'I've brought my lute, as you see. Can't have a wedding without musick, song and dance, can we now? Somebody fetch me a stool!'

Hal sat beside Seb's front doorway, tuned his lute by torchlight, sipped the wine that was handed him and began to play a lively air. Adam and Mercy opened the dancing, cavorting up and down the street and others joined in. Torches appeared, set into pots and barrels, lighting up Paternoster Row.

The Watch arrived, with their staves and cudgels, to determine whether this was some gathering of ill intent, decided it was innocent enough and accepted cups of ale. One fellow went so far as to claim his kiss from the bride. The guardians of Farringdon Ward Within seemed content to stay until Seb's good friend, the City Bailiff Thaddeus Turner, came to tell them to attend their duties. Who could say, though, how tidings had reached Thaddeus' sharp ears all the way over beside Guildhall?

Seb and Rose stood framed upon their doorstep: the happy couple indeed. Seb had been smiling so broad and so long that his jaw ached. Even so, he could not cease to smile. Every glance at Rose beside him, her joyous laugh, her merry eyes, made him smile anew.

Rose kept looking at the ruby on her finger as if to make certain it was real and still there. Such a day was this as she had dreamed of these years past and now it was come so unexpectedly, she could scarce believe it.

Later that eve, the bedding ceremony was conducted with much laughter and bawdy jests amongst the menfolk and a deal of encouragement from the womenfolk. Seb wished that this aspect of a wedding day could be avoided, not wanting to recall the embarrassments of this moment when he had married Emily. Soot everywhere, he remembered. At least Jude – the guilty party on that previous occasion – had been given little opportunity to do his worst this time.

Alone at last in the bedchamber at the front of the house, Seb and Rose lay side by side. The revelry continued below for a while but, eventually, the Watch dispersed the last few merrymakers from the street and all fell quiet. Mercy had taken Dickon and Julia home with her family to Distaff Lane, determined the little ones should not disturb the newlyweds' night of bliss. Hal and the other clerks had returned to Westminster. Only Jude stayed, sleeping in his old chamber and, no doubt, suffering from Ralf's legendary snores. He might yet regret not having gone back to Mistress Baxter's leaking lodging house in Thieving Lane.

'I beg pardon, Rose,' Seb said, staring up into the darkness, his hand toying with a silken strand of her hair. 'I ne'er meant to rush you into this. This afternoon, I intended to ask you, if you would consent to be my wife when all should be prepared beforehand. But, I confess, fearing my nerve might fail me, I made my vow unto you, there and then. I…'

Rose made no answer but stopped his words with a long, lingering kiss.

'But now 'tis done, you shall have no regrets,' she whispered. 'Dearest husband, be mine, as I am yours.'

Thursday, the ninth day of February
The Foxley house

Seb left his bridal bed early, not from choice but forwhy he must be at Westminster all too soon and there were things to accomplish afore that.

Nessie had kindled the fire in the kitchen hearth and was heating water.

'God give you good day, Nessie,' Seb greeted her. 'I trust you slept well?'

'I trust you didn't sleep at all, master?' she said, attempting to wink at him. 'No bridegroom should.'

'Enough of such talk, Nessie. 'Tis not your place to make unseemly remarks. I would have you take a pitcher of hot water upstairs to Rose, if you will?'

'O' course, she's a fine mistress now. S'pose she'll want to wash in hot water ev'ry day.'

'We shall be attending mass at St Michael's shortly. I wish Father Thomas to bless our marriage after the office be done. What is this?' Seb picked up a fold of paper lying upon the table board. It was sealed with a drip of wax without any indentation but his name was written thereon in bold, black ink.

'Don't ask me. Can't read, can I? Reckon someone left it last night. It was there when I woke up.'

Seb broke open the wax and read the neatly penned script. So few words but they sent a shiver through his blood:

Do not return to Westminster, if you know what is good for you and yours.

The brief missive was unsigned, not surprisingly. Seb screwed it up and put it in his purse, out of sight, as Rose came down the stair, still smiling.

'Come, sweeting, let's away to church,' he said to Rose, taking their cloaks from the pegs by the kitchen door. 'Once we have God's blessing, I shall be utterly content.'

'I wos thinkin' you'd both be utterly content already, after last night.'

'Nessie! Such talk is improper. Behave yourself,' Rose told her.

'Or wot? S'pose you'll be takin' a broom t' me like Mistress Em used to do, now you're all high-an'-mighty like she wos.'

'You and I will be having a long discussion after I get back from church,' Rose said. The stern tone was unheard before.

Things had certainly changed since yester morn when Rose had been plain Rose Glover. Now that she was Mistress Foxley, even Nessie had sense enough to realise the household would be different with Rose having its governance. The wench hoped the change wouldn't be for the worse.

Hand in hand, the newlyweds nigh danced to the church of St Michael le Querne on the corner where Paternoster Row joined Bladder Street to become Cheapside. The office of low mass was already begun but heads turned as they entered. Smiles and knowledgeable looks greeted them, not to mention much whispering behind hands. Rose giggled and waved to Mary Caldecott, their next-door neighbour and the loudest of the whisperers.

'We could hear the bed creaking and groaning 'til nigh cockcrow,' Mary called out. 'Or was that you moaning in ecstasy, Seb?'

'You heard naught of the sort, Mary,' Rose told her, hoping to spare Seb – turning red to the ears – further embarrassment.

'Why's that? He disappointed you on your wedding night, did he, Rose? Oh, the pity of it. Must have been you complaining about the lack that we were hearing through the wall.' Mary laughed loudly and her fellow gossips joined in. Matters were beginning to get out of hand.

Father Thomas turned, frowning, from his Latin recitation of the office 'neath the chancel arch.

Seb pulled Rose away towards the font and they stood quietly, watched over by St Christopher from the mural on the wall. Seb inspected the painting. He had repaired it three summers since, making good the flaking plaster and repainting it but, in truth, it was becoming a patchwork of old, new and entirely lost areas of pigment and should be wholly plastered over and begun anew. Yet it would be a sorrowful thing to obliterate the image, forwhy St Kit was like a friend of long acquaintance. Besides,

St Michael's had not the money to pay for a new mural, unlike the more wealthy churches further along Cheapside, where the parishioners were rich merchants with fat purses. Mayhap, Seb would volunteer his services, *gratis*, and make repairs once more, sufficient that the protecting saint would smile benignly upon them for a few years more.

The Eucharist bell rang and Seb turned his attention to the Elevation of the Host and sacred things, murmuring the appropriate Latin prayers, which he knew by heart, along with the priest. Others did not bother but continued their chatter. Seb shook his head at so blatant disregard for the solemnity and wonder of Our Lord's redeeming sacrifice of blood. Mary Caldicott and her cronies should be ashamed.

The office was done; the Benediction bestowed. The parishioners hastened away to begin the labours of the day but Seb and Rose lingered, watching as Father Thomas washed the sacred chalice and pix in the piscina and dried them upon spotless linen before locking them away in the small coffer beside the High Altar.

'You wished to speak with me, Sebastian?' the priest said, smiling, his misshapen arthritic fingers folded together as in prayer. 'I believe I know the reason.'

'Indeed, good father, the whole parish seems to know,' Seb said. 'But Rose and I wish you to ask Almighty God's blessing upon our union, if you may.'

'From what I heard, 'twas somewhat of a hasty union. Am I correct in supposing the reason for it? Tongues are wagging to that effect.' He looked at Rose, his meaning plain.

'Nay, father,' they both answered.

''Tis the way of my life being at hazard these days,' Seb explained. 'I fully intended that we would wed after Emily's year-mind be passed upon the sixteenth day of April, but I feared leaving Rose so uncertain in her position, if the worst befalls me – I pray God it does not. I love Rose most dearly and would do right by her. The beginning of Lent next week adds urgency to my cause, so we made our vows yesterday, each to the other, and asked God's witness to the same. A blessing would seal those vows forever.'

Father Thomas nodded and led them to the holy water stoop by the door. He marked their foreheads with a cross then their clasped hands before binding them together with the length of his stole. He recited much in Latin before repeating the Benediction, naming their names.

Rose understood little of what was said. Once outside the church, she asked Seb to explain.

'He asked God's blessings upon us both, just as we desired.'

'But he said more than that,' Rose insisted.

'Aye.' Seb pulled Rose to him within the lychgate to the churchyard. 'He begged that we be granted the heritage and gift of children to be raised in Christian wise to the further glory of God. A finer request I ne'er heard.' He kissed her. 'Does that please you, wife?'

Rose returned his kiss.

'Indeed it does, husband.'

'Now. I fear I must return to Westminster, sweetheart, loath as I be. And that idle brother of mine must come too, if he be yet arisen from his bed.'

Back in the workshop, Adam, Ralf and Kate were setting out the day's tasks. Adam had brought Dickon and Julia back from Distaff Lane and was relieved to give them into Rose's care. The little lad was attempting to dip his finger in the ink wells and Julia was fractious with another tooth coming through. The workshop was no place for them.

'Ah, Seb, God give you good day,' Adam said.

'The Almighty has done so already,' Seb chuckled. 'And all of you likewise,' he added, smiling at those he employed, all eager at their desks.

'But we have need to speak of those new commissions,

cousin,' Adam continued. 'You recall the letter I sent you on Monday? You did receive it?'

'Aye. An impressive list, Adam.'

'Well? Which of them do we accept and which refuse? I cannot decide about Bishop Stillington's portrait. 'Tis up to you.'

'Accept them all, Adam,' Seb told him. At that moment, his spirits soaring, he felt as though he could achieve anything or everything the world might demand of him.

'All? Are you certain?' Adam was of a different mind.

'Aye. But make the agreed completion dates well spread. I may confirm the contracts upon Saturday, if you draw them up, provisionally. Consult Master Collop at the Stationers' Hall concerning the wording, if you be in doubt.'

'You trust me with so much?'

'Of course. Now Jude and I must hasten back to Westminster. Where be the idle fellow? Not still abed, I hope.'

Seb and Jude were walking along the Strand, returning to Westminster, to Secretary Oliver's domain, but neither man was eager to reach their destination, although Seb's conscience pricked him. He had Lord Hastings' commission to complete but had not the heart to search out murderers and espiers any longer. Rose had put more salve upon the raw skin of his hands and rebound them with fresh linen. The injuries looked to be healing well this morn but were sore yet. Was that sufficient reason to excuse his labouring at his desk alongside his fellow clerks? In truth, it was not. The weather seemed to sympathise for it had begun to drizzle, chill and melancholy, on a wind blowing in from the west.

'Have you settled upon the guilty parties yet, Seb?' Jude was asking as they passed the weather-worn edifice of Queen Eleanor's Cross at Charing and turned down King Street. 'Sowbury and that bloody Frenchman are most likely, by my accounting.'

'Forwhy you like them not?' Seb ducked to avoid a dripping eave. ''Tis hardly a crime to be disliked by you. How would it sound in a court of law? Jude Foxley does not like the accused, so the fellow must be guilty. Half London would be hanged by that criterion.'

'And all of bloody Westminster, especially King Great-Bollocks himself. He'd hang first, if it were my choice to make.'

'This lay upon the kitchen board this morn,' Seb said, taking the crumpled letter from his purse and handing it to Jude, changing the subject well away from such treasonous nonsense. 'What say you to that? I wish I might forget it but...'

Jude turned his back to the rain to read it, in order that the paper shouldn't get wet and the ink run.

'Ah, well. That reduces the possible miscreants to those who came to the celebration last eve.' Jude wiped moisture from his face and returned the letter. 'So, unfortunately, le Clerc couldn't have left it in the kitchen, now could he? It has to be Sowbury, as I've said all along, the bastard.'

'Not necessarily,' Seb said, stepping hastily aside to let a horseman pass on his way, splashing mud. 'Eustace did not come either but sent money for ale, nonetheless. Le Clerc could have given one of the others this note, telling them he was sending me his congratulations. The letter was sealed. Whoever delivered it need not know what it truly said.'

'Sowbury. I wager he wrote it and delivered it.'

'Nay, Jude. He least of all wrote it. As yet, I be not familiar with every clerk's hand but his I know well enough and le Clerc's also, from working with him on Monday concerning those Welsh documents. Neither man wrote this note.' Seb fell silent as they turned along King Street, the Great Gate ahead upon the left hand.

'The Welsh documents! Les Pays de Galles!' Seb cried aloud. 'Dear God, Jude, what have I done? I knew something to be amiss... I must warn the king.' With that, Seb broke into an unaccustomed run.

Jude, mystified, loped after his brother, cursing as he splashed through a patch of mud and horse shit.

'Warn him about what?' Jude called out but Seb did not pause to answer him. Muttering obscenities, Jude followed him to the Great Gate.

'Let us pass in haste,' Jude heard Seb telling the guards at the gatehouse. 'You know us well enough by now. 'Tis a matter of life and death.'

Chapter 15

Thursday morn
Westminster

SEB HASTENED to the Great Hall where the denizens of Westminster Palace were yet breaking their fast. No time to waste, he made straight for the door beside the dais and lifted away the curtain. The chamber beyond was unoccupied; Lord Hastings and Sir Nicholas not at their posts as guardians of the king. Seb knocked courteously upon the inner door on the far side of Hastings' desk. No one answered but Seb could hear muffled sounds from the royal apartments on the other side of the sturdy oaken barrier.

The matter being of such importance, he entered without awaiting permission.

Horror!

He burst in upon King Edward and Chesca, she half-naked upon a silk-draped couch, the king grunting atop of her.

'Pardon; pardon.' Seb shielded his eyes, half turning away, but he knew this could not wait. Neither could the sight be unseen. Chesca... merely a translator for the king? Jude was correct all along. 'Forgive me, your Grace, but...'

Seb got no further with his explanation afore Sir Nicholas was manhandling him out of the chamber and slammed the door upon a scene of such intimacy.

'How dare you!' Sir Nicholas was spluttering, hardly able to speak for indignation. 'You rogue. You rapscallion. You... you...'

Seb broke free of the man's grasp and ran back to shout as loud as he was able before the door, in the hope that the lovers might hear.

'Chesca. Look to my translations. 'Tis not France but Wales. I was mistaken. The young prince...'

At Sir Nicholas' order, two liveried men-at-arms rushed in and seized hold of Seb, dragging him away so fast his feet could hardly keep up with them. He stumbled, protesting all the while, but they did not let him fall, not until they were across the Outer Courtyard to the Great Gate, up the winding stairs to a lock-up above the guardroom. The door was unlocked with a mighty key and creaked on ungreased hinges. The men flung him inside to land on a pile of foetid straw that stank of human waste and rat droppings. He landed hard, knocking the wind out of him. The door banged and the key grated. Seb was imprisoned at the king's pleasure. Or rather displeasure.

'Ah, company. That's welcome,' a voice greeted him. 'But still no breakfast, eh?'

Seb struggled to his feet, brushing evil-smelling straw from his attire – clean on this morn. Already, he began to stink. He leaned against the wall whilst he recovered his breath, then thought better of it, realising it was slimed with the Lord alone knew what. Squinting in the gloom of the cell which daylight seemed to be avoiding, its arrow-slit windows forbidding the entrance of God's good light, Seb made out the source of the voice.

A dark shape lay at ease in the least noisome corner.

'Ne'er thinking to see yer kind in this midden-hole,' the fellow said. His voice had something familiar about it.

'You be the pedlar at Charing Cross from whom I purchased the colourful braid,' Seb said, remembering. 'Jake Parslow, if I recall aright?'

'Aye, master, that's me. So wot did you do t' land in 'ere, eh? Robbed another honest man of 'is livelode, did yer?'

'Nay. Naught of the kind. I fear I disturbed the king's grace at an inopportune moment... 'Twas ill done, indeed.'

'Ah,' the pedlar said, seeming to comprehend Seb's meaning entirely. 'You got any use fer a packet o' pins? I have a few here though they took me pack o' goods fer sale, may the Devil rot their souls. I see they let you keep yer purse. A couple o' pence might buy us bread an' ale from them guards.'

'I broke my fast afore,' Seb said. Nevertheless, he unfastened his purse and took out a penny. 'Here, buy yourself whatever the guards allow.'

The pedlar took a packet of pins from inside his tattered jerkin and tossed it to Seb in exchange. Not that Seb could think how such a thing might serve in this dismal place. The fold of blue paper lay before him, the pins piercing it in neatly aligned rows, just like the packet he had purchased for Rose not long ago... just like those he had seen... where was that? For the moment, he could not recall. This situation was not conducive to clear thinking. And his head ached. Mayhap, he had struck it when the guards threw him down? There was a tender place above his right eye most certainly. Yet he must contrive a means of informing the king that the life of the little Prince of Wales was in jeopardy.

How had he been so foolish as to mistake the meaning of *Io consiglio rapire il Galles* for 'I advise the plundering of France', thinking *Galles* referred to Gaul – France? Nay. The Italian word *Galles* was as the French *Pays de Galles* – Wales! And *rapire* in Latin means to seize as well as to plunder. Therefore, the phrase could as well say 'I advise the seizing of Wales': the king's elder son, the Prince of Wales, who was to be at Westminster to celebrate Eastertide with the royal family. If his guess in applying the Latin meaning to the Italian was correct, Seb had to warn King Edward that the lad might be abducted, or worse, upon his long journey from Ludlow in the Welsh Marches. But having failed in his first rash and discourteous attempt, the king was hardly likely to grant him audience now.

What a coil! And it was all his own fault.

Seb picked up the packet of pins for no reason other than the vague idea that he had seen a number of similar packets in some unlikely place. Idly, he toyed with the spot of wax that kept the paper folded. A strip of paper fluttered out.

The pedlar leapt to retrieve it but Seb caught a glimpse of writing upon it.

'Not that packet,' the fellow shouted. 'Here, 'ave this one. I gived you the wrong one.' He swept up the first and tried to snatch away the written paper, too late.

Seb recognised what he held in his hand.

''Tis a meaningless note,' the pedlar said, shrugging and making out that it was now of no importance.

Seb knew he had hold of another Italian letter in code, addressed to *Il Leone d'Oro* and signed at the bottom by *Il Scudiero del Rubino,* the Esquire of the Ruby, just like the others.

'I know exactly what this is,' Seb said. 'And 'tis far from being a "meaningless note", as you insist. Be you the wretched intelligencer we have been seeking? The Italian espier? Nay. I misdoubt that. But I suspect you may be a go-between, delivering and returning letters betwixt the espier and a courier for his master. Be that the way of it, Jake Parslow? How much do they pay you for your rascally intrigues as their messenger?'

'Not enough! I didn't bargain for them demons locking me in 'ere fer no reason, takin' me pack. Bastards, all 'o them.'

'Why did they lock you in here?'

'Like I told you: no reason. They said I touched 'er, laid 'ands on 'er titties wot I never did. I wouldn't dare. I ain't stupid. Touch the king's daughter? I wouldn't, would I? Not in a 'undred years, though she does look to 'ave a fair pair o' bubbs on 'er.'

'You touched the king's daughter?'

'No. I told you I didn't. Might 'ave brushed against 'er by mistake, as you could say, but that's all. That young Lady Bessie's got a fair pair right enough.'

'Never mind your lewd nonsense. Tell me who gives you these notes in the packets of pins? I swear to speak on your behalf concerning your predicament here, if you will but answer my question. Tell me, I pray you, in the king's name.'

Parslow laughed, a humourless cackle which sent a rat scurrying.

'Oh, aye, as if yer not in the same mess as me. Nobody's goin' t' listen to you or me. B'sides, I tell you an' I'm good as dead.'

'Do you not realise the treasonable content of these notes you carry?'

''Ow would I? Can't read, can I? Why d'you reckon they chosed me as their messenger?'

'Who chose you?'

'Not sayin'. Me life won't be worth a tin groat, if I does, so don't ask me.'

'Was it one of the clerks in Secretary Oliver's scriptorium? Or someone else?'

'Whose? Never 'eard of 'im, whoever 'e is. Now stop yer damn questions 'cos I ain't answerin' 'em.'

With the pedlar disinclined to divulge any intelligence, Seb was at a loss what to do. Idleness was never his way. But he had the coded letter. Sitting on the floor, he cleared a space of wispy straws, leaving a damp layer of filth. Without pen, ink or paper, finger marks in the dirt would have to serve. He wrote out the first letter which occurred after each of those odd little symbols. Being used to the method by now, it did not take him long.

Jake Parslow watched him, head on one side like a curious bird.

'Wot you doin'?' he asked.

'Working out the cypher of your treasonous communication to discover what it says.'

'Treasonous? They never said anythin' about treason. Wot does it say then? It looks like yer made worms in the filth to me. 'Ow can that be treason?'

'Believe me: this be treason of the worst order. 'Tis more imperative than ever now that I get to speak with King Edward directly. This confirms my utmost fears. His son's life be at hazard.'

'Them worms tell you that?'

'Indeed they do. My lack of the Italian tongue hardly matters in this case. *Mercoledì primo giorno di marzo,*' Seb read aloud. 'My knowledge of French suggests this to be the date: Wednesday the first day of March. And *all'abbazia di Sant'Albano* no doubt refers to St Alban's Abbey.'

'Them squiggly things say all o' that? I wouldn't 'ave believed it. But wot's it got to do with the king's little lad, Prince Richard?'

'Naught at all. This concerns the elder, the Prince of Wales.'

'But 'e don't bide 'ere, nor at St Alban's. I've been there a few times on me travels... fine church an' all. Bad-tempered brother cellarer, though. Didn't like 'im: a mean body in every way. Right tight-'anded wi' the ale.'

'Forget your belly for the present. The other messages you have been passing on tell of a plot to seize the prince. This note confirms the day and place. All Westminster be aware that the lad will be here to celebrate Passiontide and Eastertide with his family. My knowledge of England's geography – '

'England's wot?'

'The lay of the land; where towns and villages are, relative one to another – be not so extensive as yours as a travelling man – but I believe St Alban's Abbey on the Great North Road could well be upon the way the prince may come from Ludlow. Someone here in the king's palace appears to know precisely where the prince will be upon a certain date. So, I ask you again, Jake Parslow, who gives you these letters and to whom do you deliver them?'

'I don't know no names, I swear. Some foreign wight in Lombard Street's been payin' me t' stay around London and Westminster, taking notes, to an' fro, folded inside them packets o' pins, like you saw. But I don't know nobody's names. An' I'm losin' trade, wot with all their nonsense. Now them devils 'ave taken me pack. That's my livin', that is!'

The pedlar looked so forlorn, Seb almost felt sorry for him

but reminded himself right swiftly that the fellow was involved in treason, whether he was aware of what he was doing or not. Ignorance was no excuse in the eyes of the law, as Seb had learned from assisting his friend, City Bailiff Thaddeus Turner, in the past.

Whilst the morn dragged by, slower than a reluctant scholar upon his way to school and Jake Parslow found solace in chewing his filthy fingernails *in lieu* of dinner, Seb begrudged so much waste of God's good day to no purpose. He looked out of the window, such as it was, narrow and deep sunken in the thickness of the stone walls of the gatehouse. By twisting his neck awkwardly and pressing his face close to the embrasure, he could see a thin slice of Westminster's Outer Courtyard. Rain fell steadily from a doom-coloured sky and folk were keeping within doors, if they had the wit and no necessity to brave the downpour. Thus, there was little to distract his thoughts from the melancholy and morbid situation.

'Where have I seen a multitude of pin-packets?' he mused aloud, not expecting any reply from the pedlar who was now propped against the wall in the far corner, arms folded, eyes closed.

'In my pack o' course,' Parslow mumbled. Not asleep but listening then.

'Nay. Elsewhere...'

'Lots o' ladies 'ere at court buy 'em by the dozen.'

'I do not delve into ladies' coffers. Even at home, my goodwife be permitted her privacy.' Seb smiled to himself. My goodwife. Those words were well said and tasted sweet upon his tongue. Rose. What would she say if she saw him now, confined here in this vile place, filthy, unfed? The smile was gone. Rose would be outraged, if she learned of it.

He ran to the door of stoutest oak, hinged with iron, and pounded upon it.

'Guards! Guards!' he yelled. 'Release me. I must speak with the king. 'Tis a matter of life and death.'

'Shut yer clack, you verminous half-wit. The king don't want to speak wiv you.' The words were muffled by the thickness of wood but clear enough.

'Then permit me to speak with Lord Hastings. 'Tis imperative that I do so.'

'Shut yer stupid mouth or I'll shut it for you. One more word an' yer'll be eatin' yer own teeth. Mark me?'

Seb gave up. The guards were not about to aid him. His was a lost cause. He joined the pedlar, sitting on the begrimed floor, shut his eyes and thought of Rose and his children – the one good and beautiful thing in his life at present. And the workshop... Adam, Kate and Ralf diligent at their desks. And his home with its welcoming kitchen and comfortable bed. Mayhap, he should not be so melancholy. If King Edward refused to give him audience then so be it. Seb Foxley had done what he might and blame could not be laid upon him if the Prince of Wales came to harm. Murderers, espiers and traitors were his concern no longer and Secretary Oliver must find a new clerk. He was done with Westminster, no matter what.

With naught else to do, like an old man, Seb must have dozed but was brought sharp awake by the jangle of keys and the creak of ancient hinges.

'The bloody things I have to do to save your skinny neck.' Jude looked weary and wore a frown, deep and dark as Satan's eyes. 'Come on, get off your idle arse; the fat bastard's agreed to see you. God alone knows why he should. Even I don't want to bloody look at you. And you stink.'

'Oh, Jude. I know not what you did to achieve this but I shall be forever in your debt.'

'Bloody right you will. Forever,' Jude said.

Seb followed in his brother's wake, out of the door as the guard stood aside to let them pass before relocked the door on the pedlar.

'What of me?' Jake Parslow whined, hammering on the timbers.

'Keep the pedlar here,' Seb told the guard. 'Whatever you do, do not release him afore I have spoken with the King's Grace.' Head held high, despite the odours emanating from his attire and grimy person, he walked down the stairs, confident he would shortly be at liberty: a free man once more.

'How did you arrange an audience?' Seb asked Jude as he washed his face and hands at the conduit in the Outer Courtyard. He could do naught about his clothing but his skin would be clean. The water gushed icily and Seb shivered. As for his hair, he removed his cap and let the rain refresh it. He was not so rash as to douse his head in the conduit and, like as not, catch his death as a result.

'You owe me, little brother.' Jude stood back so as not to be splashed. 'I had words with that deceitful, disloyal bitch of mine, though I'd vowed never to speak to the slut ever again. But I did, all for your sake. Whatever devil possessed you, bursting in on the king like that? Fortunately for you, he was in a good humour – no doubt because the bastard had just fucked my wife – and was bloody amused at the thought of what you'd seen. He sent Hastings to find me in the scriptorium, thinking I would know what you were about – which I bloody didn't and still don't.

'What was that nonsense you were shouting as you ran off? Something about warning the king; a matter of life and death? I don't know what possessed you of a sudden, little brother. Our father begat a fool in you, that's for certain. I always suspected you were cracked-brained. Now I know it.'

'I realised the mistake I had made in my attempt to translate the Italian message. It was not France but Wales.' Seb wiped his face and hands on his kerchief. Having kept it tucked in his sleeve, as usual, it was reasonably clean. 'The Prince of Wales will be in gravest danger when he journeys from Ludlow. Some foul deed be planned to waylay him and I now know when and where. What is more, I have discovered that Jake Parslow be the espier's messenger.'

'France? Wales? What of them? And who's this Jake fellow?'

'Parslow... the pedlar.'

'What pedlar?'

'No matter. We must hasten to the king and you shall hear all, Jude.'

The King's Privy Chamber

Seb made his obeisance before King Edward as low as he dared without pitching forward on his face and making a worse show of foolishness than earlier that day. Thankfully, the monarch was now splendid in blue velvet and damask with silver threads. Seb closed his eyes for a moment, attempting to fix this new image in his mind to replace the previous undignified one of the royal buttocks, pale and hairy, grinding away.

Jude's courtesy was so brief as to border upon insolence. He had no intention of showing more respect than necessary to the wretch who was cuckolding him, just sufficient to avoid rousing the royal wrath – if only for Seb's sake. Even so, he was curious to learn what his little brother had discovered.

Sir Nicholas FitzAlan and a servant were the only other persons present but Seb hardly noticed them.

'Ah, the Foxley brothers... again,' the king said, wrinkling his nose as if assailed by a stench. Seb feared he might be the source. 'Well?' Edward continued. 'Every time I set eyes on either of you, it usually means trouble and/or expense. What is it upon this occasion? I heard mention of "life-and-death". So tell me.'

'Your Grace,' Seb began, still on bended knee.

'Oh, cease your grovelling. Get up.' The royal humour was sorely tried.

'Thank you, my lord'. Seb got to his feet. 'I fear I have been at great fault in my previous translations of the coded messages from the Italian tongue, being unfamiliar with it. I took *Galles* to mean Gaul – France – but, in truth, I now believe it to mean Wales. Therefore, the phrase which we – er, I understood to refer to the plundering of France... I fear it speaks of the seizing of Wales and not the Principality but the Prince thereof. And I now have...'

'What!' roared the king, leaping from his comfortable chair by the fire. 'You discover my son's life is in danger and say naught of it!'

'I-I attempted to inform you, my lord, as soon as I realised...'

'Who would dare? I'll have him torn apart by wild dogs, boiled alive, rip out his vitals and feed them to the fishes. Tell me who!' Edward was spitting, blustering.

Seb took a step back; two steps; more.

The infamous Plantagenet rage boiled over. A silver goblet was thrown at the wall, spilling ruby wine down a priceless tapestry, denting the jewelled cup. A velvet-covered gilded footstool was flung across the chamber as though it weighed no more than a length of kindling, smashing one leg as it crashed against the marble hearth, sending chips of stone and wood splinters flying. The abused tapestry was torn from its tenterhooks and trampled upon.

At last, the king paused to draw breath. His shoulders slumped and he subsided into his chair. Gradually, the hectic flush of blood faded from his countenance as Edward recovered himself.

'Get this mess cleared away,' he told the servant who had shrunk back into a shadowed corner during the outburst. 'And bring more wine... and a new cup. God's bones: such useless dolts I pay to serve me. Do it, you imbecile!'

The servant scuttled off, knowing a fresh cup of wine was more urgent than tidying broken furniture or rescuing a ruined tapestry.

'Tell me the name of this Devil's minion, Foxley. Tell me directly.'

'I-I do not know his name.' Seb hastened his speech. 'But

I know the date and place chosen to attack my lord prince.'
He held out the note that he had discovered folded within the
packet of pins.

'This is gibberish,' the king snarled, eyes flashing in
dangerous wise.

'But I have deciphered it. St Alban's Abbey upon Wednesday
the first day of March is the place.'

'Yet you know not who will commit this monstrous deed.'

'Nay, my lord, but I know the messenger who carries these
infamous letters. You already hold him in custody in the lock-
up above the Great Gatehouse. Jake Parslow, the pedlar, has
been passing them betwixt someone in Lombard Street in
London and the espiers here at Westminster. Mayhap, he can
be persuaded to name the conspirators.'

'Persuaded! I'll torture the pig with red-hot irons myself until
he tells all. Then he shall be strung from the nearest tree and
I'll dance on his corpse whilst it's yet warm.'

'M-my lord, if I may venture...' Seb said, his voice a-quiver
with the reticence of a lowly clerk daring to advise his king,
'Might not the promise of mercy, if he reveals the names, meet
with better success? If he knows he is to hang whether he
speaks or not...'

Edward gave Seb a look so stern and fierce, enough to chill
any man's blood.

'Mm. I shall think upon it for the time it takes to fetch the
devil from the lock-up. Sir Nicholas. Go, bring this wretch to
me. Now. And make haste; I want this done before I dine. You
hear me, Nicholas?'

'Indeed, my lord.' Sir Nicholas bowed and departed.

Seb noted the fellow looked pale as lead-white pigment.
Mayhap, the royal explosion of wrath had affrighted him as it
had Seb. Attending upon the king so closely must be a fraught
means of service.

'As for you two,' Edward said, sounding calm now as he
watched the serving-man return with a pitcher of wine and pour

the liquid into an undamaged cup which he proffered to the king. 'Return to your duties in Secretary Oliver's scriptorium. I'll send for you, if needs be.'

Dismissed out of hand without a word of thanks, Seb and Jude withdrew.

'Bastard has no more manners than a bloody coney-catcher,' Jude muttered even as they were passing through the door. 'He could've offered us wine for our bloody trouble. Bastard. Give me five minutes in a dark alley with that great lump of grease and he'd rue the day he ever took a fancy to what's mine.'

'Hush, Jude. He be the king. Have a care what you say. You know espiers lurk in every corner. Some ill-wisher may report your words.'

'I don't care.'

The Scriptorium

Seb and Jude arrived at their desks, the latter still muttering insults and threats against the king and in no mood to suffer Secretary Oliver's reprimands.

'I don't want to hear your excuses. Just get on with your work. I'm docking half a day's wages from you, Jude Foxley, and a day and a half's worth from you, Sebastian, seeing you did naught at all yesterday and none this morn. Duffield's been summoned upon the king's business most urgently, so we're short-handed again. Those warrants won't write themselves and you'll both forego dinner to get your share of copies completed.'

'We will not.' Jude thumped his desk with his fist, knocking the inkwell to the floor. Fortunately, it hadn't yet been filled but the little earthen pot shattered on the stone flags. 'I'm sick and tired of this accursed place and I'm not in need of your petty few pence. But I am in need of a good dinner, so you can...'

'Master Secretary,' Seb intervened. 'My brother be out of

humour. We have attended upon the King's Grace and the audience was not of an entirely solicitous nature. Please forgive him. We will begin our copying directly.'

'We bloody won't,' Jude said, heat flaming his face and neck.

'Jude. I beg you; do as I say this once,' Seb whispered, nudging his brother to silence. 'Here. Have use of my inkwell. I shall fetch another.'

Seb took a spare inkwell from the shelf, filled it from the communal ink bottle and took both to his desk. He filled Jude's inkpot also then resumed his seat, having a care for the split wood. He prepared his pen and began copying.

'There be something amiss here, Jude,' he murmured so Oliver should not hear and kept his eyes upon the parchment.

'Everything's amiss here – as always. We should walk out.'

'Nay. What think you of Lawrence Duffield's summons? Who does the king send when 'tis a matter of great urgency? Who but Sir Nicholas FitzAlan? But we were there when the king sent him to bring the pedlar from the lock-up. Has there been time enough for the groom to fetch the pedlar to the king, receive the new command and come here to fetch Lawrence all afore we arrived? I think not. And Lawrence be yet absent from his desk.'

'What does it matter? Perhaps the king sent another groom. The business could be taking a while. Who cares, anyhow?'

'I believe Sir Nicholas came here first to fetch Lawrence afore going to the lock-up.' Seb dipped his pen and began a new paragraph.

'Why would he do that? He's an arse-licker and wouldn't dare disobey his high-and-mighty paymaster.'

'Why? I know not but I mislike the smell of it.'

'That's just the gaol-stink off your clothes,' Jude laughed, poking Seb on the arm.

'Silence!' roared Oliver, bringing his staff down with a crack across Jude's desk, making all the clerks jump in their seats.

Jude was on his feet, tearing up the warrants of which he

was supposed to be making copies, flinging them all about. Then, with a great heave, he overturned his desk and stormed out. The scriptorium would not see Jude Foxley again. Ever. No matter who tried to persuade him. He was done with the likes of Oliver and hours of mindless labour. He had better things to do with his life.

Seb shook his head and continued writing.

Chapter 16

Thursday afternoon
Westminster

SEB WENT without dinner, as Secretary Oliver demanded, but the call of Nature was not at Oliver's command. Thus, Seb left his desk whilst his colleagues were in the Great Hall, eating their meal, and made his way outside, through the Inner Gate into the Outer Courtyard, towards the house of easement. At least the drizzle had relented for the present, although the clouds were the colour of unpolished pewter and heavy with the weight of rain yet to come. Pulling his cloak close about him, he shivered in the chill easterly wind blowing off the river.

A crowd was gathered by the Great Gatehouse. A deal of shouting and commotion could be heard. Although he would hardly admit to it, Seb possessed his fair share of the London citizens' native curiosity. His need forgotten for the moment, he could not resist the temptation to learn what was amiss.

As he reached the scene, the crowd parted to allow the passage of Westminster's coroner, Sir Thomas Burns, leaving the gatehouse. The presence of the cherub-faced coroner meant only one conclusion was possible: a death had occurred in unnatural circumstances. Mayhap, a guard had slipped upon the narrow stair and fallen, or choked upon his dinner. Yet Seb had the cold sensation in the pit of his stomach that no common mishap was the cause.

It came as no unexpected revelation to Seb to see two burly

225

guards lugging the limp form of Jake Parslow in the coroner's wake. The crowd murmured and muttered. Some, like Seb, removed their caps in respect. The Lord God knew the pedlar was given little respect otherwise. They had not wrapped the body in any kind of covering, nor even concealed the face from view.

Once clear of the gatehouse, the body was laid down on the wet cobbles for Sir Thomas's inspection in the best of the daylight. Seb pushed through the crowd.

'Coroner Burns?' Seb said. 'I may be of assistance to you in this case.'

Sir Thomas, reluctant to soil his robes by kneeling in the mud, was content to have some other ruin theirs in his stead.

'Ah, Master Foxley. Why am I not surprised to find you here?'

'I happened to be passing by, sir. No more than that.'

'A coincidence, nonetheless.'

'Aye. I suppose so. I would inform you, sir, that I spent some hours with the unfortunate pedlar this very morn, in the lock-up here. He was fit and well when I departed to make report to the King's Grace.'

'You were interrogating him?'

'Well, no. Not officially, leastwise. Rather I was, briefly, upon a most unfortunate misunderstanding, his fellow prisoner. Once the matter was resolved, I was released.'

'When was this?'

'Afore dinner. In truth, 'twas a long morn; I quite lost all sense of time. After I made my report to the king, His Grace sent for Jake Parslow – that be this fellow's name, if you know it not – to question him. It would seem those questions are not to be answered. Did he die by some accident?'

Coroner Burns rubbed his smooth-shaven chin in thought.

'That's what I'm here to determine and, since you're here also, you may as well assist. I see no obvious outward injuries.'

'Where was he discovered?' Seb asked, crouching to see more closely.

'In the cell, where he should be. The guards say all seemed in good order. They had heard naught untoward: no cry for aid nor groans of anguish, if a seizure took him. I myself viewed the body where it lay and, to all appearances, death looked to have come upon him peacefully enough.'

'Who first discovered him?'

'The groom of the chamber sent by the king to interrogate the fellow, together with the clerk to record the questions and answers.'

Seb raised his eyebrows. To interrogate?

'But that was not the way of it, sir. The king sent Sir Nicholas FitzAlan to fetch the pedlar, not to question him. The king intended to do that in person on so delicate a matter. I was there and tell you true what was said.'

'Well, the guards tell it otherwise: that FitzAlan – for you are correct in saying it was he – stated that he was acting under the king's direct instruction to interrogate the prisoner. He and the clerk both bear witness that the fellow was already dead when they entered the cell.'

'Did the guards also witness this?'

For a moment, Sir Thomas gave no reply.

'I know not,' he admitted. 'The matter will be looked into. But you told me you were with the prisoner earlier. If you're attempting to lay an accusation of foul play upon FitzAlan, is it not the case that you had the opportunity to do the same? Did you commit murder by some devious means, Master Foxley?'

'I most assuredly did not and my brother and the guard who came to release me saw the pedlar alive and protesting as I departed the cell. And the clerk with Sir Nicholas: do we know who he was?'

Whilst they were speaking, Seb had been examining the body. He and the coroner and their melancholy charge were now hemmed about by the crowd, closing in and craning necks for a better view of the deceased. 'I pray you,' Seb said to a fellow who jostled closest, 'Aid me in turning the body, if you will.'

The man shrank back, reluctant to touch a corpse, but another obliged, helping Seb lay the body face down.

Seb had no hesitation in lifting the coarse, greying hair of Jake Parslow to reveal his grubby neck. Lice were abandoning the fast-cooling body and Seb was slapping them away as they leapt to his own warm flesh. But this would not take above a few moments. He knew what he was looking for and found it as expected: a mere pin-prick of blood betwixt two vertebrae in the neck.

'There you have the cause of death, Sir Thomas, exactly as found in the case of Piers Creed and young James Penny.'

'I see you knew to look for it,' the coroner said accusingly. 'Are you his killer?'

'I told you, sir, no. I will swear upon the Gospels, if you so require of me. However, I know for certain the perpetrator of this felony.'

'Are you accusing Sir Nicholas FitzAlan, the king's own groom of the chamber? That's outrageous.'

''Tis a fact that he be close involved but the murderer be another: the clerk who accompanied FitzAlan – a man known to me and likeable, such that 'tis hard to credit. It pains me to conclude that the clerk, Lawrence Duffield, did this and worse besides. FitzAlan fetched him from the scriptorium to silence the pedlar who knew of their schemes. The king must be informed directly for this concerns treason.

'But I leave that in your hands, sir. I have other matters to attend to.' With that, Seb pushed through the crowd, all a-gape and stunned by his words, to continue upon his delayed errand to the latrines.

The shocks were not over yet for Seb. As ever, the house of easement was deserted. Few had Seb's respect for the cleanliness of the palace. Having done as required, he became aware of sounds. He was not alone as first thought. Some poor soul was in difficulty, groaning. Leaving the stall, he wondered whether to offer aid or leave whoever it was in peace. After all, what could he do in such a case? As it came to pass, the decision was made for him.

The soul in difficulty was not within a stall, as Seb had supposed. A prostrate form lay not far from the entrance to the place. How could he not have seen it when he came in for he nigh had to step over it in order to leave? For certain, it could not have been there before. He bent to tend the unfortunate and was startled to recognise him.

Lawrence Duffield. The very man he had lately named for a traitor and killer. A length of old but stout rope was tight about his neck.

Seb hastened to remove the rope, his cold fingers clumsy. God be thanked; Lawrence was yet alive and gasped frantically for much-needed air as Seb loosened the noose.

'Who did this to you, Lawrie?' Seb asked, much confused by this occurrence. He aided him to sit, propping him against the wall but he slumped forward and Seb had to hold him up.

Lawrence gave a feeble cough and tried to clear his throat.

'That wretch... the groom,' he croaked, his hands going to the pale red welts across his throat.

'Sir Nicholas? He did this?'

The injured man made no reply but fell limp against Seb's shoulder.

Seb lay him down, rolling his own cloak for a pillow, before seeking assistance.

The crowd at the gatehouse had begun to disperse now that there was naught else to interest their morbid curiosity but Seb's shouts for aid had them running towards the latrines to observe this new calamity.

Sir Thomas Burns abandoned his directions for dealing with Jake Parslow's body and came in haste.

'Another corpse?' the coroner enquired with a sigh.

'Nay, sir, but not so far removed,' Seb told him, leading the way. 'Lawrence Duffield has suffered a close call but lives still.'

'Is this the man you accused not ten minutes since of being

a killer?'

'Aye, the same.'

'Perhaps someone else has drawn that very conclusion and acted upon it. You,' Sir Thomas chose a fellow at random among the gathering of the curious, 'Find Surgeon Curran and bring him. And make haste.'

The young fellow sprinted away. The crowd was fast diminishing. Unlike the open courtyard, the latrine was no place to linger, if it could be avoided, but Seb had grown used to the stink by this time.

'Afore he fell senseless,' Seb continued, 'Duffield said the groom did this to him. I think it likely he refers to Sir Nicholas FitzAlan.'

'I hesitate to suspect a close body servant to the King's Grace but, if you are correct, could this be a falling-out amongst thieves, as it were? A failed attempt to silence a fellow conspirator?'

'It could be, if Sir Nicholas did this? I be uncertain of it, though. Where was Sir Nicholas after he supposedly discovered the pedlar dead in the lock-up?'

'I had his testimony as a first-finder and then he went straightway to inform the king. At least, he said that was his intention.'

'And the clerk with him: what of him?'

'This Duffield?' The coroner frowned at the shallow-breathing form at their feet. 'I paid no attention to him once he had told me his version as a first-finder. Which reports agreed in every detail. Obviously, he came to this foul jakes.'

'I wonder why he did so.'

''Tis plain enough.'

'Nay. The clerks be ill-bred and use any convenient corner within the palace as necessary. Lawrence Duffield be as guilty as any upon that score. I refuse to do likewise and take the trouble to come here... as my colleagues know full well. They make jest of it.' Seb ran his hands through his hair, considering the perplexing events. 'Could it be that it was supposed and intended that I should find Duffield here?' he mused aloud. 'Oddly, I would testify upon oath that he was not lying thus when I entered but was looking to be upon the brink of death within such a short space. In truth, sir, I begin to suspect this was but a mountebank's performance for my benefit; to mislead me.'

Lawrence Duffield stirred and groaned, regaining their attention and in good time as the surgeon arrived, clutching his bag of mysteries.

Lawrence lay abed in the clerks' dormitory. Surgeon Curran had dosed the patient with an elixir to soothe his abused throat and a sleeping draught. Rest was required. And no interrogation! That was the surgeon's order.

What better way to avoid answering questions, Seb thought. But he had already observed the sleeping clerk close enough. The lesions upon the fellow's neck, made by the noose, were deepest at the back, not at the front. If attacked from behind, as might be expected in an attempt at strangulation, the welts in the flesh would be worse across the throat. Conclusion? The noose was pulled tight from the front. Lawrence had been looking at his would-be murderer. There were also the rope burns across Lawrence's palms and the inside of his fingers to be considered.

Seb hated that a man he believed to be a friend could betray everyone, from his king to his fellow clerks, but that was the truth of it. And for what reason? To what purpose, he could not comprehend. Even so, it was now up to him to assemble the facts and prove his case, much as he wished it otherwise.

Another clue had fallen into place when he opened the coffer beside Lawrence's bed to find the wretch a shirt that wasn't befouled from the latrine floor: within lay dozens of the blue packets of pins as sold by the pedlar. Seb was annoyed at not having recalled this far sooner. Jude discovered them days before when they tried to determine whether Seb was alone in having his belongings searched. If only he had remembered that, Lawrence might have been revealed as the traitor earlier – or maybe not. The pins were of no importance afore he knew of the pedlar's involvement, carrying letters folded within the pin-papers. Such a tangled web of intrigue was sufficient to baffle the sharpest mind, as Seb made excuse to himself.

However, one vital object had not yet been uncovered: the murder weapon. But Seb had a feeling he knew where it was. However, he had no intention of seeking it out. That would be a scawager's unsavoury task; a dung-collector could have the likely but dubious honour of finding the weapon in the ordure from the house of easement. Seb realised Duffield had not had time enough to conceal it anywhere else since it was not hidden in the lock-up cell nor found upon his injured person. Dropping it down the shaft from a latrine stall would have taken but a moment.

Instead of returning to his desk in the scriptorium, as he should, to make order of his notes and compile his evidence, Seb set out to enquire as to who was responsible for cleaning the latrines. Nobody in the palace seemed to know. Little wonder then that the place was so befouled. Seb thought the steward or the chamberlain must have overall charge of such matters but each household officer directed him to the other.

The steward said he recalled that the house of easement had been cleansed two years before, or thereabouts, during the king's absence, of course, and could not require further attention so soon when few folk made use of it. But it was naught to do with his office anyway.

The household chamberlain admitted responsibility for cleaning the palace but the latrines, being quite separate, thankfully, were not within his authority. He suggested that Seb speak with the marshal who oversaw the king's stables and the mucking-out thereof.

The marshal said his duty, under the king's master of horse, was to see the stables befitted the fine beasts kept there. It was not his business to see that the courtiers were likewise fittingly housed. He cared not if men lived in squalor, so long as the horses had spotless, comfortable stabling of the highest order.

The falconer with charge of the king's hawks and hunting birds in the mews and the kennel-man, who oversaw the keeping and care of the king's hounds, were both of a similar opinion to the marshal. Wherever Seb turned, it seemed the king's beasts were better housed than his servants. However, when Seb, nigh despairing of his quest, told the kennel-man his reason for wanting the latrines emptied had naught to do with cleanliness and more to do with the possibility of a reward for finding a murder weapon, the fellow became interested.

'How much? This reward.' The man chewed on his nether lip, considering.

'A shilling,' Seb suggested upon the spur of the moment.

The kennel-man shook his head.

'Nah. Not worth the muck and trouble for a shilling. Ten shillings.'

'Impossible. I, er, the king cannot afford so much. Two shillings.'

'For wading in shit up to the armpits! Never. Eight shillings.'

'That be nigh one hundred pence. Far too costly. I shall find a scawager in the city.'

'Nah, master. Not so hasty. I didn't say I wouldn't do it. Half a mark. That's my price.'

'Six shillings and eightpence? 'Tis yet high indeed.'

'Me and two lads will make quicker work of it. Half a mark shared between us is not so much.'

'Oh, very well. You drive a hard bargain,' Seb conceded. 'Half a mark it shall be, if you carry out the task directly.'

'Payment beforehand.' The kennel-man grinned and held out a grubby palm.

In the event, Seb hardly received value for his coin.

The kennel-man did not so much as sully the toes of his

boots but stood back, arms folded, directing two skinny kennel-lads with shovels in the process of emptying the latrines. They began with the stall closest to the door, being the one most often used. For that reason, when needful, Seb preferred the stall at the far end in which the stench was somewhat less vile. But Duffield would have had to be swift in disposing of the weapon before making the pretence of an attempt upon his life. Since Seb found him slumped just within the doorway, the first stall seemed the most likely place.

Within a few shovelfuls, one lad cried out that he had found something. The kennel-man snatched the shovel from the lad and presented it to Seb, covered in muck. A bucket of clean water, fetched from the courtyard conduit by the other lad for the purpose, revealed an enamelled brooch in the shape of the White Lion of March, King Edward's badge. The object was valuable, no doubt, but not a killer's weapon. The kennel-man tucked it into a pouch at his belt. This was proving to be quite a profitable day.

Just a few minutes later – barely time to recite a Paternoster – the other lad shouted. The procedure was repeated. This time, when the filth was washed away, there lay a thin-bladed knife, fine as a needle. Seb had the murder weapon, he was certain. He dismissed the kennel-man and his lads with thanks before taking the knife to the conduit to wash it more thoroughly. The final piece of the puzzle was discovered.

Later that evening

For the third time in a single day, Seb stood in King Edward's privy chamber. Upon this occasion, at least he wore clean, sweet-smelling attire, no reminders of either the noisome lock-up or the stinking house of easement. He was in the company of Sir Thomas Burns, the coroner, to inform the king of the appalling events. Only Lord Hastings and Sir Nicholas FitzAlan were present beside the king. The groom's presence was going to make this an awkward audience indeed.

Having made their courtesies, the coroner stepped back with the king's consent, leaving Seb standing alone in the midst of the tiled floor. He could not have felt more vulnerable if a contingent of archers had surrounded him with drawn bows, prepared to loose their arrows at him at less than five paces distance. How this matter might conclude, he had not the least idea. Despite the blaze in the hearth, he felt chilled, yet sweat dewed upon his upper lip. He wiped it away with his sleeve.

'Y-your Grace… m-my Lord Hastings…' he began, his voice quavering.

'Sir Nicholas, give Master Foxley a stool before he falls down,' the king said.

'I be grateful, indeed, sire,' Seb said, sitting on a finely carven stool with a brocade seat.

'Just get on with it.' King Edward scowled mightily which did naught to calm Seb's jangling nerves. 'I want an end to this business of treason and murder and Sir Thomas and Lord Hastings tell me you have solved it.'

'I believe I have done so, sire, though my solutions do not include any reasons why. I can but describe what has occurred without knowing of any cause.

'I may say with certainty that intelligence has been past betwixt Westminster and the city, carried by the pedlar Jake Parslow, lately deceased. The information was enciphered in otherwise innocuous letters in Italian, folded within packets of pins. I be sure now that the clerk Lawrence Duffield wrote those letters, having made close comparison of his scribal hand in the scriptorium with that of the letters. The numerous packets of pins in his bedside coffer testify to the means of conveying the letters, as I have described.

'Sorrowfully, forwhy I considered Lawrence to be a friend, I must also name him as the murderer of Piers Creed, James

Penny and the pedlar, as well as making an attempt upon my life in collusion with another. The needle-thin blade with which he pierced their necks was retrieved from a stall in the house of easement a few hours since, close by where he was found this afternoon, to all appearances half slain.' Seb turned to the coroner who handed him a linen-wrapped item. Seb unwound the cloth and placed the murder weapon at the king's feet. Now clean, the fine steel stiletto blade glinted ominously.

'As for the other half of this treasonous alliance that signs itself the Esquire of the Ruby and Duffield's partner in crime,' Seb continued, his attention fully upon the king, 'I believe him to be the espier who has listened in on your highness's council meetings and divulged that intelligence which Duffield then encoded into the Italian tongue and dispatched to their master, the Golden Lion, via Lombard Street, using the pedlar as the messenger.'

'What! Who could possibly listen in on Privy Council business? That would require a trusted man.' The king had lost colour, his knuckles white as he gripped the arms of his chair. 'None of my counsellors would dare and none have the slightest connection to Italy. You have it all wrong, Foxley. A pox on you! You must have.'

'It would please me mightily, sire, to be proven in error, but at least the man did not attempt to kill his fellow traitor, though he likely assisted in the pedlar's death and that of Penny.'

'So who else is involved? Who did try to kill this clerk, Duffield?'

'None harmed Duffield but himself, despite what he told me.'

'How do you know? Did the wretch confess?'

'Nay, sire, but when a man fights for his life, struggling to loosen a rope about his neck, he breaks his fingernails and claws at his neck. There were no such signs but rather what appeared to be rope burns across Lawrence's palms and the inside of his fingers, as would happen if he had pulled strenuously upon a rope. Also, the noose was pulled from the front, not from behind, as revealed by the deep gouges on the back of his neck. If strangled from behind, the welts would have been across his throat.

'I believe that Lawrence's near-death was self-inflicted. There was no other involved, no inept would-be killer. The close call was intended. Lawrence did not want to die by his own hand but would make out another tried to end his life. As Sir Thomas Burns suggested: this was a falling-out among thieves – or rather murderers and traitors.

'In truth, I do not believe there to be any reason why Lawrence Duffield may not speak since his throat has suffered so little injury.'

'But to what purpose would he fake his near-death?'

'To avoid questioning, at least for a while. And Lawrence was also hoping to cause his fellow conspirator to carry the burden of guilt as far as possible; to lay the blame at another's feet... upon the espier himself.'

'Name this treacherous devil and be done with it.'

'I fear, my lord, the espier be here with us. Sir Nicholas FitzAlan has betrayed your Grace and planned the abduction of the Prince of...'

Sir Nicholas leapt at Seb, a bejewelled dagger in his hand. The blade descended, shining in the firelight.

There was an instant movement, a flurry of fine cloth, a cry. Who knew that King Edward, despite his size, could act so swiftly when he had need?

Lord Hastings was at the door, yelling for the guards.

The coroner assisted Seb to his feet. He was shaken but unharmed.

The king stood over Sir Nicholas's sprawled form, one royal foot still hard upon the groom's right wrist. The dagger had skittered under the king's chair and the fellow's arm lay in a position Nature had never intended – useless. He was whimpering and making feeble protest but Edward was not inclined to mercy.

'You treasonous cur! How dare you betray me? I put my trust in you, you two-faced Janus; you bloody Judas. You would kill my son! Death is too good for you, you loathsome serpent. You eat my food, sleep in my chamber, wear clothes I provide and then… How could you do this to me? To England?'

'I spit on England,' the groom managed to say betwixt teeth gritted in pain. 'What has England ever done for me? The FitzAlans were the most loyal family and yet what good has it done us? Reduced to poverty, relying on royal whim for charity. Duke Sforza of Milan has already paid me more in three years than you'd pay me in three lifetimes.'

The king stamped on Sir Nicholas's broken arm, making him shriek in agony. He repeated the action twice more – once for each year of the groom's term of betrayal.

Seb could not help but flinch each time in sympathy.

Finally, guards rushed in, halberds at the ready. Then they stood, perplexed, wondering who they should apprehend. The white-faced clerk upon the stool, mayhap? Had they not arrested him before, earlier this day?

'Take this bastard,' the king snarled, indicating the man on the floor by kicking him in the ribs. 'And strip him of his royal livery. I want him in chains in the foulest rat-infested hole you can find. And don't have a care for his injuries – the more, the better. On the morrow, he goes to the Tower to suffer the worst torments that can be devised until he tells all. I will know every detail of their wicked plots.

'Oh, and arrest Secretary Oliver's bloody clerk, Lawrence Duffield. He gets no better treatment but keep them apart. I don't want them concocting some fantastic tale between them. I shall have the truth out of them… even if it kills them,' Edward added, his eyes black and fathomless; no hint of blue.

Seb had not seen this side of the king's character before. The blazing Plantagenet temper was one thing; this ice-cold cruelty was something else. King Edward was truly a man to be feared.

The Clerks' Dormitory

The hour was late by the time the king dismissed Seb – too late to go home. Too late even to go to Jude's lodging in Thieving Lane. With no other choice, he went to his cold bed in the dormitory, hopefully, for the last time. He was done with Westminster, no matter what.

A streak of moonlight through a grimy window was the only illumination but sufficient to see his fellow clerks, each huddled 'neath their blankets. Only Lawrence's bed was empty, a tangle of pale sheet showing white under the moon.

Exhausted, Seb crept to his bed and climbed in without any attempt to undress. He could not cease to shiver, unsure whether the cause was the cold of night, the groom's attack or, more likely, the king's air of menace. He shuddered, unable to forget the face of his monarch as he had witnessed it this eve.

'Seb? Seb. We must talk.' Hal Sowbury was at his bedside. 'They took Lawrence away. Did you know? Called him a murderer. Can you believe it? I can't think how this could be. They've made a grave mistake, for certain.'

Seb gathered his wits and sat up in bed, wrapping the thin blanket around him.

'Nay, Hal. I fear 'tis no mistake. Lawrence deceived us all.'

'Not Lawrie. He wouldn't. He's my friend... and yours.'

'Hal, it grieves me to inform you but Lawrence killed Piers Creed, James Penny and a pedlar who was an accomplice. He, it was, who attempted to kill me more than once. I be that sorrowful...'

'Someone has done this to incriminate him. Lawrie would never harm anyone. I've known him for years. I trust him. But some rascal tried to kill him in the latrines. Mayhap...'

'The only rascal, in that case, was Lawrence himself. In truth, I be too weary for this conversation, Hal. All will be made known on the morrow and, meanwhile, I should make less of my friendship with Lawrence, if I were you, for your own sake. I am truly sorry that this be the way of things but you will hear the truth in the morning, no doubt.' Seb turned away. 'God keep you safe, Hal,' he said as he lay back and pulled the pillow over his ears.

Chapter 17

Friday, the tenth day of February
Westminster

THE FOLLOWING MORN, in the dormitory, before breakfast, Seb did Hal Sowbury the courtesy of telling him all that had come to pass concerning Hal's friend, Lawrence Duffield. Of course, 'twas natural that Hal did not want to believe a word of it. The chief clerk's voice echoed to the rafters with recriminations and curses flung at Seb.

Seb sat silent upon his unmade bed whilst Hal ranted. He had but told the truth and could do naught to sweeten it for Duffield's friend.

Disillusioned and confused, Hal quieted eventually.

'He truly did kill Piers? And James?'

'Aye.'

'In cold blood... and with their sins upon their souls, unshriven?'

Seb nodded.

'Will there be a trial?'

'No doubt.'

'Why would he do those things? I do not understand.'

'Forwhy he was sending intelligence to Italy, he and Sir Nicholas FitzAlan. Piers and James and myself, all unknowing for the most part, had seen the encoded letters they wrote. Discovery had to be avoided. Murder was the result.'

'Lawrie betrayed the king? Why?'

'I know not, Hal. Only he can explain that.'

'He'll be tortured, won't he?'

Seb did not answer, though he knew full well from the king's own lips.

'Shall we go, break our fast, Hal?' Seb suggested. 'I cannot recall when last I ate a meal.'

Together, they went down to the Great Hall, although neither man had much appetite for food nor the company of their fellow clerks. The likelihood of having to retell Lawrence's story to them had no appeal.

Seb allowed Hal to do the telling, making no corrections to the clerk's softer version of the tale which made Lawrence simply a man misled by the real culprit. What did it matter now? He nibbled bread and sipped ale – ashes and vinegar upon his tongue. He gave up the attempt to eat and returned to the empty dormitory.

There, he made a bundle of his few possessions in the bedside coffer and prepared to depart Westminster. If he ever set eyes again upon this miserable place, it would be too soon. He had completed the onerous task set him and paid for by Lord Hastings on the king's behalf. Now he was going home, back to Rose and the children. Back to his proper work at the Sign of the Fox in Paternoster Row. There were all those new commissions to be dealt with and he had lost two weeks of what could have been busy and worthwhile days. His only pleasant thought concerning this last fortnight was that, thanks to his efforts, the little Prince of Wales would be safe from the king's enemies upon his journey to spend Eastertide with his father.

The Foxley House

At Paternoster Row, Seb was greeted like a long-lost love. Rose flung her arms about him, uncaring who saw her zealous gesture of affection.

'Seb, what an unexpected arrival. I never thought to see you before tomorrow's afternoon.' Rose's smile lifted his spirit.

'Sweeting, I could not wait so long, not once my work for Lord Hastings and the king was done.' Seb kissed his new wife, long and tenderly, in no haste to end it until the intervention of two small persons, shouting 'Papa, Papa!', and a tail-wagging dog forced them apart.

'Jude told us you had solved the riddles,' Rose said as Seb set down his bundle of belongings and stooped to greet Dickon and Julia who hung about his legs. Gawain forced his wet nose into the embrace, determined not to be ignored.

'Jude has been here?' Seb ruffled the dog's fur then moved the creature aside so he might kiss Dickon and Julia.

'Aye and still is. He slept the night in his old bed. Let me fetch you ale, husband. Have you broken your fast, as yet?' Rose kissed Seb again, a swan's down brush upon his cheek, just to be certain he understood the rapture of his welcome. As if he might forget.

Jude was still at the board in the kitchen, lingering over a third serving of pickled herrings and newly baked bread – it being Friday and a fasting day. Seb joined him, murmuring a hasty Latin grace over the platter Rose set before him. This time, the food tasted as it should and the ale was sweet and fresh, though he was somewhat hampered by the children, both of whom wished to clamber upon their father's knee. Rose shooed them away, finding Dickon's rag ball to amuse them.

'Leave your father to eat in peace,' she told them before bringing more bread to the table for Seb. 'So, 'tis done at Westminster? You are home to stay?' Rose asked.

'King Edward's own army will not drag me back to that place,' Seb told her when he'd swallowed his mouthful. 'The deceitful complexities of politics I leave to others. I tell you, Rose, there is not a wholly honest man in that dung-heap of Westminster. Overweening ambition, connivance, self-seeking and wickedness... 'tis all there, steaming like the Devil's own cess-pit. Though there will likely be a trial that I may have to attend but that could be held at the Tower or Guildhall. At least, I pray it will be.'

'My poor Seb. You've hated this last task, haven't you?'

''Tis a relief to be home with you, dearest one. How I have longed to see you, sweetheart.'

Jude snorted and pushed his empty platter aside.

'Spare me St Valentine's bloody hearts and flowers, little brother; it's not his feast day 'til next week. Tell me what I missed. You weren't done when I walked out of that damned scriptorium, were you? Did you unmask the killer at last? It was that bastard Sowbury, wasn't it? I knew it!'

'Nay. Hal was innocent. Lawrence Duffield committed the murders.'

'Duffield? Aye, well, I suspected it was one of those two.'

'You were convinced of Le Clerc's guilt at one time.'

'It's only natural to suspect a bloody Frenchman. More ale, Rose.' Jude held out his cup.'

'Pour it yourself, Jude. The jug is full and to hand. I'm not one of your Westminster servitors nor some common tavern wench.' Despite her words, Rose refilled her husband's cup, whether he had need or not, driving home her point like a bodkin from a bow before taking up her cloak and basket. 'Come, Nessie. We need butter and worts from Cheapside market. We shall eat well in these last few days before the Lenten fast.'

The women departed, leaving the children to the care of the menfolk.

The brothers exchanged glances. Seb wondered what Jude had done to earn Rose's disfavour. Likely he would learn of

Jude's transgressions later. He finished his meal, giving the last morsel to Gawain, and made to leave the table, intending to go to the workshop.

Julia had tired of her game with Dickon and tottered over to her father and uncle.

In a most unusual show of avuncular affection, Jude swept the little maid into his arms. It was probably the first time he had seen her so close and she stared, large-eyed, at her uncle.

'Well, little maid, and how... Christ's bloody bones, Seb!' Jude burst out. 'You never told me she was another man's by-blow.'

Seb snatched the child away more roughly than he meant to, setting her howling.

'She is not! Julia be *my* daughter!'

Jude laughed mirthlessly.

'She has mismatched eyes, little brother. Only one devilish rogue in England bears that trait: Gabriel bloody Widowson. That's who. You're as hapless a cuckold as I am. What is it about us Foxleys that other men think they can help themselves to our wives just as they please? Do they think we're so stupid, we won't find them out?'

For months now, Seb had been telling himself that the differing colours of his daughter's eyes were but a trick of the light, if a constant one. And none else in the household ever remarked upon it because all understood the token was not to be spoken of.

'Are you willing to raise another's bastard as your own?' Jude continued. 'I wouldn't. Get rid of her.'

'How dare you suggest...' Seb spluttered, outraged. 'Julia be an innocent. I cannot blame her for the sin of her begetting.' He stroked the infant's chestnut curls – so like her mother's – to soothe her whimpering.

Gawain growled. Being their self-appointed protector, he had no liking for raised voices when the little ones were involved.

'Likely, she'll be as wayward as Widowson and as contrary as the Moody Mare ever was.' Jude used the insulting name by which he always referred to his brother's late wife, Emily.

'We shall raise her as our own, to be courteous and obedient. She be family, no matter what you think or say.'

'We? You mean you and Rose? Well then, you're mad, little brother. Consider the cost of raising another man's sprig. She's not of your blood. Not one single drop, you fool.'

Seb said naught, shaking his head.

'Disown her. Give her to the Sisters of Charity,' Jude insisted, grabbing Seb by the shoulder and setting the dog growling again. 'One payment and she'll be off your hands forever. You can forget about her.'

'Julia be *my* daughter and there's an end to it.' Seb's raised voice came as a shock. 'One more word upon the matter from you, Jude, and you shall be the one disowned.' Still with the child in arms, Seb strode to the workshop. With one wary glance at his uncle's stormy countenance, little Dickon quietly followed his father along the passage, his rag ball in his hands. Gawain came along behind.

In the workshop, whilst Ralf and Kate were at their desks, diligent at their allotted tasks, Adam was huffing and muttering over a pile of papers.

'Seb! God be praised. I heard your voice. Now you can sort out this mess. So many commissions... so much work... I know not where to begin. There's this book of John Lydgate's verse due to be delivered first thing next week and 'tis barely half stitched, the binding not started. And this... and these...' Adam brandished the open order book and a sheaf of loose papers under Seb's nose. 'In truth, cousin, we have neither room enough nor scribes to do so many. Ralf's doing the work of three men, as am I, and Kate has to labour like a journeyman.'

Seb took a deep breath to calm anger. How dare Jude...? He murmured a silent Ave Maria to steady himself, forcing aside his ill-humour with his brother afore attempting to recall their present business and situation.

'Adam. What of the contract for the Bishop of Bath and

Wells' portrait? Did you get the legal side of the matter set down?'

'Not yet. There's been no opportunity. We need more hands here, Seb.'

'I know and have given much thought to the problem,' Seb said. He leafed through the papers with his free hand but Julia tried to grab them, so he set her down.

'Thinking about it doesn't help, Seb. You must do something practical, such as taking up a pen and getting some work done yourself. All this time you've spent away from the workshop…' This was no way for a journeyman – even a kinsman – to speak to his master but Seb knew Adam was right.

'Give me leave, cousin. Another hour and I shall return.'

'But Seb! Hey! Don't leave the babes with us. They cause no end of…'

Seb was gone once more, taking Gawain, leaving Adam angry and despairing. This was not the way a workshop should be run, with the master never present and toddlings running amok amidst the desks. His patience was so sorely tried. Then he thought of that idle rogue, Jude, doing naught to earn his keep, despite being fully trained as a scribe and book-binder. Why should he not finish stitching and binding the Lydgate book in readiness for Monday? That would be one less task to do.

Adam went to the kitchen in search of his quarry.

As expected, Jude was lounging on a bench, feet up on the board, swigging ale.

'Get up, you lazy oaf. We're working our fingers to the bone in the workshop.'

'So? It's nothing to do with me how my brother manages his affairs.'

'That's the trouble: he isn't managing his affairs at all and hasn't been for these two weeks past. You get free board and lodging here of late. The least you can do is help us in our labours. There's a poetry volume needs binding…'

'Go to hell, Adam. I don't work for my brother and I certainly don't work for you, cousin.' How was it that Jude could make so foul an insult of the word 'cousin'?

'What do you do, then? You're a damned parasite, Jude Foxley, living off the charity and goodwill of others at every turn.'

As ever, with these two hot-blooded kinsmen, the quarrel turned to violence. Blows were exchanged, resulting in grazed knuckles, bloody noses and swollen lips. Rose's tidy kitchen was soon littered with splintered furnishings, shattered pots and dented pans.

A bucketful of icy water ended it, setting the combatants spluttering.

Rose was returned from Cheapside.

'Out, you knaves. Out of my kitchen this instant,' Rose cried. 'And don't ask me to tend your hurts and salve your bruises. See what you've done! How am I supposed to prepare dinner amongst this wreckage with all my pots broken? Seb will throw the pair of you out on the street and serve you right. Where is that husband of mine?'

'The Lord only knows,' Adam muttered, righting a stool and slumping down on it. He took a spotless napkin to dry his face and dabbed at his bloody lip. 'Reckon you've loosened my teeth, you devil,' he snarled at Jude.

'Good. I'm glad of it. You'll not forget your place again, you upstart cur.' Jude wiped gory snot from his nose with his sleeve and examined his skinned knuckles, flexing his fingers – not broken, at least. Water yet dripped from his fair hair.

'Go away, both of you. Take your disagreements elsewhere. I must put my kitchen straight, may St Mary aid me. Look what you've done to the best ale jug! Broken beyond repair. And I'll have to ask Stephen Appleyard or Jack to mend this bench. Men! Why God didn't give you the sense he gave a sheep, I'll never know. Nessie, fetch the broom…'

Seb entered the kitchen by the back door. His moment was ill-chosen indeed. He retreated swiftly, back out to the yard, doing his best to block his young companion's view of the chaos.

'We shall go by way of the shop door, Hugh, 'tis more direct,' Seb said.

'Looks like a battle took place in there,' the young man said, having seen more than Seb hoped.

'Aye. My brother and our cousin be the cause, no doubt. A wolf and a wild cat be more amicable than those two.' He sighed. 'I fear, if you should choose to work for me, Hugh, 'tis a fact to which you must become reconciled.'

Hugh Gardyner chuckled.

'I have elder brothers just as bad. And two of my fellows in apprenticeship to Master Collop knock each other about like skittles whenever master isn't watching. Fear not, Master Foxley, I'm used to such conflicts. I am eager for this trial in your workshop. Master Collop says I could not do better than become your journeyman when my term of apprenticeship ends soon.'

They entered the shop. Kate was serving a customer, showing the woman a Latin primer in a soft leather covering. The lass's eyes brightened with joy when she saw Hugh.

Seb didn't appear to notice but doffed his cap to the customer. Hugh followed his example.

'You may change your mind, Hugh,' Seb went on, 'When you discover how many commissions we have in hand and, as you be aware already, matters do not always proceed as smoothly as we desire.'

'I enjoy a challenge, Master Foxley,' Hugh said, winking at Kate who smiled at him and nigh forgot the customer she was supposed to be serving.

'Aye, and likely you will find it here,' Seb said. He straightened some pamphlets upon the counter board where a breeze had disturbed them.

'My hope is that you'll approve my work and want to keep me.'

'You come with Master Collop's recommendation. He speaks most highly of you and I have always found his judgement sound. Come through to the workshop, Hugh, and I will show you your desk and our way of working.'

If Seb had hoped to impress Hugh with a busy workshop, abuzz with activity, he was disappointed. The only one at work was Ralf, bent over his desk, working methodically at his transcription.

'Ralf, this be Hugh Gardyner, come to aid us in our time of need. He has nigh completed his apprenticeship and Master Collop sends him with compliments and glowing recommendations to ease our load. Hugh, meet Ralf Reepham, a fine journeyman and worker of small miracles with gold leaf. You may learn much from him.'

The two men, the ageing and the youthful, greeted each other warmly.

'We've met, of course, lad,' said Ralf, his Norfolk burr obvious. 'A good scribe is ever welcome. I could do with a bit of help, as you see. Could you rule up some more pages for me, according to this template? Young Kate was doing it but had to tend to a customer.'

Seb showed Hugh to the spare desk, used in the past by Tom Bowen before his employment had ended abruptly and resulted in tragedy. The lad's initials were carven deep in the wood: the only memorial to that unhappy youth. Seb hoped Hugh's time with them would result in joy rather than sorrow. He laid a selection of quills for Hugh's use, an inkpot and the straight edge required for ruling pages, along with pins and string.

Ralf passed him the template and Hugh began his work, smiling broadly.

Seb observed for a moment, noting the lad's methods for coping without a thumb upon his right hand. Despite the appearance of awkwardness and being cack-handed, Hugh worked fast and efficiently, pricking through the pages so the lines were marked the same on every sheet. Such a task was more usually performed by a junior apprentice, not one upon the eve of completing his term, but it would serve as a means of settling Hugh into his new place.

Seb wondered at the wide smile, though. Was it for the pleasure of coming to work at the Sign of the Fox? He suspected not – not wholly, leastwise. Kate was a more likely cause for there was the possibility of a betrothal betwixt the youngsters when Kate's father, Alderman Edmund Verney, and Hugh's guardian and uncle, ex-Lord Mayor Gardyner, could come to an agreement. Apparently, money was the thorny issue, as was so often the way of such things.

Having seen the newcomer settled, Seb turned his attention to the Lydgate poetry book required for Monday next, half stitched. It was a long while since he had last stitched and bound a book, illumination being his particular task, and he felt out of practice. The pages were already fixed in the press with the stout linen strengtheners in place, hard against the comb around which the stitches would be evenly spaced. Jude had always been good at this particular task but there was another who owed him a favour or two: his neighbour, Jonathan Caldicott.

Jonathan's shop was next door, adjoining Seb's house, where the fellow did naught but collate, stitch and bind books written by others. His work was of a reasonable standard, if not the very best. Jonathan was rarely busy and, therefore, ever in debt. What money he earned ran through his hands like water through a holed pot. Seb had lost count of the times and the amount of coin he had lent to his neighbour. Every quarter day, when the rent fell due, Jonathan would come knocking, begging a few groats or a shilling or so to make up the deficit. Seb owned his own place so never had that concern.

At Christmas last, the Caldicotts had been in worse difficulties than usual, being a quarter mark short on the rent – which was nigh the whole of the sum required. Seb had paid it in full, having been reassured that repayment would be made in haste. Indeed, threepence of the three shillings and sixpence owed had been repaid at Epiphany, only to begged back on the twelfth day of January when Mary Caldicott broke the wooden sole of her patten overshoe in the first snow and required a new pair. Not so much as a farthing had been forthcoming since. No doubt but Jonathan would return, pleading for monetary assistance for charity's sake, come Lady Day next month, when rents fell due once more.

Having determined upon the matter, Seb picked up the weighty stitching device in his arms, with the thick wedge of pages still aligned in place, and carried it from the workshop.

'What in the name of Creation are you doing?' Adam asked as Seb squeezed past him, almost tripping over Gawain in the workshop doorway. 'Where are you taking our stuff?'

'To another pair of hands. Fear not, I be reducing our workload and labour, as well as making more room in the workshop.'

Adam watched him go, fearing his cousin was run mad. Events at Westminster had addled his wits for certain.

Jonathan Caldicott's shop

'God give you good day, Jonathan,' Seb greeted his neighbour.

'What do you want, Foxley?' The discourteous response indicated Jonathan's fear that Seb was about to demand the repayment of money. 'Business has been slow of late. I'm owed considerable sums by my customers. And the wretched cat pissed on the new binding leather to its ruination. I'll have to buy more.' The excuses flowed readily and in advance of any request for coin being made.

Seb put the heavy device on the counter board which sagged alarmingly 'neath the weight, so he moved it to the floor.

'I have not come to ask for the money you owe me, Jonathan. Rather, I have a proposition for you.'

'Proposition?' Jonathan's eyes narrowed. 'What do I want wi' propositions? Likely, it'll cost me coin I don't have.'

'It will cost you naught, save a little rearrangement.'

'I don't like the sound of that.'

''It may be to your advantage.'

'Oh? How come? Nothing, er, underhand is it? I don't want no trouble wi' the law. I can't be doing wi' paying fines and that. Can't afford it.'

'Nay. Naught of the kind. What say you, Jonathan, if I propose paying your quarterly rents, in full, from henceforth?'

'And why would you do that? I don't understand. You'd be wanting something from me in exchange, I know.'

'May we speak of this privily, without half Paternoster Row learning of our business?'

Grudgingly, Jonathan led Seb through to the kitchen. His goodwife, Mary, sat by the feeble fire, plying her needle over some mending. Seb noted that the work – like the poky kitchen – was not particularly neat. Mistress Caldicott couldn't hold a candle to Rose's expertise as a needlewoman.

Seb greeted her, touching his cap, but she ignored both him and his mannerly gesture.

'Bring us ale, woman,' Jonathan told her. 'Then be gone. We have a matter to discuss which is none of yours. And don't go gossiping about it either.'

'How can I tell of it when I don't know what it's about? And if it involves money, tell him we haven't got any since you lost it in that foolish wager. Playing knuckle-bones, indeed, at your age.' The plump woman rolled up her mending anyhow, poked the needle into it as if to kill it and stuffed it behind a stool.

Two dusty cups were slammed down upon the rickety board that served as a table and an earthen jug with a chipped spout, hardly containing three finger-breadths of cloudy ale, was set beside them. No wafers nor cakes were offered. Christian hospitality was as scarce as courtesy in this house.

Jonathan wiped the cups out on a stained, grey-tinged napkin, fraying at the edges.

'Help yourself to drink,' he told Seb.

More than three hours passed before Seb returned to his own workshop. Having missed dinner, he wore a look of considerable satisfaction upon his face.

Adam, Ralf and Hugh were all at their desks, pens busy. Kate was with customers in the shop.

'You look pleased with yourself, cousin.' Adam glanced up from the page he was working on. His lip was badly swollen, a clot of dark gore forming a scab upon the injury. 'So, what have you done now? Won at dice?'

'Better than that, Adam. I have taken on new premises and employed another journeyman. Also, we shall have the contracts drawn up and signed at Stationers' Hall by this time next week. 'Tis all in hand.'

'You haven't been idle then? Who's the new man? And where's this new place? Convenient, I trust?'

'It could not be more so. We now have the use of Jonathan Caldicott's shop next door and he will do all our stitching and binding.'

'But Seb, the fellow's workmanship isn't good enough for us.'

'It will be, else he shall not receive his wage. He and I have discussed the matter at length. I deem him capable enough, so long as I keep watch upon his standards and make certain his materials be of best quality. For the present, I shall pay his quarterly rents but he and Mary may live there so long as he works exclusively as my journeyman. If he wishes to labour for anyone else, I shall require a token payment of rent from him.'

'In which case, I doubt you'll ever see a penny of it.' Adam was unimpressed by this new arrangement. 'And what of the landlord who owns his house? Is he agreeable to this?'

'Oh, aye. The good dame in question be well pleased. In truth, she has already suggested that I could purchase the place outright and save her the trouble of dealing with unreliable tenants.'

'Who is she?'

'Dame Ellen Langton, our own dear lady. She holds the leases on other places along Cheapside and says she be too old to suffer the annoyance of Caldicott's lack of payment and the upkeep of a building when, in his case, the tenant makes so little effort himself.'

'How fortunate for you. And will you buy it?'

'With the money from Lord Hastings – of which a goodly sum yet remains – and payment for Bishop Stillington's portrait – when I get to it – I believe my finances will allow it. But I needs think on the matter and discuss it with Rose afore I decide. All in good time, Adam. All in good time.'

Chapter 18

Saturday, the eleventh day of February
The Foxley House

IT BEING A HALF-DAY, at the dinner hour, Seb was about to put up the shutter on the shop and pay his employees' weekly dues when Jonathan Caldicott rushed through the shop door, book in hand.

'It's done,' he cried, waving the volume like banner. 'Where's my wages? And money for materials is extra.'

'Patience, I pray you, Jonathan. I have paid no one as yet. Besides, I will be certain of the workmanship first.' Seb took the book to the doorway where the light was best. He examined the stitchery, the execution of the binding and the embossing the customer had required. Every detail was observed minutely – without comment.

'Come on, Foxley, you owe me. That's a good piece o' work, that is.'

Seb passed the book to Adam, since his cousin was so doubtful about taking on Jonathan as a journeyman.

'What do you think, Adam?'

Adam repeated the close inspection, running his fingers along the raised design, feeling for undesired discrepancies, slight wrinkles in the wine-red leather or dirt trapped in the glue betwixt the wood and leather layers.

'It will do, I suppose,' he admitted, returning the book to Seb. 'Though the metal corners at the bottom are misaligned.'

'What! They never are. I took an age over getting them straight.'

'See for yourself.' Adam returned the book to Jonathan who scoffed at the criticism of his handiwork.

'A hair's breadth... if that. Nobody'll notice.'

'God will notice,' Seb said.

'God ain't the damned customer.'

'At the Sign of the Fox, we work as though He is. I will put the corners to rights myself this afternoon. Otherwise, this book will do – just. For the future, I expect you to pay attention to every detail.'

'That embossing is bloody beautiful: took me an age, that did.'

'You did well with that, I grant,' Seb said, ever fair in judgement.

'So, where's my pay and cost of materials?' Jonathan held out a greedy hand. 'Two days' work...'

'Two *half*-days,' Seb corrected. 'You did not begin until after I left you yesterday, which was nigh unto the dinner hour, and a morning's work this day is all.'

'And materials.'

'Nay. We supplied those: the leather, wood, linen and metal fixings.'

'Not the stitching thread. That was mine. And I used my own embossing tool and glue.'

'I doubt so little cost a farthing.' Seb took a groat from his purse and a few pence beside. Usually, he paid the wages from the coin box in the shop but did not wish Jonathan to have knowledge of their takings nor where they were kept. He did not trust him so far. 'Here. Seven pence. That far outweighs both your earnings and expenses but take it as a gesture of goodwill.'

Jonathan snatched the money with a scowl and ill grace, omitting any gesture of thanks but hastening to take his leave.

Seb called him back.

'Wait. Here, take Monday's work.' Seb gave him a set of

loose folios. 'Those require collating and trimming afore you commence stitching. The book is to have a soft cover only. Adam will bring you the leather Monday morn, when we have it. And my wife, Rose, may call by any time to check your stitching thereof, she being an expert glover and thus understanding such details better than any.'

'No woman will oversee my work.'

'Indeed she will.'

'He's going to give us naught but trouble, cousin,' Adam said when Jonathan was gone. 'You'll regret the day, Seb.'

'Mayhap, but Jonathan knows the penalty if he fails me: he and Mary shall lose their home. They will not want that.'

'And neither will you, in which case I'll wager your soft heart will get the better of you. Jonathan will likely rely on that and abuse your charity. Buy the house over the wretch's head and put him out. Be done with him, his miserable wife and their troublesome chickens. Recall what one of their damned birds did to our workshop not so long since. Jonathan hasn't compensated you yet for the damage done.'

Seb held up his hands to bid Adam cease his ranting.

'You speak truly, I admit, but every man deserves a second chance.'

'Second chance! More likely a fifth, sixth or seventh, one way or another.'

'Aye, then so be it. Now, let me see to paying the wages of those most deserving...' Seb said, taking the coin box down from its place on the shelf. 'Ralf... sixpence per day for six days...' He counted out three shillings worth of coins and gave them to the old journeyman who touched his cap in acknowledgement and thanks.

Evening came. Having attended choir practice in St Paul's to appease the precentor, Seb was now sitting by the fire in the parlour, Gawain snoozing at his feet. He was reading a book concerning ways of preparing pigments for painting, using linseed oil instead of egg tempera – an intriguing notion, indeed. A Netherlandish artist, Jan van Eyck, had used this method for painting portraits half a century ago and Seb was considering whether to try it. He would need to practise mixing and applying these oil paints, learning their nature and use. On the other hand, the book told that they took months to dry, unlike tempera which dried whilst a man recited the Paternoster and an Ave. Did he have so much time to spare, waiting to put on the next layer of colour? Maybe not with so many commissions in hand, but it was a possibility for the future.

Rose stood by the hearth, brushing dried lavender out of their Sunday best clothes, ready for church on the morrow. As the tiny flowers fell into the fire, the pleasant scent of lavender filled the parlour. Kate sat darning her stocking by candlelight. The little ones were already abed, cosy in their cradle. Nessie was in the kitchen, chopping worts, ready for dinner on the Lord's Day.

Jude had disappeared, off to some tavern or other, no doubt. Adam was gone home to Mercy and the children in Distaff Lane, Ralf was visiting his widowed friend Joanie and Hugh was returned to his uncle's fine house in Poultry. All was peaceful in the Foxley household.

Gawain stirred and awakened, alerted by some sound a man could not hear. Seb gave the dog a soothing pat without looking up from his reading and turned the page.

A great crash and a screech from Nessie in the kitchen startled them all.

'What has she done now?' Rose said, sighing and laying aside Seb's best doublet. She went along the passage to find out the reason for Nessie's cry. Kate, eager to leave her mending, went also.

But Gawain would not be quieted. The creature stood with ears laid back, tail down and teeth bared. Why he should behave so for some mishap in the kitchen, Seb could not understand.

He marked the place in his book with a parchment strip and closed it.

Once out in the passage, he could hear Rose speaking loudly and clearly:

'Whoever you are, my husband isn't here. He is attending choir practice at St Paul's across the way. I do not expect him home for another hour at least.'

A growl rumbled in Gawain's throat. Seb hushed him, wondering why Rose had lied concerning his whereabouts.

'Then I'll wait,' a man's voice replied. 'I am a patient man.'

Seb turned and led the dog to the front door. He opened it, thanking the saints that he remembered to keep the hinges well greased with lard, such that it opened silently. He went out into the dark street.

In the light from the torch burning beside his door, he espied a couple of urchins making mischief, throwing stones at a cat. Seb would have chastised them for their cruelty in the normal way of things but, instead, he gave them a penny and promised another after, if they fetched the City Bailiff, Thaddeus Turner, from Guildhall.

'Make haste. Tell Bailiff Turner that Master Foxley has an intruder in his house and the womenfolk be endangered. He will know where to come,' Seb instructed the lads.

The pair ran off. Seb could but hope they wouldn't abscond with the penny and not bother to deliver the message. Whatever the case, the women were in the kitchen with a stranger and must not remain so.

'Come, Gawain, we have work to do.' Seb lifted the torch from the sconce to light his way and he and the dog went down the alleyway to the side gate which gave entrance to their yard. A night creature rustled in the garden plot somewhere in the darkness and the laughter of revellers sounded from The Panyer Inn at the end of the street.

In the yard, a thin shaft of light came from the back door to the kitchen, showing it was not quite closed. Since the door opened inwardly, if he shoved it wide of a sudden, he should have the element of surprise upon this patient stranger. He wondered who it could be. And why had Rose lied to the fellow, saying he was not at home? She must have good reason.

Seb tip-toed across the cobbles with Gawain close at his knee. Supposing the stranger intended harm? He went to the woodpile under the lean-to with its canvas awning and chose a good straight log, not too thick, such that he could have a firm grip upon it. Thus, he was armed, if need be. If not, then he was but fetching more wood for the fire. He set aside the torch, leaning it up against the water trough. It would be ready, if required. Though never a man renowned for aggression, he braced himself and moved to the back step, testing the weight of the makeshift club in his hand. He dared delay no longer.

Seb put his shoulder to the door and burst in. Gawain barged betwixt his legs, barking, claws clattering as his paws slipped on the flagstones.

'Gawain, down!' Seb ordered.

Such a scene faced man and dog.

The stranger stood, leaning against the chimney, half in Nessie's chimney-corner where the wench slept. He held Nessie close, her back against him, the long kitchen knife, stained green with worts, pressed to her neck. She looked frozen in terror.

Rose and Kate were seated at the table, up against the wall with the board, strewn with chopped leeks, cabbage and the end of a wedge of cheese, forced close, keeping them in their place. Kate was sobbing. Rose had one arm about the young lass. If anger had a face, Rose wore it now.

'Seb. About time,' the stranger said. 'And drop that lump of wood.'

Seb did as he was told, the rough-hewn log thumping on the floor. The moment of surprise was passed.

'Who is this devil that invades our home, Seb?' Rose demanded.

It took Seb a few moments to realise he knew the man, so

greatly had his appearance changed in just a day – filthy, clothes torn, his features bruised and gashed, his hair tangled.

'Lawrence Duffield,' Seb said, his tone sounding flat, giving no hint of his racing heart. Now was not the moment to succumb to inner turmoil.

'I prefer Lorenzo, as my mother named me.'

'I care not what you prefer. Lay down that knife and get out of my house.'

'Ah. I see this wench means little to you. Suppose I hold the blade to your wife's lovely neck? We've all heard you singing of your love for her.'

Lawrence shoved Nessie away in one swift movement, so she fell to the floor and grabbed Rose, pulling her from behind the table.

Seb gasped but Rose made no sound, though her eyes blazed. She was not a woman to be cowed in her own kitchen.

Lawrence looked exhausted and slumped upon the nearest bench, forcing Rose to sit beside him. She cast a hasty glance down and to the side, repeating it. What did she mean?

Seb risked a glance also. He noted that the bench, one leg broken earlier by Jude and Adam in their quarrel, was propped precariously upon two blocks of wood.

'How did you escape? Why are you here? What do you want, Lawrence?'

'How I got away from a few drunken fools on a Saturday eve is no great tale. Like most of their kind, my guards were inept, incompetent. What does it matter? I need money and safe passage out of England. You can arrange that. I know you have Italian connections. Otherwise, I'll make you a widower a second time. And it won't end there. Have you heard of *vendetta*?'

'My sister-by-marriage spoke of it once, I recall. I know not its meaning.' Seb inched closer.

'Well you shall learn its meaning first hand, if I'm executed over this because it will be all your fault. Vendetta is a blood feud. My family will seek vengeance upon you and yours down the generations. Your children will never be safe.'

'I cannot imagine the family of a respectable Englishman behaving so.'

Duffield laughed humourlessly.

'As you say, my father's family is unlikely to take retribution but my mother's brothers, being Milanese, will have other ideas. As will my sons and cousins and my wife's kinsmen also. Italians have long memories. My godfather was Francesco Sforza and his grandson, Lorenzo, the Golden Lion himself, will avenge my death for the excellent service I have done him.'

'How come you have connections to so noble a family in Italy? Your speech sounds only of England.' Seb was intrigued, despite the situation. Besides: keep the man talking and who could say what chance might offer.

'My father was a cleric, a deacon, serving in the household of old King Henry of blessed memory. When the king fell into madness, my father was sent upon a pilgrimage to Rome to pray for his recovery. This my father did but, upon his homeward journey, he fell sick of the ague and was forced to rest and recover in Milano. As a priest upon a pilgrimage, Francesco Sforza was honoured to give him hospitality. Whether it was in the delirium of fever or the enchantment of my mother who nursed him, my father fell into temptation. I was the result. My mother, Maria, was Francesco's daughter by a courtesan, said to be more lovely than Helen of Troy. My father dared not return home a disgraced priest, so he remained in Milano, doing all he could to serve the Sforzas and make amends. He taught me English and Latin. My mother taught me Italian.

'When news came to us nine years ago, that this Edward of York had slain King Henry at the Tower of London, it broke my father's heart and killed him as surely as if a Yorkist sword had pierced his breast for he ever loved the old king whom he had served. When I was of age, my mother bade me come to England to seek *vendetta*, both for my father and the House of Lancaster. Lorenzo Sforza gave me money and his blessing, along with a secondary purpose: to keep him informed of doings at the English court with permission to take revenge upon York and, if it should happen to benefit Milano, then that was all to the good. Your so-called king plans to invade Scotland this summer coming. That will draw French Louis to the north to aid his ally against England. With French interest turned from Italy, Piedmont will be Lorenzo's for the taking, as he has long desired.'

'But what of your plot to slay the Prince of Wales? What has that to do with Piedmont or aught else?'

Duffield only smiled.

'I see,' Seb said softly. 'This be your act of *vendetta* against King Edward, revenging your father's death?'

Duffield nodded.

'Then you be worse than a traitor to your king, Duffield. You deserve to die and naught that I may do shall help you avoid that fate.' Seb took a step closer to the table board and idly fingered the chopped leeks, picking up a pale green circle of onion-tasting flesh and eating it raw.

'Not *my* king. He is a Yorkist devil.'

'He was crowned and anointed by God!'

Duffield shifted a little on the bench, his thoughts returning to the present.

'Enough talk. I have a blade at your wife's throat, Foxley. Do you forget that? I have nothing to lose: she'll be just another useless body to add to the list.'

'How many innocents have you slain?' Seb reached out for the piece of cheese.

'Too many for her to make any difference. You want her death on your conscience? It won't weigh on mine, I can tell you.'

'What is it that you think I could do to prevent you? I be but a scribe – a man of the pen, not the sword.' Seb could see Rose's expression of horror at his seemingly-nonchalant words. He took the cheese in his right hand and let his arm hang loose at his side. He felt a cool dampness press against his fingers but kept his eyes on Duffield. He moved back a half step to a better position.

'You will give me food, money, decent clothing. I look like a scoundrel in these rags.'

'You *are* a scoundrel.'

'I need passage on a ship –'

'Fetch!' Seb shouted and threw the cheese under the table.

Gawain, having waited patiently, his snout nigh in his master's cheese-scented hand, leapt to retrieve his favourite morsel, jumping over the end of the bench where Duffield sat, holding Rose.

Startled, Duffield jerked away from the dog in full flight, tipping the bench off its makeshift supports. The bench toppled and he tumbled to the floor. Rose fell on top of him, beating him with her fists.

Seb grabbed the kitchen knife and cast it aside, into the basket filled with linen awaiting washday from which he took a bedsheet.

'Rose, you may leave off now,' he said, standing ready with the crumpled sheet.

Rose complied reluctantly.

It took all four of them – Seb, Rose, Kate and Nessie – to wind the sheet around Duffield as he flayed and cursed, securing it with Seb's belt, pinioning the wretch's arms within the linen 'til he was bundled up like a pudding. For good measure, Kate took one of Julia's soiled napkins from the basket and stuffed it in his mouth to end the litany of foul words pouring forth in English and Italian. Now Duffield could do naught but drum his heels upon the floor, uselessly. He soon tired of hurting his feet against stone.

Rose stepped back to admire their handiwork, dusting off her hands as for a task well done. Now her assailant lay helpless, she had her revenge, kicking him hard in the ribs.

Nessie wanted her own retribution and spat in his face,

watching in satisfaction as the gobbet of spittle slid across his nose and into his left eye socket, knowing he couldn't wipe it away.

'That's for scarin' me t' death, you stinkin' fat mouldywarp.' She could think of nothing worse to call him but name him for that troublesome little creature that was forever digging up mounds of earth in the garden plot. It was hardly comely behaviour or language for the Foxley household but neither Seb nor Rose reprimanded her.

'As for you…' Rose turned to Seb, her hands on her hips. 'What do you think you were about, eh? You practically gave him permission to slit my throat.'

'Nay, sweetheart, I did no such thing but I had to keep him talking, did I not? I was but distracting him. You know that.'

Rose gave him a doubtful look and shook her head, causing Seb to wonder what he had said amiss and trying his best to recall his precise words to Duffield.

Fortunately for Seb, at that moment of awkwardness, Thaddeus Turner hastened into the kitchen accompanied by two stalwart constables and trailed by the pair of urchins, eager for their promised reward.

'Thaddeus, God be praised. You be a welcome sight, my friend,' Seb greeted the bailiff.

'What's this?' Thaddeus poked the sheeted form lying on the floor with a stout, muddy boot.

'A traitor, a murderer and an espier. He escaped from the king's custody; I know not how. He was on his way to the Tower to await trial.'

'An espier, eh? Don't think I've had one of those in custody before, not that I know of, leastwise. How come he's in your kitchen?'

''Tis a long tale but the short of it is that he threatened to kill Rose…'

'And me.' Nessie added her pennyworth.

'Aye, and Nessie also,' Seb said. 'He has killed three people at Westminster, of which I know for certain, and more besides, maybe. Lord Hastings employed me to find out this murderer and his fellows in treason. I have done so and this be the outcome.'

'So he is not yet tried and condemned?'

'Nay.'

'But you have him ready shrouded for the grave. It's as well to be prepared beforehand.' Thaddeus was grinning at his own grim jest. 'Does the devil have a name?'

'Lawrence Duffield was his name at the scriptorium in Westminster but he prefers to be addressed as Lorenzo, so he says.'

'A foreigner as well! This gets ever more interesting. Get him on his feet,' Thaddeus instructed the constables. 'Come on, Lorenzo, you great sack of turds. It's the Guildhall lock-up for you until the king sends his men to collect you. If they don't bother by Monday, I'll hang you myself.'

'Be wary of him. He be slippery as an eel and more cunning than a serpent.'

'Fear not, Seb. He's in safe hands now. He won't escape us. Put the ropes on him before we go outside,' the bailiff told his men.

The constables had brought ropes and quickly made a noose of each which they slipped around Duffield's neck.

'Any attempt to flee or otherwise misbehave and the ropes shall pull tight. I don't care whether you die tonight or at the king's pleasure. Now get moving.'

'I want that sheet returned when you've finished with it,' Rose called out as Thaddeus and the others departed. 'It's my best linen. Oh, and Seb will want his belt and my daughter has need of the napkin.' She closed the kitchen door and leaned against it, blowing out a sigh. 'Ale for all,' she said, having to ladle the drink from a bowl, since the jug was broken earlier that day. She handed the urchins a treenware beaker each, seeing they deserved it, having run to Guildhall and back.

Seb paid the urchins their penny and thanked them for their service.

'We're goin' t' watch the bugger swing, master,' one lad said. 'Will yer let us know the day?'

'You be of an age to be at your school books, not waiting around at the gallows-tree,' Seb said. 'Now get you home. The hour grows late and your parents will be concerned for you.' He fetched the torch which he had left in the yard. Its flame had died and he rekindled it at the hearth before putting it back in its sconce by the front door to light the way for passers-by, observing the urchins as they scampered off, into the dark, turning into Bladder Street and the Shambles.

'Thank the Lord Jesu that ended as well as it did,' Rose said, sitting on a stool and sipping her ale. 'Have a care with that bench, Seb,' she reminded him as he was about to sit on the broken form, now propped once more on wooden blocks.

'I was that scared,' Kate admitted.

'And me,' said Nessie. 'Nearly wet meself, didn't I?'

'Gawain saved us all, didn't you, lad?' Kate was making much fuss of the dog. 'Wait until I tell Hugh about it. He'll be shocked to hear how imperilled I was and so glad to see me safe.'

Seb nodded. Hearing the lass speak of Hugh, seeing the spark in her eyes, it was pleasing to know how she felt about the young man who, God willing, would become her husband one day. Aye, God willing, Seb thought. But what of Duffield's threats? This *vendetta*? Were any of them safe now? Were the children's lives to be blighted for the future? He prayed they would not be. After all, this was civilised England, not barbarous Italy. He refused to dwell upon the matter.

The events had to be retold when Ralf came home, having passed a pleasurable eve with Joanie, his widow friend. Seb said little, leaving the women to tell the story. Now the danger was done, they seemed to be making light of the encounter, laughing as Kate recounted how, with Gawain's aid, they had got the better of the ferocious felon. Seb's part was scratched out and obliterated, like a mistake in a manuscript. He did not mind but was glad of it.

Weary, he returned to the parlour, threw a fresh log on the fire, arranged the cushion in the fine chair that had been a gift from the Duke of Gloucester and took up his book. He hoped Jan van Eyck's ventures in oil painting would distract his thoughts before bed. But, as was ever the way of it, peace was not to be had.

Jude's voice could be heard coming from the kitchen. If Dame Fortune looked kindly, the women would tell him the tale over again and keep him there. Likely, his brother had been around the taverns and was drunk as a brewer's pig and Seb could not face another challenge. But Jude was not long detained.

'Seb, where are you, little brother? I have tidings to tell.'

Seb sighed as though the weight of the world had been shirked by Atlas and loaded onto his narrow shoulders.

'In here...' he called. 'If you must,' he added under his breath. He ran a hand across his brow; a headache lurked: a heavy, grey, river fog behind his eyes, likely to spread and envelop his senses.

Jude came striding in, full of himself.

'You'll never guess, Seb...'

'Probably not.' Seb frowned over a complex receipt for mixing woad pigment with walnut oil. Apparently, blue hues turned greenish, if mixed with linseed oil. He would have to remember that. He put the marker in the page but was reluctant to leave his reading.

'Go on... guess,' Jude insisted.

'I be not of a humour for games.'

'I'm setting up in business! Are you shocked?'

'Jude, go to your bed. Tell me when you be sober in the morn.'

'I'm not bloody drunk, if that's what you think.'

'Did you win at dice this once?' Seb reopened his book.

'Will you bloody listen to me? Put that damned book down.'

Jude snatched the volume away and threw it on the settle where it lay open, the spine stretched. 'This isn't a drunken jest. I've bought a place, just around the corner from here, in Ave Maria Alley, off Amen Lane, two doors up from the Stationers' Hall. Do you recall it? It used to be a cap-maker's shop, the one that always has a puddle outside whenever it rains. You must know it – you fell in that puddle often enough when you were lame. I was always having to save you from it.'

'Then I wish you well in your new home,' Seb said, attempting to reach the book and close it so as not to damage the spine further. 'Chesca will be pleased to move out of Thieving Lane.'

Jude made himself comfortable in the chair across the hearth from Seb. Unfortunately for Seb's aching head, this conversation was likely to be of some length.

'That little slut's got naught to do with it,' Jude explained. 'Well, hardly anything. It's like this, Seb, the king – may the Devil rot his bollocks – has paid me handsomely not to take Chesca to the Court of Arches over her adultery with him. He doesn't want his good name – ha, ha – dragged into the midden because of his "dalliance". Aye, that's what he calls my utter humiliation. Can you believe it? Anyhow, this is, well… a sort of business transaction: he's paying for the use of my, er, property, as it were.'

Seb's eyes went wide, his mouth hung agape. It took a few moments before he could speak.

'You have sold your wife to the king! Dear God in heaven, Jude. Chesca is not a milk cow to be sold at market. Whatever are you thinking?'

'It's not like that. It's more of a lease upon a warehouse. He may have the use of it, so long as is convenient for us both.'

'This be immoral… unChristian, Jude. And shall Chesca be returned to you when he tires of her?'

'Aye, well, maybe. I haven't thought so far ahead as that yet.'

'Plainly.'

'But never mind her. I told you I wasn't going to work for

that bastard Oliver anymore, didn't I? It's all in hand. Next week I'll be sorting out the place, getting ready to bring in what's needed for my business. I've ordered it from Flanders.'

'It? What have you ordered from Flanders? When did you do that?'

'A while since; when you-know-who paid me the first instalment.'

'But why from Flanders? Their paper is best, I grant you, but what else can you possibly need as a stationer that cannot be obtained here, in London?'

'I never said I was going to be a stationer. In truth, little brother, I'm here out of courtesy, to warn you.' Jude brushed a dog-hair from his hose. He could not look at Seb nor meet his eye.

'Warn me?'

'I shall be in competition with you.'

'Aye, I understand that but London ever has need of good scribes.'

'I'm not going to be a bloody scribe. Can't you get that fact into your dullard's brain? I've done with scribbling my life away. And I want nothing to do with those bloody interfering busy-bodies at the guild either.'

'But the guild will not let you...'

'They won't be able to stop me. There's no legislation covering my new business and I have a royal warrant as part of the deal with his High-bollock-ness.' Jude paused to breathe deeply. 'I'm going to be London's first printer!' He threw his hands wide. 'There! I've said it. So now you know.'

'A-a p-printer?' Seb's voice hardly sounded like his own. 'A-as Master Caxton at Westminster?' He stared at his brother. He could not have been more horrified if Jude had just admitted he was King Herod who slew the Holy Innocents.

'Aye, but better. Much better and far more profitable. Are you shocked, Seb? I knew you would be.'

Shocked? That was too mild a word for what Seb felt at that

moment. Devastated. Betrayed. It appeared that his own brother – thoughtless and heedless as ever – was intending to ruin his business, destroying the livelihoods of all at the Sign of the Fox.

Chapter 19

Sunday, the twelfth day of February
St Michael le Querne Church

EVEN WITH ROSE slumbering softly in his arms, Seb couldn't still his turbulent thoughts enough to rest. It seemed a miracle that she could sleep soundly after the ordeal of last eve whilst he did not. Yet it wasn't their encounter with Duffield which kept him awake for that, so he felt, was resolved. As ever, it was Jude who made peace and quietude impossible.

Little wonder then that Seb's mood this morn was sullen as the rain-laden clouds outside. He had not yet told anyone of his disturbing conversation with Jude, not knowing how to break such news so, unsurprisingly, Rose and the others were perplexed at his ill-humour and sharp words to everyone.

Even Dickon could do naught to cheer his father who refused to play peep-bo or even give encouragement to the little lad's attempt at reciting the Ave Maria as they waited in the nave for old Father Thomas to begin the office of Low Mass.

'Avay-mia-grass,' was the best the child could manage but, since his use of English was yet barely a dozen words, it was a good effort. Rose had been trying to teach him for some while now. A good Christian's education could not begin too soon, as Seb insisted.

'For pity's sake, Dickon,' Seb scolded. 'Can you not do better than that? The correct wording be: *Ave Maria, gratia plena, Dominus tecum.* Have you not learned that much at least?'

The lad dissolved into tears and clung to Rose's skirt. Such a reprimand from Papa was unheard of 'til now.

'Have a little patience.' Rose put her hand on Seb's sleeve. 'He's not yet two years of age. I'm certain I couldn't have managed to say even the first word so young.'

Seb nigh shook her off but refrained.

'I have matters lying heavily upon my mind,' he made the excuse.

'Then you'd best lay them aside. Don't vent your spleen on the children or anyone else. I know this is Jude's doing – whatever is amiss – as it usually is. Shout at him, not the little ones.' Rose bent down and wiped Dickon's snotty nose and tear-streaked cheeks upon her apron. 'Turn your thoughts to God, husband, you know that will calm you. Besides, you need to be in better humour to sing well at High Mass in St Paul's later. Don't waste your voice berating little Dickon; save it for the motet you told me of. 'Tis the last chance you'll have to sing beautiful music before Lent will silence it.'

'I have not the heart for it this morn. I shall send word to the precentor, saying I cannot sing.'

'You will do no such thing, Seb, if I have to drag you into the quire myself. Singing will restore your humours like no other remedy. Now cease your moping and listen to Father Thomas.'

Chastened, Seb did as Rose said. She was correct, of course. She always was. He took little Dickon up in his arms, holding him close and whispered his apologies into a small, soft ear. The child responded, chuckling and grabbing a handful of his father's unkempt hair. Seb was forgiven right readily. His hair did not fare so well as a clump of dark strands, interspersed with too many grey, was entwined around the child's fingers and pulled out.

He managed to stifle a yelp of pain at the loss and did his best to disentangle himself from Dickon's grasp. He supposed it was no worse than he deserved. Seb turned his attention to the chancel arch beneath which, beyond the rood screen, Father

Thomas began to recite the opening prayers for the spoken office of Low Mass. Singing was reserved for High Mass later and Vespers in the evening, for which Seb's presence would be required in St Paul's. Famed across London for his angelic voice, he wished he might be spared the effort this day.

It proved nigh impossible to keep his mind upon any matter but Jude's intention to ruin them all by setting up a printing press and robbing them of the means to earn a living. Seb was not so concerned for himself. He could turn his hand to painting tavern signs, coats-of-arms, portraits and such like. But what of Adam and Ralf who relied in the main on penmanship to gain their wages?

Seb considered: printed books still required stitching and binding, embossing and gilding but was that enough to keep the workshop busy? Young Hugh's would surely be one pair of hands too many which was indeed a pity. The young man was likeable and worked well. As a journeyman, he would be an asset at the Sign of the Fox, if only Jude's new venture did not deny them their trade.

Rose nudged Seb, bringing him back to attending God's service at the Elevation of the Host. He must keep his thoughts upon the present. He bowed his head as required, remembering, belatedly, to make the sign of the cross. He gazed at the great wax tapers burning on the altar, their flickering light blurring before his eyes as his thoughts wandered off again, like straying sheep.

Mayhap printed books were but a fleeting fashion and Jude's schemes would come to naught. Did Jude have even the slightest notion of how to work a printing press, he wondered? Seb had never seen one but Master Collop once visited William Caxton's place and watched the procedure for himself. He later reported back to the guild that the press was a huge, cumbersome contraption, requiring the strength of Hercules to work it. And the process of compositing the type – whatever that meant – was a slow and fiddly one. The printed pages were done with glutinous ink that got everywhere. To judge from Master Collop's description, it was a right messy procedure.

Like most of his fellow stationers, Seb was of the opinion that a few good scribes were far more efficient, undoubtedly superior and less bothersome. Besides, Caxton had yet to produce anything with even a hint of illumination or a single colourful miniature. Perhaps Seb's workshop had naught to fear from this recent invention that seemed best suited to producing cheap pamphlets by the dozen but little of any quality or distinction. No doubt but he was worrying needlessly, he tried to convince himself.

Back at home, everyone was eager to break their fast, including Jude who had bothered to rouse himself from his bed, belatedly. It was the case that the Church fined those who failed to attend at least once a week but having his lodgings in St Margaret's parish at Westminster whilst sleeping at Paternoster Row in St Michael's parish, Jude reckoned he could avoid any fine by telling each parish – should the authorities enquire – that he had gone to mass at the other. Not that a sixpenny forfeit was of any concern, not when he had the king's bribe weighing his purse right heavily. He could click his fingers at meddlesome clerics, aye, and at God and the pope, come to that.

Seb said grace over the bacon collops and bread and the meal began. All was quiet until the edge was taken off their hunger and Jude spoke first.

'Have you told everyone my glad news, little brother?' he said, lifting a second helping of bacon onto his platter with his knife. Somehow, he succeeded in chewing and grinning at one time.

Seb did not look up, pushing his food about, watching the grease congeal. He had no interest in eating.

'Are you ailing, Seb?' Rose asked, concerned to see good food could not tempt him. 'Shall I fetch you a posset, instead? Something to settle you?'

'Nay, Rose. I know not what will improve my humour this morn. And I apologise for my surliness earlier.'

''Tis forgotten. I realise that wretch Duffield last eve upset you most of all... thinking he was your friend.' Rose was finding reasons to excuse his behaviour. She moved the dish of bacon away so Jude could not take any more than his fair share. 'And what is this glad news of yours, Jude? Have you shocked Seb mightily by telling him you have found some worthwhile occupation to earn your bread? I thought your work at Westminster paid well.'

'Keep your nose out of my bloody business, woman. I'm worth more than those buggers were willing to pay. Now I have a new venture...'

Rose sighed.

'Little wonder then that my Seb is out of humour. We all know your ventures inevitably end in trouble.'

'This one cannot fail. Seb should've told you: I've already taken a house in Ave Maria Alley.'

'You'll be moving out then.' Rose couldn't conceal her relief and hers wasn't the only barely hidden smile. Kate had little liking for the brash braggart who came to the house whenever he wished, disturbing Master Seb's humours and causing trouble with Master Adam at every opportunity.

On the other hand, Ralph could hardly object to sharing the chamber that had once been Jude's alone but the fellow frequently returned late at night and drunk, making a din and spoiling the old man's sleep.

Nessie – who had once believed herself in love with the man – realised now she'd been more enamoured of his fashionable red-leather high boots and jaunty cap than of the wearer himself.

And Gawain had suffered Jude's bad temper too many times, being kicked about.

It seemed that no one would miss Jude, if he departed Paternoster Row.

'Can you afford to pay the high city rent?' Rose asked.

'You always seemed to be owing payment to the woman in Thieving Lane.'

'I told you to keep your nose out of my affairs,' Jude yelled at her across the board.

'It became *my* affair too when I wed your brother, since he so often uses *our* coin to buy *you* out of your difficulties. Don't think I don't know what my husband does to aid you... either of you.' She glanced at Seb, wondering if he'd hoped she was unaware of coin disappearing from the coffer most weeks. She was not to be fooled and, now she was mistress of the house, she had the right to speak out.

'Quietly, I pray you,' Seb said, rubbing at his brow. 'Do not raise your voice to my wife, Jude. I will not have it.'

To make matters worse, Julia began to wail as she sensed discord all about. Rose picked her up from her blanket on the floor and tried to calm her.

'Now see what you've done, Jude Foxley. She's teething and miserable as it is. I'll not keep her quiet once you've set her off. Why don't you just get out? Go to your new place or the tavern. I don't care which. And don't come back, you idle rogue!'

''Tis the Lord's Day,' Seb reminded them. 'Curb your ire, both of you, for pity's sake.' He left the board, his platter hardly touched, and climbed the stairs, intending to comb his hair and fetch his chorister's garb, in readiness to go to St Paul's. It was somewhat early but he could bear no more dissent in his household. At least one good thing would come of Jude's move to Ave Maria Alley – he would not bide under their roof any longer and they could live peaceably without the constant bickering and argument he caused, ever stirring up trouble like an ill wind. In the meantime, Seb must trust to the beauties of the cathedral to soothe him.

St Paul's Cathedral

It being the Lord's Day, the stationers had dismantled their stalls in the nave and the dairy wives had removed their baskets of butter and cheese. St Paul's was returned to its rightful use as the house of God, not a street market.

Seb was in the south transept where the choir formed up, awaiting the officiating priests, the Dean and Chapter before processing into the nave and entering the chancel. There was to be no long procession from the Bishop's Palace this day since Bishop Kemp had taken to his bed with gout and would not attend. It was as well for the dour clouds of earlier were now shedding their load with a vengeance.

Seb was glad he had arrived before the rain, seeing some of the young choristers were soaked in the time it took them to run from the school across the precinct. Seb nodded a greeting to the firm friends and fellow choristers, Simon Hutchinson, Adam's stepson, and to Will Thatcher, Beattie's lad whom he had rescued last year. Water dripped from Will's pale hair and Simon was wringing out the hem of his surplus. The precentor called them into line, counting heads, before hastening off with the bellows-boy to play up the organ.

The crucifer came first with the great be-jewelled cross, flanked by the servers with the candles and followed by the thurifer, swinging the gold incense-burner on its long chain, scenting the air. Then the choristers came in pairs – from the youngest trebles to Seb and the adult vicars-choral – all singing a joyous processional anthem as they walked at a measured pace. The organ huffed and wheezed like an old man well past his three-score-years-and-ten, being just as temperamental and disliking cold, wet weather, as did its ancient human counterparts.

The nave stank of wet wool with a hint of dusty lavender and the odour of two hundred or more not-so-clean bodies.

No wonder the thurifer applied himself to his task with such diligence. Not that it made much difference. Even in the quire stalls, shielded from the congregation by the rood screen, the pungent reek of the choristers' damp woollen gowns could not be disguised by any perfume from the Holy Land, however costly.

Once in his allotted stall, as the anthem ended with a harmonious 'Amen', Seb looked to the great east window. It was a miracle in stained glass and Seb never tired of watching its hues of ruby, sapphire, emerald and amethyst shift across the tiled floor of the chancel as the sun moved. But this day, there was no colour. The dreary grey light cast no tapestry of gemstone tints. In truth, because of the gloom which the candles did little to dispel, it was difficult to read the music written out in the great songbook, propped upon its stand, facing the choir. It was as well that Seb knew his part by heart and did not require to read it.

The antiphonal psalms, sung in two parts, were done and now Seb and two of the vicars-choral were to sing the motet, practised at such length last eve with the precentor criticising every phrase. The three left the quire stalls to stand 'neath the rood screen, Seb in the centre. He breathed deep, closed his eyes for a moment, then looked, not to the roof beams above but beyond, to heaven itself. Being pitch-perfect, he did not require the organ's note. He sang the first word '*Ecce*', high and clear, then his fellow songsters added their voices: '*Ecce filii matris tuae*'. 'Mother, behold thy son.' These were the dying words uttered by Our Lord Jesu upon the cross. The motet would be sung again on Good Friday but this day it was a reminder of the reason for Lent which began three days hence. Seb ended the gentle 'Amen', fading to nothingness, with tears in his eyes.

Rose was correct. Singing had restored his humoral balance and thinking of Christ's agonising betrayal and death put Seb's problems into perspective as minor inconveniences. Better yet, the rain must have ceased and the sky cleared for the stained glass was once more strewing jewels of light across the floor.

When the recessional anthem was done, Seb left St Paul's with a smile upon his lips.

Back at home, his appetite regained, Seb realised he was hungry for this last Lord's Day dinner afore the Lenten fast.

Rose hadn't come to the cathedral to hear Seb sing, having determined upon a fine dinner and invited their good friends to share it, as she often did. Kate was sent with a covered platter of choicest morsels to Dame Ellen's place in Cheapside. For weeks past, the old woman had been too frail to walk to Paternoster Row but she was not forgotten.

Stephen Appleyard and Jack had arrived before Seb. Jack appeared to have grown another hand-span since the previous visit, his shoulders broader than ever. It seemed impossible he had once been an undersized street urchin – all spit and chicken bones, as Emily had once described him. Likely, Jack would be one of the few men who could look King Edward in the eye, if they ever dared, before the lad was done growing. However, this day, he caught Seb's eye with a pleading look – one which Seb could not quite comprehend. And was that a smear of dirt upon his jaw? Or a bruise? What mischief had Jack embroiled himself in now?

Adam, Mercy and her three lads, Kate, Ralf along with his beloved Joanie, Pen and Bennett Hepton were all invited and Old Symkyn joined them also, glad to leave his begging bowl by St Paul's Gate. Seb made certain his crippled friend ne'er went hungry. With Nessie and the little ones, it was quite a gathering which spread from the kitchen into the passageway but Jude and Chesca did not appear – for which mercy Seb was thankful.

Seb said a Latin grace, thanking the Almighty for the bounteous dishes set before them and the meal began. Juicy mutton pieces and parsnips with cinnamon spice in a pastry coffin, worts and leeks in cheese sauce and rolled bacon strips stuffed with onions, oatmeal and sage, served with thyme- and marjoram-flavoured bread. It was a feast fit for King Edward at Westminster and ignored the sumptuary laws, stating 'no more than two dishes in a course for humble folk', as though they'd ne'er been written. Nobody bothered with such nonsense these days, anyway.

As she brought forth and served a platter of honeyed wafers with a sweet pottage of apples and dried apricocks, cooked in wine and topped with thickened cream – a last treat before Lent – Rose caught Seb's eye and mouthed 'What of Jude's news? May we know of it?'

Seb made a gesture that could have meant anything from 'Better not to' to 'I care not' but it seemed he did not forbid the telling. It would be a fresh matter to discuss, other than the changeable February weather, seeing more rain was falling outside.

'Jude had eager tidings to tell this morn, did he not, Seb?' Rose said when everyone was served. She took a spoon and began to help little Julia with the fruit pottage whilst Dickon preferred munching on the wafers, dropping crumbs to Gawain, hiding 'neath the board.

'Aye, and I dare say the whole of London shall know of it soon enough,' Seb admitted, wiping honey from his fingers on his napkin. 'He has a madman's scheme to set up a printing press in Ave Maria Alley to rival Master Caxton's at Westminster.'

For a moment, no one spoke until each had taken in the words.

'But he can't do that,' Adam said. 'Caxton has the king's licence.'

'It would appear that my brother has also received the king's blessing and relevant documents, amongst other, er, favours.'

'Ah,' Adam was quick to discern the reason, 'To compensate him. But who will regulate his work? Do the stationers have the right of it? What will it mean for us scribes?'

'In truth, I know no more than you. 'Tis your livelihoods at stake, as well as mine, so I thought you should know of it. How it may affect our business 'tis impossible to tell until Jude has all set up and printing commences. Even then, it will take time for him to build a reputation.'

'Which, knowing your scapegrace brother, he never will.' Adam drank his ale and seemed more at ease. 'We worry needlessly, Seb. It will come to naught in the end. When has Jude ever made a success of anything but emptying your coffers and causing trouble?'

Before Seb could reply, likely by leaping to his brother's defence, a knock upon the kitchen door interrupted the conversation.

'Thaddeus. God give you good day,' Seb greeted City Bailiff Turner as he made his breathless entrance, rain dripping from his hood. 'Rose, do we yet have food sufficient for our friend?'

'I haven't come for dinner... but to inform you...' Thaddeus managed to say. 'I was intending to return your linen sheet and napkin, Mistress Rose... and your belt, Seb, but both are now deodand – forfeit to the king. I fear you cannot have them back.'

Rose handed the bailiff a towel to dry himself.

'How can that be, Master Turner? The sheet is of good Holland cloth and Seb's belt was a gift from Warden-Master Richard Collop and finely worked. Now he has but his old one, nigh worn through at the buckle.' She took the damp towel from him and hung it by the hearth to dry, followed by his sodden cloak and hood which were leaving puddles across the floor. 'We used them to tie the devil. The king can but take weapons used in a crime: is that not the case, Master Turner?' Rose's anger was apparent in that she addressed him formally, not as Thaddeus, as was usual since the bailiff was Seb's good friend.

'Aye, mistress, but I have to report that Lorenzo Duffield made use of them this morn ... in the lock-up... as a means to avoid standing trial for treason. He contrived to make it seem he had hanged himself, using the sheet and belt. I apologise for the loss of your belongings.'

Mercy and Pen gasped at the horror of it. Seb and Joanie

made the sign of the cross – none other bothered.

'The devil is not dead, good women. He wrapped the sheet about the straw-stuffed palliasse provided for his bed, then tied the belt as though around a neck, making it look as if it had a head and hung the belt from the window bar. When the guard brought him bread and water this morn, he was distracted by the seeming body. Duffield was hid behind him, to the side of the door. He overcame the guard and made good his escape from the lock-up. Again. This one is more slippery than any eel, just as you said, Seb. I've come to warn you that he's at large once more.'

'So we are all yet in danger,' Rose said, wringing her hands. 'This is too bad, Master Turner, that you cannot keep folk safe, even when Seb has brought the felon to justice twice over.'

'Well, this is a tale you must tell, Seb,' said Bennett Hepton, refilling his ale cup and making room upon the bench for Thaddeus to join them. 'What's come to pass? Have you been apprehending villains again? Pen, you best not listen if 'tis too gory,' he told his wife.

Rose handed the bailiff a cup of ale, offering him the platter of honeyed wafers to follow, but her countenance wore such a look of worry.

'Let's leave the menfolk to this bloody story,' she said. 'We can take the children and sit in the parlour to talk of more wholesome things. I would not rehearse it again.'

'What of the soiled pots and dishes, Rose?' Pen asked, renowned as she was for her spotless, tidy kitchen. Likely, that would change when her babe was born.

'They'll yet be there an hour hence and will suffer no harm for the delay. Come Kate and Nessie, you know the worst of this already.'

'If 'tis allowed, Mistress Foxley, by your leave, I'll stay,' Joanie said. 'I've heard naught of this story and, as Ralf will tell you, being once wed to Hamo, that beast of a man, there's little I haven't seen of mankind's misdeeds done upon his fellows.

Besides, I enjoy a good tale.'

'As you will, mistress,' Rose said, lifting Julia from her seat. 'But you have been warned.'

With the women departed and cups replenished, Seb began the story. As he related the happenings of recent days at Westminster, he noted Jack fingering his jaw and wincing now and then. Seb reckoned that was another tale waiting to be told, if there was time afore Vespers when he must go to Paul's once more. This time of year, when nights were long, Vespers was sung early.

'So what did these secret messages concern of the king's business?' Bennett asked.

'They intended to either abduct or kill the young Prince of Wales at St Albans, during his journey to Westminster to pass Eastertide with the royal family.'

'To what end?' Bennett wanted to know. 'The king has another son, so it would not affect the inheritance of the throne too much.'

Seb felt shocked at Bennett's words. The loss of a child – whether prince or pauper – would devastate and anger the parents. He had observed how Will Thatcher's mother and father were afflicted when the lad went missing the year before. He knew if anything happened to Dickon or Julia he would be distraught. Mayhap, when Pen's babe was born – God willing – and Bennett felt the responsibility and joys of fatherhood, he would understand better.

'As far as I can tell,' Seb continued, 'Since the scheme was not enlarged upon in the short messages, nor was every encoded letter discovered, the Italians planned to leave evidence of French involvement. They intended to have King Edward make war on France in retaliation for the murder or imprisonment of his son – for I have learned the way they think, calling it *vendetta*.'

'What would these foreigners gain by having England and France fighting each other?' Adam asked.

Seb shook his head.

'Lawrence – the felon calling himself Lorenzo – said something to the effect that his lord, Duke Sforza of Milano, would invade and take some disputed lands in the south whilst King Louis was engaged to the north by the English. Piedmont, he called it, though I have no knowledge of such a place, presumably at the "foot of a mountain".'

'I never trusted those folks,' said Joanie without any hint as to whom she referred.

'And now he's on the loose,' Adam said. 'It's not good enough, Thaddeus. You have to find the rogue, else Seb and his family can't sleep safely in their beds.'

'I know.' The bailiff was pale and worn. 'I have every constable searching but my purpose here was not only to warn you but to ask you, Seb, to draw a likeness of this Lorenzo, that folk may know whom we seek. It's worked before, showing your drawings. I realise it's the Lord's Day but...'

'Aye. I should have thought of it myself. A quick sketch will not take long.' Seb rose from his stool. 'Help yourselves to ale and wafers. I shall be in the workshop.'

Seb sat at his desk, charcoal in hand and paper before him. He closed his eyes, the better to picture the clerk, Lawrence Duffield, looking like any other decent, law-abiding fellow. He had to forget the snarling, desperate killer, Lorenzo. Upon the London streets, Lawrence would do his best to act the part of a common man.

Once he had the image in his mind, Seb's hand moved deftly across the page: a curved line here, a little shading there as the likeness of the living man was conjured upon the paper, as if by some magick or wizardry. It was done in the time it took to say a dozen Paternosters. Seb blew the charcoal dust away and returned to the kitchen. He handed the image to Thaddeus.

'Are you sure of him?' Thaddeus asked, frowning at the likeness. 'The devil looks so pleasant... quite handsome, in truth.'

'Aye, he fooled us all at Westminster,' Seb said. 'I liked him

and took him for a friend. How wrong was I? His disguising
was perfect. I ne'er suspected him until the last, although Jude
had his suspicions. I should have paid more heed to my brother.'

'Jude got something right? I don't believe that.' Adam took
the last wafer.

'Almost. Though he suspected Hal Sowbury also. Hal is the
chief clerk at Westminster. He and Lawrence appeared to be
good friends of long-standing, so Jude had reason to think him
involved – mainly forwhy my brother so disliked the chief clerk.
But Hal was innocent and utterly distressed when he learned
how he had been duped for some years by Lawrence's pretence.'

'And Lawrence managed this devious plot all alone?'
Stephen asked.

'Nay. As a clerk, he had no way of securing knowledge of
King Edward's plans. His fellow conspirator and espier, listening
in to the Privy Council's deliberations, was the king's own
groom of the chamber, Sir Nicholas FitzAlan. In truth, I find his
treasonous behaviour the most reprehensible in that he betrayed
the king's intimate trust in him. What kind of scoundrel does
such a thing? And why would he? That, I cannot answer.

'And then, apart from those two, they made use of a pedlar,
Jake Parslow, to convey the secret letters to Lombard Street, to
some Italians there. I know no names.'

'And where is FitzAlan now? And what of the pedlar?'
Adam asked.

'As far as I know, FitzAlan be imprisoned at the Tower where
he rightfully belongs and remains secure – as I trust.' Seb looked
to Thaddeus who nodded.

'I have heard naught to the contrary,' the bailiff said. 'But I
must leave you. My constables must be shown this likeness.' He
rolled up the sketch and tucked it into his belt under his cloak
to keep it from the wet weather. 'Good day to you all and my
thanks for the ale and wafers. Oh, and be sure to bar your doors
and shutters this night, Seb, for safety's sake.'

'I shall not forget, my friend. Fare you well.'

With the bailiff departed, looking at his guests, Seb saw Jack sigh with relief upon the bench. He recalled that the lad had not said a word since Thaddeus arrived.

'What did happen to the pedlar, Parslow? I know of him and I've bought ribbons from him in the past,' Joanie said.

'Lawrence killed him to silence him. I fear you will purchase no more from Jake Parslow.'

'Pity that. His ribbons were of good quality,' Joanie said. 'Will you walk me home now, Ralf? I have a goodly supper prepared that I know you'll want to share.'

With that enticement – not that it was needed – the old journeyman fetched their cloaks.

'I'll not be back for supper, Master Seb, thanking you,' Ralf said with a sparkle in his eye. 'If you will tell Mistress Rose for me, I'll take that as a kindness.'

Old Symkyn departed with a blessing and Adam and Bennett Hepton collected their womenfolk from the parlour and left, Adam with his gaggle of stepsons trailing behind. Rose, Kate and Nessie were awaiting the water to heat before washing the cups and platters. Dickon and Julia had been put in the cradle for a belated nap.

Stephen Appleyard nudged Jack.

'Come, lad, let's thank these good folk for a fine dinner and leave Master Seb and his family in peace.'

'I, er, I want t'ave a word wiv Master Seb,' Jack muttered, staring at the empty board before him, a deep frown furrowed his youthful brow.

'If Master Seb's agreeable… I suppose you may,' Stephen said.

'Aye, so long as I be not delayed for Vespers in Paul's,' Seb agreed. 'Come away into the parlour, Jack, that we may speak privily.'

Seb sat upon the cushioned chair before the hearth, adding another log to the fire.

'Well, Jack? You have hardly said a word all this while. Does this have to do with the bruise on your jaw?'

'Yer noticed then. I 'oped yer wouldn't, didn't I?'

'For my craft as an artist, I needs must observe small details. Besides, you have been poking at it ever since you arrived.'

''Ave I? I never meant to...'

'You be in trouble.' Seb stated. 'What have you done amiss upon this occasion?'

'Nuffink, not really. I jus... 'Er goodman took a swipe at me, caught us unawares like, didn't he.'

'You were with a married woman and her husband caught you?'

'Aye, but we wasn't doin' nuffink... jus' a kiss on the cheek... sort of. Bessie told 'im that woz all but the bugger wouldn't b'lieve us.'

'How is it that I be unsurprised, Jack? And more to the point: why do you tell me? What would you have me do concerning this foolishness of yours?'

Jack stood there, inspecting his muddy boots, knotting his fingers and chewing his nether lip.

'Well? I do not have so much time to spare. Speak now, Jack.'

'The bugger's sayin' I must pay 'im, or 'e'll tell the parish or take us t' court even. I ain't got no money, 'ave I? I 'oped yer might lend us a few coin, 'cos yer a kind master an' the best...'

'So you think to flatter me? Sweet words do not beguile me, Jack.'

'I wasn't bigillin' yer, whatever it is. I need a few coins is all, don't I?'

'How much money does her husband demand?'

'Er, I, er... 'alf a mark, the bugger wants, don't 'e?'

''Tis a high price to pay for one kiss.' Seb sat silent then, watching the lad fidgeting, knowing the truth would come out, eventually.

'Aye, well, we might've, er, bin doin' a bit more'n kissin'. We woz in 'er bed... wiv no clouts on and... yer know 'ow it is wiv a buxom wench...' Jack could say no more.

'Not a wench but another man's wife! How could you be so

irresponsible?'

'I wasn't irrysposable. I wasn't even drunk, was I?'

'Then how do you excuse your stupidity?'

'Me an' Bessie... we luv each uvver, don't we?'

'May the saints preserve us!' Seb threw up his hands. 'What do you know of love, Jack Tabor? You be but sixteen years of age or thereabouts. Marriage comes afore love, according to the law.'

'But I can't marry 'er, can I?'

'Exactly so. Stay away from other men's wives.'

'Can I 'ave the money? I needs it t'night.'

'If I had the sense the Almighty gave a worm, I should refuse, leaving you to suffer the consequences of your actions.'

'I ain't got no connerqwencies nor no money, so will yer lend it me, please, master?'

'And no doubt but you will promise to repay me the sum of six shillings and eightpence in due course?'

'Course I will?'

'When?'

'Whenever I...?'

'How?'

Jack shrugged. They both knew full well the money would never be forthcoming.

They went along the passage into the shop and Seb took down the coin box from the high shelf. He sorted out the appropriate money.

'Here. Take it. But do not expect me to repeat this favour. Any subsequent unwarrantable transgressions of a like nature will be entirely accountable to you. Do you understand me, Jack?'

The lad nodded, though he had not the least idea what "subsequent unwarrantable transgressions" might mean. Nevertheless, he now had the money, enough to buy his way out of trouble – hopefully.

Chapter 20

Monday, the thirteenth day of February
The Foxley House

SEB ROSE EARLY and lit a rushlight. For once, it wasn't raining when he drew aside the shutters on the glazed window of which Emily was always so proud and looked out upon Paternoster Row from the bedchamber. It was yet dark and the torches in the cressets that folk put by their doors to light the street had burnt out long since but a few stars showed beyond St Paul's spire, cold and clear. Frost sparkled on rooftops and cobbles, making the filthy city seem a place of enchantment.

Rose stirred and turned over in her sleep. Her nightcap had gone askew and a long fair tress dangled down, brushing her well-worn slippers set beside the bed. The babes slumbered in their cradle, Julia sucking her thumb, Dickon's arms flung wide as though to welcome the new day.

Seb's family. How he loved them all.

He washed his face in the laver bowl, breaking a thin skim of ice and shivering at the touch of cold water. Then he knelt before the image of Our Lady in its heavy frame. The picture had been there in Matthew Bowen's day, when Seb was but newly qualified as a journeyman, concealing the secret aumbry where Bowen hid his fortune. Their household monies and savings were kept there still. Seb said his prayers, as he always did, mentioning by name those he would have Christ Jesu take into His special care. His family came first, then his relatives, then employees and friends. Dame Ellen Langton received particular mention for her health had been failing of late and Old Symkyn, whose crippled limbs would cause him discomfort on so chilly a morn. And for Jack to stay out of trouble.

Seb felt he ought to pray for Jude in his new venture but it seemed madness to beg divine assistance for something that could destroy his livelihood, if it met with success. Thus, Seb prayed rather for his brother's safety and good health, for his contentment in his new place and reconciliation with Chesca – if such were possible – knowing not what else to say to the Lord Christ on Jude's behalf. He wondered, fleetingly, if Jude ever prayed for him in like wise.

Rose sat up, pushing her hair from her face. The chamber was cold but her early-morning smile warmed him like a brazier.

'May God bless you this day, sweetheart,' Seb said, kissing her cheek.

'And you also, husband mine. 'Tis washing day and I've slept over long.'

'Nay. The hour be right early. Even Jonathan's wakeful cockerel has yet to crow and rouse the neighbourhood. Rest awhile. I know you tended to Julia in the night.'

'Aye… those coming teeth do plague the poor mite.'

'I shall see to the kitchen fire, ready for you to heat water. Likely the conduit could be frozen so Nessie will have much of which to complain but the rain be gone for the present. I have a deal to do to prepare for the day. I must go to Master Collop about the contracts for our new commissions. Adam had a lawyer draft them but I must check and sign them and have them witnessed by the guild. Then to Dame Ellen about our renting Jonathan's place next door and how that should be best arranged.'

'Mary will want a say in that. You know she dare not trust him with any important matter. She'll still want the use of her kitchen and bedchamber even if Jonathan shares the workshop with you.'

'I shall expect more than that alone, if I be paying the rent in full. We be over cramped here and require more room to store materials.'

'Mary won't like you taking ownership of her home, Seb.'

'In which case, Jonathan should have paid the rent regularly and not borrowed the coin from me each time it fell due. Dame Ellen would be within her rights to throw them out, as shall I when I take on the lease but, being both of us Christian souls and soft of heart, we neither of us intend to do so. But changes will come to pass.'

'Seb, are you certain we can afford to take on so much when your brother could be about to ruin our business with his printing works?'

'Fear not, sweetheart. All will be well.' Seb went to the window. The sky over Aldgate in the east of the city was showing a paler hue and lights appearing in the tenements hunched against the precinct wall opposite as folk stirred their fires to life, lit tapers and opened shutters. Smoke began to rise from rooftops and the few chimneys, climbing vertically in the breathless air.

Dame Ellen Langton's House in Cheapside

'God give you good day, Dame Ellen,' Seb greeted the old woman, removing his cap and dipping his head in respect. 'And you also, Mistress Hepton.'

Dame Ellen waved him to a lowly stool from her cushioned chair by the fire, to remind him he had once been her most humble lodger. He looked around the kitchen where he and Jude used to share Sunday dinners, served by Emily as Dame Ellen's apprentice silk-worker and servant. Em's brother, John Appleyard, had always been there, too, he being the dame's apprentice to the craft of tailoring which had been her husband's business. The kitchen was well ordered and clean as a fresh parchment. It had always been thus but now Peronelle, who dwelt around the corner, kept it so, tending to Dame Ellen's needs.

'Will you take ale, Master Foxley?' Peronelle asked with due formality in the old woman's presence.

'Aye, a drink would be welcome. I thank you.'

'Peronelle, mull it and spice it for Sebastian on this cold morning.' Dame Ellen huddled into her wolf-skin coverlet despite the fire's heat. Elderly folk ever felt the cold more deeply, did they not?

Seb regarded her as close as he dared without giving offence. Once plump, Dame Ellen was now sparrow-bone frail. It was as if age had leeched away every trace of colour from cheek, lip and eye. Not a hair showed around her spotless wimple but Seb thought it likely to be of a colour with the frost-white linen.

'Peronelle, summon John from the shop,' the old woman ordered, her voice harsh, stronger than Seb expected. 'I have matters to discuss with you all. Sit down Pen, John, both of you, and listen well to what I say. I haven't got much time to spare.'

Seb wondered that the good dame yet had business matters demanding her urgent attention but then realised her meaning.

'I'm not long for this troublesome world.' She shook her head as Pen made objection. 'And I have drawn up my will with my son Dick's agreement but since he lives down Deptford way, I have appointed you, Sebastian and John, as my executors. It will not be an arduous task for my bequests are straightforward.' She paused and Pen held the ale cup for her to drink. 'Dick will inherit the lion's share of my estate, as is right and proper, with token bequests made to the Mercers' Company and the Cutlers' Company in recognition of both my husbands. Donations go to St Peter's in Cheap and St Michael le Querne's… but all such matters are set out in my will.

'More importantly, you, John, will have this house and shop and the tailoring business. Since you've been running it for me of late, I dare say that comes as no surprise to you.'

'My thanks, Dame Ellen,' John said, beaming with pleasure.

'Aye, and in return for living here, you and your wife – when you find one, John – can pray for my soul, everlasting.'

'Of course. I would do so anyway, even without such a generous bequest. You've taught me so well, not just tailoring but how to run a business. I owe you everything, Dame Ellen.' There was no denying the tears in John's eyes as he spoke, whether of gratitude or sadness at the thought of his old mistress's passing.

'And find yourself a decent wife,' Dame Ellen ended sternly, then turned to Pen. 'Now Peronelle, you've been a good lass and the most kindly of neighbours. You took on the silk-working when Emily died so unexpected – may God care for her soul.' All made the sign of the cross. 'I expected her to be looking to that side of my affairs,' the dame continued, 'But you've done well and I am proud of you, young woman, so you will receive the tenement that I own in Milk Street, by Blossom's Inn. Whether you and Bennett choose to live there or use the income from the rent will be up to you to decide.' Dame Ellen fell back in her chair, seeming exhausted by so much speech but Pen helped her to another sip of ale and she rallied her strength.

'Sebastian. You are a good man and trustworthy... almost a son to me... unlike that brother of yours. How your father sired two so different, I cannot tell. But that's by the way. You were a fine husband to Emily, so I'm bequeathing to you that which I would have left to her, apart from the silk-work, of course, which Peronelle has already. Emily was the daughter I never had and I would be generous to her, accordingly, in the hope her children will benefit, God willing. We spoke of this matter the other day, Sebastian: that you might take on the lease of your neighbour, Jonathan Caldicott. Well... I have decided against it.'

Seb was shocked, dismayed.

'But,' she went on, 'Instead, you shall have the freehold of it. The place shall be yours, to do with as you will and...' She paused to breathe deep and steady herself. 'Also, I own four tenements and a small shop in Distaff Lane. You didn't know that, did you? I use an agent to collect most of my rents so few are aware of what I own. Your cousin Adam and his new wife live in one of the houses. What you do with those properties, Sebastian, is down to whatever proves convenient to you but I could hazard a guess concerning the place your cousin occupies.' She closed her heavy-lidded eyes but was not quite done speaking.

'Now go, all of you. I am wearied by this. Leave me. But I promise you, you'll not have long to wait for your legacies. I am done with this life. Remember me in your prayers... properly... no hasty Paternosters and a couple of mumbled Aves. Proper heartfelt prayers for my soul when I am gone, you hear me?'

Seb left Dame Ellen's house, his mind awhirl with thoughts of this new status and its possibilities. Aye, and its responsibilities. He would become a man of property: Caldicott's place, Adam and Mercy's house, three other tenements and a shop besides. But Dame Ellen was not gone yet and, for all her declarations that she was nigh her end, she might well live on for months to come. He wondered how he should proceed regarding Jonathan's place now. After all, the dame had denied him the lease and the freehold possession was not yet his. This made matters awkward indeed. And was it wise to assume that Dame Ellen's last will and testament would be executed swiftly and smoothly when the time came? Others' last wills had been contested before through the Court of Chancery. She might even change her mind and rewrite it in the meantime.

The Foxley House and Workshop

Adam greeted Seb upon his return to the workshop with a list of queries and complaints.

'Ah, Seb, thank the Lord God you're returned. I've had Lord Mayor James's man here, demanding to know when you will be going to Guildhall for his first sitting, since he's paid the first instalment for his portrait already. He said this afternoon, at three of the clock, would be convenient. I think you should heed the request. His man said his lordship is angered at the delay. It's been two months now since terms were agreed.'

'I know that, Adam, but other matters be pressing. I passed the morn with Dame Ellen.'

'A social call when we are so busy?'

'Nay. She has made me an executor of her will, in company with John Appleyard. There were matters to discuss.'

'Maybe so, but she's not dead yet; that could have waited. Our customers are more important. You're risking our reputations here. And Bennett Hepton wants to know when the little Book of Hours for Pen will be ready and we haven't even begun work on it. You insisted you must do the illuminations, so we need to talk of the design before we can so much as rule up the pages. And we're all getting under each others' feet now Hugh is here. You told me we could likely move some of us into Caldicott's workshop this week. Is that arranged yet? And you have those contracts to get signed: the one for St Mary-le-Bow's large illuminated Gospels and the Bishop of Bath and Wells's portrait. Have you read through those contracts yet? I had them drawn up last week, as you said.'

'Nay, not as yet. I shall do so now, by your leave.'

'And what of next door's workshop? Can we move Ralf's desk there? He is agreeable to it, so he says – isn't that so, Ralf? – and our stitching press is there already.'

The old journeyman nodded without looking up from his pen and the page of beautiful script.

'Nay. There has been a development concerning that. We may speak of it later. I shall see to the contracts firstly then visit the lord mayor this afternoon. Do we have fresh paper? I noticed we be somewhat short of it in the storeroom.'

'There's enough for you to make your preliminary sketches of the lord mayor, if that's what concerns you?'

So much to do. Seb took the contract documents from his desk and retreated to the quietude of the parlour, the better to understand the convoluted legal Latin. He could ill afford any errors. He shook his head over a mis-declined noun which made a nonsense of one clause, crossing it through and making the correction, putting his initials 'SF' in the margin to authenticate the change. You would think lawyers ought to have a better knowledge of basic Latin second declension regular nouns.

Satisfied, he went out once more, leaving Adam to take charge, as always. He must take the documents to the Stationers' Hall, in Ave Maria Alley, to be witnessed and put for safe-keeping in their secure coffers.

Ave Maria Alley

His business at the Stationers' Hall completed, the contracts witnessed and secured, Seb intended to hasten home for dinner. He must prepare what he required to take to Guildhall, to begin work on Bartholomew James's portrait in his lord mayor's regalia of office. It would be good to return to his true craft at last after so many weeks of copying out other folks' execrable handwriting and collating tedious documents. He would enjoy the use of fine pigments, creating things of beauty once more.

But as was the way of late, Seb's intentions came to naught.

As he departed from Stationers' Hall, he had little choice but to pass by Jude's new place of abode. It was a large building on the corner of Ave Maria Alley and Amen Lane which became Paternoster Row, half-timbered with modern brick-infill and jettied upper storeys to give more room. It was only natural that his brother, espying him from the open window, should drag him within, insisting he view the place, inspecting all four floors, from attic to cellar, and sharing wine to celebrate the acquisition. It was a fine building, indeed, Seb had to admit.

Despite having no time to linger, Seb found himself caught up in Jude's excitement for his latest scheme.

'And you have the audacity to set up a printing press upon the very doorstep of Stationers' Hall! I know not how you dare, Jude.'

'Why not? It'll shake those old grey-beards, wake up the buggers. They've been stuck in the past since King Arthur's time, never moving on.'

'You forget, I be one of those 'grey-beards' now as an Assistant Warden. Not all of us be in our dotage.'

'Aye, well, maybe you're the exception that proves the rule, little brother. Have you seen the fine plasterwork on the lintels above the door and windows? Come outside and see it. There's a particularly fine grotesque which looks just like King Bollocks himself.'

The brothers were standing out in Ave Maria Alley, looking up at the house.

'See the scroll work and vine leaves? Good as anything you do in the margins of a manuscript. And there's the grotesque.' Jude pointed out the plaster head above the door lintel. 'You can't deny the likeness to that royal arse-wipe.'

Seb admired the craftsmanship, as demanded, but thought his pen and brushwork far exceeded a few marks made in plaster, although he did not say as much.

'What do you know of printing?' he asked. 'What of the method and equipment required?'

'I saw a working press when I was in Flanders. In Bruges, it was; a huge thing,' Jude explained. 'I reckon those upper windows will have to come out.' He pointed to the fine glazed windows above. 'It's a pity but I don't see that we'll ever get the bloody great contraption up the stair.'

'Must you have it above stairs?' Seb enquired. 'If you have it down on the ground floor, will folk not be intrigued and drawn in to watch the procedure? It could attract customers.'

'Aye. Maybe. But then we'll likely have to remove these lower windows just the same. It'll not go through the doorway, wide as it is.'

''Tis a problem, I agree, but tell me, honestly, brother: will you know how to use it?'

But Jude had no opportunity to reply, even if he intended to, for their conversation was ended abruptly by a commotion and screaming.

'Beware!' someone shouted.

A horse was hurtling down Warwick Lane, towards Seb and Jude, dragging a cart behind. Eyes white with terror, the beast was scattering folk like panicked chickens. It was coming straight toward the corner of the house.

Jude saw the danger first and shoved his brother aside but the horse swerved into Paternoster Row. At such a speed, the cart overturned, catching Jude and sending him flying.

Folk came running – some to give aid but others for no better reason than to see the spectacle. A group of stationers came from the hall, Master Collop among them.

Seb was clambering to his feet, somewhat dazed, having landed heavily when Jude shoved him out of the horse's path. A crowd gathered, though the horse was long gone, having disappeared beyond the Panyer Inn, leaving a trail of broken bits of wood and wreckage from the cart in its wake.

A man came puffing and waddling down Warwick Lane. Likely, this was the carter.

Master Collop took charge of the situation, giving orders and allotting tasks to bystanders, as well as to the stationers. He was much concerned for Seb who was now sitting upon his brother's doorstep, bleary-eyed and confused.

'Take Sebastian to the hall. Settle him, give him wine,' Master Collop instructed. 'Summon a surgeon, if he requires one.'

'Nay.' Seb's senses were returning. 'What of Jude? My brother?'

A shapeless pile of dark cloth lay beside the heap of kindling wood that had once been the cart's tail.

'Jude! Dear Lord God in heaven.' Seb limped over to the sorry form that lay upon the churned mud. 'Jude, Jude. Please...' Seb fell on his knees and pulled aside the gown to reveal his brother's face whiter than pounce dust, blood-smeared. 'My brother...' Seb turned to Master Collop. 'I cannot tell if he breathes.' In truth, Seb was too afraid to find out for fear he would discover Jude drew breath no longer.

Master Collop crouched down, put his ear to Jude's chest and then held his cheek to the injured man's lips.

'He does but only just. Fetch a priest, someone. You: go into the cathedral. Find a priest. Make haste!'

One of the younger stationers scuttled off to do the Warden-Master's bidding.

'And the surgeon,' Seb called out. 'He has need of a surgeon.'

Seb knelt beside Jude, holding his brother's chill hand, every word he uttered a prayer, every sigh a heartfelt plea to the Almighty to spare this life, this beloved Christian soul. A sizable crowd had gathered around the sorry scene but Seb was unaware of anything but Jude's crumpled form. He took off his torn and mud-stained cloak and folded it, taking the trouble to do it neatly before using it to pillow his brother's head.

'Do not leave me, Jude.' He stroked the fair hair away from those closed eyes. 'You saved me. You know I need you so. You must not...' Seb was unable to say the word. He dared not speak it for fear it might come to pass. Tears coursed down his face but he knew it not.

The crowd parted to let the priest through.

'Has he spoken?' he asked Seb.

'Nay. Not one word.'

'No confession then. Who is he?'

'Jude Foxley. My brother. But his last act did save my life. Will so selfless a deed not serve instead of confession? 'Twas an act of fraternal love... Our Lord Jesu will surely make allowances...'

The priest scowled at this presumptuous layman who dared

to put his opinions into the Saviour's mouth.

'It's no business of yours what allowances Almighty God may make. Now stand away and let me do what must be done.'

Seb struggled to his feet, aided by an onlooker.

Then Master Dagvyle, the surgeon, arrived, his apprentice trailing behind, encumbered with a weighty bag of the surgeon's paraphernalia.

'Is he dead?' Dagvyle demanded, elbowing the priest out of the way.

'As good as. You've wasted your time,' the priest said, shoving the surgeon back.

'Not until he's dead.' Dagvyle pushed the priest and the pair began squabbling over Jude. It was all most unseemly.

Seb pulled them apart.

'Tend my brother, for pity's sake and cease your arguing.'

The Foxley House

Just when life had seemed poised upon the verge of all things good, disaster had struck. A new and loving wife, a thriving business ready to expand. That morn, Seb had thought their future looked so bright and full of promise.

Now his brother lay here, in his old chamber above the outside stair, life hanging by a thread, his broken body carried here upon a hurdle. Surgeon Dagvyle had done his best, setting broken bones in splints and stitching gashes but the blackening bruises to head and body betokened hidden hurts within and none could guess their extent or severity. Jude was in God's hands now, whether he might heal or no.

Seb kept vigil. Sore from head to foot with cuts and bruises of his own, his knees ached from kneeling so long beside Jude's bed, praying, working through the rosary beads, over and over, until Rose took them away.

'You blister your fingers then how will you hold a pen or use a brush? How will you work tomorrow?' Rose asked.

He stared at her blankly, as though 'pen', 'brush' and 'work' were words of some foreign tongue he knew not.

'I'll sit by him,' she went on. 'You go have supper in the kitchen with the others. Go on. You've been kneeling here for hours. It's not good for you and you have your own injuries to heal. I'll take care of him, fear not.'

Seb rose stiffly, grabbing the bedpost for support, realising his right foot had lost all feeling.

'He saved my life,' he said – not for the first time. He had been saying the same all afternoon.

'I know,' Rose said, not unkindly, though she tired of hearing the phrase. 'Go eat your supper; you need food. And I've put out a clean shirt for you. You can't wear that one: it looks like a butcher's apron.'

'Jude's blood.'

'No. Mostly it's your blood from that cut on your shoulder. You should have let Surgeon Dagvyle stitch it for you.' She ushered him to the door. 'Have a care on those stairs. I see you are uncertain on your feet.'

'Cramp.'

'Adam has stayed to supper, having much to discuss with you. Lord Mayor James was greatly angered when Adam had to go tell him you wouldn't be coming to start his portrait this day, as you'd promised. He is cancelling the contract and demanding you return his payments made so far.'

'Aye.' Seb nodded. He cared not one jot about such matters. He returned to the bedside, reaching out to touch Jude's cheek to assure himself it was still warm. He had ne'er seen his brother so still, so silent, for so long. It was unnatural.

His brother's broken leg was splinted and propped upon cushions. Bloodstained the bindings around his head.

'Oh, Jude, come back to me. Dear Christ have mercy: I cannot lose you.' Seb knelt once more, beginning his prayers for his brother's recovery over again. Supper was of no consequence.

Rose remained, watching from the shadowed corner of the chamber, brushing aside her tears, concerned for her husband in his obvious distress. As for the man in the bed, her feelings could hardly be more entangled. Jude was ever the cause of so much strife and discord in the Foxley family yet, without his swift actions this day she, so lately a bride, would likely now be clad in widow's weeds. She should be overwhelmed with gratitude towards her brother-by-marriage but, Christ and St Mary forgive her, she tended him for Seb's sake alone. Not for Christian charity's sake and certainly not with the least morsel of affection.

Only her deep love for Seb could make her care in the slightest for his brother. But care for him she would for as long as Seb wished it so. Even if she were not her beloved's wife, she would have done the same. Seb was her life. And ever had been since they first met, if truth be told. And thus he would remain as long as she drew breath.

Epilogue

Monday, the third day of April and the day following Easter Sunday
St Paul's Cathedral

S EB HAD PROMISED Rose when they made their hasty vows before Lent began, that upon the first day after Passiontide, they should have a proper public wedding. And that day was now come. At the hour of Terce, as Paul's clock struck nine, he waited at the porch by the west door.

Memories of the previous occasion kept intruding, when he had stood here, fearing that Emily Appleyard might have a change of heart and not come. Jude stood by him as groom's man then. Dame Ellen Langton took charge of organising the bridal procession, he recalled. Neither was here this day.

Seb felt nervous. He knew not why. This time, he did not doubt the bride would come.

'You have the ring, Adam?'

'Of course. Rose will never forgive me, if I lose her precious ruby. And that's the fourth time you've asked me, at least.'

'And all is in readiness at Stationers' Hall for the wedding breakfast?'

'You know it is. Mercy and Pen have it all in hand, as you know full well. Now cease fretting, Seb, and enjoy the day.'

The distant sound of merry pipes grew louder, heralding the arrival of the bridal party.

Seb murmured a hasty prayer and crossed himself.

Adam gave him a quizzical look, raising his eyebrows.

Seb just smiled hesitantly in return, having no intention of telling Adam of that for which he prayed. But then his smile broadened. His eyes lit with love as he caught the first sight of his bride.

Escorted by Warden-Master Richard Collop who would give her into Seb's safekeeping in lieu of the bride's father, Rose was a vision of heaven.

She wore the gown of rose-coloured silk velvet that had once been Emily's, hardly worn but it was utterly remade. She and Pen had unpicked it and restitched it in the latest fashion, adding length to it, Rose being somewhat taller than Emily. They had trimmed it at neck and sleeve with the gorgeous braid Seb purchased not so long since from a certain, not-to-be-named pedlar. Both the gold threads of the braid and the bride's golden hair caught the early morning sunlight, gleaming and sparkling. Rose wore a circlet of primroses and violets about her head and carried a posy of the same. Kate had gathered the flowers at first light, still wet with dew, and woven the circlet with her nimble, artist's fingers.

Adam nudged Seb and grinned.

'You're a lucky man, cousin. Not sure you deserve her.'

'I do not, in truth, deserve such a wife, Adam. I know that and thank the Almighty daily for such immense favour as He has seen fit to grant me.'

'Was that your prayer just now?'

Seb shook his head. His words, begging protection for his dear ones and, especially, to guard against any possibility of *vendetta*, were a secret betwixt him and Christ Jesu. The dread Italian word would otherwise ne'er pass his lips. Rumour had it that Lawrence – Lorenzo – Duffield was escaped across the seas and may he remain there for evermore. His partner in treason, Sir Nicholas FitzAlan, had been tried, condemned and executed a fortnight since. This was to Seb's great relief, although that emotion had been overshadowed by sorrow at the time forwhy Dame Ellen passed from this life the day previously and Seb was much involved in arranging a fitting funeral for her, along with his fellow executor, John Appleyard.

But such matters must be banished this day.

Rose was at his side and the priest began the marriage ceremony.

Afterwards, Seb recalled them remaking their vows but the rest passed in a haze of happiness. It was the most splendid occasion, just as he had promised Rose.

Their marriage was now official and undoubted and Rose wore, forever, the ring, the colour of rubies, to prove it.

Important Characters featuring in 'The Colour of Rubies'

The Foxley Household

Sebastian [Seb] Foxley – an artist, illuminator and part-time sleuth

Rose Glover – Seb's house-keeper, a glover [rescued by Seb in a previous adventure]

Dickon & Julia – Seb's children by his late wife, Emily Appleyard

Ralf Reepham – Seb's elderly journeyman scribe [acquired by Seb in the previous adventure]

Kate Verney – Seb's apprentice

Nessie – Seb's maidservant

Jack Tabor – once Seb's apprentice, now Stephen Appleyard's

Gawain – Seb's 'colley' dog

At Westminster

Jude Foxley – Seb's elder brother, now the Italian clerk in the King's Scriptorium

Francesca-Antonia Baldesi-Foxley [Chesca] – Jude's Venetian child-bride

Mistress Baxter – Jude's landlady in Thieving Lane

The King's Scriptorium at Westminster

Secretary Oliver – the King's French Secretary [based on the real secretary Oliver King]

Hal Sowbury – the Chief Clerk

Piers Creed – the most industrious clerk

Lawrence Duffield – a clerk, Hal's friend
Barnabas Newson – a red-bearded clerk
Robin Beckton – a mannerless clerk who gambles
Eustace Dane – an elderly clerk
Andre le Clerc – the French clerk

Some Illustrious Persons at Westminster Palace [real]

King Edward IV
Queen Elizabeth Woodville-Grey
William, Lord Hastings – the King's Chamberlain

Others at Westminster Palace

Sir Thomas Burns – the Westminster Coroner
Master Curran – a surgeon
James Penny – a servitor
Sir Nicholas FitzAlan – Groom of the King's Chamber

The Armitage Household in Distaff Lane

Adam Armitage – Seb's cousin [actually his nephew] from
     Foxley, Norfolk, also Seb's assistant at Paternoster Row
Mercy Armitage – Adam's new wife
Simon Hutchinson – Mercy's eldest son by her first husband,
     a schoolboy
Nicholas & Edmund [Mundy] Hutchinson – Mercy's
     younger children

Seb's Fellow Stationers

Richard Collop – Warden Master of the Stationers' Guild
     and Seb's one-time master [real]
Hugh Gardyner – one of Collop's current apprentices, the
     previous lord mayor's nephew

Friends and Neighbours

Stephen Appleyard – Seb's father-in-law [Emily's father], a carpenter,

Dame Ellen Langton – once Seb's landlady and Emily's mistress as an apprentice silkwoman

Edmund Verney – an alderman, Kate's father

Jonathan Caldicott – Seb's neighbour in Paternoster Row

Mary Caldicott – Jonathan's wife

Joan [Joanie] Alder – a washerwoman and friend of Ralf Reepham

Peronelle [Pen] Wenham-Hepton – a silkwoman, used to be Emily's co-worker

Bennett Hepton – Pen's new husband, a well-to-do fishmonger

Beatrice [Beattie] Thatcher – a silkwoman, used to be Emily's co-worker

Harry Thatcher – a thatcher, Beattie's husband

Will Thatcher – Beattie and Harry's son, rescued by Seb and Adam in a previous adventure

The City Authorities

Thaddeus Turner City Bailiff and Seb's friend

Bartholomew James – Lord Mayor of London [real]

Richard Gardyner – last year's Lord Mayor [real]

William Fyssher – Deputy Coroner of London [real]

Others

Jake Parslow – a pedlar

Giles Honeywell – a purveyor of stationery in St Paul's Cathedral

Robert Stillington – the Bishop of Bath and Wells [real]

Thomas Kempe – the Bishop of London [real]

John Dagvyle – a surgeon [real]

Author's Notes

Spies. Every age and every culture has them. Spying is the second oldest profession, mentioned in the Bible. (If you're wondering, according to the Bible, the oldest profession is prostitution.) I don't know what sort of espionage and treasonous schemes were hatched at this time in England, whether there was ever any plot to harm the Prince of Wales, but King Edward's treaty with the Scots ran out the previous summer and he intended to go to war against them in the near future. The French Auld Alliance with Scotland was also true, as was the fact that King Louis XI and Lorenzo Sforza of Milan were squabbling over the region of Piedmont. But the crimes and the persons of Lawrence Duffield and Sir Nicholas FitzAlan are entirely my inventions.

The king's French secretary was real but I've changed his name somewhat because he was Sir Oliver King which would be rather confusing for readers as to whether the king or his secretary was meant. Dame Ellen was also real, although her surname was Langwith, not Langton. Her will exists and was granted probate in the spring of 1480 although, of course, Seb wasn't one of her executors and neither did he receive any bequests. Richard Collop, Lord Hastings the Chamberlain, Lord Howard, Lord Stanley, Lord Mayor Bartholomew James, Bishop Robert Stillington of Bath and Wells and the Deputy Coroner William Fyssher, mentioned briefly, were all real, too. The motley band of clerks is my invention.

By the way (spoiler alert), in the fifteenth century, a marriage contracted between two people in private, without a priest or even witnesses, was recognised as a legal union by the Church, if both had made their vows willingly in the present tense and sealed the deal by consummating it. Therefore, Seb and Rose didn't require the 'proper' wedding to make their union legal but I have found evidence that, if there were any doubts, the Church could ask the couple to repeat their vows in a public ceremony, so this second wedding has precedents.

I hope you enjoyed this novel. Look out for the next Seb Foxley medieval mystery, *The Colour of Bone*.

Meet the author

Toni Mount earned her Master's Degree by completing original research into a unique 15th-century medical manuscript. She is the author of several successful non-fiction books including the number one bestseller, *Everyday Life in Medieval England*, which reflects her detailed knowledge of the lives of ordinary people in the Middle Ages.

Toni's enthusiastic understanding of the period allows her to create accurate, atmospheric settings and realistic characters for her Sebastian Foxley medieval murder mysteries.

Toni's first career was as a scientist and this brings an extra dimension to her novels. It also led to her new biography of Sir Isaac Newton. She writes regularly for both *The Richard III Society* and *The Tudor Society* and is a major contributor to MedievalCourses.com.

As well as writing, Toni teaches history to adults, co-ordinates a creative writing group and is a popular speaker to groups and societies. Toni is also a member of the Crime Writers' Association.

This novel is Toni's the tenth in her popular *"Sebastian Foxley Murder Mystery"* series.

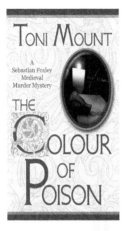

TONI MOUNT

A Sebastian Foxley Medieval Murder Mystery

THE COLOUR OF POISON

TONI MOUNT

A Sebastian Foxley Medieval Short Story

THE COLOUR OF GOLD

TONI MOUNT

The Third Sebastian Foxley Medieval Murder Mystery

THE COLOUR OF COLD BLOOD

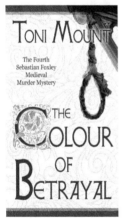

TONI MOUNT

The Fourth Sebastian Foxley Medieval Murder Mystery

THE COLOUR OF BETRAYAL

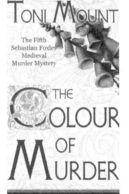

TONI MOUNT

The Fifth Sebastian Foxley Medieval Murder Mystery

THE COLOUR OF MURDER

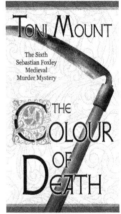

TONI MOUNT

The Sixth Sebastian Foxley Medieval Murder Mystery

THE COLOUR OF DEATH

TONI MOUNT

The Seventh Sebastian Foxley Medieval Murder Mystery

THE COLOUR OF LIES

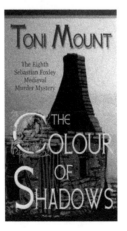

TONI MOUNT

The Eighth Sebastian Foxley Medieval Murder Mystery

THE COLOUR OF SHADOWS

TONI MOUNT

The Ninth Sebastian Foxley Medieval Murder Mystery

THE COLOUR OF EVIL

THE COLOUR OF BONE

Prologue

The Charnel House,
St Paul's Cathedral in the City of London

MY GOODWIFE believes I be quite mad to wish to spend time in such a dismal place as this.

'Who would want to pass time willingly with the remains of our ancestors long dead?' she asked when I informed her of my intentions. 'Why do you crave the company of their empty skulls and crumbling limbs?'

'Though my art does not demand it, the knowledge I acquire there will aid me in my portraiture,' I explained. 'Understanding the shape and underlying form and structure of the skeleton will make my representations of the living of more substance and, well, more lifelike.'

I realised that argument sounded perverse, if not absurd, but it happens to be true.

Thus, upon most Saturday afternoons of late, when the shop closes for the half-day, you will find me in St Paul's Charnel House, with the permission of the Dean and Chapter, of course. I sit in this chill, heartless ossuary with chalks and charcoal, drawing scores of images for future reference, surrounded by a thousand hollow-eyed skulls. Silent they may be, yet they have much to say and teach me.

I see that the skeletal forms of men and women be different in ways other than simply height and sturdiness and that there be every degree in between, from the daintiest female to the burliest male. I learn to know and recognise the signs of age upon teeth and joints, the lesions left by injury or long sickness. Even years of abiding in poverty leave their mark. The forgotten citizens of London each have a story to tell.

And so I work to my great profit, garnering new knowledge here amongst the dead, where the very dust itself is the colour of bone.

Chapter 1

Monday, the fifteenth day of
May in the year of Our Lord 1480

The Foxley House in Paternoster Row
in the City of London

MY BROTHER Jude hates me. I know he regrets having saved my life.

In that instant when his love for me caused him such dreadful hurt... he can ne'er forgive me. If he had let the horse run me down, his life would not have been torn asunder; ruined. Now his continued existence will be one of pain and humiliation; his bodily torment made worse by the taunts of those who will call him 'cripple', laughing and deriding him.

I know these things forwhy I was called thus until five years since, limping and twisted as I was when God saw fit to create a miracle for me out of another man's wickedness. I still recall the hellish flames edging ever closer to me as if it came to pass but yesterday. Throughout my life 'til then, Jude had been my protector, a safe arm to steady me, assisting me at every turn and driving away those rascals who would mock my affliction. Shall I have to do the like for him henceforth and, in good heart and patience, bear with his complaints and aid his disabilities, as he did mine in those days?

All these weeks he has lain abed in his chamber above the outside stair, impatient and irascible. Ralf, my journeyman who shared the chamber with my brother, has suffered much insult such that he asked to be permitted to sleep elsewhere. I arranged for his bed and belongings to be moved to the house next door, that which was known as Jonathan Caldicott's place but is now in my possession since Dame Ellen – may God assoil her soul – did bequeath the property to me. Jonathan and his goodwife yet bide there also, and the three of them seem to rub along together well enough.

Of late, whenever I offer assistance to my brother as he learns to walk about his bedchamber, he berates me, tells me to let him be and shakes off my helping hand. Such things he has said, names he has called me, be better left unrecorded. Little wonder Ralf desired to sleep elsewhere.

I believe Jude loathes the sight of me in very truth, and I know not what to do to set matters aright betwixt we two. Mayhap, they never can be since his sacrifice cannot be undone. Likely, he will regret having saved me forever and 'tis a debt I can ne'er repay. He refuses to allow me to make the smallest gesture of recompense. He has lived here 'neath our roof since the accident, cared for and nursed by Rose who serves with saintly patience the man who once jilted her at the church door. Such a true Christian soul is she. Giving him a home be the least I may do, but even that, he can withstand no longer.

Upon this day, he insists, he will remove himself to that great house of his upon the corner of Ave Maria Alley, so lately purchased but standing empty these months past. I asked how he will manage living alone in a place of three floors and a cellar with countless stairs to climb. He bids me mind my own affairs.

Dressed and taking naught but the staff that was once my constant companion (but rarely used nowadays except when snow and ice cause me to require its aid), Jude departed after we had eaten dinner. I went with him. 'Tis but a short walk to the end of Paternoster Row and onto Amen Lane where his house stands upon the corner, its front door opening into Ave Maria Alley, but this was his first time outside, and I feared he might come to grief on the uneven cobbles and cartwheel ruts.

Also, though I dared not mention it, I had much anxiety concerning the local street urchins, ever a plague upon those less able than themselves, recalling how I used to suffer at their hands. Stones and dung, as well as insults, used to be flung at me, and their favoured pastime was snatching away my staff and knocking me down in the mire, then laughing at my feeble and ungainly efforts to recover my feet. I was concerned that it could be Jude's fate.

Indeed, but a dozen steps from our doorway, four urchins lurked as though they had been lying in wait all this time since February last. One took up a handful of mud and filth and hurled it at my brother as he went by, head down, watching his step, his stiff-legged hobble marking him out as infirm. I hastened after, but Jude turned to face his tormentors, braced himself to stand unaided and swung the staff like a club. It caught the lad who threw the mud squarely across the ear.

'Let it be known,' my brother shouted, 'That any bugger who thinks Jude Foxley is a man to be baited like a toothless bloody bear must think again. You little bastards ever dare repeat this assault, and you won't live long enough to regret it.'

They ran off, as urchins usually do, but one turned and thumbed his nose at Jude. As soon as he turned away, my brother changed his grip on the staff and cast it like a spear. It struck the lad on the back of the head. Had it been a spear, in fact, the youngster would be dead but its blunt end served only to knock him down, fortunately. He scrambled up, but seemed somewhat dazed and unsteady as he disappeared down a narrow passageway into St Paul's precinct.

I knew Jude would have difficulty bending to retrieve the fallen staff, what with his broken knee unable to flex, so I obliged. Of course, I received no word of thanks as I returned it to him, neither did I expect it.

'Get away!' he snarled, snatching the staff from my hand. 'Cease following me like a foul stink I can't be rid of. I don't need a bloody nursemaid. Go back to your damned desk where you belong and stay there. I don't want to see your miserable face again. Ever.'

I stood in the midst of the street, watching him limp away and turn the corner. I wiped my eyes upon my sleeve.

Aye, he was right: I belonged at my desk. My business was thriving, the workshop order book replete with commissions. There was always much work to be done.

But not this day, as matters fell out.

Thaddeus Turner, the city bailiff and my good friend, was awaiting me upon my return. He was taking his ease at the kitchen board, drinking ale, eating wafers and talking with Rose as though he had the entire day to spare for naught more arduous than good companionship.

'God give you good day, Master Bailiff,' I said. ''Tis unlike you, Thaddeus, to have missed a good dinner.' It was true that my friend most often succeeded in making a timely arrival just as a meal was served.

'Aye, but he's made up for it by scoffing most of my fresh-baked wafers,' Rose laughed.

'Ah, forgive me. I hadn't realised I'd eaten so many. Your apricock wafers are the best in London, Mistress Rose.'

'Flattery will get you nowhere with me, Thaddeus Turner. And just look how tight your belt is becoming: let out another notch, I see, like a woman with child.'

Thaddeus pulled his jerkin straight, attempting to conceal his growing paunch.

'Aye, well,' he muttered. 'I have business with Master Seb, if you'll allow. This isn't a social visit.'

I helped myself to ale and refilled his cup as Rose went on folding clean linen and straightening creases from the morning's laundry.

'I'll take the little ones into the garden,' she said, smoothing the last napkin in readiness for the linen press. 'Leave you menfolk to your no-doubt urgent business.'

I saw the mischievous twinkle in her eye as she ushered little Dickon and Julia out to the courtyard and the garden plot beyond.

'Let's go count the chickens, shall we?' I heard her say. 'See if they've laid any more eggs since this morn. Nessie may well have overlooked one or two.'

I sat at the board with my ale, facing the bailiff.

'So what brings you here, Thaddeus? You want to commission me to paint your portrait? 'Tis becoming quite the fashionable thing these days. Or is it just a fondness for my goodwife's baked delicacies?'

'Much as I wish that were the case, I fear it is the matter of a suspicious death, Seb.'

I sighed.

'Have I not said often enough that the city should bear the expense of providing you with a proper clerk to take notes in such situations? Besides, if 'tis a suspicious death, as you say, then the Deputy Coroner must deal with it, incompetent as he be.'

'He's worse than incompetent, as you well know, but we ought not speak ill of a man on his deathbed.'

'William Fyssher be dying?' I asked, shocked. The man had been the bane of my life at times and Jude's before me, paying us a pittance for our services as scriveners at sixpence per day but rarely remembering to do so without our insistence upon payment. Working for the coroner usually involved us becoming mud-stained, bloody and stinking whilst he looked on, covering his nose with a perfumed handkerchief.

'So it's said,' Thaddeus continued. 'At least there won't need to be an inquest in his case, God be thanked. No mystery about a splinter in his backside turned morbid. Spent too long sitting around, idle, on a cracked seat, no doubt.'

I sucked air through my teeth and shook my head, recalling the stool I was forced to use at Westminster, in the king's scriptorium. That, too, had been a hazardous seat.

'It sounds a nasty, painful way to die.'

'But justly deserved.' The bailiff felt no sympathy for a man he despised. 'So, until a new Deputy Coroner is appointed to replace Fyssher, I have the unpleasant task of investigating any inexplicable and unexpected deaths, and this latest has me quite mystified. I need your sharp eye and quick wit, Seb, rather than your scribal talents.'

'As my good wife told you afore: flattery will get you nowhere with me either, Thaddeus.'

'So you won't help me?'

'I did not say that. When have I e'er refused to aid you? Tell me of the case.'

'In St Helen's Church in Bishopsgate Street, a woman's body was discovered this morn beneath a tombstone…'

'And how be that amiss?'

'She isn't the rightful named incumbent of the tomb.'

'Ah.'

'The tomb belongs to the founder of St Helen's Priory, one William Goldsmith, dead for two hundred years and more. A deal of building work is going on in the nave where the tomb stands. It has to be moved to a new position, and the founder's bones were to be removed from their resting place to a temporary one whilst this is done. The disinterment was intended to happen this morning with all due reverence and ceremony. Apparently, the masons were asked last week to see that the stone was loosened and prepared in readiness for its removal with pulleys and ropes, it being a weighty thing. However, when the stone was lifted, they discovered more than a few ancient bones. The body of a young woman – one of the convent's novices, as the prioress confirmed – lay atop the founder's remains, still garbed in her novice's habit.'

'Had none missed her?'

'Aye. She had not been seen since Compline last Friday eve, but that had happened previously. She was known for a repeated runaway with no desire to take her vows.'

'The poor lass. So you suspect foul play, no doubt? She would hardly have climbed into the sarcophagus and closed the lid upon herself.'

'Indeed not. I believe she fought against her assailant. But that's where the matter becomes difficult… it requires a delicate hand.'

'She was misused?'

'I know not. It would be the Deputy Coroner's task to enquire about that, if we had one.'

'You need a midwife to examine her.'

'Whether she was harmed in that way or not... Seb, I would have your opinion on this awkward matter.'

Thaddeus would not meet my eye. For certain, he had not revealed all to me, and I wondered what he was not telling.

St Helen's Priory Church, Bishopsgate

London was abuzz on this fine afternoon: traders crying their wares, youngsters at play with a barrel-hoop, goodwives chatting and laughing, and cattle lowing somewhere nearby. A soft zephyr blew up from the Thames, scented with river salt, fish and the sharp stink of the distant tanneries. Sunlight sparkled on yesterday's grimy puddles, turning them to silver tissue. Dandelions sprouted in odd corners of Cheapside and Poultry like fresh-minted gold coins, bold as you please. As Thaddeus and I turned up Broad Street, the old elm tree which overhung the church of St Bartholomew the Less was showing the promise of new leaf at last.

This year, winter had lingered too long, and spring came tardily as an unwilling scholar to school, but now the land was waking to life once more, God be praised. The sun's warmth on my back was most welcome, and I was reluctant to enter the cold stone church of St Helen. That our purpose here was sorrowful did naught to entice us 'neath the grand portal of the west door.

A solemn-faced nun greeted us, her face creased as crumpled paper, so at odds with her smooth linen headdress.

'Bailiff Turner,' she said in a voice cold as marble. 'Is this the man you promised would assist us in our time of great disquiet?' She looked at me, up and down, appraising me. Her eyes missed naught, and I recalled the fresh stain of ochre pigment upon my jerkin, acquired this morn. She would espy it for certain. I felt like a scruffy urchin compared to her in her pristine veil and wimple and black habit of finest wool, lavender-scented. A silver cross caught the sunlight through the doorway, dazzling us for a moment as it hung from her white rope girdle: the token of her office.

'Madame Prioress; Dame Ashfield,' Thaddeus said, removing his cap and bending the knee. I did likewise. 'This is Master Sebastian Foxley of Paternoster Row. He will help solve this monstrous crime.'

'Then you'd best be about your business, both of you. If she was slain here, within this church, the building has been desecrated and cannot be used until cleansed and re-sanctified. I need to know. 'Tis of the utmost urgency.' With that, the prioress departed, her shoes – not the expected convent sandals – clacking on the encaustic floor tiles, leaving us breathing in the perfume of last summer's lavender. Neither patience nor courtesy appeared to be among Madame Prioress's particular virtues.

'The tomb is this way.'

I followed Thaddeus to the centre of the long nave, St Helen's being one of the largest churches in the city, serving, as it did, both priory and parish. The nave was vast, wide enough that a wooden screen, exquisitely painted with much gilding, divided the nave along its length, keeping the holy sisters on the north side from the parishioners on the south. But I hardly had leisure to admire the gorgeous panels, shocked to see them being demolished.

Three carpenters were taking axes and saws to such beauty, and the crashing and ripping asunder of wood was an agony to me. As Thaddeus said, "a monstrous crime" had been perpetrated in this place, but, mayhap, the assault on a young maiden's life was not the only vile act of destruction here.

'What are they doing, tearing that screen apart? A thing of such beauteous workmanship... be they quite mad?' My thoughts turned upon some limner of old creating his masterwork, pleased and proud of his creation, taking weeks and months of loving care to fashion something worthy of God's house. Now it was smashed to kindling in a few hours. Such wanton obliteration by Christian men of a holy piece of art was anathema to me.

Thaddeus shrugged.

'Ask the carpenters. We'll have to speak with them anyway. They may bear witness to what came to pass when the lass died. And the masons also. They set up the block and tackle to raise the stone from above the ancient grave. John Atwood, the master mason, is likely hereabout somewhere. I met him earlier, before dinner. But come. I need your observations concerning the dead novice, and you heard the prioress: all must be done in haste.'

'Haste, indeed,' I muttered to myself. I would not be rushed in serving either the unfortunate maiden or seeing to it that she received the justice she deserved. Clearly, the church was unusable at present in any case. I knew not and little cared where the nuns and parishioners were attending mass, but it was not here. Every niche and ledge wore a coat of stone dust and sawdust, all little disturbed. Such noise and upheaval would make conducting any sacred office impossible, and, likely, the church should be re-consecrated anyway when the building work was completed. That was the customary way of it. The cold-hearted prioress must wait upon the slow turn of legal process, whether she would or no.

'See here, Seb. The stone slab has been set aside. Help me lift this wooden cover. I ordered it put here to keep the grave from further damage or interference, as well as to make it seemly and avoid any fool falling in.'

Whatever I had expected to see, it was not what lay in that yawning grave afore us. No peaceful form laid out, shrouded, hands in an attitude of prayer, perhaps, or crossed upon the breast, quietly awaiting the sound of the Last Trump.

She was wedged, hunched in a corner, her novice's habit screwed up above the knees, one bare foot showing, the other shod. But that was not the worst of it. Her mouth was open wide, gaping in a perpetual, silent scream, and her hands were clawing at naught, all bloodied and broken.

I made the sign of the cross. Her death had been a torment of agony. God save us. I hardly knew where to begin. What did Thaddeus believe I could do in such a case? I stepped away, staring towards the door and the shaft of blessed sunshine that illuminated the myriad dancing dust motes.

'I know,' Thaddeus was saying, crouching beside the pit. 'Fearful to behold. I had to walk outside this morn twice before I could force myself to look closely. Take your time, Seb. This one's harder than most. She was so young.'

'Does she have a name?'

'Aye: Anne Russell, shortly to become Sister Ursula. Her father is a vintner from Kingston-upon-Hull, wherever that is.'

'You do not require me to draw this… this grave, do you?'

Thaddeus shook his head which was a relief to me. It was not an image anyone could desire to preserve, even for the sake of justice.

'Then what?'

'Come nearer. You cannot see from there. What do you make of the torn hands... nails missing?' Thaddeus asked.

'Can you not lift her out, lay her straight, for pity's sake? She has suffered enough.'

'We could lift the corpse but can't lay it out. Me and my constables were going to do that earlier, but the body's stiff as a paling.'

'Surely, that cannot be? If she died upon Friday eve, after she went missing, the rigours of death would be passed by now.' I braced myself and knelt beside the bailiff. 'You realise what this means, Thaddeus?'

'Nay?'

'To be certain my assumptions be correct, I require to see the underside of the stone slab that covered the grave.'

'We'll need the masons to help with the winch then. Why do you need...'

'Just call the masons, Thaddeus, I pray you. When did they first lift the stone?'

'This morn, as I told you. I don't like this... the way you're thinking, Seb.'

'No more do I. But you said the masons had prepared for its removal beforehand.'

'Aye, but I'll find Atwood; he'll know more of it.'

Whilst the bailiff was gone, I did peer closer and sniffed. There was a hint of incipient decay but naught so much as I would expect from a body three days dead in warm weather. Mayhap, the chill of the surrounding stone had kept Sister Ursula's remains cool. That could also delay the onset and passing of rigour, but I was coming to suspect the explanation was otherwise.

Thaddeus returned with two fellows: one lean and hawk-like, the other burly and rugged of feature, rough as oak bark. The hawk introduced himself as Atwood but did not trouble to introduce his companion.

'I can't be doing with this delay,' Atwood complained. 'All ready to do the deed this morning, we was, then this! Blasted female!'

'That's no way to speak of Madame Prioress. Mind your language, or I'll inform your guild master,' Thaddeus threatened.

'I am the Master! And I wasn't talking about the prioress. I meant her.' He pointed to the grave. 'Wretched little cow, upsetting all our arrangements.'

'You think to blame the deceased for her death? You heartless rascal.' I had ne'er felt more tempted to knock a man down and raised my fist. All my anger at those urchins' abuse of my brother earlier rushed through me, heating my blood.

'Steady, my friend.' Thaddeus gripped my arm – hard – and the moment passed as my rage abated. Such a moment of ill-temper was a rare thing for me, but I had been hard put this morn. However, it was a sober realisation how easily my anger had flared. I must beware of further outbursts and wondered at this change in me. I prayed it was not permanent.

'When was the stone first made ready for lifting?' I asked the mason, making an effort to calm my voice and ease my taut stance.

'Last week sometime. We was ready to…'

'When precisely? We require to know the time and day exactly.'

The mason muttered and sighed.

'We was going to fix the callipers last Thursday, wasn't we, Martin?' Atwood looked to the rough-hewn mason, who nodded. 'But we found one of the wooden pulleys was split. So Hardacre, one of the carpenters, had to fashion a new one. Took him all night, so it was Friday before Sext that we finally got the rig set up. Tried it out just to make sure the stone would come free. It didn't, so we took chisels to it then tried again. We lifted it a few inches, and all was well. That was it. We lowered the stone back in place, and left it; went home.

'We thought the business of moving the bones would be Saturday, but the prioress said it weren't convenient, so it waited 'til today. And then when we finally lifted the stone... well, you know what was found.'

At my instruction, the rough-looking mason, Martin by name, winched the stone higher that I was enabled to observe the underside of it. I noted as he did so how easily one man might raise so heavy an object as the gravestone. 'Twas not beyond the bounds of possibility that another could do likewise, even one quite lacking the strength and knowledge of a mason. In other words, anyone might have moved the slab once the winch and pulleys were set in place last Friday. A skinny fellow like me... a woman... or even a novice nun.

The nether side of the stone was not so smooth as the upper, which had been polished and yet bore the much-faded design and chiselled lettering of the Latin inscription. Despite knowing the likely standard Latin phrases used and the founder's name, William Goldsmith, it was nigh impossible to read anything but the odd faint letter here and there. The story of the incumbent of the grave was almost lost to history.

Not so the story of the grave's more recent occupant. Sorrowfully, that was told all too clearly upon the underside.

Thaddeus stood, pulling his earlobe, watching me.

'See here, Thaddeus, if you care to look,' I beckoned him over.

'Must you stand 'neath it, Seb? If the stone slips or the ropes snap...'

'Have a little faith,' I told him.

Atwood nodded agreement.

'You think we don't know our business, bailiff? In thirty years, I never had a stone fall from its callipers.' The mason was scowling.

'It will take but a moment,' I encouraged.

With a wary expression, Thaddeus did as I asked.

Together we examined the sorry evidence of Sister Ursula's last hours. There were multiple scratches and smeared blood at one corner, precisely where the stone would have lain above the poor lass.

'I fear she remained alive in that tomb for some while.' I spoke softly that none but Thaddeus might hear. ''Tis the explanation of her torn and bloody fingers. This stone be sharp on the underside.'

'She tried to claw her way out. Buried alive. By the saints, what a terrible end. How long do you suppose she was in there?'

Thaddeus stepped back, as did I, nodding to Martin that he might lower the stone to the floor, which he did. It landed with a loud 'thunk' upon the tiles, seeming to fall the last few inches, raising a cloud of dust.

'I cannot tell,' I said. 'Sister Ursula has probably been dead for a day or a little longer.'

'So likely died… when? Saturday eve?'

'Or Sunday morn. Some such time.'

'And how long could she have been trapped within before the air became too befouled to breath? Can you tell?'

'I cannot know certainly. There be little enough room within for air, so probably not longer than an hour or two? Also, calling out for aid and battering the stone above her would take a deal of breath. But then we must consider that the stone had already been moved somewhat, and these callipers, as the mason calls them, gripping the edges of the slab, may have meant the grave was no longer perfectly sealed. 'Tis a possibility that a little fresh air may have trickled through the gap.'

'Meaning she could have been in there, alive, for much longer? Since Friday, maybe?'

'I fear so.' I wiped my eyes upon my sleeve. It did not bear to think overmuch about the maiden's end.

'And nobody knew? Nobody heard her cries? Nobody came to her aid?'

'You told me this was a hard one, Thaddeus. Hard to solve? Who can say? But hard indeed to ponder upon and consider when my mind would rather shut it away, banish it from my memory and bid my eyes forget what they have seen. But the maiden deserves justice, and we must make sure that she receives it. Some vicious devil be at large, and he has to pay for this act of wickedness'

With reluctance, I drew a sketch, showing how the poor novice lay in her dreadful death bed for a reminder, should one be required.

Two nuns had come to observe the proceedings, bringing a sheet and a flask of holy water. Then Thaddeus and I had the task of lifting Sister Ursula – a solemn duty neither of us relished since, to accomplish it, one of us had to go stand down in the grave. I reckoned it was the bailiff's part to do so, since I had no authority in this matter.

'But Seb, you weigh far less than I do, and your shoes will cause less damage to the founder's bones beneath than my great boots. I'll lower you, if you need help.' Thus were Thaddeus' arguments – sensible and irrefutable, unfortunately.

I eased myself into the grave without his aid – getting out again might be another matter – taking care where I put my feet. I pulled the maiden's habit straight to cover her in more seemly wise before touching her body. Rigour was abating now, for I could move her limbs. I bent low, taking hold of her torso, slipping one arm underneath her. Even as a dead weight, she weighed no more than a half-sack of grain.

'Can you reach down and support her head, Thaddeus? I would not have it fall back and strike the floor's edge here.'

Together we raised her with as much dignity as we were able, lifting her head and shoulders onto the sheet provided by the nuns. As I held her, making certain she should not slip back, the loose sleeve of her novice's habit caught upon the fastening of my jerkin and was pushed up, revealing her forearm.

'Hold. Hold,' I said. 'See the mark there on her arm.' I looked at the indentations in her flesh: clear evidence of a bite.

The elderly sister and the younger one gave aid to the bailiff in lifting her free of her unwarranted tomb and laying her straightly on the sheet. Holy water was sprinkled, and prayers intoned for their lost sister in Christ.

Having handed up her fallen sandal and searched about among the founder's skeletal remains for any other item that might more rightly belong to the novice, I noticed a scrap of brightly coloured textile that appeared to be too new to belong to the original burial, so I put it in my purse for safekeeping, if need be.

Being so used to examining the bones in the charnel house, of habit, I looked more closely at William Goldsmith's remains, lying amongst the last shreds of his ancient shroud. What I saw surprised me somewhat, and I crouched down for a closer look to study the skull, the pelvic bone and the heels. It would come as a shock to the prioress and the holy sisters if I ever revealed my suspicions to them.

'Are you going to stay down there all day?' Thaddeus asked, offering me his hand. He was grinning. 'You're getting far too companionable with the dead, Seb. It's not good for you. Come, let's go find the nearest tavern. I'm in need of some strong ale after that. *The Bull* across the way serves a decent brew.'

'Trust you to know that,' I said, relieved to be standing upon the floor once more. 'You have sampled the brewings of every tavern and ale-house from Bishopsgate to Ludgate, no doubt. But first, I must draw the bite mark on her arm. I pray you, good sisters, give me a few moments.'

The nuns left off their ministrations for the dead, eyeing me suspiciously as I took out my drawing stuff and knelt beside the poor corpse. It took but the time to say three or four Paternosters for me to make an accurate drawing of the bite. When I was done, I nodded to the nuns that they might continue their work.

NEXT IN THE SERIES: THE COLOUR OF BONE

Thaddeus laughed as he brushed the white dust of the tomb from my shoulders and back whilst I did likewise to the front of my attire. I could even feel the grit on my teeth. I took my cap, which I had tucked in my belt, and shook the dust from that also. Mind, Thaddeus was nigh as dusty as I. What a pair we must look to be, ghostly apparitions in daylight as we left the church and priory precinct to return to the everyday world of bustling London.

Get your FREE BOOK!

https://www.madeglobal.com/authors/toni-mount/download/